This plantation saga about the Old South began in the late 18th century when Lucien Bouchard, the second son of a French nobleman, dared to seek a new way of life in the New World. The first book, *Windhaven Plantation*, ended in 1834 with the building of the stately mansion called Windhaven Plantation in Alabama.

From that one man's dream and indomitable spirit came generations of Bouchards, a proud family who over the decades were torn by passion, greed, lust, and the Civil War, but who never forgot old Lucien and his legacy. Thriving against all odds—first at Windhaven Plantation and then at Windhaven Range in Texas—the family continues to be blessed.

* * * *

The Windhaven saga marches on in this tenth epic volume, as the beautiful widow Laure Bouchard falls in love with her adopted son's benefactor, Leland Kenniston—a wealthy and attractive New York entrepreneur. Back in New Orleans, her lawyer son seeks revenge against the men who kidnapped him and took him to Hong Kong.

In Texas, Lucien Edmund promises to deliver 2000 head of cattle to the Arkansas River, east of Pueblo, Colorado, where a rancher will meet the herd with his own men and drive it to the Wyoming spread. But on the way, the trip is fraught with new dangers, and Ramón discovers a silver mine, opening up the way for a new region of endeavor for the Bouchard clan.

*Ever expanding and always changing, the Bouchard Legacy will survive in the South and in the new West . . .*

*The Windhaven Saga:*

**WINDHAVEN PLANTATION**
**STORM OVER WINDHAVEN**
**LEGACY OF WINDHAVEN**
**RETURN TO WINDHAVEN**
**WINDHAVEN'S PERIL**
**TRIALS OF WINDHAVEN**
**DEFENDERS OF WINDHAVEN**
**WINDHAVEN'S CRISIS**
**WINDHAVEN'S BOUNTY**
**WINDHAVEN'S TRIUMPH**

# WINDHAVEN'S TRIUMPH

*Marie de Jourlet*

Created by the producers of
Wagons West, White Indian, The
Australians, Rakehell Dynasty, and
The Kent Family Chronicles Series.

*Executive Producer: Lyle Kenyon Engel*

**PINNACLE BOOKS**                    **NEW YORK**

**WINDHAVEN'S TRIUMPH**

An original Pinnacle Books edition, published for the first time anywhere.

Produced by Book Creations, Inc.; Lyle Kenyon Engel, Executive Producer.

First printing, August 1982

ISBN: 0-523-41111-1

Cover illustration by Bruce Minney

*Printed in the United States of America*

PINNACLE BOOKS, INC.
1430 Broadway
New York, New York 10018

If indeed there is a triumph for Windhaven, it has been made possible through the loyalty and interest of thousands of readers, whose enthusiasm for this series has motivated the author to achieve her creative best. Therefore it is only just that she dedicate this book to the devoted readers of America who believe, as she does, in the greatness of our nation as a bulwark of freedom for all mankind.

## Acknowledgments

The author wishes to express her gratitude to Joseph Milton Nance, Professor of History, Texas A & M University, College Station, Texas, for providing vital historical data; to Mary Barton of Carrizo Springs, Texas, for her helpful verification of facts of weather, topography, flora, and fauna in Texas; and to Dorothy Gardner of Chicago, who has provided much valuable information on Rush Medical College.

In addition, the author wishes to commend gratefully and enthusiastically the contribution of her transcriber, Fay J. Bergstrom of Chicago, who often provides highly effective editorial commentary, which eliminates errors in advance.

*Marie de Jourlet*

# WINDHAVEN'S
# TRIUMPH

# THE BOUCHARD FAMILY AT WINDHAVEN PLANTATION

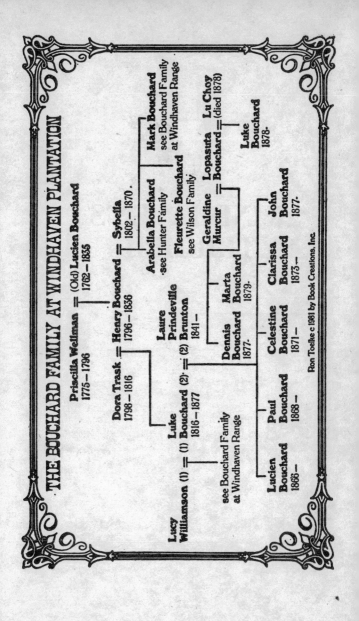

Priscilla Wellman = (Old) Lucien Bouchard
1775–1796          1762–1835

Dora Trask = Henry Bouchard = Sybella
1798–1816   1796–1836      1802–1870

Arabella Bouchard
see Hunter Family

Fleurette Bouchard
see Wilson Family

Mark Bouchard
see Bouchard Family
at Windhaven Range

Laure
Prindeville
1841–

Luke
Bouchard
1816–1877

Lucy
Williamson (1) = (1) Bouchard (2) = (2) Brunton

see Bouchard Family
at Windhaven Range

Geraldine
Murcur

Lopasuta   Lu Choy
Bouchard = (died 1878)

Luke
Bouchard
1878–

Dennis
Bouchard
1877–

Marta
Bouchard
1879–

Lucien
Bouchard
1866–

Paul
Bouchard
1868–

Celestine
Bouchard
1871–

Clarissa
Bouchard
1873–

John
Bouchard
1877–

Ron Toelke c 1981 by Book Creations, Inc.

x

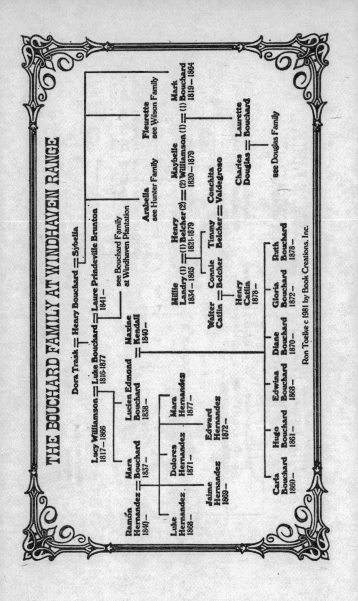

# THE BOUCHARD FAMILY AT WINDHAVEN RANGE

Dora Trask = Henry Bouchard = Sybella

Lucy Williamson = Luke Bouchard = Laure Prindeville Brunton
1817–1866 | 1816-1877 | 1841–

see Bouchard Family
at Windhaven Plantation

Arabella
see Hunter Family

Fleurette
see Wilson Family

Mark
(1) Bouchard
1819–1864

Lucien Edmond
Bouchard = Maxine
1838– Kendall
1840–

Mara = Bouchard
1857–

Ramón
Hernandez
1840–

Henry
(1) Belcher (2) = Maybelle
1821-1879 Williamson (1) (2)
1820–1879

Mittie
Landry (1)
1834–1865

Timmy
Belcher = Conchita
Valdegroso

Charles
Douglas = Laurette
Bouchard

see Douglas Family

Dolores
Hernandez
1871–

Mara
Hernandez
1877–

Luke
Hernandez
1868–

Edward
Hernandez
1872–

Jaime
Hernandez
1869–

Walter
Catlin

Connie
Belcher

Henry
Catlin
1878–

Carla
Bouchard
1860–

Hugo
Bouchard
1861–

Edwina
Bouchard
1868–

Diane
Bouchard
1870–

Gloria
Bouchard
1872–

Ruth
Bouchard
1878–

Ron Toelke c 1981 by Book Creations, Inc.

xi

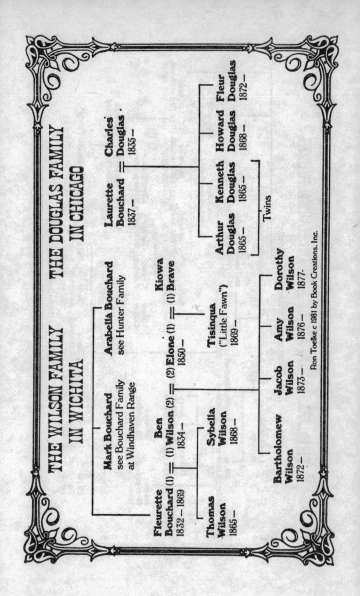

THE WILSON FAMILY
IN WICHITA

THE DOUGLAS FAMILY
IN CHICAGO

Mark Bouchard
see Bouchard Family
at Windhaven Range

Arabella Bouchard
see Hunter Family

Laurette
Bouchard
1837 –
=
Charles
Douglas
1835 –

Fleurette
Bouchard (1)
1832 – 1869
= (1) Ben
Wilson (2)
1834 –
= (2) Elone (1)
1850 –
= (1) Kiowa
Brave

Thomas
Wilson
1865 –

Sybella
Wilson
1868 –

Tisinqua
("Little Fawn")
1869 –

Bartholomew
Wilson
1872 –

Jacob
Wilson
1873 –

Amy
Wilson
1876 –

Dorothy
Wilson
1877-

Arthur
Douglas
1865 –

Kenneth
Douglas
1865 –

Howard
Douglas
1868 –

Fleur
Douglas
1872 –

Twins

Ron Toelke c 1981 by Book Creations, Inc.

xii

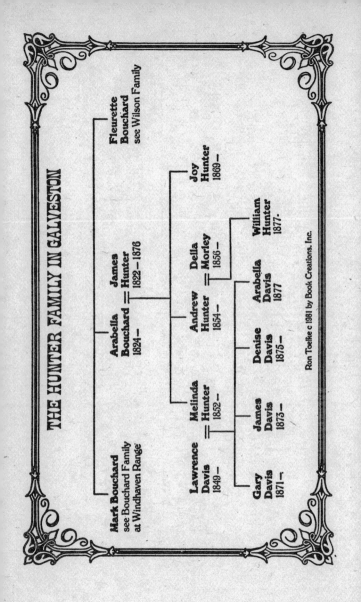

THE HUNTER FAMILY IN GALVESTON

Mark Bouchard
see Bouchard Family
at Windhaven Range

Fleurette
Bouchard
see Wilson Family

Arabella     James
Bouchard  =  Hunter
1824—       1822—1876

Lawrence     Melinda          Andrew     Della        Joy
Davis     =  Hunter           Hunter  =  Morley       Hunter
1849—        1852—            1854—      1856—        1869—

Gary       James       Denise          Arabella    William
Davis      Davis       Davis           Davis       Hunter
1871—      1873—       1875—           1877        1877.

Ron Toelke c 1981 by Book Creations, Inc.

xiii

## Prologue

With the onset of 1879, Rutherford B. Hayes began his third year as President of the United States under happier auguries than had prevailed since the great panic of 1873 and the scandals of the Centennial under President Ulysses S. Grant.

The crop failure in Europe had raised wheat prices for American farmers, resulting in an increase of cultivated acreage, the extension of railroad mileage, and the fortuitous signs of the return of a prosperity longed for over the past decade.

It was the year of the founding of Chicago's great Academy of Art, and the opening of F.W. Woolworth's first five-and-ten-cent store in Utica, New York. It was the year in which Thomas Alva Edison invented the incandescent lamp and William Deering's twine grain binder appeared. For those who looked for the emancipation of the "weaker sex," an act of Congress authorized women to practice law before the United States Supreme Court. And, on January first, came the very best sign of all: the resumption of specie payment by the United States Government, for the first time since the end of 1861.

Yet there were still dark clouds on an otherwise bright horizon. Though the frontier was constantly expanding, and fertile land continued to attract industrious homesteaders, the raw emotions distilled by material greed and the ruthless lust for power over that land still caused hardships, violence, and death. Federal troops at last ended the bloody cattle war in Lincoln County, New Mexico, in which a young orphan by the name of William Bonney, who had become the legendary Billy the Kid, had played the role of prime avenger. In the South, blacks had gained their freedom and even free land under the Reconstruction imposed

1

by the victorious North after the Civil War. However, they found little paid work and still less opportunity to vote. Because of this, there was a huge exodus of blacks from the South to the abolitionist state of Kansas, the home of "God's Angry Man," John Brown, the firebrand who had helped to kindle that terrible war that had pitted brother against brother and divided a young nation.

In Kansas, this winter, even the elements seemed to be at variance with the forecast of a peaceful and prosperous year. A bitter blizzard raged in December and January, ruining crops and killing livestock and people as well. . . .

Two miles west of the Kansas hamlet of Coldwater, on a flat, dreary plain covered with blindingly white snow, a man sat slumped on a brown mare under a gray, desolate sky. The wind whistled across this bleak landscape, the remains of a ferocious blizzard the day before. Now it was ebbing, moving away toward the east, after having wrought its pitiless havoc. The sound of the wind and the occasional snorting and wheezing of the mare, and the choking gasps of the man who rode her with his head bent—partly to ward off the cruel bite of the wind and seemingly as if he could not endure the bitter cold and desolation a moment longer—were the only sounds to be heard.

He was perhaps twenty-six, though his thick black beard and mustache so glistened with bits of ice that it was hard to determine his age. The heavy, shapeless Stetson pulled down low on his forehead against the wind and the cold almost completely concealed his swollen, bloodshot eyes. His greatcoat had been patched a dozen times or more and was nearly threadbare, as were his tattered breeches. His boots were old, the toes and heels almost worn out. A single saddlebag was attached to the pommel of his old, well-worn saddle; it contained some dried meat, half a sack of flour and as much of beans, and perhaps half a pound of coffee. Also in the saddlebag were a small pouch of gunpowder and at most a dozen rounds for his pistol, an old .36 he wore holstered at his hip. These possessions, his tinderbox, and his two-year-old mare were all he had left in the world. The mare had been a gift to him last July from Ramón Hernandez, who had saved him from being lynched by the Windhaven Range vaqueros when they had caught him trying to cut a stray steer from the herd out of desperation for his starving wife and daughter.

2

His name was Robert Markey. After marrying his sweetheart, Marcy Hildebrand, he had come out to Kansas in the summer of the Centennial. His father's failing farm in Indiana had been seized by creditors; the elderly man had been ailing for several years, and even young Robert's help had not been enough to save the farm. So he had come to Kansas with his young wife, hoping that this land would produce wheat and rye and barley in abundance so that he could begin a new life. In June of '77, Marcy had borne a daughter, Lucille, named after her mother. Though young Markey worked even harder with this additional responsibility, he had found that all the skill his father had taught him about working the land had been to no avail: Kansas soil was dusty and untillable. Little by little, money he had salvaged from his father's farm—money obtained by selling off some stock before the creditors could seize it—had gone into the new venture, into food for Marcy and for the baby, and had dwindled.

Yesterday morning, at the height of the blizzard, both his wife and child had died before his eyes. Holding Marcy and Lucille in his arms, he wrapped them in his greatcoat to keep them warm. But the raging wind had smashed the shutters of the tiny house; it had blown out the pitifully small log fire he had been keeping alive in the fireplace, and the aching cold driven by the lashing wind had done the rest. Little Lucille had whimpered for a few moments, and then stiffened, her face turning blue in a last convulsion. Agonized, he had prayed aloud to God and clung to Marcy with all his strength. But the birth of the child had been difficult and debilitating, compounded by a mild touch of fever she had contracted in the fall. She had, or so he had thought then, recovered after keeping to her bed for a week and dosing herself with sassafras tea. However, her resistance had been severely weakened.

Marcy suddenly began to gasp—shallow spasms instead of breathing. Then she had given a rattling moan and her head had turned to one side. He had slowly risen, cradling her lifeless body, and begun to weep. Everything that he had loved, everything he had worked for, had been taken from him in a single day.

He had spent many hours digging a grave for Marcy and Lucille, battling the frozen ground, forcing himself to continue although he had long passed the point of exhaustion. Then he had prayed aloud for his dead wife and child, inwardly cursing a wrathful God, his voice breaking with agony. He did not know why it had happened or why he had been thus devastated.

All he had left of the past was the horse that Ramón Hernandez had given him. He had named the mare Jenny, in tribute to an elderly aunt who had been kind to them and had given him a few dollars when he and Marcy left Indiana. He had no other companion now.

At the grave of his wife and child, he had wearily concluded that only work could take his mind from the annihilating loss he had endured. All he knew was that he must go south—certainly it would be warmer there. But he also remembered that the man who had stopped the vaqueros from hanging him that July day—and who had given him the mare and some food to take back home—had said that he was from Windhaven Range, the Bouchard spread near Carrizo Springs, Texas. If somehow he could get there and tell Ramón Hernandez what had happened, perhaps there would be a job for him, where he could work off his indebtedness. He wanted Ramón Hernandez to know that he wasn't a thief.

And yet ruefully he knew, even as he had decided on this course of action, that he was really not a very good farmer. His father had taught him a good deal, but perhaps it wasn't in his nature to till the soil for unending years and live from it the way his father had done so well until his illness. But he was willing, he was strong, and he would work or die.

He was grateful that the wind at last had abated and now, as the mare dutifully plodded on through the thick snow, he saw the sky darken with the approach of twilight. He had ridden for hours without knowing it, out of a dogged will to survive, and now a dull, sickly glow from the sun that had finally emerged from behind the thick clouds had begun to sink below the horizon.

Here and there, like forlorn waifs, trees burdened with snow drooped from the force of the wind, which had humbled and buffeted them. He was bone-weary, but the ache inside of him was more than the hurt of overtaxed flesh and sinew. He felt a dreadful guilt oppressing him: perhaps he could have saved both Marcy and the baby. He tried to tell himself he had done all that he could before they had slipped away from him, but he would never forget

4

how sweet Marcy had died in his arms with hardly a murmur of complaint.

He began to cry, but the bitter cold froze the tears, and he could feel his eyelashes grow weighty until they were nearly frozen shut, and he could hardly blink them.

He halted the mare for a moment and looked bleakly around him. A soft snow had begun to fall again, and the tracks he had made were already beginning to be covered up. And then he gasped as he turned to look south again: there, about a mile or so away, was the outline of a small frame and sod house. Perhaps there he might find warmth, shelter, maybe a cup of hot coffee. And the mare deserved rest and warmth too, after the terrible long journey she'd made today with him.

"Just a bit farther, please, Jenny girl," he hoarsely urged the mare. He tried to draw in deep breaths, but the air was still so frigid that it seemed to cut like a knife into the raw wound that his lungs had become. But the cheerful light from the kerosene lamp behind the window of that isolated little farmhouse became a beacon, urging him on at a moment when he felt unable to exert any more effort to go on riding through the desolation of the barren winter scene.

The mare moved wearily toward the farmhouse. Robert Markey saw that behind it to the left was a ramshackle barn whose roof had begun to sag from the heavy weight of the snow piled upon it. Next to the barn stood an old wagon, beside which lay a plough nearly covered by drifting snow. It was the sort of plough even a farmer's wife might handle, wrapping a broad strap around her while gripping the handles and letting her horse pull it to minimize her own exertion. These people, Robert thought to himself, were not much better off than he; what kind of crops must they raise on land so grudgingly yielding as this and visited by the cruelest of elements?

He slid down from his saddle, holding on to the mare's neck for support while he tried to get his balance and regain some vestige of his strength. The mare turned its head toward him and nuzzled his cheek, and he uttered a choking sob. That seeming gesture of compassion and affection only served to remind him of his irreparable loss and the black anguish that consumed him.

He staggered to the door of the house and, as a wave of fatigue swept over him, leaned his forehead against it.

5

Then, forcing his cold-numbed fingers to ball into a fist, he struck weakly.

The door was opened by a gaunt, gray-bearded man who peered curiously at him and then demanded, "Who are you, mister?"

"I—I've been riding all day—my name's Robert Markey—I—I'm looking for work."

"Work, is it?" the tall homesteader snorted contemptuously. "In weather like this?" Then, catching sight of Robert Markey's mare, standing with its head drooping, he growled, "You've ridden that horse a spell, I can see that."

"Who is it, Jed?" a woman's voice called from inside.

"Fellow wants work, Ruth Ann." Then, to the exhausted widower, he growled, "You can put your horse in the barn with mine and the cow. Ruth Ann 'n me was just about to sit down to supper. You're welcome to share it with us, such as it is. Mind you hurry; it's too cold to stand here passing the time of day with the door open!" With this, he closed the door, and Robert exhaled a long, shuddering breath, as he wearily trudged back to take the mare's reins and lead it to the snow-covered barn. Opening the door, he could see in the obscure darkness several stalls, and he heard the mooing of the cow the farmer had mentioned. The mare pricked up its ears at the sound of the whinny from the sturdy black gelding at the far end of the barn.

Robert led the mare to an empty stall and pushed on the gate. As his eyes grew accustomed to the darkness, he made out a small hayrick at the back and trudged toward it. Without bothering to look for a rake, he tugged at the pile with his arms and made his way back with an armful, which he tossed into the stall. The mare gratefully bobbed its head and began to eat.

With his shoulders slumped from fatigue, Robert trudged back to the house and again struck the door with his fist, wincing at the pain in his frost-bitten fingers. Again the gray-bearded man opened the door, curtly ordering, "Stamp your boots off good, mister. Don't need any snow in here. When the Lord sent it, I don't think He meant it to come inside folks' houses."

Robert dutifully stamped the snow off his boots and then bent his head to pass through the low entrance. The farmer shut the door hard behind him and then demanded, "Where are you from?"

"I—I had a little farm near Coldwater, mister. . . ."

6

A small fire flickered cheerfully in the stone fireplace, and a placid-featured, gray-haired woman in homespun stooped to it to stir up the embers. She gave him a brief, cheerless smile and then straightened. "I'll be having supper in a jiffy, Jed," she informed her husband, and then went back into the kitchen.

"Sit yourself down in that old chair," his gruff host ordered Robert. "Guess you can't hurt it none—varnish was taken off quite a spell ago. But then, as I always say, man proposes and the Lord disposes. I'm Jed Bowland."

"It's—it's kind of you to take me in on a night like this, Mr. Bowland." Robert gratefully seated himself on the chair as he fumbled with the buttons of his greatcoat.

The old homesteader stood over him, scowling down at him. "You wanted work, you said?"

"That's right. I—my wife and baby died yesterday in the blizzard—"

From the kitchen there came a sympathetic clucking sound as the farmer's wife, overhearing this, paused at her work and turned to stare into the drab, sparsely furnished living room.

"You must ask His help in your time of need, brother," the gray-bearded farmer sententiously declared.

"Yes, sir," Robert sighed. He began to rub his eyelashes with the tip of a forefinger, and the melting ice mingled with a sudden well of tears.

"I'm a Methodist. Deacon in the church here. What's your persuasion, Mr. Markey?" the gaunt man asked almost truculently.

"My wife and I were Episcopalian."

"Humph!" Jed Bowland's face hardened. "Well, I suppose a man has a right to choose what church he'll abide by. But my father and grandfather before me were Methodists, and that's what I'll be till the day I die. Ruth Ann, too. Now, Mr. Markey, you said you wanted work. Can you milk a cow? My Daisy's due by morning, at the latest. Ruth Ann has herself a spell of rheumatiz; can't properly do her chores."

"I—I never milked one, to be honest with you, Mr. Bowland."

The gray-bearded farmer gave him another contemptuous "Humph!" and was silent for a moment, as if meditating over the answer. "Well now, just what *can* you do to earn your keep? Tell you what—that barn's weighed down

7

by snow and needs the roof braced up. There's a pile of rough-cut timber in the barn, and if you're handy, you could fix it in a jiffy."

"I—I'm afraid I've never done that, either," Robert apologetically confessed.

"I see. Well now, Mr. Markey, looks like I got to depend on myself, which is what the Lord originally intended for all of us, I reckon."

"Supper's ready, Jed," Ruth Ann piped up, as she came out of the kitchen with a large bowl of stew, which she set on the rickety rectangular table near the center of the room.

"I'll give you your supper anyway, Mr. Markey, but I don't rightly guess you can help me much. And as you can see from this house, there's no place for anyone else 'ceptin' for Ruth Ann 'n me to sleep. So you'd best be ridin' on. Mebbe if you find the Richters—they're about fifteen miles or so south of here—they might have something for you. Mrs. Richter's got a flock of chickens she's mighty proud of."

"Th–thank you, Mr. Bowland. I—I'll go see her, then."

At the farmer's almost imperious gesture to come to the table, Robert rose and, divesting himself of his greatcoat, carefully draped it over the old chair, as he waited for the farmer and his wife to seat themselves before he did.

Jed Bowland bowed his head and clasped his hands and began to say grace. Robert emulated him in bowing his head and closing his eyes. He almost felt like falling asleep, and the pleasant warmth of the fire made him try not to think that he would have to go on riding once he'd had his meal.

There was no conversation at the table. Several times the woman peered quizzically at him, but when he caught her gaze, she meekly lowered her eyes and resumed eating. The stew was mostly filled with potatoes. There was a plate of cold biscuits, strong but stale coffee, and for dessert, a small piece of rhubarb pie and a hard wedge of mousetrap cheese. Nonetheless, it tasted like a banquet to the exhausted, famished young widower. His host watched him from narrowed eyes and, when Robert had finished, sourly commented, "You'd eat us out of house and home if you were a hired man here—I can see that, Mr. Markey."

"I—I'm sorry—I rode all day—and I guess—"

"No need to make excuses. A man's born with the appetite he's got, and that's the good Lord's doin' too," Bowland stolidly remarked.

His wife began to clear up the dishes at once, continuing to send Robert covert, wordless glances. When she had gone back to the kitchen, Bowland turned to the widower and averred, "I don't want to seem hard about it, but like I just told you, the long and short of it is there's no place for you to sleep here. You'd best be on your way and see if you can find the Richters. If you ride hard, more 'n likely you'll be there by midnight."

Robert wanted to protest that he could make himself an improvised bed in the barn, but thought better of it, seeing the sour look his host gave him. He rose from the table and made his way toward the chair, where he put on his great-coat. "I want to thank you for supper, Mr. Bowland, and for your advice about the Richters."

"You're welcome. Sorry I can't do more for you, but out here a farmer has to do the best he can or go under. I guess you know that yourself, though. Only good thing for me this winter was I got my wheat in a week early. I'd just about be wiped out if I hadn't. Kansas is the kind of place that tests a man's faith in his Maker."

"I agree with you there, Mr. Bowland. Well, thank you for the supper—and you, Mrs. Bowland. I'm mighty grateful," Robert said in a dull, hopeless voice.

"That's quite all right, Mr. Markey. I'm sorry about your poor wife and child," the woman turned back to say.

Robert eyed his host for the last time, but Bowland stared back at him coldly with his jaw set unflinchingly and his gaze impassive. "Much obliged again, Mr. Bowland. I hope you make out in the spring." He hoped the old homesteader would change his mind and ask him to stay, but there was no word in return. So, buttoning up his great-coat, Robert walked to the door and let himself out, pulling it closed as fast as he could to keep out the cold.

There were stars in the sky now, but they too, like the sun that day, seemed lusterless and dull. His face downcast and his head bowed, he trudged to the barn and entered it. The mare pricked up her ears at the sound of his footsteps, and the cow let out an anguished moo. Robert shrugged. "Sorry I can't help you, Bossy," he muttered. "Jenny, I guess we have to be going. I'm sorry, I surely am, but at least it's not quite so cold outside. Let's go now." As he opened the gate of the stall, he noticed that the mare had

9

eaten all of the hay he had strewn down. "That's good! We've both got something in our stomachs now, Jenny, so we ought to be able to make it till we find the next farm. Maybe they'll take a shine to us both—I surely hope so." He pushed open the barn door to lead the mare outside, and then methodically closed it.

He had broken bread with this couple, the first human beings he had seen since that terrible yesterday, yet he had remained untouched by human warmth and compassion. He did not exist for them, and he would be forgotten as soon as dawn broke, he was certain. Or perhaps Jed Bowland might use him to illustrate some sanctimonious sermon, describing the ne'er-do-well who had knocked at his door one night and gone on to nothingness.

He straightened himself as best he could, weary though he was: such thoughts were self-pitying, unmanly. He would not seek any favors because of his bereavement, nor would he dwell on his hard luck. If there was any hope in whatever future remained for him, it must be through work, not lamentation over the ill luck with which he had been cursed.

Thus heartened, he lofted himself into the saddle, took up the reins, and clucked his tongue to start the mare on this seemingly never-ending journey.

The mare plodded doggedly on, but Robert Markey did not attempt to quicken its slowly ambling pace. He could only marvel at the animal's stamina, which surely surpassed his own.

He wondered at the obdurate patience of the beast. It made no complaint over the frigid atmosphere, nor the dreary monotony of bearing him to an unknown destination without even hope of reward. It dumbly accepted his orders, whether they were right or wrong or involved danger. Men, he thought bitterly, would rarely show such self-denial and perseverance. There was a lesson to be learned from Jenny, and perhaps it was all the inspiration left to him now in his lonely anguish.

The muffled hoofbeats of the mare, making its way through the thick snow, provided the only sound to be heard. Once Robert looked back, staring at the mare's receding prints; after a few hours in the shifting snow, even these would be erased. To him it was a kind of symbol of the past that had been wiped out, and that what awaited him—the unknown, the challenging, the dangerous—must be faced as if he were beginning a new life, with neither privilege nor guarantee.

Slowly he lifted his head to the sky and prayed aloud: "Marcy, my love, I hope you and Lucille have found peace now. I wish to God I could have given you that peace. Forgive me. I only hope I can earn my keep without charity. I want to be a man again, if I can ever forget how I let you both down."

As he stared yearningly up at the unrelentingly immense sky, he thought for an instant that he saw the sudden bright twinkle of a star, quickly extinguished in the dark vault that arched beyond the reach of his vision. He closed his eyes and murmured a silent prayer, and clung to the reins, letting Jenny go as she would, without direction. The mare seemed to be content with journeying southward, directly and without veering to any degree, and soon, lulled by the soft muffled thud of the mare's hooves on the snow-packed earth, wearied by emotional stress and physical exhaustion, Robert Markey fitfully dozed.

He suddenly jerked awake, listening to the sound of his breathing and the mare's, and her persistent plodding. Gusts of steam were rising from the mare's nostrils as her warm breath hit the frosty air. There was an eerie silence everywhere, as gradually the sky grew lighter with the advent of a wintry dawn. He presumed they had somehow missed the farm the old homesteader had spoken of, for surely they would have reached it by now. He had passed by two abandoned houses with their barns barely standing. Near one of them had lain an old wagon wheel, making a circle in the snow on which was perched a crow, black and lean, searching for pickings in this barren plain. The crow had cawed twice at him, then flapped its wings and headed toward the west.

The pervasive loneliness of the landscape was borne in upon him with each passing moment. Far beyond, illuminated by the red and purple of the coming sunrise, he thought he could make out the outlines of several houses, a small farm community. Perhaps there would be work at one of them.

How tired he was! He could not remember when he had ever felt such crushing fatigue, not even when he had worked on his father's farm from sunup till sundown. But

11

then there had been purpose to it, and inquisitiveness and a zest for living. Then, as a boy, he had not known what conflicts and atrocious strokes of fortune awaited the unsuspecting.

He turned very wearily in his saddle, as if looking back for this happier time, and he started with surprise. About two hundred yards behind him was a mongrel with a long muzzle, a long tail, and a white hide with black spots. He reined in the mare and waited a moment. The dog came closer and then stopped, sniffing and raising its face.

Robert groped with his numbed fingers into his saddlebag and drew out a piece of dried jerky, which he held up. "Come get it, boy!" he called. His voice was hoarse and unsteady; it did not sound like his own, and it was so loud in this predawn stillness that it startled him.

The mongrel lowered its muzzle and began to come forward, paw by paw, slowly advancing in the thick snow. He waved the meat again, and the dog smelled it and quickened its pace toward him. Robert eased himself down from the saddle, stifling a groan of pain at the effort it cost him. He turned to face the mongrel and offered the piece of meat.

The dog bounded forward, wagging its tail. It took the meat almost daintily, gulped it down, then wagged its tail again. Its brown eyes fixed Robert with an unwavering look, and he turned back to his saddlebag and took out a second piece of meat.

This time he squatted down, wincing at the swirling pain of his cold-stiffened body so long in the saddle. The mongrel did not hesitate this time: it came up to him at once, furiously wagging its tail, and once again daintily picked the jerky from his fingers. Young Markey began stroking the dog's head with his left hand, and the mongrel whined softly, remaining immobile till the caress was over.

"You're lonely, too—a stray like me. I wonder how far you've been following me," Robert mused aloud. This time, the sound of his own voice revived him. It was as if he had returned to the world of the living, and this dog had been the catalyst that had brought this miracle about. He felt tears sting his eyes and, mounting Jenny, he called down to the dog, "Come along then, we'll see what we can find. Maybe we'll bring each other luck, if we work together!"

With renewed vigor, he jabbed his heels against Jenny's belly, and the obedient mare began to trot forward. The mongrel followed, looking up at him and wagging its tail. Robert suddenly felt very melancholy, and it would have taken very little for him to pour forth all the tears of his frustration and loneliness and bereavement.

# One

On the morning of December 25, 1878, the *Southern Belle* steamed majestically into the harbor of San Francisco. Captain Jasper Jackson smiled as he approached Lopasuta Bouchard and Leland Kenniston standing together at the rail, admiring the harbor with the hills beyond. "Gentlemen, didn't I promise you we'd be here for Christmas Day?" the genial captain chuckled.

"You did indeed, Captain Jackson," Lopasuta responded happily, "and you'll never know how grateful I am for the speed of the voyage. I'm almost home now, after all this time—it seems nearly an eternity."

"I hope before the two of you continue your journey you will have a chance to enjoy something of this colorful port," the captain commented. "It's really a remarkable city, and it's growing by leaps and bounds on that hilly peninsula between the Pacific Ocean and the Bay. As a matter of fact, the very same year that the United States declared its independence from George III, it was founded by the Spanish, who named it Yerba Buena."

"I didn't know that," Leland Kenniston averred. "Did you, Lopasuta?"

"No, I confess I know very little about this part of my country," the young lawyer admitted sheepishly. "My people, the Comanche, lived inland—to the south and east."

"Well, gentlemen," the captain continued, "the United States naval force took it over in 1846 and renamed it San Francisco. But it was the Gold Rush, two years later, that really got it growing. In the days of the Forty-niners, it was a city of complete lawlessness, famous most of all for the Barbary Coast. They eventually organized vigilantes to keep the peace until a police force was finally established."

"And I daresay," Leland Kenniston put in, "that a great

14

many innocent men were shanghaied in some of those waterfront dives along the Barbary Coast and forced to labor on ships—not unlike what happened to you, Lopasuta."

"I know how they must have felt, from my own despair when I first found myself on that ship going around the tip of South America to here and then to Hong Kong," the tall, handsome young man agreed. His face sobered. "I was luckier than most of them, I'm sure."

"Well, sir," Captain Jackson beamed, "you surely aren't at the end of the world when you get off my ship. San Francisco was linked with the East Coast by the Pony Express back in 1860, and nine years later it was connected to the rest of the country by the transcontinental railroad. And speaking of railroads, Mr. Bouchard, you'll be able to get back home to Alabama in a good deal less than two weeks, I'd say, if you can make the right connections. I have a few friends who work on the railroads, and if you need any assistance, please call on me. I'd be proud to do you a service. It's been a privilege having both of you gentlemen aboard."

"We've had a wonderful voyage, Captain Jackson, and I'm very grateful to you." Lopasuta shook hands with the middle-aged captain. "But the first thing I want to do is send a telegraph wire to my wife in Montgomery. I want her to know that I'm coming back to her as quickly as I can."

"There's a telegraph office on the Embarcadero, Mr. Bouchard. I'll have one of the stevedores take you to it as soon as we've docked and passed customs—which shouldn't take long. But first, I'd like both of you gentlemen to come to my cabin for a Christmas libation."

"Very kind of you, Captain Jackson," Leland Kenniston nodded, and shook hands with the captain. "We'll just take you up on that."

Then, as the captain walked away to give orders to his first mate, the businessman turned to Lopasuta. "I know how you must feel now, Lopasuta; I know you're worried about how your wife, Geraldine, is going to receive you. My feeling is that she'll understand perfectly. From all the things you've told me about her during our voyage here, she seems to be a sympathetic and warmhearted young woman. She'll understand that what happened to you wasn't of your own choosing."

"You know I sent her a letter, and I explained every-

15

thing to her, and I asked her forgiveness, Leland—I admit, I still feel I should call you Mr. Kenniston."

"Now don't go back to formalities!" The tall, black-haired Irishman shook his head. "We're friends, and I think we'll be more than that, if you'll think about the offer I made you. I've told you that my parents were immigrants out of County Mayo and poor as church mice. They sacrificed and slaved to get me some schooling so I could amount to something—and what I've accomplished has been mainly due to their own wonderful love for people and their complete lack of snobbery. I'll always be Leland to you, Lopasuta."

"I'll never be able to thank you enough for your friendship."

"Oh yes, you will—you're going to go to work for me! As soon as I open up my New Orleans branch, I want you to play an important role in it. As I've told you, I'm setting up a New Orleans office because it is highly important for me to have a southern branch of operations in order to secure the best price for cotton. Suffice it to say that my mills in England and Ireland depend on raw materials—like cotton and also wool—for dry goods, and I depend on getting the best price to turn the best profit. Of course, you will only be involved in the legal end—there'll be a factor for the business side. You'll have to take the bar examination in Louisiana so you can practice there, but I think you, your wife, and your children would love New Orleans. It's even more cosmopolitan than San Francisco, with a great deal more tradition and culture."

Lopasuta smiled, then looked down at the deck and hesitated.

"After I send that telegraph, Leland, I'd like to do something else—and I'd like you to join me."

"Of course! What is it?"

"Well, I want—I want to go to church and give thanks to both the God whom my Geraldine worships and to the Great Spirit of my people—who I know are one and the same—for having brought me back home to my native land."

"That's a wonderful idea. I've something to thank God for, too, Lopasuta. I almost think you were heaven-sent: you saved my life when I nearly toppled over the rail during that storm at sea, and I know what a definite help you can be to me in my own ventures. You see, I'm a loner in a

16

way, but I made my money honestly through hard work, and I've cheated no one. And you have the same character. You're upright, and you also believe in hard work and dedication to duty. Those are the virtues my own parents taught me, so when I find them in a man like you, I'm all the more grateful—that is, if I can induce you to take my offer."

"I'm thinking a good deal about it, but of course I want to discuss it with Geraldine."

"Naturally you will. Well now, let's go back to the captain's cabin and have that libation. After we dock, since I'm sure we won't be able to get a train out today, I'd like to have a fine Christmas dinner at a nice restaurant where we can talk over the times ahead for us, Lopasuta." Leland Kenniston put his arm around Lopasuta Bouchard's shoulders, and the two tall men walked to the captain's quarters.

Afterwards, Lopasuta went back to his stateroom and knocked on the door of the adjoining cabin. The door was opened by the eighteen-year-old Chinese girl, Mei Luong, who held his tiny son in her arms, and Lopasuta smiled fondly at Luke. Mei Luong was learning English at a remarkably fast pace, although she understood it better than she could speak it, and the Comanche lawyer found himself using less and less of the pidgin Chinese that he had acquired during his involuntary stay in Hong Kong, and more English. "Mei Luong," he now told her, "we are going to leave this ship very soon. But please come on deck with me now; I want both you and my son to see America for the first time."

"I, too, wish to see it, master," Mei Luong replied eagerly, her eyes respectfully lowered and her head inclined in Lopasuta's presence.

Lopasuta knew Chinese women showed an extraordinary amount of humility in the presence of men, and it saddened him. While he had been working in Hong Kong for the miserly Scotsman, David Brorty, he had been informed of the inferior status of Chinese females. He had learned that, especially in the villages, the birth of a girl child was regarded as a disaster because it represented a useless mouth to feed. Many impoverished families sold their girl children to mandarins or to the owners of teahouses that were little better than houses of prostitution. This was one reason why, it had been explained to him, many young Chinese sought to immigrate to the United States, in the hope of

17

finding work and a better degree of equality among the sexes.

As they stood at the rail, Lopasuta took Luke from Mei Luong and cradled him tenderly in his arms, saying in English, "Look, my son; this is the country in which you and I and Mei Luong will live. It is a country of opportunity and freedom for people from all over the world. And I will see that you learn, as I learned, how to help those who are in need and who are victimized by others who think that because they have wealth through an accident of birth, they can rule over their financial inferiors in the way that the feudal lords of the Middle Ages did."

Mei Luong's eyes were wide with curiosity as the *Southern Belle* approached its dock in the great wharf. As she looked toward the bow, there lay the beautiful city of San Francisco. The city seemed remarkably familiar to Mei Luong, for, like Hong Kong, here too were bustling wharfs, steep hills to which hundreds of buildings clung tenaciously, and many church steeples piercing the sky. As they steamed past dozens of different kinds of vessels, she thought to herself that if it weren't for the lack of her beloved sampans, she would truly feel as if she hadn't sailed thousands of miles to an alien land. Mei Luong hadn't known what to expect when they finally reached their new home—this America—and now that she was here, she no longer felt quite so fearful.

"There are so many ships, master," she exclaimed. "It must be larger than Hong Kong."

"Not quite yet, but one day it will be, Mei Luong," Lopasuta prophesied. "And you and Luke are seeing it for the first time on the day that Americans celebrate as the birth of the Son of their God. It is a good omen, Mei Luong."

"I will try to learn the ways of the *wai kuo jen*, master. Although I am only a worthless sampan girl, I do not want to be useless in this new country."

"You must never think that way of yourself again, Mei Luong," Lopasuta interrupted fiercely. "Because of you, Luke is alive. I want you to be with him as his nurse for as long as you yourself wish it, Mei Luong. You will teach him the ways of your people. The Chinese are an honorable and kind race, and their word can be trusted. This is what I myself believe, and I want my son to learn that there are other people and other ways in this great world of ours.

18

Knowing how they live and think will make a better man of him. I do not know the Chinese word for it—in English we call it education, Mei Luong. But," his tone softened, "now let us get ready to go ashore."

As they stood outside the telegraph office on the Embarcadero, Lopasuta clutched in his hand a copy of the Christmas message he had just sent to Geraldine. Leland Kenniston suggested they go immediately to the new Palace Hotel straight up Market Street, a hostelry recommended by Captain Jackson. As Lopasuta turned his head to view the broad thoroughfare, he noticed a tall spire two blocks away—Trinity Church.

"Leland," the Comanche began, "I wonder if you would mind if we went to that church before we secure our lodgings."

"I think that's a fine idea," Leland assured him. "However, I suggest that we disencumber ourselves of our luggage first." With this, he hailed a passing hansom cab and directed the driver to take their belongings on to the Palace Hotel. The driver smartly stepped down from his seat and carefully lifted in Lopasuta's battered traveling case and, after a bit of a struggle, with Lopasuta assisting, Leland's large, unwieldy steamer trunk. Mei Luong, however, was reluctant to hand over her meager possessions to a total stranger, and clung tenaciously to her small bundle.

Ten minutes later, the little group of travelers sat at the back of the lovely church, listening to the choir sing the Christmas hymns and to the priest delivering his heartening sermon on how Christ was born for the redemption of the sins of man.

As Mei Luong looked around in awe, Leland gave her a warm smile of reassurance. Lopasuta bowed his head and silently prayed. He was grateful to God and to the Great Spirit for his deliverance from the toils of William Brickley, who he now firmly believed had not only drugged him in New Orleans, but also arranged for his being put aboard the ship bound first for this very city, and then transferred to one destined for Hong Kong. For all his long hours of anguished thinking, though, he still could not understand why.

He then thought longingly of Geraldine. How loyal she had been, since that first day when she had come up to

19

him in the courtroom to congratulate him, after he had won a case defending an illiterate black stonemason who had done work for a corrupt scalawag. He remembered how they had courted in secret, eating lunch at a little restaurant on the outskirts of the city owned by an elderly black man and his wife and rarely patronized by the white citizens of Montgomery; how she had alienated her parents by deciding that she was going to marry him; and how idyllic life had been for them, beginning with their New Orleans honeymoon.

He had been gone from her almost two years, and it had only been a little over a month since he had discovered that his miserly employer had never mailed the letter he had written to Geraldine when he first arrived in Hong Kong explaining what had happened to him after his visit to New Orleans to consult with William Brickley. The months had dragged by with no reply from her, and he was sure Geraldine had given up on him.

He prayed for the soul of Lu Choy, the young woman who had found him left for dead in an alleyway when he was first dumped off in Hong Kong and had taken him back to her sampan, where she nursed him back to health. He remembered that one spontaneous and unforeseen liaison with the Chinese woman who, in a moment of terror during a terrible storm, had clung to him for comfort—resulting in the birth of his son Luke and the death of Lu Choy. Afterwards, he had learned of his employer's perfidy, and immediately sent another long letter to Geraldine, telling her all that had happened.

And so he prayed fervently that Geraldine would not reject him because of his infidelity. If she would not take him back as her husband, he hoped she would accept this child. Among his own people, the Wanderers, adultery was an unpardonable sin. Often the wife was put to death, and sometimes the guilty man was banished from the tribe and sent out into the desert to take his luck with the pitiless elements.

He thought, too, of his child by Geraldine, the child he had never seen. He could not wait until he reached Montgomery to see that child, who had been created in their love for each other. It was all he asked from a kind and merciful God.

When the service was over, Lopasuta turned to Mei Luong, who had sat very quietly beside him. "Luke is a wonderful baby—he didn't make a sound," he murmured. "And you're a wonderful nurse, Mei Luong."

She lowered her eyes self-effacingly. Soon after she had come aboard Lu Choy's sampan to nurse the child, she had reluctantly told Lopasuta of her own life. Like Lu Choy, her own parents had been very poor, and she represented an economic burden to them. Finally, when she was only twelve, they had sold her to a brothel keeper in Peking. She had escaped one night and made her way along the dusty road toward Hong Kong, for she had heard that it was a free port and the British authorities would not let people be sold into slavery. There, she had worked sewing garments in a dingy, airless shop for only a few pennies a day, enough to buy her food and little else. And then, when she was fifteen, a young coolie had come into the shop to pick up some garments for his mistress. He had seen her and smiled at her, and it had been the first kindness she had known in all her life. Even her own mother had hated her, she had told Lopasuta.

Thanks to the coolie's infatuation for her, she had been recommended by him to the steward of the wealthy household where he worked, that of a dealer in precious jade who was patronized by many of the wealthy British. She had worked there for a year and then, when her young benefactor had been given a generous gift by his employer so that he might marry her, she had talked Li Kuo into buying a sampan. She had argued that this would be an investment in their future, since they could earn their living by fishing. And he had consented.

Four months after she had found herself pregnant, her young husband had slipped and fallen off the sampan in deep water beyond the port and drowned. When her child was born, it was malformed, and mercifully it had died a day later. And then the miracle had happened, she had told Lopasuta: a little more than a week after her baby's birth and death, the old midwife had come for her and told her that there was a foreign devil who needed a wet nurse for his newborn child.

Lopasuta thought that, if Geraldine could listen to Mei Luong tell her story, she would understand the desperate, poverty-stricken lives so many Chinese led and how it was that, out of the will of fate, he had met Lu Choy, who had saved his life and then given him, without his having sought it, her love.

The little group walked out of the church and were momentarily dazzled by the sun after the dimness of Trinity's interior. There was scarce traffic on Market Street, where normally its hundred-foot expanse would be pulsating with horse-drawn vehicles of every description, and Lopasuta expressed a slight worry that perhaps they should walk back to the Embarcadero to find a carriage. But just as the travelers began to walk down the wide sidewalk, an open carriage-for-hire pulled up to the curb, and the driver asked if they wanted his services.

As they clambered into the cab's interior, Leland directed the driver to take them to the Palace Hotel. A flick of the reins sent them briskly on their way. Although the hotel was only a short distance up Market Street, the travelers craned their necks as the sights and sounds of San Francisco presented themselves for inspection. As the cab pulled around onto New Montgomery Street and into the courtyard of the hotel, even Leland Kenniston, seasoned traveler though he was, gaped in wonder. Standing seven stories high, the Palace Hotel was a monument to its deceased builder, William C. Ralston, then president of the Bank of California. The interior courtyard, where passengers were picked up and discharged, was actually an atrium, ringed by balconies and roofed above by opaque glass to let in light. As he stepped from the carriage, Lopasuta momentarily thought he was back in the lush bayous of Louisiana, for he found himself amidst a forest of potted plants. Leland led the way into the lobby, stopping to peer into the hundred-and-fifty-five-foot-long main dining room, and stepped up to the front desk.

The dapper clerk looked frostily at Mei Luong cradling Luke in her arms, and then turned a scornful eye on Leland, who crisply ordered, "I wish three rooms: one for myself, one for this gentleman, Mr. Bouchard, and one for Mr. Bouchard's child and nurse. You have already received our luggage."

"I'm terribly sorry, sir," the clerk declared haughtily, "but it *is* Christmas, and I'm afraid we are all booked up."

"My good man, I think this will interest you," Leland began, withdrawing from his inner coat pocket a crisp white sheet of paper and displaying it ostentatiously to the clerk. The latter's demeanor immediately became more respectful, almost fawning.

22

"I do apologize, Mr. Kenniston. I can't imagine what I could have been thinking. Of course! Three of our finest rooms are at your disposal. I'll have a bellman bring your luggage directly, sir. The number four elevator will take you up, sir. Rooms seven-o-five, seven-o-seven, and seven-o-nine, sir. They are all exterior rooms and the bay windows will give you a lovely view of the harbor. Thank you for your patronage, Mr. Kenniston."

The travelers strode into the elevator, and Leland was bemused to watch the expressions on Mei Luong's and Lopasuta's faces as the elegant paneled car with its padded benches and mirrors glided them upward.

Mei Luong was shown to her room, and stared in wonder first at the fireplace, then at the huge double bed covered with a satin spread, the silk hangings, and the elegant dressing table near the window. She clapped her hands with glee when Leland turned the taps on the marble washstand, and she ran her hands over and over again through the water streaming out. When he showed her how to use the commode, she giggled like a little girl, then blushed and put her hands over her smiling face. Lopasuta laughed with delight over her pleasure, hoping that it erased the initial hostility of the desk clerk's reception of her.

As the young lawyer and his friend and benefactor turned back into the hallway to find their own rooms, Lopasuta stared at Leland and asked, "Why did the clerk change his manner so quickly?"

"Unfortunately," his friend responded, "money talks everywhere. I showed him a letter of credit from my New York bank, which is the largest in the country. The amount it shows is enough to convince even that awful snob that we won't skip out as deadbeats—and enough to gloss over the fact that we have a Chinese in our party.

"You see," he went on, "since Oriental labor has been coming to California, the good citizens not only of San Francisco, but also of towns farther along the northwestern part of this country resent the 'heathen Chinee,' as they call them. The Chinese are cheap labor, and they replace whites who feel they've a God-given right to work simply because they're white."

"I understand. My own people were treated that way," Lopasuta remarked gravely.

"And your mother was Mexican, as I recall. Well, I don't think we can be particularly proud of the way we

23

treated the Mexicans. Of course, it was partly because of Santa Anna and the Alamo. I confess to wondering what might have happened in the relations between our two countries if that egotistic opportunist hadn't ordered the no-quarter signal be given by his bugler when he attacked that gallant handful of men with his huge army. Oh, well, anyone can be an amateur historian and second-guesser—and just listen to me! Here it is Christmas, we're in this wonderful city, we're all starved, and I'm prattling on about the Mexican-American War!" Leland chuckled. "Let's freshen up, and then see if we can't find some quiet, homey place in which to have a nice Christmas dinner. I'm sure we can get an excellent meal downstairs in the dining room, but I think Mei Luong might feel very uncomfortable under the scrutiny of hundreds of pairs of eyes."

Lopasuta agreed, remarking to himself that this was yet another example of Leland's kind, thoughtful manner.

Half an hour later, they were all downstairs in the lobby, and Leland excused himself while he walked over to the desk clerk. He returned after a few moments, and said, "The clerk—who has become extremely obliging after his initial rudeness—has recommended a place that might be open today. It's called Chez Marianne, and it's not far from here. I've a partiality for French food—doubtless acquired not only in some of the better New York restaurants, but also in New Orleans. And by the way, Lopasuta, I think that you and your lovely wife will not only fall in love with New Orleans for its color, its history, and its luxury, but, above all, for its marvelous Creole restaurants."

"That is, if she takes me back," Lopasuta replied somewhat glumly, with a deep sigh. He glanced at Mei Luong, who stood holding his son, and he added, "I prayed that she would take me back. But it is for the Great Spirit to decide."

"I've a feeling she will, and you'll only torture yourself if you keep brooding about it till you reach Montgomery, Lopasuta. When we take the train tomorrow, I want to talk to you in more detail about what I have in mind for you in New Orleans. It would be good to get your mind back to something substantial like that. You're a very gifted person, and what you've done in the legal profession in Montgomery, where you ran into so much prejudice, has greatly impressed me. Also, now that I've come to know you well, I admire many other qualities about you."

24

"It's kind of you to say that, Leland. And I feel a deep bond of friendship for you, as well. I'll say only that if I do accept your offer, I'll devote as much of my energy as possible to work on your behalf."

"I've known that from the beginning, and that's why I want you with me. Well now, here comes a carriage; let's tell the driver to take us to Chez Marianne. It's five o'clock, and I could eat a horse, to be frank with you."

"So could I." Lopasuta again glanced at Luke and then nervously added, "Perhaps the restaurant won't allow babies."

"If the place is run by a woman, I think I can appeal to her maternal side. Besides, judging from the way your son behaved during the church service, he won't bother any of the patrons there," Leland rejoined, as he hailed the carriage driver.

Chez Marianne was owned and run by Marianne Valois Anderson. Marianne had come to San Francisco after leaving Galveston, where she had had an affair with Lawrence Davis, the son-in-law of Arabella Hunter, Luke Bouchard's half sister.

Originally a milliner, Marianne had always wanted to open a bistro like the one her parents had run in France, and her initial success, plus her subsequent marriage to young Kevin Anderson, convinced her that she should expand her establishment. Her restaurant was becoming known and frequented by some of the finest citizens of her adopted city, who appreciated not only the excellent Creole meals but also her charming hospitality.

Now thirty-five, Marianne exulted in life and was grateful for her good fortune. Although Kevin was nine years younger than she, he had proved to be a devoted husband and considerate lover, and gradually he had begun to take greater responsibility in the running of her restaurant. He had suggested advertising posters, as well as printed flyers, which were delivered to various hotels and other business establishments to increase patronage—and he was still young and vigorous enough to act as a bouncer, in the event that customers became rowdy.

But best of all—and it was something that she had secretly hoped for since her teens—she had had a child by him. This Christmas Day marked the four-month anniversary of her baby Danny's birth. That was one of the reasons that had prompted her to keep the restaurant open, although Kevin had argued that everyone else in town had closed down to celebrate the holiday. "No, darling," she insisted. "I'm so grateful for the wonderful luck I've had in being married to you and having Danny, in doing such wonderful business, and being complimented all the time by people we haven't seen before. Surely in this growing city, Kevin, there must be many people who would love a good meal in congenial surroundings—maybe they're traveling and away from home and their loved ones, and some hospitality and good food would be welcomed—and remaining open today for these people is my way of expressing my gratitude."

She had prevailed on him, and so the restaurant was beautifully decorated with fir boughs hung on the moldings and red candles in glass holders on each table. At the base of each candle, a circlet of holly with its red berries added a further festive note.

A carriage halted before the restaurant. Leland Kenniston peered through the window and declared, "We're in luck: not only are they open, but it looks absolutely charming. Our train won't leave until ten o'clock tomorrow morning, so we can enjoy a leisurely Christmas dinner and sleep late if we want to. Come on, Lopasuta. Here, Mei Luong, hand me down Luke."

"I'm afraid he'll have to be content with his usual fare," the tall Comanche lawyer humorously declared as he took his tiny son from Leland and kissed him on the forehead.

The tall, black-haired Irishman paid the carriage driver and reached in to lift Mei Luong out, much to her embarrassment. Lopasuta stared at his new friend: this considerate act underlined his respect for the man whose life he had saved aboard the *Southern Belle*. More and more, his instinct told him that a relationship with Leland Kenniston would create boundless opportunities—which he could never achieve in Montgomery, regardless of how hard he worked—due in large part to his new friend's forthright and energetic personality.

Mei Luong drew back, her black eyes widening with surprise, for Leland's gesture had been one which evinced a feeling of equality between him and herself: feeling an inferiority imposed by the centuries-old Chinese tradition of male domination over the female, she could not believe what she saw. She understood that he meant it, but all the

26

same she hesitated until Leland again beckoned to her with an impatient smile. Lopasuta gave his son back to Mei Luong, and then the little party proceeded into the bistro.

Marianne Anderson, wearing a burgundy satin gown, came forward with an ingratiating smile. "A merry Christmas to all of you, and welcome to Chez Marianne. I do believe that you are new here, and you have come on a very special day."

"We have indeed," Leland avowed. He continued with a smile, "We've just come all the way from Hong Kong, and tomorrow we take the train back east. I was told by the clerk at the Palace that you had the finest French restaurant in all of San Francisco."

"Edmund Carlson is somewhat prejudiced, but I'll try to live up to our reputation," she declared graciously, as she led them to a table.

Seated around a small table near the entrance sat three men, none older than thirty. Waiting for their first course to be served, they had imbibed Christmas cheer more ardently than wisely. One of them, dressed in a black frock coat over a stiff white shirt and a cravat at the collar, glowered as the pretty young Chinese girl carrying Luke walked past his table. Then he turned back to his two companions and, in a slurred voice, grumbled, "What the hell is this? I thought this was a decent place, yet here we have a chink bitch walking in and showing herself off. Hey, Marianne, come on over here, quick!"

The attractive proprietress handed menus to Leland, Lopasuta, and Mei Luong, then murmured, "Excuse me, if you please. I'll be right back to take your order." Then, straightening her shoulders and frowning at her rowdy guests, she went over to their table and bent to the young San Franciscan who had made the scurrilous remark about Mei Luong. "Please, boys, no trouble on Christmas Day, hm? You can see that these are people of quality, and there's no reason for you to be so rude."

"Lissen, Marianne," the irritated, partly inebriated man in the black frock coat growled, "don't tell me you've become a chink lover all of a sudden! We've got too damned many of those yellow-skinned heathens coming into San Francisco—and I for one don't want any part of them. Now you just get her out of here."

"I am sorry, Mr. Cabot, but I must decline to do your bidding. I opened this establishment to offer good food and

27

hospitality to anyone who wishes to enjoy it—unless he or she proves to be objectionable. And these people are quiet, they've come a long way—one of the gentlemen said that they just sailed in from Hong Kong—"

"In that case, Marianne, to hell with your place! All I have to do is tell my friends, and you'll be off limits to them, you hear me?" the man named Cabot hissed as he tried to rise and then sank back in his chair, panting heavily.

"Really, Mr. Cabot, that's not fair. You're good customers, all three of you. But just once, since you'll probably never see these people again, be nice," Marianne pleaded.

"Oh, to hell with it! Maybe if I get some of your good French food in me, I'll feel better about it—but I don't think so," Cabot growled. His two friends, both owlish from the liquor they had already consumed, nodded solemnly.

Marianne gave the trio a worried smile and then went back to the table where the foursome waited and murmured, "I'm sorry if they've offended you. I didn't expect anything like this. Now, would you two gentlemen like a drink to start with, while you make your decision? Of course we have roast turkey, and I also have some wonderful crabs fresh from the Bay this very morning."

"I think we should have the crab as an appetizer," Leland decided, "and a bottle of good French white wine —perhaps a Chablis, if you stock it."

"I do indeed, and it will be my pleasure to let you enjoy the wine with my compliments."

"That's very kind of you, Mrs.—" Leland hesitated.

"It's Anderson. Marianne Anderson."

"A pleasure to meet you, Mrs. Anderson. I'm Leland Kenniston, from New York, and this is my good friend, Lopasuta Bouchard. The Chinese girl is the *amah*—that's Chinese for nurse, you know—to his little son, Luke."

Marianne's eyes widened. "Did you say Bouchard? Bouchard—that name is familiar to me—" she exclaimed.

"The Bouchards are a large family, Mrs. Anderson," Lopasuta explained. "I was adopted by Luke Bouchard, of Montgomery, Alabama. But there are also Bouchard relatives in Texas—Carrizo Springs and Galveston."

Marianne had gone very pale and put her hand to her mouth. Now she remembered: Arabella Hunter, the mother of Melinda Davis—wife of Marianne's secret lover,

Lawrence Davis—was a Bouchard. Lawrence had once mentioned this. Decidedly, she told herself, it was a very small world. She collected herself and murmured, "Very likely that's where I heard the name. You see, I spent some time in Galveston before coming out here. But forgive me—I am keeping you hungry! I might suggest, if you don't care for turkey, a delightful *canard aux cérises*. I have a New Orleans chef who is a wizard at elegant Creole cooking, and I promise you that you won't be disappointed if you try his duck. It's cooked with cherries, a little brandy, and wild rice with almonds that are sauteed in butter before they're introduced into the rice."

"That sounds magnificent and mouth-watering, Mrs. Anderson," Leland chuckled. "I leave myself entirely in your hands. And you, Lopasuta?"

"The duck, of course. Mei Luong, I know that the Chinese enjoy duck, though this is not cooked Peking style. Mrs. Anderson," he looked up at the attractive proprietress, "might I ask for some soup, and possibly some soft fruit as well, for my son?"

"Of course. It's a pleasure to serve all of you."

"We're very grateful for your hospitality. It will make this holiday all the more meaningful," Leland replied sincerely. She gave a little nod and went to the kitchen.

But at the far end of the bistro, the young San Franciscan named Cabot had turned in his chair to glower at Mei Luong and the baby, and now he could no longer contain himself. Stumbling to his feet and lurching forward, he raised his voice. "I don't fancy breaking bread with a goddamned chink around me!"

"Quiet, you fool," one of his companions muttered. But it did not deter the truculent man as he unsteadily made his way toward the table that the travelers shared.

It was Leland Kenniston who rose to his feet and confronted the half-drunk man. "Now, we don't want any trouble with you. Just go back to your table and enjoy your dinner and remember it's Christmas Day," he murmured placatingly and put out a hand to pat Cabot's shoulder. But the latter struck it down with his fist and glared at the now thoroughly terrified Mei Luong. "I'm talking about you, you yellow-skinned devil bitch! You don't belong with decent men in a place like this, you hear?"

Lopasuta Bouchard rose, although Leland made a move to halt him. "You're going to take that remark back. It's

29

not worthy of a *decent* man," he said in a voice trembling with rage.

"And if I don't? Oh, I get it, that's your brat by that chink bitch—*owww!*" At that vicious phrase, Lopasuta had smashed his fist into his interlocutor's face, felling him to the floor, where he lay inert. His two companions hurried from their table to lift him by the arms and drag him back, propping him up in the chair. One of them said, "I'm sorry this happened. We'll take him out of here as soon as we bring him to and get some black coffee into him."

Mei Luong was trembling and crying softly. Lopasuta Bouchard turned to her and whispered, in a mixture of Chinese and English, "You did nothing; he is a hateful man who knows nothing about you. What he says about you is out of ignorance. Please forget it. We shall enjoy our dinner now. And remember above all else, Mei Luong, how grateful I am that you have come with me to take care of my son."

Despite the fact that their train was not due to leave for hours, Lopasuta was awake and out of bed at six o'clock the next morning, unable to contain his excitement over, at long last, leaving for home and his beloved Geraldine.

After pacing his room for an hour, feeling like a tiger in a cage, he walked down the hotel corridor to Leland Kenniston's room and knocked softly. Leland, too, was awake and dressed, and he suggested that Mei Luong also be awakened, so they could spend their last few hours in San Francisco taking in some of the sights.

Leland rode the elevator down to the lobby, and requested of the desk clerk that a hearty breakfast be sent up to his room. After dining on what seemed like mountains of scrambled eggs, bacon, and sourdough toast, the party packed their bags, paid their bill, and strode into the courtyard, where they hailed a hansom cab for a leisurely drive to the train station.

They boarded the Southern Pacific at ten o'clock, finally heading east. The first leg of their journey would take them to St. Louis. Leland had arranged for Mei Luong and the baby to have a separate compartment from his own and Lopasuta's. Aside from reasons of propriety and comfort, this would give him ample time and privacy to talk to the Comanche lawyer regarding the latter's possible future with him in the New Orleans branch of his business.

To Lopasuta's embarrassment, Leland had insisted on paying the others' fares all the way to Mongomery. When Lopasuta had protested this magnanimous offer, his benefactor winked, saying, "Think of this as a business conference."

As they settled into their compartment, Leland turned to Lopasuta and said, "I'll be getting off this train at St. Louis and changing there for New Orleans. In the meantime, I hope we can more or less settle things between us. As I have mentioned, I hope you will contact the Louisiana Bar Association about taking their examination; it will be imperative for you to be licensed in that state."

"Leland"—Lopasuta broke in—"before we go any further discussing the nature of your business and my duties, there is one thing that worries me."

"What's that? If it's the money—"

"Oh, no, not that in the least," Lopasuta declared, shaking his head. "As I've told you, I've made enemies in Montgomery because I stand up for those who are poor, illiterate, and in the minority—my *jefe*, Sangrodo, of the Wanderer tribe of the Comanche, recommended that I speak for my people. It is because of that that Luke Bouchard offered me the chance to study with a wonderful old man, a great lawyer himself, who had not a single bone of prejudice in his entire body. Thanks to him, I became a lawyer in Montgomery. What I am getting at is, I am concerned about being able to devote as much time as I can to those who have no one to speak for them."

"I know exactly what you're talking about, Lopasuta; that's one of the reasons I particularly admire you. Let me assure you that if you come to work for me, once you are accepted to the bar in Louisiana, I'll give you all the time you need to do what we might call clinical work, helping the unfortunates."

"That's very understanding of you, Leland. I'm tempted to say now that I shouldn't pass up the opportunity you're offering me. But I still have to contend with my domestic life and be prepared to be separated from Geraldine if she won't accept me."

Leland had turned for a moment to watch the magnificent California landscape pass by the train window, but now he turned back, his eyes narrowed, and a hint of impatience in his voice. "Look, Lopasuta, you've unwillingly been to hell and back. I'd be ready to stake my reputation

31

in the belief that your wife is going to accept you. And as for the child—why, no one can blame you for what happened: you thought yourself lost forever, and you took what comfort you could from a fellow human being who had saved your life. If Geraldine is half the woman you've made me believe she is, she'll forgive you readily enough when you're reunited with her."

Tears glistened in Lopasuta's dark eyes, and he turned his face away to hide his feelings; Comanche did not reveal their secret selves. But Leland Kenniston was one of those rare, communicative spirits who had made him feel thoroughly at ease, as if he had been a friend for many years. At last he said, "With what you've offered, Leland, if Geraldine *does* take me back, I'll be able to provide for her as I've always wanted to, and make up to her for my long absence. I long to see her again—and the child I've *never* seen. We'll be a family—two wonderful children— that is, if she will accept my son by Lu Choy."

"This is the Christmas season, Lopasuta," Leland said kindly, as he put his hand on Lopasuta's shoulder and smiled reassuringly at him.

"I shall never forget how kind you've been to me. I can't wait to tell Geraldine about you. And I bless the Great Spirit that we met, and have so quickly progressed from strangers to loyal friends."

## Two

Before they went to the dining car for lunch on that first morning of the journey, Lopasuta inquired, "You told me that you run an importing and exporting firm in New York, and that you had gone to Hong Kong to open a branch there?"

"Yes, that's right. I was more interested in Hong Kong than San Francisco because, as a free port, it's the source of shipments of the most varied and salable cargoes my firm can obtain. I've a factor in San Francisco who handles the transference once the ship docks at the Embarcadero, and conveys the goods on to New York at my direction. Eventually, I'll more than likely open an office there, and I'm already looking for some trustworthy and knowledgeable men who can supervise that part of the operation. As a matter of fact, I've only been to San Francisco on the way to Hong Kong and back."

"That rowdyism in the restaurant last night when that drunken fool abused Mei Luong," Lopasuta said thoughtfully, "is that something that happens frequently?"

"Yes, unfortunately," Leland said with a shrug of distaste. "There's what we Europeans call a ghetto in San Francisco, along Grant Avenue, where all the Chinese are quartered. It's their only way to protect themselves against the insularity and belligerence they're beginning to encounter—and not only in California, but also, as I mentioned last night, in some of the states and territories like Nevada, Washington, and Wyoming—wherever big ranchers, railroad subsidiaries, and mine owners are anxious to get cheap labor."

"I see." Lopasuta shook his head as he stared out the window at the California countryside. "I know that the South is rife with bigotry and racism. Perhaps that was why I wanted so much to become a lawyer: I felt that I could be at least one voice standing against the injustice I began to observe. And in all the time I've been away from my country—for I feel it to be this, Leland—these evils haven't lessened. I feel it is more incumbent upon me than ever to take a stand against intolerance wherever I see it."

"I'm glad you're an idealist, but I hope at least you're a practical one," Leland chuckled humorlessly. "Don't go so far as to be a martyr for a cause, Lopasuta. Be shrewd enough to measure the possible dangers from your adversaries."

"I know that, and frankly, Leland, that's one reason I'm thinking very seriously about the offer you made me, working for you in New Orleans. I think Geraldine would be happier there."

"I know she would. With the division of the Queen City into American and French Quarters, there's a good deal more tolerance there than you'd find in a place like Montgomery, or even your Tuscaloosa and Birmingham. In

33

states like Georgia and Mississippi—and perhaps a great part of Louisiana—which sheltered the huge plantations that exploited black labor before the Emancipation Proclamation, you're certain to find an inflexible intolerance against any humanitarian principles such as you espouse."

Leland suddenly grinned and shook his head. "I'm doing it again—going off on a tangent! Getting back to business matters, Lopasuta, any firm that does a good deal of international business, as I do, is bound to run up against legal complications periodically. Now, I know that this isn't the type of law that you are normally involved with—I believe it's called corporate law—but statutes and rules are statutes and rules, no matter which side of the legal coin you're dealing with.

"There will be a lot of matters having to do with tariffs and contracts—simple and cut-and-dried, for the most part, but occasionally people like to make things difficult. Sometimes you'll run into some fellow who wants his palm greased before he lets my goods either into or out of the country—and I won't stand for that sort of behavior."

"I understand, Leland. But from the sound of it, I don't feel right about accepting the kind of money you've mentioned for what seems like so little work on my part."

"Nonsense," the Irishman declared. "The salary is more than justified, as far as I'm concerned, just knowing that I'll have someone as trustworthy and ethical as you on retainer to me at all times. That is, of course, if you accept my offer."

"Well, I certainly want to keep in touch with you, and after I see what Geraldine decides about my future with her—if I'm to have any—I will let you know."

"That's fine. I'm still certain that she'll take you back with no recriminations. She sounds like a young woman with spunk and a good sense of humor—invaluable traits for a long and happy marriage."

"I certainly pray this is true, Leland. When we reach St. Louis and I find out what the train connections are to Montgomery, I'll wire her again so that she can be there to meet me—that is, if she wants to," Lopasuta declared.

"Cheer up. I tell you, you're worrying about nothing. You've a whole future ahead of you, a life of opportunity, and you've had that marvelous leavening of experience which will help you survive where weaker men would fail. After what you told me about how you managed to keep

34

alive in Hong Kong and how you worked so doggedly and stubbornly to subsist, I've nothing but admiration for you. I don't intend to look for any other man to handle my New Orleans business."

"I'm very grateful for your confidence in me, and I swear to you it won't be misplaced if I do accept. But now, if you'll excuse me a moment, Leland, I'd like to see how my son is and also if Mei Luong is getting along all right."

Leland gave him a cheerful wave and reminded him that luncheon would be served in about half an hour. Lopasuta nodded and left to go to the compartment next door. Mei Luong sat looking out the window, holding Luke in her arms. As Lopasuta sat down in the seat opposite her, she started, and then smiled and lowered her eyes, while a soft blush spread over her pretty face.

"The baby is well?" he asked.

"Oh, yes, master! He is such a healthy, happy baby, and he almost never cries. My mother once said to me that if a baby does not cry, it is the sign that he will have a happy life all of his days."

"I hope your mother was right! Now tell me, Mei Luong, are you comfortable?"

"Oh, yes, master, you must not worry about this unworthy person."

"You must not refer to yourself that way," Lopasuta told her. "I meant to speak to you about last night—in the restaurant, you remember. I apologize for what that man said to you."

"I was not afraid for myself, master, only for the baby. I did not want him to hurt the baby."

"He wouldn't have had a chance, believe me," Lopasuta declared fiercely as he put out his forefinger and playfully touched Luke's nose.

"Yes, master."

"We did not have very much time to see San Francisco, of course. But Mr. Kenniston told me that there is a section where the Chinese people live. In this way, they can keep up their traditions, maintain their families, and keep out of trouble, such as what happened last night in the restaurant."

"That is interesting, master. I know that my people ask for very little, only a chance to work with dignity and to support themselves. I am not afraid of work, but I know that because I am from such a low-caste family, there

35

would be no hope for me at all if I were back in Hong Kong or Peking. I told you how my father sold me to the keeper of an evil house, and there are many girls like me to whom that is done. Perhaps this is why they come here and try to live among their own kind, so that they will not be outcasts."

"That is true, Mei Luong. And it is true also that there are many men like that one who said bad things to you, with whom I fought. But these are people without knowledge or understanding of you and what you represent. But I promise you that you will have nothing to fear while you are in my household."

Luke reached out his tiny hands and grasped his father's finger, and Lopasuta uttered a sigh of delight as he regarded Mei Luong. "Just think, Mei Luong, I still do not know if my other child is a boy or a girl. It won't be until we reach our destination that I shall finally see the other one who was born while I was in Hong Kong. It is quite a family now."

Mei Luong nodded, her eyes still downcast, as she shifted the baby to a more comfortable position in her arms and then leaned forward to smile down at him. "I know that I am very lucky, master. You have been very kind to me. I will serve you for as long as you wish me to, and I will try to cause you no trouble wherever I go."

"You never will, Mei Luong, and I am more grateful to you than I can say. Now, in a little while, there will be luncheon served in the dining car up ahead. You will join Mr. Kenniston and me."

"Thank you, master. You are sure that if I sit at the same table with you, I will not disgrace you?"

"Of course you won't!" Lopasuta assured her.

"I thank you, master." She hesitated, then continued, "Master, my English is yet not too good, but I think I have understood the words that you have spoken to your friend. Please excuse my impertinence, master, but I understood you to speak of your wife and how long you had been away from her and your fear that she would not take you back because you are bringing her this child. Forgive me, I do not mean to speak out of place—"

"There's nothing to forgive. Tell me what you wish to say, Mei Luong," he urged.

"It is only—if you wish, I will tell her how you behaved

toward Lu Choy and how all of the boat people thought you to be a kind, decent man."

"Again I am grateful to you. I will come for you at lunch, then, in a little while." He abruptly rose, not wanting to show that there were tears in his eyes from the gentle humility of her words and her innate tenderness.

The heavy snow left by a Kansas blizzard delayed the train a day, and it was not till the thirtieth of December that Leland Kenniston and Lopasuta Bouchard reached St. Louis, where both men were to change trains. The enterprising black-haired Irishman almost immediately boarded one headed for New Orleans, while Lopasuta had to wait two hours for his connection that would ultimately, after one final change, take him into Montgomery.

The railroad station was cold and damp, but for Lopasuta being so close to home made him so exhilarated that he barely saw the dingy surroundings of the railroad yard, with the gusts of steam and the whistles and the redcaps scurrying with baggage and the flow of passengers who often jostled him as he stood smiling at his departing friend.

"Well now, Lopasuta," Leland said, "if you're wanting to wire Geraldine when you're coming home, you've plenty of time to do it. Now, I intend to spend about a week in New Orleans to open up an office. You mentioned that you were familiar with the Brunton & Barntry Bank in the Queen City, and you also said that if I didn't have a particular bank in mind to handle my finances there, you couldn't recommend that institution more highly."

"I still say it, Leland. Jason Barntry is getting old, but he's the soul of honor. Laure Bouchard trusts him blindly, and he's never let her down. He's made money for her in investments, and he's a sound, sober man, who doesn't believe in speculating or plunging wildly."

"And that's exactly the sort of banker I want to represent me. I told you before, Lopasuta, that piece of information is worth a good deal of money to me, and already you've solidified your position with me. As soon as I get back to New York, which ought to be about the middle of January, I'll be in close touch with you. I have your home address in Montgomery—"

"Yes." For a moment, Lopasuta's face fell, and he glanced glumly over at Mei Luong, who held Luke and waited passively, her eyes lowered. "I have your address too, Leland, and I may have to wire you from a hotel—if Geraldine rejects me."

"Now that's a trait in you which I can't say I admire," Leland declared, as he clapped the tall Comanche lawyer on the back. "You're normally such a positive person, and you went through hell and you stood on your own two feet and you got back safely. Why should you be pessimistic now? That wife of yours, she knows what she has in you. And even if she considered what you've done a transgression—which I personally don't, considering the circumstances—she'd be sure to think twice before she turned you out of her life forever. Don't forget, you've had a child together. You go on home thinking that you're going to be man and wife again and happier than you've ever been. And when the two of you move to the Queen City to work for me, she'll know that she made the right choice when she married you—I'm sure of it."

"I can never forget what you've done for me and the hope you've given me, Leland. Even if I shouldn't be privileged to work for you, you're a friend I shall value to the end of my days," Lopasuta said, as he solemnly extended his hand, which Leland shook heartily. "I promise that, as soon as I speak with Geraldine, I'll wire your New York office to let you know how things stand."

"Excellent! By the way, I very much want to meet Geraldine. I'm not sure if I'll be able to get back to New Orleans when we're ready to finalize matters, so I'd love you to bring Geraldine to New York. You've drawn such a fine picture of her, I feel I already know her—just as I do Laure Bouchard, your adoptive mother."

"I respect and admire her—and quite apart from her being the wife of Luke Bouchard. She was born in New Orleans, and she knows the city backwards and forwards, Leland. Maybe I can persuade Luke and Laure Bouchard to come along with Geraldine and me, if we do get to New York. And when you meet my adoptive father, Leland," he continued, "you'll understand why I honor the name of Bouchard, which he gave to me. His grandfather, Lucien, came here at the time of the French Revolution. He hewed a prosperous plantation out of wilderness, and divided his profits with the Creeks and freed his black slaves who helped him do it. My tribe will honor his name long after you and I have gone to the Great Spirit, Leland, believe me."

"I do Lopasuta. Well now, I'd best be getting on my train. I wish you and your wife the happiest of reunions. God bless and keep you and your family." Leland turned to Mei Luong and the little baby she cradled in her arms. "Thank you, Mei Luong, for helping my friend. Like all your people I dealt with in Hong Kong, you are honorable and upright. I am ashamed of my own countrymen for treating you and your people so badly, when you come to us in search of freedom."

The young Chinese crimsoned and shifted uneasily, not used to such lavish praise. "The master is too kind to this unworthy person," she murmured.

"No, only just. This man for whom you work, Mei Luong, is a good man. Take care of his child, and I shall see you again one day."

With this, he shook hands a last time with Lopasuta Bouchard, and then, after directing a porter to take his trunk to the baggage car, he picked up his leather valise and walked down the ramp toward the gate from which his train to New Orleans would depart.

On this frigid January morning, Geraldine Bouchard had hired the carriage of an elderly black driver to take her to the red-brick chateau of Windhaven Plantation. Her eighteen-month-old son, Dennis, was at home under the supervision of Mrs. Emily Norton, the middle-aged midwife who had delivered him and still came to visit Geraldine frequently. When Geraldine had learned from her parents that it had been Mrs. Norton who had gone to them and told them of the birth of their grandson and fiercely urged that they not condemn Geraldine for marrying the man of her choice, a tremendous empathy had grown up between the two women.

Geraldine hurried to the door of the chateau and, seizing the knocker, rapped it thrice. A few moments later, it was opened by Amelia Coleman. The attractive octoroon had married Burt Coleman some months after Lopasuta Bouchard had freed her from her indentured servitude to the unscrupulous Carleton Ivers after her father had embezzled money from Ivers's bank. She was expecting a baby in April; if it was a son, he would be named Mason after Burt's favorite uncle. Laure Bouchard, grieving over her martyred husband, had invited the young woman to live in the chateau with her husband and child. This had made them fast friends and confidantes, and Amelia felt that she owed all her happiness to the Bouchards. She went out of her way to comfort Laure in the long, anguished months that followed Luke's untimely death.

Because she was an excellent cook, Amelia had accepted Laure's offer to be official cook of the chateau, with an increase in her wages, after the death of Hannah Mendicott. This, together with Burt Coleman's appointment to the role of assistant foreman working with loyal Marius Thornton, had given Burt—who had been tragically widowed when his first wife, Marietta, had died in childbirth—a new purpose and dedication in life. Burt continued to be responsible as well for overseeing Andy Haskins's acreage downriver, but he had said he was glad to be living at Windhaven Plantation, for Amelia's sake as well as his own, and he had assured Laure that he did not at all mind riding over to Andy's land two or three times a week. Burt's willingness to shoulder additional responsibility, as well as his devotion to Amelia and readiness to make sacrifices for her, had touched Laure's heart and helped to alleviate some of the anguish of her own bereavement.

Amelia uttered a joyous cry of greeting when she saw Geraldine Bouchard. "Oh, my, Miz Geraldine, how nice it is to see you! But what in the world are you doing over here so early in the morning? It's such a long ride from Montgomery!"

"It's because I've the most wonderful news. Lopasuta is finally back from Hong Kong, and he should be arriving at the Montgomery railroad station today! Is Laure here, Amelia?" Geraldine's face was radiant.

"Oh, Miz Geraldine," Amelia exclaimed, "I'm so glad for you! I'll go tell Miz Laure; she's tending John." John Bouchard had been born a month before his father's heroic death, and perhaps because Laure had sensed that this would be the last child she and Luke would ever create, she had from the baby's birth tended to him herself as much as possible, graciously refusing the offers of the older Bouchard children's nurse, Clarabelle Hendry, to look after the baby.

Laure hurried ahead of Amelia, carrying young John in her arms. His hair was as blond as Laure's herself and he had a lusty pair of lungs, which he now demonstrated as he was jostled while his mother fairly ran to meet Geraldine.

"Oh, my, Laure, he's angry!" Geraldine exclaimed. "I

didn't mean for you to hurry so—but I've the most wonderful news!"

"I know, Amelia told me! Well now, young man, I see you want to be the center of attention. But you have to learn that you'll just have to take your turn." Laure stared lovingly down at the little boy and playfully chided him by wagging a forefinger in his face. "Would you mind if I came along with you to welcome Lopasuta back home?"

"Would I mind?" Geraldine echoed, and she laughed gaily. "I came to see you because I wanted so much to ask you if you'd come along with me. I—I'm so excited and anxious, I don't—I really wouldn't want to be by myself at such a time. You know—his letter explaining everything—"

"I know, my dear." Laure's face sobered, and she put a hand out to touch Geraldine's cheek. "And I hope you still feel as you did then, when you read the letter, that you want him back—"

"Oh, yes, with all my heart!"

"And the child by that Chinese girl?" Laure added in a very low voice.

"Oh, of course! He's Lopasuta's, and I understand how it happened. He thought he'd never see me again—and that storm, and—he's not the sort of man who would leave his wife for another woman—Oh, I'm so excited! You're sure you want to come along?"

"Yes, of course. I don't think John is quite up to the long ride into Montgomery, dear, so I'll let Clarabelle Hendry look after him. She's been clucking around me like a mother hen ever since I had him, wanting to take charge!"

"I want to go back home first and get Dennis. Lopasuta will finally see his son—our son." Then, her eyes widening, she mused, "Goodness! He doesn't even know that our child *is* a son!"

Laure turned to Amelia, who stood respectfully behind them. "Amelia, dear, would you give John to Mrs. Hendry and tell her that I'll be going into Montgomery with Geraldine?"

"Of course, Miz Laure." Amelia came forward and took the little boy from Laure's arms, crooning to him as she walked up the stairs to find the amiable nurse.

"Just let me get my wrap—it's so chilly for January, even if this is Alabama," Laure remarked.

A few moments later, both women got into the carriage. Geraldine had begun to worry that perhaps they would miss the train. "I wanted to get there ahead of time, Laure, so we're certain not to miss him. He couldn't tell me exactly what train it would be, but he did know the day—and it's today. And I'd feel awful if I missed him!"

"Hush, darling. You won't miss him, and it's going to be wonderful for you both." For a moment, Laure's face was melancholy as she reflected on Geraldine's imminent happiness, which only served to remind her of her own loss. Even though she had reconciled herself to Luke's death—and been proud of the way in which he had offered his life to save that of Governor Houston—the beautiful widow realized with each passing day how much she had lost in this man who had been lover and father, friend and bulwark of strength, ever since she had agreed to leave New Orleans and be his wife and live with him in the red-brick chateau by the Alabama River. Her great need of him had been sorely underlined by her having realized how susceptible she had been to the specious and devious charm of her dead partner, William Brickley. Having realized her vulnerability after Lucien Edmond Bouchard had come from Texas and exposed Brickley and his plan to bankrupt the plantation and destroy the Bouchard fortune, Laure Bouchard had told herself that never again would she allow her loneliness to lead her into the arms of a man who, on the surface, seemed more than usually attentive and considerate to her.

Geraldine urged the old driver to ride as quickly as he could back to her home, and she was restless through most of the journey. Laure smiled and tried to reassure her. "My gracious, darling, after all this time, I'm sure we won't miss him."

"But suppose his train was early and he doesn't find me there and thinks that maybe I don't ever want to see him again?" Geraldine worried aloud.

Laure put her arm around the younger woman's shoulders and consoled her. "The very idea! I think I know Lopasuta pretty well myself, and I'm sure that if he's gotten there ahead of us, he'll wait until you come. He loves you, and that letter of his was one of the most beautiful things I've ever read. He was honest and he threw himself on your mercy—if he had been a philanderer, he would have been arrogant. But he's not that sort of man at all, and he knows that you know it. So you just hush up and sit back and relax. We'll be at the station very soon!"

The elderly driver of the carriage, doubtless spurred by the thought of the bonus Geraldine Bouchard had promised him for making the drive to Lowndesboro, then back to her house, and thence to the railroad station, drove expertly—though sometimes, in rounding bends in the road, both women were jostled more than they enjoyed. But this did not in the least irritate Lopasuta's beautiful young wife, who clung to Laure's hand and from time to time cast the honey-haired widow eloquently fervent glances, which bespoke all her inward emotions at the thought of this long-delayed, dramatic reunion.

The carriage drew up in front of the house, and Emily Norton had Dennis dressed and ready and hurried out to lift the little boy into Geraldine's arms. But Laure proposed with a laugh, "Do let me take him, Geraldine; you're so nervous, I'm afraid you might drop him!"

"That's very kind of you, Laure. Frankly, I didn't want to do this by myself," Geraldine confessed with a nervous laugh. As Dennis nestled in the cradle of Laure's arms, Geraldine leaned to him and kissed him on the forehead and murmured words of endearment. "Thanks so much, Mrs. Norton," she called to the friendly midwife-nurse, "and I'm ever so grateful at your offer to make lunch. But please don't trouble too much; just a little something that Lopasuta and I can share together."

"I completely understand, Geraldine," the woman gaily called back. "I'll have something nice for you when you get back here. Now you go on to the station and don't worry your pretty head about anything."

The elderly black driver glanced back, assured himself that his passengers were comfortably seated, and then started up the horses again. "Now to the railway station, ma'am, ain't dat right?" He turned back to glance at Geraldine for confirmation.

"Oh, yes, and don't delay a minute!"

Then she sobered, remembering. "Oh, Laure, how dreadful of me—I forgot—Lopasuta's been away all this time, he doesn't know about Luke at all—"

"No, very likely he doesn't."

"It will be so dreadful for him—Luke meant so very much to Lopasuta. Oh, how proud your Luke would have been of my husband—oh, my, I really don't know what I'm saying, I'm so excited!" Geraldine confessed.

"That's all right, honey. We'll both tell him. Or, rather, I

43

will. After all," Laure forced a tiny smile, "I'm his adoptive mother and probably the news should come from me."

"Yes, I suppose you're right. Oh, my, the driver is really going fast, isn't he? Well, I can hardly wait to get there. I wonder if we've missed any of the trains. Lopasuta didn't know exactly what one he'd be on, but he was sure he'd be here today," Geraldine repeated nervously.

"Then we'll wait till he comes, it's as simple as that," Laure stated patiently.

Geraldine fretted, "But I do hope it won't be past noon, because otherwise poor Dennis will be all off schedule and get cranky. And if Mrs. Norton prepares a nice lunch, then Lopasuta will miss it. Oh, dear!"

Laure burst out laughing, but there was a tender look in her eyes as she quietly said, "What you're saying, dear Geraldine, jumbled up though it may be, is that you're still very much in love with him."

"Well, of course I am! He couldn't help it if someone drugged him and sent him off on a ship around the world! My goodness, Laure, I'd be a fine one if I blamed him for that when it wasn't his fault!" Geraldine seemed to bristle.

Laure laughed even more. "The way you defend him only proves to me how much the two of you need each other." Then, her face solemn for a moment, she added almost wistfully, "It's wonderful to have love. I know now what it is all the more because I don't have it. And yet, I'm at an age, I suppose, when women are supposed to begin to recede into the background and grow old. Only I don't want to—and Luke would never have approved of that, I'm sure."

"Do you think you'll marry again?" Geraldine hazarded with a quick look at her friend.

"I can't tell. I know that I loved Luke very deeply; I loved John Brunton, too, although in a different way. It's possible for a woman to have several loves in her life, for each means something special in its own right. I haven't met anyone, of course, nor has there been time to think of that. But, yes, to answer your question, I'd like to have someone I could admire and respect and love and live with to the end of my days. Well now, here we are at the station!"

The driver halted the carriage at the side of the railroad station, made of limestone and bricks of the red clay so abundant in this region of Alabama. The clay had given the area its Creek name, "Econchate," which meant red ground. The ticket window was on the outside of the rectangular one-story building, and a modest waiting room with hard wooden benches occupied most of the inside. Outside, between the station and the railroad tracks, were two additional benches. Geraldine urged Laure to take one of these benches so that they could see the trains coming in, while she paid the driver. She told the kindly old man, "If you're still at the station when my husband comes in, I'd like to hire you to take us home."

"Mighty fine with me, ma'am." He tipped his old stove-pipe hat and gave her a wide, almost toothless grin. "I ain't plannin' to go nowhere. It's mighty chilly, and you been real good to me, payin' me what you did, ma'am. I'll just sit inside and have me a chaw of tebacky till you're ready for me agin'."

Geraldine thanked the old man, then hurried over to where Laure sat with Dennis. She was talking to him and making certain that his clothing kept him well covered from the cool January air, but a bleak sun had emerged and had begun to warm the chilly atmosphere. Geraldine was impervious to the weather: she could not sit still, but hurried around to the ticket window and demanded of the agent, "Have there been any trains from the west in already?"

"Oh, yes'm, sure have. One was in here about half an hour ago."

"Oh, dear!" Geraldine made a wry face. "When is the next one due?"

"Lessee now—'bout ten minutes, ma'am. You expectin' a loved one, maybe?"

"Indeed I am! Well then, we'll just wait for it. Thank you very much," she said, and walked back to Laure.

"My pleasure, ma'am," the bespectacled, nearly bald clerk called after her.

"The agent says a train came in half an hour ago, but there's another one due in about ten minutes. Oh, my, I'm so nervous I can hardly sit still—am I ever happy that you came along with me today, dear Laure!" Geraldine fussed.

"Now you sit down and close your eyes and just rest. Save your energy for the time when Lopasuta arrives. He can't miss us—we're right in front of the train," Laure sedately advised.

Geraldine nodded distractedly, glancing up and down

45

the platform. On the other bench, a man and his teenage daughter sat. He was reading a Bible, while the girl self-consciously clutched her coat collar and huddled closer to him, her badly worn gray coat missing a button at the neck. Geraldine sighed and closed her eyes and waited.

Soon there was the mournful hoot of the train whistle as it approached, and she at once sprang from her seat, clasping her hands and looking down the rails to watch it coming. "Oh, I just know he'll be on this one, Laure!" she exclaimed.

Chugging and grinding its wheels, the locomotive halted at last and the porters began to lower the metal step-down stools for the disembarkation of their passengers. A florid-faced, stout man in a beaver-trimmed coat was first to descend and made for the man and his teenaged daughter with a bellowing cry of "Fred, damn it, good to see you! My, Agnes honey, you've grown at least three inches since I last saw you two Christmases ago!" His heavy suitcase in one hand, he adjusted his bowler hat more firmly on his head with the other, and led the two off. Three other passengers got off the train, but not Lopasuta.

Geraldine uttered a cry of dismay as the porters picked up the stools, clambered aboard, and gave the signal to the engineer to start the train up.

"Oh, Laure, whatever could have happened to him?" Geraldine twisted her slim fingers together and her eyes misted. Glancing down at Dennis, she groaned, "It's really nippy, and I'm so afraid you'll catch cold. Maybe I shouldn't have brought him, Laure, but I was so sure Lopasuta would be back by now—"

"Hush, Geraldine, don't be upset," Laure soothed. "Dennis is dressed very warmly and I'll see that he doesn't get a chill. I'm sure Lopasuta will be on the next train. Go ask the ticket agent when it's due. That'll put your mind at ease, honey."

"You're right. I'm being foolish," Geraldine determined and, abruptly turning, strode swiftly toward the ticket agent's window. She returned with the news that the next train was due from St. Louis in forty minutes. "Good gracious, Mrs. Norton's lunch will be just spoiled and everything," she lamented.

Laure smiled knowingly. "Geraldine dear, you're being peevish over things that don't matter. I know it's trying, but just think of how nice it is will be when Lopasuta finally gets off the train. Think how lucky you are. Think how devoted he is."

Geraldine sighed and nodded, a rueful look replacing the somewhat petulant look on her lovely face. "You're right, Laure, you always are. Yes, I am lucky and I know it," she finally said with a flash of her characteristic spunkiness.

"Now that's more like it. Just sit here and think about what it's going to be like between you two when you're reunited again. And before you know it, the train will be in. My, Dennis is a lovely child; he's good and warm and happy—and he's waiting for his daddy."

Laure's appeal had its effect, and Geraldine sat back on the bench, a happy smile on her lips as she waited for the train. Soon, once again, there was the mournful hoot of the train whistle from afar, and again Geraldine sprang to her feet, her eyes wide with eager expectancy. "I just know he'll be on this train, Laure, I know he will!" she exclaimed.

"They say the third time's the charm," Laure quipped as she rose, glancing down at Dennis, who was fast asleep in her arms. A wave of maternal tenderness engulfed her: she was thinking of John. The last child she and Luke had was perhaps because of that the dearest, the most vulnerable and helpless, and so more in need than any of the others of all her love.

Wide-eyed, tense with eagerness, Geraldine watched the train come in and chug to a noisy stop. Then, with a cry of delight and joy, she saw Lopasuta's tall, wiry frame come down the steps, turning back to hand down a Chinese girl carrying a little baby. Her eyes filled with tears, and Laure, still holding Dennis and watching Geraldine closely, was as deeply moved.

Although she had wanted to remain poised and self-assured and let Lopasuta be the first to make overtures, she forgot all this as she saw him and hurried to him. "Oh, my darling, God has given you back to me—and I shall thank Him for the rest of my days—oh, my dear, my love!" she exclaimed tearfully.

He took her in his arms and held her close. For a long moment, there were no words between them. He could feel and hear her muffled sobs, and a surge of contrition arose in him. "I—I can't believe you've forgiven me," he began in a voice that trembled with anxiety and love.

Geraldine disengaged herself from his embrace. Her

47

eyes were wide and bright with tears, but there was a teasing little smile on her lips as she exclaimed, "But after all, I received your letter, my dear one. It told me how much you love me, even when you were far from me, even when you could get no word to me. And you know that I respected you from the very first day I met you, because I knew then—yes, even then—you weren't the sort of man who would ever abandon me."

Mei Luong stood patiently behind him, carrying the baby in her arms. From under thick lowered lashes, she gave Geraldine a covert look, wondering exactly how this white wife would accept the man who had fathered a baby from one of her own kind.

"And so you truly do not blame me, then. It's all I've dreamed of, Geraldine," Lopasuta murmured huskily.

Geraldine straightened, and her eyes sparkled with animation more than tears as she retorted, "Of course I don't blame you! After all, even though I'm not the silly, naive girl I was when I first sought you out in that courtroom, Lopasuta, and I'm an old married woman now, I still have the same nonconformist outlook on life as I've always had. You know, dear, someone like myself doesn't easily give up on or walk away from the people we love and respect. Besides, my darling, I should think you'd have more faith in me than that. Even when I didn't hear from you, never once did I think that you'd given me up or believed that you no longer loved me."

"I thank God and the Great Spirit." Lopasuta reached for her hands and held them tightly, staring deeply into her eyes, a tremulous smile on his lips.

"I've missed you horribly, my dear one," she went on, "more than you can ever know." Then, as if wanting to countermand that total admission of love, she saucily added, "All the same, if I do say so myself, I've managed quite nicely on my own—so I expect you to behave yourself from now on."

He started at this, staring at her. Then he realized that in the time he had been in Hong Kong, he had been almost mesmerized by Lu Choy's way of kowtowing to her man. He knew that he would have to learn all over again a modern American woman's ways of thinking and reacting. Then a slow, wide grin came over his face and he burst into uproarious, happy laughter as he lifted her up into his arms and twirled her around. "Well now, Geraldine, I promise you that you'll never have any reason to doubt me—after what you've just said, I don't think I dare!"

They dissolved in each other's arms, while Laure looked on. She turned to stare at Mei Luong, who met her gaze and flushed, but who could not suppress an amused little smile to see that this beautiful, mature foreign woman understood exactly what she herself was feeling about this reunion. For herself, Mei Luong had been quite certain that no American woman, certainly not one married to Lopasuta, would reject him. Secretly, though she would never dare let him know even the tiniest hint of it, she was more than a little in love with her master.

At last, Lopasuta released his wife and turned to Mei Luong, beckoning her forward. "Geraldine, I'd like you to meet Mei Luong. And this is the child," he murmured. Geraldine looked down at the baby and reached out to touch him very gently on the forehead, just as Lopasuta added, "I've named him Luke, after my father."

"That was a beautiful thought, my darling," she said, biting her lip. "And now, I want you to meet *our* son, Dennis, to whom Luke will be just a wonderful playmate. Laure, dear . . ."

The lovely widow approached and Lopasuta turned to her. "Laure, how good it is to see you after all this time! There were times, black horrible days, when I thought I'd never come back here to see the people I love the most in all this world."

"It's so wonderful to see you again, Lopasuta," Laure replied softly, biting her lower lip to keep her threatening tears in check. "But never mind *me*," she added in a lighter tone. "It's time you met your son!"

As she held Dennis out to Lopasuta, the handsome lawyer gazed with awe at the toddler, then clasped him tightly to his chest. "My son!" he whispered. "My wonderful son! At last I meet you! All this time I have wondered about you, wondered if you were a boy or a girl. Dennis, my son, I am your father." As he spoke the word "father," Lopasuta glanced quizzically around the station platform. "But where is *my* father, Luke?"

Laure's face was grave for a moment, and she glanced knowingly at Geraldine with an implicit look in her eyes that bade the younger woman say nothing of this tragic matter. Instead, brightly, she retorted, "We'll talk about

49

that when I've taken you and Geraldine and your sons home."

Lopasuta nodded in agreement. Then, turning to Mei Luong, he beckoned to her. Unbeknownst to Lopasuta, the young Chinese girl had rehearsed a speech in English, by which she had intended to greet Geraldine. With a charming accent, in her sweet, reedlike voice, she declared, "Honorable one, I am at your service. Luke is a very good boy. I have helped to bring him up for you until you could do so yourself, but I hope that you will let me be his nurse so that I may serve you and the master."

Geraldine burst into happy laughter and spontaneously hugged Mei Luong. Then, turning to Laure and linking her hand in Lopasuta's, she exclaimed, "Let's go back home. Then I'll really know it's happened—that we're all together again!"

The old black man driving the carriage had patiently waited for Geraldine and Laure inside the waiting room. He hurried out to his carriage when he saw them leaving and now beamed to see them approaching with Lopasuta and Mei Luong. " 'Pears like you done found who you been lookin' for, ma'am," he chortled to Geraldine, as he waited while all of his passengers were settled inside the carriage. "Where to now?" Geraldine happily gave him the address of the small white frame house she shared with Lopasuta.

Emily Norton welcomed them and exclaimed delightedly over Luke. She bundled both children into her arms and then scurried to the bedroom, where she placed Dennis in his crib and Luke in his half-brother's old bassinet. Coming back into the parlor, Mrs. Norton told them, "The lunch is ready on the stove; I've been keeping it warm. I made a nice beef stew, and there's biscuits and honey and strong, good coffee—"

"My gracious," Geraldine interrupted with a giggle, "that's more than enough, Mrs. Norton. I'm ever so obliged to you!"

"It was no trouble, dear; I wanted to do my part in welcoming Mr. Bouchard back home," the genial midwife-nurse responded.

Laure, although she really did not wish to eat anything, did so to keep them company. She could see that Lopasuta was impatiently waiting for news of Luke, and this respite gave her time to prepare a story which would not overly tax her own emotions, already deeply shaken by participating in the reunion between Lopasuta and Geraldine.

As they began to eat, Lopasuta remarked with a smile, "All that's lacking is having Luke here, for I wish to honor him."

Laure looked at Geraldine and then, with a sigh, responded, "You have already honored him, dear Lopasuta, by all you've done—by your courage in finding your way back home to those who love and need you: to Geraldine and to me, and most of all to your child. You see, my dear, Luke died a year and a half ago—but he died like a hero, and I shall always remember that with great pride."

"Died—oh, no—no, it can't be true—how? What happened?" Lopasuta cried out in agony.

"He died saving the life of Governor Houston. You see, our old friend Dalbert Sattersfield ran for mayor of Lowndesboro, and his wife, Mitzi, wrote the governor asking him to make a speech supporting Dalbert at a campaign rally. Well, there was a deranged man in the audience; he drew a derringer and was going to kill Governor Houston. Luke leaped down from the platform and tried to take the gun away. But it went off and—and he died right before my eyes in the hospital."

"May the Great Spirit keep his wonderful soul forever," Lopasuta murmured.

"Amen to that, dear Lopasuta. I had him buried, as I knew he would want to be, beside his beloved grandfather on the top of the towering bluff," Laure murmured.

There was a long silence, then at last Lopasuta raised his head, and his eyes were bright with tears. "Truly he died just as he always lived—courageously and selflessly. As soon as I can, I want to go with you, Laure, to pay a visit to his grave."

"Of course. But in the days ahead, you and Geraldine and your children are to spend all your time together thinking about life, not death. For me, Luke will always be alive; he was so vital. Since we all have to die someday, I think he didn't mind going the way he did. He offered his life in return for another man's. I shan't forget that, not ever." She suddenly rose. "And now, it's time for me to leave."

Geraldine drew aside the chintz curtain and declared, "That nice driver is still outside. I think he had an instinct that you'd want to be getting back home."

51

"I'll see you again soon, both of you. Mei Luong, it was good to meet you. You're a sweet girl, and I know you'll take very good care of both the children," Laure complimented the demure Chinese girl, who blushed and nodded.

Laure climbed into the carriage and told the affable old black driver, "You've really worked hard today, and I mean to reimburse you for the helpfulness you've given us on this important day. You remember where you brought the young lady—out to the big red house near Lowndesboro?"

" 'Deed I do, ma'am. You want me to take you back where I picked you up from?"

Laure leaned back and gave a delighted little laugh. "You're omniscient. That's exactly where I want to go now."

"I don't rightly know what dat big word you used means, but I'll take you dere straight off!" he chuckled. He clucked to his horses and shook the reins, starting them trotting off toward the center of town and then southward along the trail that faithfully followed the winding course of the Alabama River.

Arriving back at Windhaven, Laure opened her reticule and handed him a ten-dollar bill. "Oh, no, ma'am, dat's too much!" he protested.

"No, it's not. You've earned it and then some. Thank you ever so much for being so kind and patient with us."

"God bless you, ma'am! You ever want anyone to drive you anywhere you say, you send word to town and ask for ol' Epetha Brown; dat's my name," he beamed.

Laure smiled, waved her hand to him in farewell, and then climbed the steps to her home. She went at once to her bedroom and closed the door, to be alone with her thoughts.

As she had left the white frame house, touched almost beyond her own strong self-control by the happy reunion of Lopasuta and Geraldine, she had beckoned to Lopasuta to walk her to the carriage. In a low voice, she had told him, "There's something else you should know, Lopasuta. It was indeed William Brickley who drugged you and then arranged to ship you to Hong Kong. Lucien Edmond found that out when he came up here after everything seemed to go wrong with my plantation. But I'm getting ahead of my story. You see, when I visited Mr. Brickley in New Orleans after you disappeared, he proposed that we become partners in a gambling salon. Jason Barntry thought it was a sound proposition, and I went into it. Then we found out that Brickley's real plan was to have some of his shills plunge the casino heavily into debt—an expense that I, of course, would be liable for. So you see, dear Lopasuta, the plot to get rid of you was tied up with Brickley's wanting to bankrupt Windhaven Plantation and to malign the integrity of the Bouchard name."

He had looked at her for a long moment, and then murmured, "Thank you for telling me. Now a good many things are clear to me. God bless you, Laure. I'll pray for you and the children." He then had gone back into the house to be with his wife and two young sons.

Laure sat by the window and, opening the shutters, stared out onto the green landscape that led to the scenic banks of the Alabama River. That river, endlessly flowing down to Mobile, had seen the red-brick chateau built by the energies of Henry Bouchard, old Lucien's only surviving son and yet a son who had been completely at odds with his father's nobility of purpose and ethical outlook on life. So Henry Bouchard had inadvertently erected a landmark to the memory of a great man—a man who had founded a dynasty of honor and family loyalty and love, based on the precepts of hard work and the tolerance of all races and creeds and colors of mankind.

These were precepts that had become a part of her own moral code, she who had been once so desolately cynical after General Butler's men had taken over her father's bank in New Orleans and had driven him to suicide after she had yielded herself to a platoon corporal, rather than be gang-raped by the rest of his men. How far she had come, thanks to the sympathy and humanity of John Brunton, who had been her father's banking partner; and then with Luke, the grandson of old Lucien, who epitomized all that his grandfather had lived for and believed in.

She wept silently, thinking of the river and the endless journeys by Luke and Lucien it had witnessed—from Econchate to Mobile, from Montgomery and Lowndesboro to Mobile and New Orleans. Over the long years, their unremitting labor, devotion, and steadfastness of purpose had founded a community that could survive against bigotry and violence.

But that knowledge did not console her now. She was

too filled with the anguish that seeing Lopasuta and Geraldine reunited had evoked within her. She turned to stare into the oval, silver-framed mirror of her boudoir table and saw herself. She was thirty-eight, in the full bloom of her mature womanhood. She was poised, she knew herself to be capable of devotion, and, even more, of the dark, swirling tide of passion. Though she had often twitted Luke about being an "old sobersides," he had thrilled her as an ardent lover, and she had held nothing back in response. When she had been younger, before the tragedy of the occupation of New Orleans by federal soldiers and the subsequent despoilment of decent women had taken place, she had naively believed that an intellectual man could not be capable of carnal passion. How wrong she had been, and how ably Luke had proved that belief to be without foundation!

As she watched the sun slowly wane and the first shadows of twilight touch the distant bluff where Luke lay at immortal rest with old Lucien and his beloved Dimarte, she made an impartial analysis of herself and her life as it now stood.

Her affairs were in excellent order because Hollis Minton, her new attorney in New Orleans, had conscientiously looked after them during Lopasuta's absence. Jesse Jacklin, who had been appointed manager of the casino following the death of William Brickley in the duel with Lucien Edmond Bouchard, had proved to be most capable, and the profits of the gambling house were steadily increasing.

There was Luke's legacy, and part of its foundation had been some of the money old Lucien had invested in the Bank of Liverpool, thereby surviving the collapse of the Confederacy. She knew that she would never want for anything materially: there was money in trust for all the children—Lopasuta had drawn up an ironclad will, which could not be shaken by the most malignant of enemies—she retained a part interest in the Brunton & Barntry Bank, and then there was Windhaven Plantation itself, with its steady, if not spectacular, profit at the end of each year. Of equal importance to her was the fact that on Windhaven Plantation there existed a commune of people who were friends and neighbors, who were part of her family, not simply tenant-owners who shared the amenities and the land with her. Luke had wrought well for her, and she thanked God for his farsightedness.

But when she looked into the mirror again, she saw the tears in her eyes and she knew why she wept. She wept for her loneliness, for the deprivation of the man who had comforted and loved her, who had been able to parry her sauciness and flightiness with a deep-rooted and long-abiding desire, tempered by common sense and, always, warm human compassion. She could not recall that they had ever had a spat, and that was rare indeed. She remembered how she used to tease him, and she remembered how she had first given herself to him when he was on his way to Windhaven Range—while he was still married to Lucy and before Laure herself had married John Brunton. Later, after Lucy had been killed by Mexican bandits and John had died of yellow fever, she and Luke had finally married. And now it was to be no more.

Was there somewhere another man who would take his place? Not yet, not on the horizon. And now she knew better than to be trapped by the lure of physical infatuation, the gambit that the treacherous, suave, and devilishly personable William Brickley had offered her so calculatingly.

She wept again, and she prayed. And then she thought of her children, and mostly of Lucien, who bore the founder Bouchard's never-to-be-forgotten name. He was nearing thirteen, and she wanted him, as the heir apparent, to have as cosmopolitan an education as he could to prepare him for the years ahead. The country was expanding, in transportation, in business and commerce, and in science. He should be more than a farmer to one day be able to meet the new developments of this ever-growing country. Perhaps an excellent Swiss school, or perhaps one in France. She would think about it, and she would ask Hollis Minton, who was well versed in many matters beyond his practice of the law, for his advice.

And she would love them all and show partiality to none of her children, because all of them had been fathered by the man she now mourned and whose memory would be in her heart and mind forever.

# *Three*

Mrs. Emily Norton had obligingly stayed on to prepare supper for Geraldine and Lopasuta, as well as for Mei Luong. Efficiently, she arranged one of the spare rooms for Mei Luong and transferred the bassinet and crib into it so that the young Chinese woman could look after both children and yet have her own privacy. She was ever so glad she had been a busybody and fiercely gone to Geraldine's parents after Lopasuta had disappeared, telling them that Geraldine had just given birth to a son whom she had named Dennis after her father's brother. That news had finally reconciled them with their daughter. Yes, from now on, everything was going to be just wonderful for this nice young couple. And she personally thought that the little Chinese boy, who looked a lot like Lopasuta, was just adorable.

Immediately after dinner, she put on her hat and coat and kissed Geraldine warmly, telling her that now that she had a full-time nurse, she could sleep late in the morning. And Geraldine couldn't help blushing when Mrs. Norton said that, for the latter's eyes had rested for a long moment on hers, as if to intimate that she knew perfectly well that a young couple wanted to stay in bed after having been away from each other for such a dreadfully long time.

Lopasuta sighed happily as the door closed, and turned to Geraldine. "She's really a treasure. I'm so glad she was here to help you, my darling, when you went through your ordeal of having our son all by yourself. And I'm happier still to know that your parents aren't angry with you anymore for having married me. I promise you I'll never give them cause to ever feel that way again."

"I just can't believe we're together at last, my darling." Geraldine slipped her hand into his and squeezed it, look-

56

ing at him adoringly. Then, remembering Mrs. Norton's meaningful expression, she continued, "And I do hope you aren't going to rush back into your law practice, not till we've had a sensible and reasonably long second honeymoon."

"You know, Geraldine dearest, what you just said is an excellent cue for me to tell you about a very wonderful thing that happened to me when I was coming back on the ship from Hong Kong to San Francisco. We had a spell of rough weather, and I saved a passenger who nearly fell overboard. He turned out to be a remarkable man, by the name of Leland Kenniston. He had gone to Hong Kong to open up a branch of his importing and exporting business—he lives in New York—and he told me that he wants to open another branch in New Orleans. We became very good friends, and in fact we traveled together as far as St. Louis. He would like very much to have me pass the bar examination in Louisiana and be qualified as a lawyer to handle his affairs in New Orleans."

"Why, that's absolutely marvelous! And you know, you'd have lots more business there than you ever will in stuffy little Mongomery—and probably a lot less prejudice, too."

"I've thought of that, Geraldine," Lopasuta reflected. "Of course, I told him that I still want to spend some time running a kind of clinic, for people who have a case where justice should be on their side and isn't, just because they can't get a lawyer to defend them. And Leland told me that the work he'd have for me would be part-time and would allow me to take such cases as I'd like to handle—for I'm sure there are plenty of poor people in New Orleans who are being taken advantage of by powerful, influential people, just as I found here."

"Well, I'm all for it. It sounds like a wonderful opportunity. When will all of this take place?"

"He was going to New Orleans for about a week to do some hiring and to see to the opening of his office. When he gets back to New York, he is going to contact me. He told me that you'd love the shops and restaurants and the wonderful French Quarter. Laure could tell us a great deal about New Orleans because she was born there."

"Yes, that's right!" Geraldine exclaimed happily. "I'm very excited by this, my love! But, in the meantime, let's just plan on being by ourselves. Maybe in a few days we'll pay a visit to my folks—I know they'll treat you properly from now on. I'm so glad we've reconciled—though in a way it was only because you were gone and I was having the baby alone. Mrs. Norton took it on herself to lay down the law to them," she giggled irrepressibly, "and I wish I could have been there invisibly and heard her."

"I shan't forget her kindness. And now, I'll do the dishes as a proper husband should, just to show you that I'm back to stay," Lopasuta chuckled as he rose from the table, helped Geraldine to her feet, and then held her tightly in a long, very satisfying embrace.

She lay on her side, a happy smile on her lips, her eyes closed; her even breathing told him that she had fallen fast asleep. They had made love with a gentle hunger, tender and consoling. Each seemed to want to give the other the utmost pleasure and the knowledge that it was as exquisite as it had always been between them, and that nothing had taken place in all this long while to mar that joy in union.

He was at peace now. He looked at his sleeping young wife, smiled tenderly, and put out his hand to touch her dark hair and to push away a wayward curl on her cheek, leaning forward to kiss it very lightly, so as not to waken her. Then he rose and went to the window and drew the curtains. The moon was full and high, and it shone down on the deserted street. It was silent, but it was not a desolate silence; rather, one of abiding comfort and reassurance. She had taken him back, she had forgiven him. And he began to think of how, when Luke grew old enough, Mei Luong could teach him the Chinese language and something of the traditions and the customs and the culture. Perhaps she was not too well educated, yet her instincts were good, and there was much about the Chinese people that he admired: their uncomplaining courage, their hard work, their refusal to take charity, or to be crushed by adversity. It would do Luke no harm to learn how to adapt to rigors that would test his character and strengthen him for the time when he would take his place in the world.

Out of these pleasant thoughts came the remembrance of what Laure had told him when she had walked with him to the carriage. Yes, it had been Brickley, the man who had sent him that sly letter offering a retainer and asking for his aid in a legal matter, who had drugged him and had him sent to Hong Kong to die. For surely if Lu Choy had not found him in that alley, he would have died. And now that he knew what other vindictive deeds Brickley had done in his grandiose scheme to entrap the Bouchards, he suspected that Brickley had not been alone.

He thought back to the cases he had won for poor, mistreated, freed black workers who had been bilked by arrogant carpetbaggers, wealthy scalawags, and the rich gentry of Montgomery who still hated Abraham Lincoln and the Emancipation Proclamation. They preferred to think of blacks as perpetual slaves, rather than as freed workers who deserved the dignity of a contract and the right of payment for services rendered.

He knew that he had made enemies from those cases. Certainly for one, there was Carleton Ivers, who had treated Amelia McAdams virtually like a slave. And there were other enemies who, like Vernon Markwell had, wanted to retaliate because he had shown them up for the greedy, selfish bigots they were.

All the same, he wondered who else had been in the scheme with William Brickley. And he promised himself that he would try to find out while he waited to hear from Leland Kenniston, and while he enjoyed what Geraldine had been pleased to call their second honeymoon. . . .

On the other side of town, another man was also wide awake, ruminating over the events of the day. Milo Brutus Henson—the man whom banker Carleton Ivers had backed to buy a piece of land and attempt to sell it on a speculative basis to gullible investors—had been standing in the shadows by the train depot when Lopasuta and Geraldine were walking toward the carriage with Laure Bouchard, Mei Luong, and the two children. He had come to the station to meet a friend of his from St. Louis, and upon seeing Lopasuta, he had thought he had seen a ghost—for to him Lopasuta *was* a ghost, a man he presumed was dead. Henson had also been in partnership with the later Homer Jenkinson and the corrupt Judge Siloway. They had worked up a scheme that had included, among its other ruthless machinations, a blackmail attempt on Andy Haskins and a vicious exploitation of an unstable ex-Confederate officer in a plot to kill both Luke Bouchard and Andy Haskins.

Milo Brutus Henson, William Brickley, and Carleton Ivers had plotted to rid themselves of the interference of Lopasuta Bouchard, for his fight for justice was interfering with too many of their own plans for self-aggrandizement.

Now fifty-two, short and dapper, with an elegantly waxed mustache, Henson was known around Montgomery as a reputable surveyor who had retired and purchased a venerable white-columned house on the eastern edge of town. There he had led a profligate life with many transient lights of love, and though he had thought of resettling in California and living like a Spanish don on the profits from his many secret investments in illicit enterprises, he enjoyed his social position and his creature comforts here in Montgomery too well to think as yet of pulling up stakes and making so drastic a move.

Moreover, after hearing from William Brickley that Lopasuta Bouchard had been sent all the way to Hong Kong and would probably never be heard from again, he had felt that there would be no further interference in his own private affairs. And yet now, nearly two years later, there was that damned Injun lawyer—tall and proud as you please—hugging that simperingly pretty young wife of his and getting off the train with a Chinese girl with a baby in her arms!

The friend he had come to meet was a middle-aged land speculator from St. Louis, whom he had met at a bordello in New Orleans several years ago and who had kept in touch with him over the years. Albert Sawyer had paid him a visit today to see whether the two of them might go into partnership in buying up some parcels of land near Tuskegee that, it was rumored, the city fathers might one day be interested in acquiring for a school or similar public institution. Albert Sawyer had been talking to Milo Brutus Henson when the latter's attention had been drawn to Lopasuta and Geraldine, and Sawyer had muttered, "You look as if you're gonna be sick, Milo boy! Or do you have eyes for that pretty, dark-haired girl that tall fellow's with? Not bad. I wouldn't mind a piece of that myself."

"No, I'm all right. Come along, Albert, I—I don't want that fellow to see me. Besides, I've got my carriage at the other end of the station," Henson had hastily averred, steering his friend abruptly away from the station exit.

They had gone to his house where the two men were greeted by Henson's current inamorata, a Natchez girl named Elaine Fairfield. She was blond, twenty-four, with a vacuous mind, but an insatiable concupiscence, and she also was cunning enough to flatter her aging, dissolute lover on the subject of his virility. He was pleased with her, and thus far she had been with him five months—which was very nearly a record for tenure in the white-columned old house.

He had hired a black cook, a widow in her mid-fifties, to whom he did not mind paying top wages because, though virtually self-taught, she prepared gourmet meals nearly as well as the chefs in some of New Orleans's finest restaurants, like Antoine's. Albert Sawyer belched at the end of the dinner and admiringly shook his head. "Damned if I've ever eaten a better meal than that, Milo boy! Where'd you get that nigger cook? She's a marvel. Maybe I should steal her from you!"

"You try, Albert, and I'll cut your tripes out." Henson grinned humorlessly, baring yellowing, decaying teeth. Then, turning to Elaine, he gave her an oily smile and said, "Laney, honey, be a good girl and go get another bottle of port for Albert and me. And have some yourself."

"Sure thing, sweetie!" The blond concubine rose with a supple movement of her hips that Sawyer did not miss with his beady little eyes, and cooed, "Now don't you nice gentlemen say anything nasty about me while I'm gone, you hear?"

After she had left, Henson eyed his friend and muttered, "I can't stand that bitch when she tries to talk in company. But she's dynamite in bed."

"I can tell that. Man, what I wouldn't give to have a try at her," Sawyer stated frankly.

"Well—I've got some thinking to do tonight. Sure, why don't you keep her company?"

"You mean it, Milo? You're a pal! Does that mean you and I can work out that deal?"

"More'n likely, Albert. Only I'll draw up the rules and I'll tell you to the penny how much your investment is going to be—and you'll cough up to the penny, too, understand?"

"Sure, Milo boy, anything you say! Oh, man, you're really a pal!" Sawyer exhaled with a sigh of lecherous anticipation.

When Elaine returned and began to fill the two men's glasses with port, Henson beckoned her to him and whispered into her ear. She made a face and started to whisper something back, but he reached under the table and pinched her thigh viciously, as he hissed, "You'll do it, or else you'll pack your duds and be out of here in an hour, you hear me, bitch?"

"Ouch—sure; please, Milo honey, that hurts—and you'll leave an awful mark. I'll do whatever you say!" she gasped, beads of perspiration standing out on her forehead, as she tried to squirm away from his fingers.

"That's better. Now then, you go over and make friends with Albert. Me, I'm going to drink my port and have a cigar in my room—I've got some tall thinking to do. You don't mind, do you, Albert boy?"

"Sure don't—like I said, you're a real pal and I won't ever forget this," the overjoyed St. Louis speculator panted, for by now the willowy blond young woman had seated herself in his lap, crooked an arm around his neck, and was stroking his cheek and nibbling at his earlobe.

Milo Brutus Henson sat on the edge of his bed clad only in his drawers, drinking whiskey out of a bottle. He had already been slightly tipsy from the port he had consumed during dinner, and the whiskey was turning him nearly sodden. But what kept him from being thoroughly drunk was the memory of what he had seen this afternoon at the Mongomery railroad station. "He must have the luck of a cat with nine lives to have gotten back from there," he said aloud to himself, and shook his head. "Goddamn it, I almost had me a stroke, when I saw him getting off that train—handsome and tall and looking as fit as ever. How the hell did he do it? I've gotta hand it to him, though, and coming back with that Chinese girl and that brat yet . . . wonder how he got it . . . wonder if it was from her . . . and yet that wife of his carried on as if it were their wedding night!" He took another swig from the bottle, belched, and shook his head. "Just listen to me! Anyone would think I've gone soft, talking this way. I'll have to take matters into my own hands, now that Brickley's gone. Somebody reliable. Sure, I know a few people down New Orleans way. Maybe I can get myself a stevedore off the docks who doesn't care what he has to do for money, as long as cash is put into his hand directly after the job is done. Sure—that's the way I'll do it! I'll have that accursed, meddling Injun put out of the picture once and for all, just see if I don't!"

His voice was so loud that it almost scared him, and he dropped the bottle with an oath. He bent down, fumbling blindly to try to retrieve it, then swore at it as a bad job, and fell back on the bed and began to snore.

## Four

It had been a mild winter in Carrizo Springs, one that had not hampered the work of the vaqueros in cutting out the culls from the herd their *patrón*, Lucien Edmond Bouchard, intended to market that spring. Indeed, it had been so balmy that on New Year's Day the Bouchards had been tempted to hold their annual feast outdoors; however, practicality won out, and that day had found all of the sofa and chairs in the large living room of the sprawling hacienda filled with the partners and principal hands—along with their wives—of Windhaven Range.

The guests had enjoyed themselves tremendously, especially when Maxine Bouchard had seated herself at her spinet to play traditional holiday melodies. Joining her in song were Mara Hernandez, Lucien Edmond's beautiful sister, and her handsome Mexican husband, Ramón.

Their other partner, Joe Duvray, had laughed uproariously when Ramón's booming baritone all but drowned out the ladies' efforts, but his wife, Margaret, quickly silenced him with a poke. Eddie Gentry, sitting with his lovely wife, Maria Elena, whom he had rescued from the life of a dance-hall girl, and then brought back to Windhaven Range and married, witnessed this exchange, and hid his own smile with his hand.

The elder Bouchard girls—the lastborn, Ruth, was just eleven months old, and had slept soundly throughout the festivities—passed among the guests with platters of food. Lovely Carla, now eighteen, sat down to chat with her aunt, Maybelle Belcher. Years before, Maybelle had been

63

abandoned by her husband, the dissolute Mark Bouchard—Luke's half-brother—and had sorrowfully followed Luke and his family to Windhaven Range. There, fate had brought the widower Henry Belcher with his children, Timmy and Connie, and now Maybelle basked in her elderly, doting husband's happiness with her.

Her stepchildren now had families of their own. Connie had married Walter Catlin, a morose cowboy who had come to Windhaven Range for work. While on a drive to Dodge City, he had found at last, after many years of searching, the man who had stolen and then abandoned his wife and child, and had finally avenged their deaths. This past November, Connie had given birth to a son, whom Walter had insisted on naming Henry, much to Henry Belcher's delight. The infant was at this moment being tended by eight-year-old Diane Bouchard.

Timmy had married Conchita Valdegroso, a shy, lovely Mexican girl of eighteen. At first Maybelle had protested to Henry that a marriage between his son and a Mexican girl was not exactly the sort of marriage she had had in mind for this strapping young man. But Henry Belcher had pointed out how successful the other Mexican-American marriages were—those of Mara and Ramón, Eddie and Maria Elena, and the humble, self-effacing vaquero, Pablo Casares, and his wife, Kate—and Maybelle's objections had been overcome.

As ten-year-old Edwina Bouchard sat down on a sofa next to Lucas Forsden and his wife, Felicidad, her sister, Gloria, now six, playfully climbed into his lap. Nacio Lorcas, the only adult of this inner circle who was unmarried, was seated across from Lucas, and despite having been made to feel welcome and accepted by his fellow guests, he felt a sharp twinge of loneliness at viewing all of this familial harmony.

That New Year's party had illustrated the spirit of Windhaven Range. For here, just as in Lowndesboro near the Alabama River, a commune had been founded in which men and women worked together, heedless of differences in their social or ethnic status. The incentive and inspiration, the driving force behind the ranch, was just as it had been from the very first days on Windhaven Plantation.

This, then, was a further legacy of old Lucien Bouchard, whose courage, tolerance, belief in God, and dedication to his own strict integrity had created a dynasty . . . not of power and greed and wealth, but of love and compassion and the strong family ties that held fast against tragedy and violence.

Now, more than a month later, the weather remained mild. The children of the ranch were able to continue uninterrupted at the school founded by the dedicated nuns who had come from Mexico. Here on Windhaven Range they had found sanctuary, and their school was the fruition of a dream long sought by Catayuna, the beautiful and mature widow of the great Comanche *jefe*, Sangrodo.

Since the weather had been so cooperative, it had been easy to enlarge and remodel some of the older structures on the ranch, such as the bunkhouses that quartered the vaqueros. Additional cottages had been built, serving as small but adequate homes for the men as they married and had families. Improvements were also made on the hacienda, where Lucien Edmond and Maxine enjoyed the comforts they had earned after their arduous years of pioneering here in this fertile valley in Texas near the Nueces River.

On this February morning, a momentous decision was about to be reached about the operation of Windhaven Range's annual cattle roundup and market drive.

Seated with Lucien Edmond in his study were his two partners, Ramón Hernandez and Joe Duvray, as well as Eddie Gentry, Lucas, and Nacio Lorcas. Simata, the Kiowa brave whom, for years, Lucien Edmond had depended on to act as scout, had married last year and had gone to live permanently near Fort Duncan. Sitting in on this conference, for the first time, was Lucien Edmond's fair-haired and blue-eyed son, Hugo. Now almost eighteen, he was as tall as his father, wiry and outwardly good-natured—but inwardly, Hugo burned with the intensity of youth that seeks recognition for its own attributes and potential. At breakfast, having heard that the men would be discussing where they would drive the cattle this spring, he had boldly asked his father if he might attend the meeting.

A year and a half ago, he had begged his father to let him go along on the Kansas cattle drive, but Maxine had protested that he was far too young, and that the dangers of attacks from bushwhackers, rustlers, and hostile Indians, to say nothing of the inevitable risks of stampedes, sandstorms, or thunderstorms, would be far too dangerous for the unfledged boy. Maxine had had her way, but this time Hugo was determined to ride with his father.

Hugo listened attentively and without a word as Lucien Edmond began the meeting by declaring, "As all of you know, yesterday a courier from our old friend Joseph McCoy rode up with a letter for me. McCoy reports that the Dodge City cattle market promises to be better than ever this year—but I know that he's eager to drum up business for the Santa Fe Railroad that services Dodge. Just the same, because he's a good cattleman second after he's a railroad man first, he did happen to mention that cattlemen are pouring into Colorado and Wyoming, eager to buy stock to build up the herds, and that they'll pay good prices for Texas cattle."

"Colorado and Wyoming—*hombre*, that's a much longer drive than to Kansas," Ramón protested. "You're talking of many months on the trail, and the need to take a larger number of vaqueros along, not only to move the herd, but to make sure they aren't stolen."

"I'd be inclined to agree with you, except for several things which I've already learned, Ramón," Lucien Edmond replied. "When we started out years ago, all of us were afraid of hostile Indians. True, we'd made friends with Sangrodo, and his reputation throughout the territory served as a protective shield in most instances, but there was always the possibility of attacks by renegades. However, the power of the Indian on the open range has been broken in the last year—understandably, after the massacre at Little Big Horn. I don't agree with the government's policy of herding Indians like sheep into reservations far north where there aren't any buffalo and where they starve, but General Sheridan put them down in his book as harmful to the expansion of our country—so there it is; most of them are on reservations. There are many army posts in Colorado and Wyoming, and there are mining towns up there eager for beef. There are railroad lines up there, too, connecting those areas to California, as well as to our usual sales markets of Chicago and St. Louis."

"Then you want to drive a herd all the way up north and northwest, Lucien Edmond?" Ramón demanded, with a glance at Joe Duvray and Eddie Gentry.

"Before I answer that question, let me tell you what else McCoy's letter said, Ramón," Lucien Edmond told his

66

brother-in-law. "He gave me the name of a fellow named Maxwell Grantham. Seems this Grantham's a wealthy Easterner who settled near Cheyenne, Wyoming, two years ago and hired himself a top foreman and the best crew of cowhands he could find. McCoy learned about him when he stayed in Dodge for a spell on his way out to Wyoming. The story is that he went out to Wyoming for his health, but back East he was married to a society-minded wife who preferred sophisticated city gigolos to the decent husband she had, so she up and left him. He decided to flee the confines of city living and move out West, and he liked it so much that he took to the life of a cattleman. The result, McCoy informs me, is that Grantham planned wisely, made a good deal of money, and is building up a fine herd. He's willing to pay at least fifteen dollars a head for good stock."

Ramón whistled softly and shook his head, as he sent Joe Duvray a speculative glance. "That's better than we've done the past few years. Still in all, you have to weigh against your market price the cattle you might lose on so long a drive, to say nothing of supplies, wages—you know the figures as well as I do, Lucien Edmond."

"That's right. And that's why I'm going to wire Grantham in care of the telegraph office at Cheyenne and ask him what his needs are. Maybe he can arrange a meeting place midway between his ranch and ours, or at least closer than you and I are figuring off the tops of our heads."

"That's a sound idea," Ramón slowly agreed after a moment's pause for thought. "There's still plenty of time to plan a drive, and thanks to this good weather, the men have had a chance to do all the branding and culling out the herd. But you don't think we should try Kansas again?"

"They still have that fear of Texas fever, and they've extended the quarantine boundaries. I don't fancy running into angry citizens armed like a posse, as happened back in the days right after the Civil War when we tried to get cattle to Sedalia," Lucien Edmond declared firmly. "But let's see what Grantham says after he gets my wire. I'll send one of the vaqueros into San Antonio this afternoon to get it off as quickly as possible. With any luck, we should have an answer back in ten days at most."

"Can I say something, Pa?" Hugo Bouchard, who had been quiet up to now, stirred restlessly in his seat as he spoke up. All the others, including his own father, looked at him with a surprised start. Lucien Edmond smiled, saying, "What have you got on your mind, son?"

"Well, Pa, I want to go along with you this time. I'll be eighteen pretty soon, and that's the age of a man. I haven't really pulled my weight here, and you know I've wanted to go with you for the last couple of years."

"That's right, you have, Hugo. Stand up a minute. Well, you're taller than I am by half an inch, I'd say, and you're strong—and I've watched you riding horses and going to the corral and breaking one or two now and again. Don't think I've ignored you all this time, Hugo."

"He's of an age when he ought to be doing some sparking," Eddie Gentry teased as he winked at Ramón.

"That's right, *muchacho*." Ramón fell in with Eddie's bantering mood. "Perhaps, Lucien Edmond, since there aren't too many pretty girls around here who haven't already been spoken for or married, Hugo is hoping he may see more than just cattle and cowboys along the way . . . perhaps some lovely young heifers of the two-legged variety, isn't that so, *mi amigo*?" He turned to give Hugo a knowing grin.

But the tall youth stiffened, and though his face flooded with crimson, he stoutly defended himself: "I don't give a damn about girls, Uncle Ramón! I can handle a rope and a horse, I can ride my share of drag, or even point—"

"*Gran vaquero* he is already and not yet on his first drive," Ramón jokingly interrupted.

But Lucien Edmond held up his hand to silence the good-natured ribbing. "Let Hugo speak for himself. I like a man with spunk, and the fact that Hugo happens to be my own flesh and blood makes it all the more important that I find out just how his mind works, now that he is of an age when he ought to have more responsibilities. Go ahead, Hugo."

"Like I said, Pa, I don't want to work in a bank, or behind a desk, or anything like that. I think I've had enough schooling—leastwise, as much as I need to work on a ranch—and I've picked up plenty of Spanish from the cooks all these years to be able to speak with the men—"

"That much is true," Ramón loyally interposed on the youth's behalf. "I've heard him talking to some of the vaqueros, and he's not bad for a *gringo*."

"What about guns?" Lucien Edmond pointedly asked his son. "If you go along with us—mind you, I'm just thinking

68

out loud and not saying yes yet—you'd have to be able to defend yourself if something critical arose. No one on the drive is responsible for anyone who can't carry his own weight. I mean, we're not going to pamper you out there. You'll stand your night shifts like anybody else, and no privileges just because you're my son."

"That's just the point, Pa! I don't want any privileges. And I'll practice with firearms all you want. I can shoot a carbine and a rifle, though maybe I haven't had any practice with a pistol." Hugo's voice was firmer now, with a mature self-assurance, which his father did not overlook, and which secretly pleased him.

"All right, then. Tell you what, this afternoon, you go out and do some shooting with Ramón. Ramón, get him a pistol, show him how to clean it, load it, draw, and then do some target practice with him."

"That I will do gladly, Lucien Edmond. And for now, we'll wait to hear from this fellow Grantham, is that it?"

"Exactly. I don't say we can't go on making a few small drop shipments of good beef to the army forts we've been servicing the past year or two, because that's always profitable and reliable. But this Wyoming deal might be very big, because if Grantham is really serious about developing the quality of the herd, then he's thinking the way I'm thinking—that's why we've been doing this crossbreeding, bringing in the Brahmas and even the Herefords. Well, I think that's all. I'll see you at lunch—and you too, Hugo. This time, we'll try to exclude your mother so that you can have your say, and you and I can talk man to man."

"Thanks, Pa. That's all I want—a chance."


Santiago Calderón, a vaquero whom Ramón had hired last spring, and one of the best horsemen on Windhaven Range, was dispatched to San Antonio shortly after lunch with Lucien Edmond's wire to Maxwell Grantham. Later that same afternoon, Lucien Edmond took Maxine aside and declared, "You know, Hugo sat in our conference this morning about the spring cattle drive, and he wants a chance to prove himself. He's asked to go along."

"Oh, Lucien Edmond, but he's still a boy!" Maxine protested. "There are such awful dangers—"

"This year, I think they would be at an absolute minimum, Maxine dear. For one thing, we're planning to ship cattle to the Colorado and Wyoming area, and we'd use a different trail. The hostile Indians are nearly all on reservations by now, so that eliminates one danger. And this new trail would bypass certain known areas where rustlers and bushwhackers have been operating. It would be very safe in comparison with the past. But mainly, I doubt that Hugo would want a job in a bank, or clerking in a store, and he does love horses and has shown a certain aptitude for them. It's as good a time as any to test him."

"I still have misgivings, darling."

"Be sure that he'll be well cared for—though he won't be pampered."

"It's curious, Lucien Edmond," Maxine interrupted, "that you've brought up Hugo's future, because I've been thinking about Carla. It's time we thought about a direction for her. She'll be nineteen soon—and I feel she's too bright to just settle into marriage."

"I know. She's lovely and quiet and she's been a wonderful help to you around the house—she likes children, too, and the vaqueros praise her for the interest she shows in them and their families," Lucien Edmond replied. "But—yes, she should have more."

"We might think of sending her to a New Orleans finishing school," Maxine suggested. "For one thing, I'd like for her to learn French—that's certainly in keeping with your family, since old Lucien came from Normandy. The French literature and culture would round out her background very nicely. As to marriage, you know how isolated we are here in Carrizo Springs and how few neighbors we have. Eligible young men aren't easy to come by, but in New Orleans it's possible she might find someone she cares for. And with Jason Barntry and Laure's attorney, Hollis Minton, there to guide her and watch over her, her opportunities for a wholesome social life would be far greater."

Maxine sighed. "My darling, it reminds me what an old married couple we've become. Yes, it's hard to realize that Carla and Hugo are both of a marriageable age, and that they will leave the nest some day soon."

"They must have their chance, of course. And yet, we've been very fortunate thus far in bringing them up on this ranch, giving them all the opportunities possible, and having them turn out so well. Hugo hasn't really found himself yet, and my personal opinion is that, once he's been on this drive, he'll have a better idea of who he is and what he can accomplish. That's exactly why I think at this point it would be well for him to go along with me. In the case of Carla, a parent usually supposes that a girl is inevitably headed for marriage, but she, too, ought to have a chance to broaden her education so that she can make a decision for herself. You know, she's shown quite a skill for drawing. Do you remember last year how she sketched this hacienda with such marvelous detail? In New Orleans, there certainly would be a fine school where art would be one of the courses offered. Then she could find out if this skill of hers can be expanded into a talent which would fulfill her spiritually," Lucien Edmond suggested.

"Why, that's a marvelous idea! I am glad, Lucien Edmond, that this ranch hasn't diminished your refinement, which appealed to me so much when I met you in Alabama." Maxine put her arms around him and gave him an affectionate kiss, which Lucien Edmond returned with enthusiasm. "My goodness, I shouldn't have said old married couple, not from the fervor of that kiss, my darling," she breathed happily.

Eight days later, Ramón Hernandez sat in Lucien Edmond's study, where the two partners discussed Maxwell Grantham's answer. The wire had come in from the telegraph office in Cheyenne and read as follows:

Thanks for your wire. Joseph McCoy has already told me about you and your successful Windhaven Range. I can use up to 2,000 head of yearlings and two-year-olds for breeding stock. Is it possible to bring them to the fork of the Arkansas and Apishapa Rivers, east of Pueblo, Colorado, by July of this year? Wire me if you can make this commitment.

Am ready to offer you $15 per head. Am eager to meet you after knowing your reputation as a top rancher and breeder.

Maxwell Grantham

"I think this is a good plan," Ramón declared, "but we'll have to get a quick start. You know yourself, Lucien Edmond, you can't figure on much more than ten to fifteen miles a day when you're on a drive, or you'll run the herd ragged and lose their weight long before you get to Colorado. We have to allow some extra time, too, for crossing mountainous country near the Colorado border. And of

71

course, since Grantham wants breeding stock, cows and bulls will be much more unpredictable and difficult to handle on a drive than steers. My guess is, without having looked at a map yet, that it will take us three and a half to four months to meet him in Colorado, which means that we should plan to leave no later than the middle of next month. Do you think that's possible?"

"We need to talk this over with Joe; since Joe's a partner, the cattle in this herd are his, too," Lucien Edmond pondered aloud. "But on the face of this, I don't see why we can't make a start within the next two to three weeks. I think we ought to go speak with Joe right now, and then I'll send Santiago back to San Antonio with a wire telling Grantham that we can meet his deadline. You know what this sale will mean, Ramón? Thirty thousand dollars—the best we've ever done since we came to Windhaven Range."

## Five

The year of 1878 had been a particularly satisfying one for Dr. Ben Wilson in Wichita. For a year now, he had been pastor of the Quaker church, replacing Jacob Hartmann, who had died of a heart attack two days after Christmas the year before. The unanimous vote of the congregation had been a tribute to his conscientiousness, both as a doctor and as a family man. His obvious love and devotion for his Indian wife, Elone, their children, as well as Elone's daughter and his children by his first wife, Fleurette, had won him the admiration not only of his fellow Quakers, but also of the citizens of Wichita.

What had once been merely a cattle town had, thanks to the quarantine urged by homesteaders and their reaction to the wide-open lawlessness of Dodge City, turned into a stable community of farmers, merchants, and traders. Many disgruntled cowhands who had wearied of the long, monotonous spring and summer drives up from Texas had decided to try their luck at farming, or even clerking in Wichita's supply and variety stores. Those who came from Dodge reported that this year, a good half-million cattle were moving through its shipping yards, and that the prairies south of Dodge were dense with cattle, obscuring the ground itself.

Part of this was due to a huge new grazing area in the Texas Panhandle, its short grass available for cattle with the passing of the great buffalo herds and the departure of the Comanche to reservations in the northwest. Three years earlier, Fort Elliot had been established on Sweetwater Creek to prevent Indian raids from the north, and in that same year, Charles Goodnight, a victim of the 1873 panic, left Colorado and began to drive remnants of his herd south to Texas. He had been the first to try the western market a decade earlier by selling beef in New Mexico to soldiers on army posts and Indians on reservations. When he returned to Colorado for his wife, he met John G. Adair, a wealthy Irishman, who financed him in a mammoth venture in a million-acre ranch, which was known as the famous J.A. Later, Charles Goodnight selected a ranging area along the Fort Worth & Denver City Railroad, developing a town named after him. He was to show Texas cattlemen the potential of the far northern and northwestern markets—and he was destined to live until 1929, dying at the age of ninety-three, a giant of the old cattle trail, when the West was young.

During most of this past year, Ben Wilson had devoted himself, as spiritual head of the Quaker church, to urging his parishioners to contribute tithes for the enlargement of the town's grammar school and the formation of a hospital. In his earlier days in that town, when the cowhands had come to Wichita to get drunk and involved in *macho* gunplay, he had had to treat many patients at a single hectic time. He was also aware that, in the event of any widespread epidemic such as scarlet fever or diphtheria—a disease he had particular reason to dread, since its sudden savage occurrence in his native Pittsburgh had taken the life of his adored first wife, Fleurette, at the tragically early age of thirty-seven—a single doctor could never hope to cope with the harrowing strain of multiple cases and the inevitable spread of the disease. Toward fall of 1878, he was happily able to announce to the congregation that some five thousand dollars had been raised for the hospital, and that the contributions toward the school were already large enough to begin the construction of a large new wing by November of this year.

Just a week before he had informed his fellow Quakers that there was every reason to hope that a hospital could be built sometime in the following year, another doctor had come to town. Dr. Berthold Mannheimer was a dapper little man in his early forties, with a neatly trimmed spade beard, enormous spectacles, a thick German accent to color his fluent English, and a perenially supercilious expression on his face. He had come from Trenton, New Jersey, he informed the citizens of Wichita in an open letter in the daily newspaper, because he had heard that there were many Germans here in Wichita, and he was tired of working in a hospital for low wages, enduring paltry medical facilities and tyrannical supervision from his superiors.

All of this was true, except that Dr. Mannheimer purposely neglected to indicate the real reason for his sudden departure from Trenton: a bachelor by preference and a satyr by nature, he had embarked upon a risky liaison with the wife of the head of the hospital where he was employed. This liaison was about to be discovered and his reputation blackened when he discreetly packed two valises, one of which contained his instruments and certain remedies by which he set great store, and took the first train west.

He set up an office across the street from the city jail, and those few citizens who patronized him after reading that he was ready for business discovered that his manner was high-handed and his prices outrageous by comparison with Dr. Wilson's. Nonetheless, there were still a few Wichita citizens who looked askance at Dr. Wilson's union with an Indian woman and, out of prim bigotry, preferred to patronize the new doctor.

In the past year or so, Ben Wilson had become increasingly interested in a new cause—that of women's suffrage. He was grateful that the Quakers' long-held belief in equality of the sexes led the men of his congregation to hold their wives and daughters in rather higher esteem than seemed to be true in the town in general. As a physician, and thus invited into many different homes, he had ample opportunity to observe how women outside the Quaker community were treated by their menfolk. He had seen all too often the cruelty and abuse that were the lot of many of the hardworking wives of the local townsmen, farmers, and ranchers.

He thought of his own Elone's subtle development—how once she had been extremely submissive, but since coming to Wichita and interacting with the women of the Quaker community, she had gained confidence in the white man's world, to the point where she could forthrightly take her place alongside any man as his equal.

Elone, too, had developed a desire to see the women of Wichita better treated; she observed how much better off the Quaker wives were, and she marveled that they alone among the white women were considered equals by their husbands. She now agreed with Ben that something should be done for women and, ideally, the first step would be to secure for them the right to vote—an essential right if women were ever to become mistresses of their own destiny. She eagerly read the letters that Ben directed back east to the chief protagonists of the women's suffrage movement, and just as eagerly read their replies to them. Echoing their words to him, she urged him to do what he could through the medium of the church to educate their town's citizens.

One evening just before the end of the year, he was sitting at supper with Elone, now twenty-eight years old. He thought, as he did frequently, of his good fortune at finding happiness with this lovely woman; indeed, after his first wife, Fleurette, had died of diphtheria back in Pittsburgh, he had despaired of ever feeling contentment again. Fleurette, the half sister of Luke Bouchard, was the mother of two of Ben's children—Thomas, a sturdy boy of thirteen, and Sybella, ten, named after valorous old Sybella Bouchard, Fleurette's mother. He smiled fondly at them as they seated themselves at the table with the other children. Sitting down next to Thomas was Bartholomew, almost seven, Ben's and Elone's oldest son. Next to him was Jacob, five and a half, and on Jacob's right sat Amy, almost three. Elone was cradling their lastborn, Dorothy, in her arms before settling the one-and-a-half-year-old girl in her high chair. Tisinqua (whose name meant Little Fawn) delighted in her half-sister's antics. At the age of nine, she showed much of the grace of her mother, whose beauty she so closely mirrored. Ben had commented to Elone that she and her daughter looked so much alike that Ben felt it was

75

as if he had known his wife as a child. Gazing at Elone, he thought she was as lovely now as she had been when he had first found her in Emataba's village on the Creek reservation. She had fled there with her baby, who was the product of Elone's abduction and rape by the chief of a Kiowa tribe. Tisinqua spoke excellent English, though she still retained her knowledge of Creek and the Sioux of her mother's origin. In Ben's opinion, it was a definite blessing for children to be able to speak more than one language, for it would broaden their awareness of the world in which they lived.

"I hope that in another year or two, dear Elone," he said to his wife, "we'll be able to give women the vote here in Kansas. It will be a tremendous step forward. You know, of course, that back in 1867, the Kansas legislature placed a referendum on the ballot, but the men defeated the right of women to vote by a tally of thirty thousand to nine thousand—a shameful referendum, because it disenfranchised Negros, also."

"I heard you say that at the meetings, my dear husband," Elone nodded, her eyes bright and intent on his homely, kindly face.

"It is to be hoped that the women of our state will not have long to wait for what are simply their rights," Ben averred solemnly.

Ben delighted in sharing with Elone this and other concerns, and now, at the beginning of 1879, at the age of forty-four, he reflected that he had never been happier. The love, security, and peace of his wife and children warmed him, as did his rich involvement with the growing community of Wichita and the inspiration of the Quaker faith—which abhorred violence and substituted reason, compassion, and humanity for the guns that still seemed to rule the frontiers—and his active life as a doctor and his frequent visits to the Creek reservation kept him physically fit.

Despite his widespread popularity, there was still one influential man in Wichita who had not yet accepted Dr. Ben Wilson. His name was Dade Torrington, and he owned a small cattle ranch on the outskirts of Wichita.

Dade Torrington had been born in Schenectady to zealous Lutheran parents, and as an only child, he had been downgraded and stuffed full of religious maxims dealing with the joy of unremittingly hard labor, sacrifice, and obligation. He had run away from home, joined a dry goods drummer bound for the Ohio Valley, and had worked with him until he was nineteen. Then, having acquired a little money, he had been determined to establish a small cattle ranch down in Texas. He had married a young school-teacher from Dennison, Iowa, whose parents had considered him little more than a vagrant and opposed the marriage. But Ruth Barnes, plain, homely, and a year older than her sturdy young suitor, had rebelled against their wishes and gone off to Texas with him. Torrington had bought about five hundred acres at fifty cents an acre near Austin, rounded up over a hundred stray longhorns, sold them for a middling profit, bought himself a pedigreed short-horned bull and two short-horned heifers, and, within five years, had a herd of a thousand, three vaqueros, and a successful *capataz* from Durango, who had helped him expand his herd and sell it to Mexican army forts and ship a good part of the herd from Corpus Christi on to New Orleans before the Civil War.

Dade Torrington had prospered and, finally, with the advent of the war, moved to Kansas, bought land near Wichita, and sold his cattle to Union Army forts. The Civil War had not touched him because he was a Unionist by background and sentiment and detested slavery.

But by the time the war was over, he had developed an ingrained prejudice against Indians, for roving bands of renegade Kiowa had stolen his cattle and, during one of their raids, had inflicted an arrow wound in his left arm, leaving it almost paralyzed.

His wife had died six years before, and his only son, a tall, gangling youth in his early twenties named Davis, had vanished the morning after his mother's death. Torrington had hoped that his strapping son and he would be drawn closer together after their bereavement; but Davis Torrington had left without a word or even a note and it was only last year, quite by accident—when a courier from California had come to town to visit a former sweetheart—that the gray-haired, stocky rancher had learned what had happened to his son.

Grief-stricken by his mother's death, and secretly hating his father for his inflexible and almost tyrannical manner—believing that his father expected a kind of servile docility from him and total obedience to his wishes—the young man had ridden westward to try to start a new life

77

for himself where he would no longer be dependent upon his father. He had never been close enough to his father to understand that the man's gruff, seemingly domineering manner actually hid a pathetically hopeful yearning that his son would achieve far more than he himself had been able to do in years of drudgery and poverty and frustration. The courier had reported to Torrington that Davis was now settled in the fertile San Fernando Valley, near Los Angeles, had married a young Mexican girl, and was earning a livelihood by planting oranges in a small grove and taking them by mule-cart into the city.

With the death of his wife and the alienation of his son, Dade Torrington had become a dour, embittered man. Frugal and thrifty, he had banked his profits, investing part of his capital with a New Orleans factor, who had tripled his investment on land speculation in the American quarter, and he had given up ranching three years ago. He lived alone, with an elderly, widowed housekeeper, who cooked and tended his white frame house and who herself hated Indians because her husband had been killed in a Kiowa raid over a decade before.

And so, when he had come into Wichita for supplies and seen Ben Wilson with Elone and heard how this Quaker doctor had married an Indian after the death of his first wife, Torrington had set his mind against him. Of robust health, he had needed no medical attention, and when he had learned that another doctor had settled in Wichita, he had told his housekeeper, "It's a damn good thing, Mrs. Paxton, because I think I'd rather kick the bucket than let a squaw man fuss over me." Nevertheless, being taciturn of manner, and turned almost into a recluse by the death of his wife and the loss of his son, Torrington kept his opinion about Ben Wilson to himself.

By the end of January 1879, the winter storms that had besieged most of Kansas had subsided, and Dr. Ben Wilson determined to visit the Creek reservation where Sipanata, the sturdy brave who had taught the Quaker the Creek tongue, ruled as *mico* since the death of Emataba not quite three years ago. Elone would be staying behind with their seven children. The oldest were now attending the one school Wichita boasted, a rural school whose expansion would enable the provision of more classrooms and teachers for the children of those homesteaders who had begun

78

to come from the Middle West and East to settle around the now stabilized and thriving town.

Ben's absence would be a good opportunity for Elone to visit more often with the late Pastor Hartmann's aging wife. Mrs. Hartmann had recently volunteered to teach in the rural school, for she had sold her store to an enterprising couple from Maryland, who had come to visit a cousin and decided to settle down in Wichita.

Elone respected Tabitha Hartmann and knew that the older woman sometimes felt great loneliness and at such times needed the heartwarming diversion of exchanging hospitality. Whenever Ben was away, Mrs. Hartmann would invite Elone and the children over to supper, or Elone would prepare a special supper with emphasis on Indian dishes for the former pastor's wife.

Ben Wilson set forth on the journey to the Creek reservation during the first week in February, using one of Jacob Hartmann's wagons to which he harnessed two geldings, and spent a considerable part of the separate bank account he had maintained for the express purpose of providing supplies for the Creeks. The wagon was loaded with blankets, flour, salt pork and jerky, sugar, coffee, salt, and beans, as well as playthings for the children and dress materials for the women. "I'm certain I'll be back by the end of the month, my dear one," he told Elone as he kissed her goodbye, and then bade farewell to all of their children. Solemn little Bartholomew—named after Friar Bartoloméo Alicante, who had so unstintingly ministered to the Creeks at Emataba's reservation—seemed sad, and so the Quaker doctor squatted down, put his hands on the boy's shoulders, and gently asked, "Are you sorry to see me go away, Bartholomew?"

"Yes, Papa, and something else, too," the brown-eyed, somewhat chubby boy replied. "I wish those Injuns you're going to see could be here. I heard you say to Mama how far away and lonesome they are."

"That is a very humane and blessed thought, Bartholomew." Ben hugged the boy, who was precocious and had already shown considerable interest in reading books far advanced beyond his school primer. "I'll bring you back a bird or a horse carved in wood by one of my good friends there. In that way, both you and the one who has whittled it for you will be close together in spirit each time you play with it."

Rising, he kissed Elone again and then got into the wagon. As he waved to them and then started off, Bartholomew turned to his mother and said, almost wistfully, "Mama, when I grow up, I want to help people, just like Papa."

"You are a good child, a wonderful son, Bartholomew," Elone murmured, "and your father is very proud of you. One day perhaps everyone will love you as he is loved, wherever he goes—as he is in the Creek village where first I met him."

## Six

For Dr. Ben Wilson, the lonely journey to the Creek reservation was a time for nostalgic reflection and for humble thanksgiving to his God for the renewed life and happiness which had been granted to him after Fleurette's death. He remembered that first time when, after having left young Thomas and Sybella at Windhaven Range with their grandmother, Sybella, he had ridden to Wichita to buy supplies for these neglected people, who had been treated like starving dogs by an unscrupulous Indian agent. That was how he had met Jacob and Tabitha Hartmann, and later, after he had cured Elone and Tisinqua of the croup and he had gone back to Wichita to buy Elone a dress, he was helped in this unfamiliar task by the storekeeper's congenial, goodhearted wife. Through his own efforts, he had convinced the Bureau of Indian Affairs in Washington to replace the disreputable agent with one who truly cared about the plight of Indians, and who had even seen to it that a capable army doctor was appointed to replace Ben when he and Elone had married and decided to move to Wichita to establish roots and reclaim Thomas and Sybella.

Yet, Ben sadly thought, even that kindness and bounty had not succeeded in brightening the hopes of these abandoned people who had once ruled the forests and glades of the South. They had come from Econchate, where they had peacefully prospered, to this forsaken plain, symbolically bordered by a rickety, rotting fence that eloquently spoke of the isolation and the contempt with which they were treated by military and governmental authorities. Where there had once been over three hundred men, women, and children banished to this autocratically defined strip of land with its ignoble fence to limit the Creeks' freedom, now there were scarcely more than a hundred and fifty. Old age, illness, loss of spirit and hope—these were the infirmities that had felled so many of the strong, indomitable Creeks.

He reached the Creek village in a week, and Sipanata warmly welcomed him. This, too, recalled Dr. Ben Wilson's first essay at a new life, after his first wife's death: Emataba, then *mico*, had ordered Sipanata to teach him their language, and at first Sipanata had grudgingly obeyed, since he had every reason to distrust the white man. But Ben Wilson and he had become fast friends, once he had observed how the Quaker doctor respected his Indian patients and treated them with dedicated care.

"Elone and the children send their greetings to you, Sipanata," the Quaker doctor told the *mico* as they sat side by side at the feast the Creek leader had ordered to celebrate the return of their white-eyes shaman. "We now have seven children, Sipanata, and we are trying to build a school and a hospital for the sick. Tell me, does the army doctor still help your people, as the agent promised he would?"

"Yes, that is so. Dr. Brenton is a good man, as I have told you in the past, and he, like yourself, does not look down upon us because we are banished here with a fence around us to remind us that we depend on the charity of the Great White Father for our existence."

"And you still receive the proper amounts of food and clothing for your people, Sipanata?"

"We do. The *wasichu* who is in charge of us sees to it that we do not starve. And what he sends us is good." Sipanata shrugged philosophically. "He is a kind man, like you, but my people still look upon this as charity, like a man tossing a bone to a dog near the campfire, wanting him to take it and be off and not bother him. Since the last time you were here, there are fewer people in my village

81

because they die out of sadness that they are so shamefully reduced from what their ancestors once were."

"I know that, and it deeply grieves me, Sipanata," Ben responded fervently.

"Then there are others," Sipanata continued, "who have left us of their own free will—some of the younger ones, who have gone to Dodge City to work for the *washichu*. They are given the lowliest of tasks, like sweeping saloons or unloading wagons. I do not say it is wrong, because the young are better off living that way than behind this rotting fence that reminds us, as it did him who was *mico* before me, of what we have come to over all these long years."

"Yes," Ben mused, "it is half a century since President Jackson wished your people to be moved far from their hunting grounds. That cannot be undone, Sipanata. But perhaps, even though the work your young braves are given in places like Dodge City is menial, it will strengthen them and give them hope that one day, when we have new leaders in our great council in Washington, justice and fairness will be granted to your people and to all other tribes. In my own faith, in the brotherhood which we call Quaker, we believe in this with all our hearts and souls."

"It is a pity there are not enough men like you throughout the land." Sipanata's lips curved in a humorless smile. Then, with a shrug, he urged, "But tonight is a night of celebration and feasting to welcome you back. Let us not talk of sad things, for there are enough ghosts beyond that fence at night to make us all remember what was once and will never be again."


Dallas Masterson was wiry and wry humored, clean-shaven, with light-brown hair. More than five years ago, he had ridden point for the big Glossup ranch in the Panhandle. Masterson, then in his early forties, had ridden his boss's herd to market that summer of 1873, then he had taken his pay and told Hiram Glossup that he was finished with riding point and would try to earn his living at the wheel, at faro and keno.

It was said of him that he had become a cowboy shortly after the Civil War after a girl had broken his heart in New Orleans, where he had been a blackjack dealer. Whether or not the story was true, it served to explain why he had gone back to gambling after just a few years on the trail.

During an altercation in the saloon where he had worked, a drunken cowboy had aimed his six-gun at a man he believed had insulted him, but the bullet had caught Dallas Masterson near the lung. The bartender had gone for Ben Wilson, and the Quaker doctor had used one of the saloon tables as his operating table. After dosing Masterson with enough whiskey to numb the pain, he sterilized his instruments in boiling water—a procedure he had learned in Pittsburgh and which few doctors at the time employed—extracted the bullet, stopped the bleeding, and then used an ordinary needle and heavy thread for sutures. Ten days later, Masterson was sitting at the faro table as house dealer. That same night, when someone had remarked that Dr. Ben Wilson was a squaw man, Dallas Masterson had felled him with a blow to his jaw and said to the silent spectators, "The next man who downgrades the doc in my hearing gets worse than that, savvy?"

More than three years ago, he had befriended a twenty-year-old waitress named Flora Colcroft, who had run away from her cruel stepfather and a squalid home in St. Louis. What little money she had saved had been just enough to buy her a railroad ticket to Wichita, a town she had chosen on the spur of the moment for her escape. She had found a job as a waitress in the restaurant in Wichita's largest hotel, and had been barely able to subsist on the paltry wages paid her. One evening, while Dallas was there eating his supper, a burly trail boss tried to bribe her into going to bed with him. When she had indignantly refused, he had made an obscene remark and pulled her to him and begun to shout at her. Dallas had risen from his nearby table, struck the man's hand away, and then drawn out his six-shooter and calmly remarked, "Mister, if you're tired of living, just go on forcing yourself on a girl that's far too good for the likes of you!"

From that moment on, Flora Colcroft had virtually worshipped the tall, wiry gambler, and having learned from one of his friends that he had nothing to do with women because of a previous disappointment in New Orleans, she had taken her courage in her hands a few months later and declared her love for him.

They had been married before the end of 1875, and Flora had borne a girl whom they had named Ardith, after

Flora's dead mother. Dr. Ben Wilson had delivered the baby and stood as godfather to the child.

On the day that the Quaker doctor left to visit the Creek reservation, Flora Masterson fell ill of a fever. Her devoted husband arranged with Mrs. Ebenezer Coulter, one of the doctor's Quaker parishioners, to care for Ardith, and he was forced to call in Dr. Berthold Mannheimer in Dr. Wilson's absence.

The bespectacled, bearded Eastern doctor examined Dallas's lovely young wife and pompously announced that it would be necessary to bleed her. He had, as it chanced, a bottle of leeches that he had brought with him when he had hurriedly left his hospital post, and although Dallas had grave misgivings, he had no choice: there was no other doctor in town.

Flora grew weaker, and by the third week of February, Dallas was frankly terrified that he would lose the one woman who had shown sincere and devoted love for him and softened his often cynical outlook forged by his struggle for survival that stemmed from a lonely, harsh background. Moreover, Dr. Mannheimer, quite unlike Dr. Wilson, began to talk at once of the expensive treatment he was providing and bluntly stated that he would like a substantial cash down payment. "It may be necessary to remove your good wife to a hospital in St. Louis—since there is none here in this Godforsaken town," he declared after his fifth visit. Scowling and caressing his spade-shaped beard, he added, "I do not like her color, and she does not respond to the leeches. Have you been giving her the elixir I left? It is a European remedy, derived from certain herbs that are not grown in this savage country, and they are usually an effective cure for all kinds of fevers."

"Yes, I have, but it doesn't seem to be working; you can see that for yourself, Doc," Dallas said hoarsely. "I'll give you your money, but frankly, I don't think you're doing her much good."

"These fevers are mysterious, Herr Masterson," Dr. Mannheimer declared arrogantly. "They come and they go, and it is difficult to control them or to diagnose them properly. It may even be contagious, so I've been treating her the way I treated patients in the East who had similar symptoms. You would be wise to trust me, Herr Masterson—ah, thank you. This, of course, is only half of what you owe me, as you know."

Dallas Masterson clenched his fists and forced himself to keep his voice steady and quiet as he replied, "You'll get the rest of it soon, don't worry. I'm good for it. Just see to it that you cure my Flora."

Dr. Mannheimer bristled, stuck out his chest like a pouter pigeon, and glared at him. "*Mein Herr*, I would not advise you to threaten me. I am well known in the East, and simply because I cannot cure your wife overnight, you must not begin to make stupid accusations. I shall expect the rest of my fee by the end of next week. Keep administering the elixir and perhaps Saturday I shall try the leeches again."

When the importunate doctor had left, Dallas Masterson knelt down and took Flora's limp hand in his and pressed it to his heart. "Honey girl," he hoarsely muttered, "I wish to God old Doc Wilson hadn't gone to visit the Injuns—he'd cure you; he really would. That old sawbones seems like a charlatan to me—you seem worse than you were when you first took sick."

"I—I feel a tiny bit better, D–D–Dallas, honey," Flora murmured faintly. She reached for him feebly with her other hand and stroked his forehead. There were tears in the gambler's eyes, which he tried to hide as he gruffly and loudly avowed, "You're just saying that to comfort me, Flora, honey. You look awful—I mean—oh, hell, why doesn't the doc get back from those Injuns? I ought to have known better than to let that faker put those slimy things on your arms and suck the blood out of you. Oh, honey—please don't die on me! You don't know how much you mean to me, you and Ardith! I love you! I never said that to anyone else—"

Flora stared at him, and then in a faint voice replied, "You know, back when I first met you, your friend Ed Percy said you'd been jilted by a girl you cared a lot for. After I fell in love with you—and after Ed Percy told me what she did—I swore I was going to make you a good wife and make it up to you for all the sorrow you had—"

"Cut it out, honey, you're making me cry like a baby." Dallas reached for a bandanna and heartily blew his nose, rapidly blinking his eyes. "You've just gotta get well because I do love you. There's never been anybody but you, Flora, all my life—and you've made me a father and Ardith is going to be just as pretty as you are—please get well, honey, please!"

"I—I'll try so hard—I want to live for you and our daughter, D—Dallas, honey," she murmured.

"That's my girl. Now you just close your pretty blue eyes, and you get some sleep. Sleep will do you more good than either those damn leeches or that elixir he's charging me so much for—there now, lie back, that's a sweet gal."

As Dr. Ben Wilson drove his two brown geldings down the main street of Wichita, a tall, gray-bearded man in his early fifties hailed him from the other side of the street. Jerking on the reins, the Quaker doctor joyously cried, "Dave Haggerson, it's good to see you!"

Dave Haggerson had been a schoolteacher in Iowa before the Civil War when he married a gentle, intelligent, mature pupil of eighteen. He had served in the war for two years in an Iowa regiment and had been wounded and mustered out three months before Lee and Grant met at Appomattox. Shortly after the conclusion of the war, a cousin of his who had moved to Wichita died and bequeathed him a small farm on the northern outskirts of Wichita. He and his wife, Elaine, eagerly moved there, but a year before Dr. Ben Wilson moved to Wichita, Elaine died in childbirth, and her sickly baby boy followed her to the grave eight days short later. Dave had gone back to teaching in the little Wichita rural school. On Saturday nights, when he felt most lonely, he would go over to the gambling hall where Dallas Masterson ran the faro table, and the two men had become devoted friends.

He had been best man at the wedding of Dallas Masterson and Flora Colcroft, and together he and Dallas had acted as a self-appointed committee of two to stamp out the label of "squaw man" with which Dr. Ben Wilson had been labeled when he had first come to Wichita. Now, his face grave and his forehead furrowed with deep concern, he hurried across the street.

"Dr. Ben," Dave had always called him that—"Flora's real sick. It came over her all of a sudden; a bad fever."

"What is it? Level with me, Dave," Ben leaned down and demanded anxiously.

"I don't know what it is, and I don't think Dr. Mannheimer, that Eastern quack, knows either. All he's done is have Flora bled with leeches, and he doses her up with some red water in a little bottle he calls a—an elixir."

"My God, it sounds like the medicine shows they used to

86

run at Chautauqua back East," Ben groaned. "Where is she now?"

"Back in her house. Mrs. Coulter took Ardith, so poor Flora wouldn't have to worry about her kid. Dallas is half-crazy—and you know something else? That Doc Mannheimer is charging him a small fortune for all these cures he's treating Flora with. You better get over there as fast as you can."

"Thanks for telling me, Dave. Thanks a lot. I'm beholden to you. God bless you, Dave."

"Likewise, Dr. Ben," Dave solemnly avowed, as he touched his hand to his forehead and went back across the street.

The Quaker doctor drove his team toward the small white frame cottage that Dallas Masterson had bought for his young wife two years ago, tethered the geldings to the hitching post outside the gate, and, carrying his black medical valise from the wagon, strode toward the door and knocked on it. A moment later, Dallas opened the door and uttered a joyous cry: "Doc Ben, thank God you're here! Please hurry, I've been praying you'd get back all this time! Flora's been sick with a fever, and that new doc has been scaring me to hell, the way he's tried to cure her—and she's weaker, not better."

"Let me see her at once, Dallas." The Quaker doctor went into the bedroom, while the gambler closed the front door and followed him, his face drawn with anxiety, and his eyes bloodshot from lack of sleep.

Flora lay propped against three pillows, and there was an unnatural pallor to her pretty, heart-shaped face. Ben Wilson drew up a small chair and seated himself, then took her pulse, put his fingertips to her forehead, and, a frown creasing his homely face, shook his head as he turned toward Dallas. "Dave told me Dr. Mannheimer has been treating her with leeches."

"That's right, Doc Ben, would you believe it? They drained all the blood out of her, so she looks like she's dying. For God's sake, don't let her die—I need her—I love her!"

"I know you do. Try to control yourself, Dallas. What else did he give her, do you remember?"

"Here—this stuff—he said it's an elixir; said it cured just about everything back where he came from."

Ben picked up the bottle of clear red liquid, opened it

and sniffed, then grimaced. "There's not much here except some coloring, water, and alcohol. You might just as well have had a traveling show medicine man give you a bottle of this and hope to cure Flora. Now, get out of here and let me go to work."

From his black bag, the Quaker doctor took cinchona bark, which the Creek as well as the Comanche, Apache, and Sioux used to treat fever sufferers. Steeping the bark in hot water produced a brew that was later to be known as quinine, the crystallized residue of salts drawn from the bark. Ben took a piece of the dark-brown bark and bade Dallas, who stood outside the bedroom anxiously looking in, "Heat some water on the stove, just a cupful, and bring it to me."

When the gambler returned, biting his lip and staring agonizedly at his pale, listless wife, the Quaker doctor took the piece of bark, dipped it into the hot water, and then held it out by Flora's mouth. "Try to suck this a little, dear. Take as much as you can. It's bitter, but it will do you good, believe me."

With a sigh, the young woman opened her mouth for the bark, then began to suck. She grimaced at first, and stammered, "Oh, my! It—it's awfully bitter."

"That's the healing part of it. Try some more, Flora, dear. Good. Now try to sleep." He rose from the bed and, after closing the shutters so that no light would filter into the room, went outside to where Dallas waited anxiously. "I'm going home now, but I'll be back this evening. Take this piece of bark and when she wakes up, soak it in hot water—let it cool a bit so that it won't burn her lips—and then let her suck on it. Oh, yes, if you could make her some nourishing broth this evening, help her drink as much as she can. Cover her up because I think the fever will sweat itself out."

"Thank God you're back, Doc Ben!" Dallas ejaculated hoarsely. "I'm afraid she would have died if I had to leave her to that fancy Eastern doc—and he's charging me a fortune."

"I had a feeling he might. When this is over, I'm going to have a little chat with him and find out more about his medical credentials. And don't you worry about his bill. I'll take care of it."

"Hell no, Doc Ben, I won't let you do that! That's my obligation!"

"I think, Dallas, after I finish talking with Dr. Mannheimer, he'll decide that Wichita's not the place for him. Not that I want to be the only doctor in Wichita, but this man is a charlatan. I thank God I came back in time, because your Flora is really very ill, and what he prescribed was absolutely the worst he could have done."

"I—I ought to kill him with my bare hands!"

"No. I think an appeal to his conscience and a reminder of the Hippocratic oath will be sufficient. I'll see you this evening."

Elone welcomed her husband with sparkling eyes and a happy smile as they embraced. "Mrs. Hartmann sends you her love. She seems much more cheerful. I think she's finally getting over Jacob's death—and do you know, my darling, she said that she hopes to be a regular teacher when our new school is finally built. I think it will save her from her loneliness over Jacob," Elone murmured.

"I think so, too, but our school is in the hands of our dear God, Elone. Incidentally, you probably know that Flora is very sick. That Dr. Mannheimer didn't help her at all. I shall go back there this evening."

"How are the people who were so kind to me?"

"Alas, Elone, many of them have died since the last time we were there. There are perhaps half the number of villagers now, but at least they will have food and warm clothing for the cold months ahead. Now—let us sit down at the table with our children and give thanks unto our merciful Savior, who brough me safely back to you, and in time to help Flora."

Flora Masterson was able to get out of her bed a week later, gradually regaining her strength. Two days before that, however, Dr. Berthold Mannheimer abruptly left Wichita forever, after a visit by Dr. Ben Wilson. And the following Sunday, in his role as pastor, Ben gave thanks unto a merciful God and for his own humble skill in saving the life of Flora Masterson.

## Seven

A hundred and fifty miles west of Wichita, the wide-open cattle town of Dodge City was the end point of the so-called Great Western Trail up from Texas. This year of 1879 saw as many cattle plodding along its dusty route as along the old Chisholm Trail farther east, which used to bring cattle to Abilene, Newton, and Wichita. This would continue for six more years, until the Kansas legislature would finally put a complete ban on all Texas cattle by extending the quarantine line all the way west to the Colorado border.

Yet history can be made in a few short years, a lurid, violent history that a century later—through the eyes of those who knew nothing of the old frontier—seemed glamorous and exciting. . . .

It was already said of Dodge City that it was a modern Sodom and Gomorrah, and there was an apocryphal story concerning a cowhand on his uppers who gave a railroad agent the last money he had and asked for a ticket to hell, whereupon the agent sold him a ticket for Dodge City. In 1872, when the Santa Fe Railroad construction gangs arrived, they found six saloons, a general store, three dance halls, and a nearby sod house for the buffalo hunters. They found men like William F. Cody, who won the name of "Buffalo Bill" because he killed 4,280 buffalo in seventeen months for the Kansas Pacific Railroad in the area of Hays City; and Tom Nixon, who by killing within a month's time 2,173 buffalo, had helped carry out General Philip Sheridan's order to destroy the buffalo herds in order to weaken the power of the Indians. Where there had been four million buffalo south of the Platte and another half million on the northern plains, five years later found almost all of the southern buffalo killed, and with it the civilization of the Plains Indians . . . paving the way for the great cattle herds which could then be directed to Dodge City.

It was a city of false-front wooden buildings, saloons, gambling halls, and theaters whose names were a byword to every cowhand on the trail: Beatty and Kelley's Alhambra, the Lady Gay, the Long Branch, the Alamo, Delmonico's Restaurant (which used the name of the famous New York City restaurant, but hardly had its quality), and the Dodge Opera House. It was a town under the control of men totally sympathetic to the cattle trade. Its mayor was James "Dog" Kelley, so named because he had once cared for General Custer's hunting dogs, and who maintained his own large pack of hound dogs, as well as a pet bear. The bear was reputed to have made a notorious inebriate turn teetotaler, when it broke its chain and crawled into bed with him one night. When the man awoke the next morning after a night of carousing, he saw the bear and fled from the room in his nightshirt, swearing off spiritous liquors from that day forth.

At the famous Long Branch Saloon, owned by Chalk Beeson and Bill Harris, Luke Short ran the gambling concessions and hired the first female pianist ever to perform in a Dodge saloon. The lawmen of Dodge were vigilant in pursuing horse thieves and train robbers, but were loyal to the mayor and his policy of letting cowboys enjoy themselves in town, especially south of the railroad tracks in the rougher saloons and houses of prostitution. The sheriff of Ford County, of which Dodge was the seat, was none other than Bat Masterson; Dodge's marshal was Charles Bassett, and his assistant was the immortal Wyatt Earp. The only restriction on guns was the rule that cowboys had to leave their firearms with the bartender when entering a saloon and reclaim them upon leaving. Nonetheless, there were still shootouts, crimes of passion, and the inevitable violence bred in a trail town.

On the next to the last day of February, in this year of 1879, three bearded, coarse-mouthed cowhands entered the Alamo Saloon. It was early evening, and the saloon was not yet filled with patrons. There were, however, several painted ladies of the establishment on hand to solicit drinks and to intimate that their extracurricular talents were available at a modest price.

The three men, challenged by the bald, stout bartender,

91

reluctantly handed over their firearms; the leader carried a shotgun, as well as a pair of Colts, while his two companions had Colts holstered at their right side, the belts adjusted to make for a swift draw in the event of trouble. They each called for whiskey and downed the contents of a shot glass, their leader laying down some greenbacks and loudly asking for a bottle of the best whiskey in the house. Upon receipt of the bottle, he and his companions ambled over to a table against the wall. Watching them, three painted hostesses moved toward the table and seated themselves beside the newcomers.

The head man, who had a long, thick black beard and bushy eyebrows and a splayed nose that he had incurred in a Newton tavern brawl eighteen months ago, was thirty-eight-year-old Ed Magruder. Born in Sedalia, he had inherited his father's small farm outside the town. But he had scarcely made a living from it, and he had taken out his frustrations with his fists on his young wife till she could bear no more. He had turned to bank robbery and cattle rustling after his wife had run away with an Eastern whiskey drummer, taking their two young boys with her.

His companions were Bill Cruxhall and Hank Everson, both thirty, and orginally from St. Louis, where they had been employed by a gunsmith. Three years ago, in a quarrel over wages, Bill Cruxhall had seized a Colt six-shooter and killed his employer. Then he and Hank Everson had taken all the money they could find in the shop as well as six of their dead employer's best pistols and twenty boxes of ammunition. They had fled the city that same night, changed their names and dyed their hair to avoid detection, and gone to work as hired hands on a large Sedalia farm. Soon tiring of this monotonous and low-paying work, they had met Ed Magruder in a tavern and cast their lot with him.

The black-haired dance-hall girl seated beside the glowering leader of this murderous little band suddenly linked her left arm around his neck and purred, "Wouldn't you like to buy me a drink, honey? I can be real sweet to you tonight, if you like. I've got a room upstairs."

"Get the hell out of here, bitch—I didn't invite you," was Magruder's surly answer, and to punctuate it, he shoved her off the chair so hard that she sat down heavily and painfully with a wail of distress.

A cowhand just entering the saloon witnessed the scene

and angrily exclaimed, "Look, stranger, that's no way to treat a lady!"

"Who the hell are you to butt in my affairs?" Magruder growled. "And who says she's a lady? She's just a common tramp peddlin' her tail, so don't be so noble!"

"I don't like that kind of talk, stranger, and I think you owe her an apology," the cowhand, a tall, lean, towheaded man in his late twenties, angrily countered as he lowered his right hand toward his holstered six-shooter.

"So you want it that way, mister? You asked for it!" Magruder snarled, as his right hand delved into his coat pocket and produced a derringer. There was a sharp report, and the cowhand staggered back, his eyes huge with disbelief and pain; then he slowly crumpled to the floor and lay still.

"Chrissake, Ed, you didn't have to go and kill the bastard," Hank Everson irritatedly complained. "Let's get the hell out of here before the marshal comes around! You ought to have checked that derringer with the bartender, and you know it."

"Don't you tell me what to do, Hank, unless you want some of the same medicine." Magruder hammered his fist on the table, nearly overturning the bottle. Abruptly rising, he added, "Hell—I'm fed up with this stinking cow town anyhow. All you see are dead buffalo bones around the station and the stink of all those damned cattle they're bringin' in. Damned shame a tired man can't find a place to relax in. Let's go, then!"

The trio moved to the bar and Magruder reclaimed his shotgun and pistols. The bald bartender, his face pale and sweating, muttered, "Best you wait for the marshal, mister—he'll be the one who says if it was fair or not."

"Don't give me that horsecrap," Magruder sneered as he leveled the shotgun and whirled around to have a clear view of the patrons at the tables, who promptly froze. "You saw and heard what went on, and that damn-fool cowhand asked for what he got. Let's go!" He glanced at his companions and jerked his head in the direction of the saloon door.

They swiftly mounted their horses and galloped toward the outskirts of town, heading east. "We'll try our hands at Wichita," Magruder decided. "It used to be a cow town like Dodge, only now it's swarmin' with dirt farmers and the like. There's bound to be a bank there for mighty easy pickings. And I haven't heard of any lawmen there who'd give us much of an argument if we separated the bank from a little of its cash—which we're gonna need."

"Sounds all right to me, Ed," Bill Cruxhall chuckled. "Let's swing around southward and double back so if they do raise a posse, they won't be able to read our tracks till we're well out of reach. Wichita it is!"

"Right! We'll get ourselves a good stake and go see what pickings there are in Indian Territory. Bound to be a lot of small farms out there and homes, and maybe even some good-looking women—not like these painted whores they got in all these saloons to bother a man's honest drinkin'," Magruder decided.

It was a crisp, wintry March morning, a memorable one for Elone Wilson. It was, in fact, her birthday. It was not the custom of her forebears to make much about such an event, particularly for a female, but Ben Wilson had remembered. As she woke, finding the bed empty beside her, she gasped with surprise to see him enter with a tray on which he had her breakfast and an artificial rose in a vase.

"My dear one, why do you wait on me?" she exclaimed.

"For two very good reasons, Elone. The first, because I love you more and more each day, and the second because it's your birthday. I've made biscuits the way you like them, and there's honey and jam as well, some little sausages, a baked apple with cloves and raisins, and—this I know you love—strong coffee. I'll sit here and watch you eat and think how lucky I am to have such a wonderful wife and mother to our children."

Elone's eyes misted as she accepted the tray. She took the artificial rose and put it to her lips, and then touched his with hers. Setting the vase down on a night table beside the bed, she declared, "My husband, you spoil me. You forget that I am from the Aiyuta. My people do not count the birth of a girl with much importance."

"And now you're teasing me," he chuckled as he leaned over to kiss her on the cheek. "Have you forgotten already that only a few weeks ago we were talking about my hope that one day Kansas would give women the vote, thus announcing that they are surely the equals of men? A great Greek philosopher named Plato said that, at the beginning of time, men and women were made of a single pole; some-

94

how the pole was divided, but through all the ages of time, they sought to be reunited and welded together. This is what I have always believed. And you, my dear one, are bound to me as I am to you by the strongest of ties, as if it had been decreed by God from the very beginning."

"I cannot say what is in my heart, dear Ben." Her voice was choked as she reached for the cup of steaming hot coffee and took a sip to regain her self-control. "I know only that I am so at peace with you, that I never think that I am Indian and you are *wasichu*."

"But that is exactly how it was meant to be from the very beginning of creation, my sweet Elone," he murmured huskily. "Incidentally, today is very important for a third reason: we have some additional money that you can put into the hospital bank account. I can hardly wait until the day we build this facility to cure the sick and those who have no money to pay for medicine. I'm sure that, too, was the intent of our Creator."

"Yes. And now that I am part of your faith, Ben, I am even more at peace than ever. I only wish all the world could know your faith and share in it."

"That is a dream of Utopia, Elone. You remember, I gave you that book written by a remarkable Englishman, Sir Thomas More. It is a kind of land that does not exist—except in the minds of those who want the most perfect of all worlds—where there is love and no hatred, justice and no wrongdoing. Perhaps if all of us think of it and work toward it, one day it will come to be." He sighed deeply and reached out to clasp her shoulders and to kiss her gently on the mouth, then leaned back. "But I've talked enough, and your breakfast is getting cold. When you're finished, I'll tend the children while you go to the bank. As soon as you return, I must go to see how some of my patients are doing."

Soon after breakfast, Tabitha Hartmann knocked on the door of their house and was welcomed cheerfully. "School is out until next week," she said to Ben, "and you know how impatient I get when I've nothing to do. I had a feeling in my bones that you'd want to make some house calls today, after having been away visiting those Injuns you always go to see. So I came over to see if I could look after the children if Elone has chores to tend to."

"You're really heaven-sent, dear Mrs. Hartmann," the

Quaker doctor smilingly assured her. "As a matter of fact, I would like to get started as soon as possible, so I'll just avail myself of your kind offer."

He turned to Elone. "Bundle up in your greatcoat; it's still bitterly cold outside." Ben carefully wrapped his neck with the hand-knit scarf Elone had given him for Christmas, and buttoned up his own greatcoat, then took his well-worn black bag from the corner of the parlor. "I'm going to walk, since both of my patients are on the edge of town. It will do me good besides—especially after all the riding I did out to Indian Territory and back. I should be back well before noon. Is there anything I can get for you, Mrs. Hartmann?"

"Bless you, Dr. Wilson, no thanks." Tabitha Hartmann grinned and patted her plump stomach. "Only one day soon I might be asking for your professional help in getting down some of this weight of mine—I'm afraid I've been overdoing it at the table. Poor Jacob, peace to his soul, he always did like my cooking—and I rather prefer it myself!"

"I can't argue with you, Mrs. Hartmann! I've certainly enjoyed your wonderful meals," Ben agreed smiling. He walked over to Elone, kissed her on the cheek, and quipped, "Maybe you can persuade Mrs. Hartmann to cook us one of her delicious suppers this evening."

Elone realized that far from being a reproach about her own cooking, her husband's intent was to make Mrs. Hartmann feel more like one of the family. She knew how lonely it must be for her older friend to have no one but herself for company every night—especially sitting alone at the dinner table. Besides, she admitted to herself, it would be a real treat, particularly on her birthday, not to have to make all the preparations for her large family by herself. "I think that's a wonderful idea," Elone said aloud, adding, "that is, if *you* think so, Mrs. Hartmann."

"I think it would be just lovely to share a meal for a change," the older woman eagerly responded.

"Good," Elone said, warmly pressing Mrs. Hartmann's hand. "And now, if you will excuse me, I shall go and put the latest contributions into the hospital account."

Ben opened the door for her; Elone turned to blow him a kiss, and then went out into the street. Ben turned back to Tabitha Hartmann. "It is wonderful for her to have friends like you, Mrs. Hartmann. Do you remember how little I knew about women when I tried to buy a dress in your husband's store the second time I came to Wichita?"

She began to laugh, and there were tears in her eyes when she finished as she said, "I have never forgotten that. And I thought to myself, what a queer, silent man he is, and yet the woman for whom he is buying that dress will surely be blessed. Yes, that is truly what I thought, Dr. Wilson. And now you be off to see your patients before you make an old woman maudlin with her memories!"

They had ridden into Wichita last night, after numerous doublings back to obscure their trail upon leaving Dodge City. Finally making camp at midnight on a grassy knoll about ten miles east of Wichita, they made a hasty supper and then rolled themselves up snugly in their sleeping blankets to waken at dawn.

"Guess that stupid cowhand I shot wasn't important enough to get a posse out after us," Ed Magruder chuckled to his two cohorts when they awoke at first light. As he stirred what was left in the coffee pot and lit a small fire, he remarked, "Coffee's all we need this mornin'. We'll mosey into town in a couple of hours. Bank won't open much before ten—not on a winter mornin', I figure."

"Anyhow," Bill Cruxhall proffered, "ain't likely to be many customers on a cold day like this, 'specially seein' as how it ain't Sattiday."

"You're right there," Hank Everson put in. "Heat that coffee good, Ed; I'm fair frozen."

"When we get the cash, we'll head ourselves south for the border—if the stake's big enough. It's better than Indian Territory for certain. I know a place near Nuevo Laredo where we can hole up for a long spell; it won't take much *dinero*, and we can have ourselves a high old time." Magruder grinned and licked his lips in anticipation. "Them señoritas know how to keep a man warm all the time—and it don't get cold like this over the Rio Grande! Here's your coffee, boys—drink up. We'll make sure we don't leave no trace of our bein' here, just in case any law comes around these parts."

Half an hour later, the outlaw trio had mounted up and ambled their horses in a leisurely gait toward the outskirts of Wichita. Magruder, head of the gang, detailed the plan. "See, what we'll do is come in separately. I'll hitch my horse to the post right outside the bank. You, Bill, stay down the street aways, but close enough so's you can cover me when I come out with the cash. You, Hank, be across the street and watchin'. My shotgun's loaded and so's my derringer. I don't figure we'll run into any trouble, but you boys have your guns out and be ready for action if you hear me whistle three times, get it?"

"Got it, Ed—don't you worry none about us," Cruxhall enthusiastically averred, and Everson chimed in with, "We had practice enough to handle this job without any hitches."

"All right, then. Let's get into town and take it real easy. Don't call no attention to yourselves when you hitch up your horses. If anyone asks, you're just lookin' the town over, cowboys done with a boss who don't pay nothin' and here to look for a job in a store, like clerkin' or somethin' like that," Magruder counseled.

He had hidden the shotgun under his *serape*, which he clutched tightly around it as he dismounted and expertly hitched the reins of his horse to the post outside the Drovers Commercial Bank. His two companions, as they had been bidden, dismounted, hands in the pockets of their breeches, Stetsons pulled slightly down over their faces, looking up and down the almost deserted street.

Elone had been the only customer in the bank after the doors were opened by the gangling, black-haired, twenty-year-old clerk, who also swept up, ran errands for the two officers, and brought in lunch for the other employees. She smiled sweetly at him, for Walter Anders was a polite, overworked and underpaid young man whose secret and still quite adolescent hope was to meet a dazzlingly beautiful girl who would choose him as her prince charming. "Good morning, Walter," she said gently. "It looks as if it's going to be a slow day in the bank, doesn't it?"

"Oh, yes, ma'am, Mrs. Wilson, ma'am." He bobbed his head and sheepishly grinned at her. "You can have your pick of the tellers."

"Thank you for telling me, Walter." Elone gave him another gentle smile and walked forward to the nearest window. At that moment, Ed Magruder entered, still cradling the hidden shotgun in his arms as he might a baby. His beady eyes narrowed, taking in the scene, and then, deftly whipping aside his *serape*, he yanked the shotgun up to waist level and growled, "Nobody make a move and nobody gets hurt. You there, baldy"——he gestured with the

98

muzzle of the shotgun toward the teller to Elone's left— "start puttin' money in this here sack!" He pulled out a gunny sack he had tied around his waist and tossed it over the cage to the horrified teller.

The three other employees in the bank, including the dignified, white-haired president, all had their hands up as Magruder waved the shotgun around to cover them. "That's nice, that's real nice. Stay that way, folks, and nobody gets shot up. Come on, baldy, get a move on! Just greenbacks—never mind the silver, hear me?"

"Why, why, yes—yessir," the teller stuttered, almost ready to faint, his face a sickly pallor.

The president, Abel Mellers, seated at his desk at the back of the bank, half turned to watch what was taking place, then stealthily eased his right hand toward the drawer in which he kept a Colt. Magruder, perceiving the movement, bellowed out, "Don't try it, mister! I'll blow your head off with this shotgun and don't think I can't from this range! Now you put both your hands inside your coat and keep them there, or I'll blast you!"

Then, to the trembling teller, "Ain't you got that money in the sack yet? Goddamn it, if I have to come around and help you, I'll leave you with a hole in your belly your guts can spill out of! I mean it!"

"I–I'm doing the b–best I can—don't—don't—sh–shoot, for G–God's sake!" the teller quavered, as he feverishly pulled out the cash drawer and began to stuff bills into the sack. "Here you are—that's all there is, I swear to God it is, mister!" he mumbled hoarsely, his eyes rolling with fright.

"Fine. Now you just lift the sack out and drop it on the floor near me—that's being smart!" He quickly stooped and retrieved the sack with his left hand, keeping the shotgun in his right with his forefinger near the trigger. Then, grinning lewdly, he stared at Elone, who remained frozen, immobile, at the other teller's window. "Honey, you're going to come along with us. This way, maybe they won't send out a posse—or if they do, you'll get it! You there," turning to the president of the bank, "you just tell any lawman that comes in that I'm taking this gal with me, and not to try to follow or they'll find her dead along the trail, savvy?"

"Why, yes, s–sir," the elderly man faintly stammered. "I–I'm mighty sorry, Mrs. Wilson—"

"Married, huh? And damned if she ain't got Injun blood in her." Ed Magruder chortled lecherously. "Means you oughta be pretty good in the sack, honey! Well, there'll be time enough to find that out once we shunt this crummy town. All right now, folks, keep it nice and easy and don't try no tricks! You keep your hands inside your coat, mister, 'cause I've got two friends outside who are watchin' you. You make a move for that gun in the drawer, you'll never get any older—I can promise you that! Okay, Mrs. Wilson, honey, let's you 'n me go out in style!" He moved closer to Elone, prodding her side with the muzzle of the shotgun, his beady eyes scanning her taut, constricted face. "Don't try nothin', if you ever want to go back to that man of yours—come on, now, stay real close to me; that's a good girl!"

He pushed her through the door of the bank onto the street, following her closely, turning to stare inside through the glass windows, waving the shotgun at the terrified bank personnel. "You know how to ride a horse, squaw?" he gruffly demanded.

"Yes. But I warn you, men will come after you." Elone courageously stared at him, her face impassive.

"So much the worse for you if they catch up with us. All right, now, clamber aboard this here gelding. I'll ride in front, and you put your arms around my waist and hold on tight. We're going to ride hell-bent for leather, savvy?" Then, raising his voice, he called to his two cronies, "Mount up and let's get out of here!"

As Elone deftly hoisted herself astride Ed Magruder's horse, she glanced frantically down the street. Thus far, the robbers had had unexpected luck: there was no one in sight coming toward the bank, and in the one store that had just opened across the street, the storekeeper was pulling aside the shutters and had his back to the scene.

Magruder mounted up, thrust the shotgun into the saddle sheath, and, clutching the sack of money in his right hand, jerked at the reins and kicked his heels against his gelding's belly. He felt Elone's arms reluctantly cling around his waist and grinned to himself. "Head east and then south, boys," he called to his cronies. Cruxhall and Everson nodded and then galloped down the main street toward the eastern outskirts of Wichita as Magruder took a last look around, then urged his gelding to catch up with them. Elone closed her eyes and tears welled on her lashes.

She prayed that her Ben and the others he would call to
help him would find her quickly before this brutal, bearded
ruffian kept his promise to assault her. She forced herself
to remain calm so that she could concentrate on ways of
circumventing his intentions.

## Eight

"How much you figure we got away with, Ed?" Hank Everson called to the bearded outlaw, behind whom Elone re-
signedly clung, as they rode along. The weather was frosty,
but not intolerable; she was grateful that she had been
wearing Ben's old greatcoat, for it would protect her
against the wind.

"I'd say three, maybe four thousand. That's plenty to set
us up where we're goin'. Don't waste time talkin', Hank;
just ride. Time enough to palaver when we make camp for
the night. Got to find some trees to give us some shelter
against this damn cold spell." He glanced back at Elone,
his lips curling in a lecherous smile and baring decaying,
yellowish teeth. "Though I got me here a hot Injun heifer,
so she'll keep me warmer 'n a heap of buffalo chips tonight."

Elone winced at this coarse threat, but said nothing.
Frantically, she strove to seize upon some way of letting
those who might pursue the outlaws find the trail. She observed that they were doubling back and forth to create
varying sets of tracks in the snow, which would throw the
pursuers off their trail. As she clung to Magruder with her
left arm around his waist, she stealthily reached back with
her other hand under the greatcoat and began to tear away
bits of her yellow petticoat. When she was certain that they
were not watching her, she dropped one small piece, and as
they rode on toward Winfield on the Kansas border and

then turned south toward Indian Territory, she dropped two more at various intervals.

"I've had me a bellyful of this damn cold," Magruder complained hoarsely. "Anyhow, plenty of little towns south of the border we can raid, if we run out of cash. I don't figure Kansas is gonna be too healthy for us from now on in. And don't forget, if you fellas are still of a mind to rustle cattle instead of robbin' banks, there's plenty of long-horns down Mexico way we can cut out with nobody no-ticin' and sell them to some of the missions, or even farmers. Hell, I had a buddy told me all about how religious folks is down in Mexico, and how the *peones*—that means they're dirt-poor—even go without food so's they can give money to the church. Those priests eat high on the hog, and they'll pay real good for beef. Christ, this wind's cold!"

It was too much to hope, Elone thought to herself, that her abductors would head directly toward the Creek reservation, where perhaps Sipanata and his braves might see them and, recognizing her, give chase. No, they were riding too far east. Her right hand dipped under the fold of the greatcoat and ripped away more of her petticoat, then dropped another piece, just as Magruder glanced back and snarled, "Look, you stupid Injun bitch, hang on with both arms or you'll fall off."

"I will do what you say," Elone replied passively.

"You damn well better, Mrs. Wilson. Hey now, that's a white man's name—you married to a white man?"

"Yes. He is a doctor in Wichita. He is a good, kind man, and he will come after me with others."

"I don't think so. Squaws are a dime a dozen, and we've got too good a head start. Not a soul in sight so far, so you better just forget your squaw man and make up your mind to pleasure me good tonight—if you want to keep on living till mornin', savvy? What do they call you?"

"My name is Elone Wilson."

"Well, Elone Wilson, I sure am lookin' forward to you peeled down bare in my sleeping blanket tonight. My pals here, Hank and Bill, they'll want a piece of you, too, so you've got three fellas to please—if you want to wake up tomorrow morning and have breakfast with us." At this, Magruder guffawed lewdly, and Elone's face crimsoned with a wave of shame.

*　*　*

102

Minutes after the three outlaws had ridden out of town, taking Elone with them, Dave Haggerson entered the bank to make a deposit of part of his teacher's salary. He walked into a scene of utter confusion, and after calming the elderly bank president, the still-frightened man told him of Elone's abduction. Dave hurried over to Dr. Ben Wilson's house, where he found Tabitha Hartmann looking after the children. She told him that the Quaker doctor had gone off to visit two of his patients, but unfortunately all she knew was that they lived nearby. With a groan, Dave thanked her, realizing that finding Ben Wilson would mean wasting precious time. He then mounted his horse and rode off to Dallas Masterson's house.

He found his gambler friend and hurriedly told him, "We've got to get up a posse right away and go after Elone. Three men came in this morning just about when the bank opened, robbed it of four thousand dollars, and took Elone off with them as a hostage. From what the clerks told me, they were riding east when they left town, but that doesn't mean anything. And they've got a head start."

"My God!" Dallas exclaimed. "We'll need four or five men who know how to ride and use guns. You know damn well Doc Ben wouldn't touch a weapon, even in a case like this. Tell you what, you got see if you can round up Jack Marley—I know he's in town because I saw him yesterday—and then go see if Sim Borland, the sheriff's deputy, is over at the jail. The sheriff's out after a couple of renegade Indians who stole some whiskey and two horses earlier this week, and he hasn't come back yet. I'll go call on some of Doc Ben's regular patients and see if I can find him. Meet you out by the railroad yard—get as many men as you can!"

Dave Haggerson nodded, went back outside and mounted his horse, then rode to Wichita's main hotel, where Jack Marley had a room when he was in town. The latter worked as a hired man for one of the nearby homesteaders, but during the last month he had been helping out at Lew Amway's farm equipment store because the owner had taken to his bed with a bad case of rheumatism.

Jack Marley was in his mid-thirties, stocky, good-natured, and had once worked as a cattle loader when Wichita had been a boom cattle town. He was an expert marksman and quite proud of his old Whitworth rifle, a gun which Confederate sharpshooters had used with deadly effect during the Civil War. Marley at once locked up the farm equipment store, saddled his horse, and joined Dave. The two men rode over to the sheriff's office and swiftly enlisted the personable, twenty-six-year-old, towheaded deputy, Sim Borland, who took along his double-barreled shotgun and a box of shells.

"That'll make four of us plus Dr. Ben. I sure hope Dallas finds him soon—the longer we stay around here, the farther those three robbers will be getting ahead of us," Dave Haggerson concluded.

"Look, I got a cousin; he's only nineteen, but he's a crack shot with a Colt," Borland spoke up. "He knows Doc Wilson, and he's been trying to get me to have Sheriff Tolliver sign him up as a deputy because he wants action. I'll just deputize him in the sheriff's absence and give him all the action he can stand."

"That's just great, Sim," Dave enthused. "You go get him, and I'll ride out to the railroad shed to wait for Dallas and Dr. Ben."

Three-quarters of an hour later, the five armed men and Ben Wilson rode eastward in pursuit of Elone's abductors. Sim Borland's cousin, Jimmy Felton, was a tall, rawboned youth who did odd jobs around the town. He lived with his ailing aunt, and spent much of his time helping out in Wichita's main stable. He had a Colt .44 holstered high on his right hip for a swift draw. Sim Borland made him blush self-consciously when he jokingly informed the others that, "Jimmy here is always practicin' his draw. Old Dan Steuben, who runs the stable, tells me he scares the horses half out of their wits, the way he pretends they're gunmen drawing on him."

"Oh, cut it out, Sim," the black-haired youth pleaded, embarrassed. "I'll show you what I can do with my Colt when we get close to those bank robbers, you just wait 'n see!"

Dr. Ben Wilson had ridden ahead, staring at the snow-covered ground to determine the direction his wife's captors had gone. The posse followed, observing the frequent circular and aimless turns Ed Magruder and his companions had taken to throw them off the track, till at last the Quaker doctor cried, "They turned off here! There's a piece of Elone's petticoat—see there on the ground near that bush?"

"That's damned smart of her," Dallas Masterson murmured, as he rode abreast of Ben. "With her savvy, she'll know how to fend for herself, don't you worry. We'll get her back before they have a chance to do her any harm. After what you did for my Flora, Doc Ben, I won't rest till I've measured those three bastards for a quick grave without a marker."

Ben Wilson said nothing, but sent Dallas a grateful look. He could hardly conceal his anxiety. The bank president had described the robbers to Dave Haggerson and repeated the lewd threat Ed Magruder had made to Elone. Although Dave had not told the Quaker doctor this detail, the latter comprehended that desperate men who would take such a hostage and mock her Indian origin would show her no mercy when it came time to forcing her to service their carnal desires. He prayed silently as they rode, his eyes glued to the marks of the horses' hooves ahead. "They've turned south, toward Indian territory!" he called. "See? There's another piece of Elone's petticoat!"

"I told you she was smart, Doc," Dallas chuckled. "And those tracks are still fresh—I'd say no more than two hours old, at most. We're closing in on them, sure as shootin'!"

Just after sunset, the three bank robbers reached a stretch of irregular terrain not far from the border of Indian territory where there had only been the faintest sprinkling of snow and where, to the southeast, about a mile distant, they could see the outlines of a coppice. "We'll head for those trees there, boys," Ed Magruder jovially announced. "This purty squaw can fix us up a meal and then we'll let her pleasure us." He glanced back at Elone and grinned lewdly at her. "Bet you're nigh frozen, but we'll warm you up plenty." Then he added to his two cronies, "No chance now any posse's after us. Just as well—these damn horses are about done in. Might have to rest up a spell in the morning before we start out again. If we reach a farm, we can latch ourselves onto some fresh ones."

The three robbers rode up to the thicket and dismounted, and Magruder reached up to pull Elone to the ground as, gripping the shotgun by its barrel with his right hand, he locked his left arm around her waist and crushed his mouth on hers. "That's for starters, you Injun bitch! Now you go fix us some chow. Bill, get a fire goin' and you, Hank, take some grub out of the saddlebag on your horse. We'll put her to work earnin' her supper and the good pokin' we're all gonna give her," he guffawed. Then, releasing her, he gave her a shove, which nearly sent her sprawling, as the other men tied their horses to the trunks of the gnarled scrub trees. It was a barren terrain, with just these few trees huddled in a pathetic little group the only protective shelter so far as the eye could see. The wind had died down, and Bill Cruxhall broke off some of the brittle branches of the nearest shrub and arranged them in a pile, then squatted down with his tinderbox and began to make a fire. Hank Everson hauled out beans, bacon, and coffee, flung down a pot and a skillet on the cold ground, and roughly ordered Elone, "Start it goin' and be quick about it! We're starved."

She had no choice, so Elone slowly began her abductors' supper. She turned her face to the north, uttering a silent prayer that, somehow, someone would find her. But she knew that she must obey, or else suffer many more indignities before they killed her.

The fire began to burn and crackle. Cruxhall produced a canteen so that Elone could make coffee, and she went about these tasks with a quiet resignation that irked her captors. "Maybe she's really glad we took her off so she could get a pokin' from real men," Magruder lecherously suggested. "Maybe her squaw man don't do right by her in bed. But I'm here to tell you this Injun bimbo is made real nice. Come on, Mrs. Wilson, get that bacon fryin' and them beans cooked right! I ain't never yet poked a bimbo on an empty stomach, haw haw!"

She would not let them bait her, but doggedly continued to prepare the frugal meal. From his saddlebag, Magruder took three tin plates and mugs and set them down on a blanket, remarking with a snigger, "Why, boys, this is really done in style. Just like eatin' at one of them fancy Dodge City chow places—'n the best thing about it is we got us a cook who's gonna take care of what we need after our bellies are good 'n full!"

At last the supper was ready and Elone filled the tin plates with bacon and beans and poured the strong coffee into the mugs, then squatted down, bowing her head, and prayed.

"You can eat what's left—you'll need your strength to take us all on, I'm thinkin'," Magruder taunted her. "Go on, eat up! Don't waste food out here!"

Elone hesitated; she wanted to tell them that to take any-

106

thing from them would be odious, but she was exhausted from the long ride in the bitter cold, and also she reasoned that the longer she took, the more chance there would be that her husband and those he had been able to enlist to come to her aid would be able to catch up with her abductors. So, slowly, she reached into the skillet and took out the two pieces of bacon still remaining, and chewed them methodically—till Bill Cruxhall, who had wolfed down his food, contemptuously tossed her his greasy tin plate and growled, "Pour your beans into this, squaw. And don't take all night to eat up. Have some coffee; it'll wake you up so you can wiggle real good for us on the blanket!" The other two men roared with bawdy laughter at this obscene sally, but Elone silently took the plate and dumped the few remaining spoonfuls of beans onto it, and then filled the mug Cruxhall had tossed to her with the rest of the coffee. The beans had cooled, so that she could eat them with her fingers, and again she prolonged this while the three men impatiently glowered at her. Her flesh cringed at the thought of submitting to their rough, brutal embraces, but she knew that if she refused, they would kill her without hesitation.

Now that they had all eaten, they sat like greedy vultures, staring impatiently at her as she forced herself to eat the beans with her fingers and to sip at the still scalding coffee. Suddenly Cruxhall spoke up. "Look, Ed, I know you were the guy that brought her along with us, but Hank 'n me, we haven't had a poke for a lot longer than you have. We oughta cut cards to see who's first to prime her up!"

"Don't push it, Bill," Magruder growled, as he reached for the shotgun beside him. "You've been mighty useful so far, and I'd hate to leave you with your brains blown out of your stupid head, just over an Injun squaw. You 'n Hank'll have your chances with her once I'm finished. Just hold your fire, savvy? All right, Mrs. Wilson, you had enough to eat by now, I figure. Start peelin' down! Get the greatcoat off. I'll go get my sleepin' bag 'n more blankets. If you get too cold, you just wiggle up tight against me, 'n I'll warm you plenty!" Once again, he punctuated his remark with a ribald guffaw, which made her cheeks burn with shame, as she lowered her eyes and bit her lip.

The six pursuers had driven their horses hard, following the few more scraps of Elone's petticoat along the trail, which now veered directly south. It was now dark, and there

107

was only a quarter moon, with hazy clouds obscuring it from view. Suddenly Ben Wilson reined in his horse and, turning to his friends, exclaimed, "I can just make out a tiny light about a mile ahead—maybe it's their campfire!"

"Damn it all, they're hidin' out in what looks like a small forest, and they've got the advantage over us. We'll have to play it real careful," Sim Borland growled disappointed. Jack Marley had taken his old Whitworth out of the saddle sheath and was priming and loading it. Jimmy Felton, a smug smile on his face, felt for his Colt. He drew it out, twirled it, made sure that it was fully loaded, then thrust it back into its holster.

Back in the coppice, Ed Magruder had drawn his derringer to order Elone to undress. Very slowly, she unbuttoned the buttons of her greatcoat and let it drop, and then, her eyes filling with tears, her head bowed, began to finger the hooks of her heavy wool dress. The three men watched avidly, and Magruder spread out his sleeping bag over a blanket, and then began to open his breeches. Elone ground her teeth, as he commented on his readiness for her: "Make it fast, bitch—I'm primed and ready. This is gonna be the best poke you ever got in all your young life, so help me!"

At last, she tugged her dress off over her head and let it fall to the ground, then began to undo her petticoats. Her flesh was goose-pimply from the cold, and, even more, from the agonizing awareness of what would befall her. Her lips moved in silent prayer to her God to save her so that she would not be shamed, or be diseased by these brutal men. She thought of her children, and tears welled into her eyes as she fumbled with the last petticoat. A chorus of lewd, appraising comments rose from the three robbers as she stood in camisole and drawers and thick, black woolen stockings inside her high-button shoes. "Jeez, she's made for pokin', if ever I saw a broad that was! For Gawd's sake, Ed, don't take all night—I'm burstin'!"

"Hurry up with your drawers and shoes, honey—and take that damn top off, so's I can see yer tits—" wheezed Ed Magruder.

She was trembling so hard she could barely stand, but she forced herself to lift the camisole and let it fall with the rest of her clothes; then she began to slowly undo the buttons of her shoes. Her dark nipples puckered from the cold wind, and Magruder lustily licked his lips as he reached up for her wrists and pulled her down onto the sleeping bag with him. "Forget the damn shoes. They won't get in my way—and I'll get rid of your drawers myself quick enough."

She saw his shotgun lying nearby, but she did not dare reach for it: the other two men stood watching, their eyes dilated and glazed with lust, their hands at the butts of their revolvers. She did not want to die; she wanted to live for Ben and her children, and that alone made her submit as passively as she could. Closing her eyes, her body rigid, she eased into the sleeping bag. She felt her ravisher's maleness prod her thigh and could not suppress a faint whimper of revulsion and despair.

"Hey, what the hell's that?" Bill Cruxhall suddenly exclaimed. "I hear horses—"

"Son of a bitch!" Ed Magruder snarled as he shoved Elone to one side and clambered out of the sleeping bag, hastily buttoning his open breeches and reaching for the shotgun. "Now how the hell could a posse follow us here?"

"Oh, I thank God!" Elone joyously cried as she huddled with her arms over her naked breasts. "They saw my petticoat—" She stopped short, realizing she had blurted out too much.

"What the—" Magruder began. "Damn that bitch! She tore off pieces and dropped them along the trail—that's how they followed us! I oughta shoot her guts out right now," Magruder snarled.

But by now the sound of the horses' hooves was louder, and the three robbers crouched behind the gnarled scrub trees and waited. "Pick them off nice and easy as they come up to us," Magruder growled to his two cronies.

"I see six of them," Hank Everson cried as he drew out his six-shooter and leveled it at the shadowy advancing riders.

"Wait till they get closer; don't waste your ammo! Hey, I got a better idea. " Magruder chuckled to himself, then laid down his shotgun at his left and, cupping his hands to his mouth, bawled out, "We got the gal, so don't come in shootin' or she'll get hit first. You ride out of here, or I'll kill her myself!"

"You better not try it! We've got more guns and ammo than you have, and you won't live to get back to Wichita to stand trial, if you harm Mrs. Wilson!" Sim Borland yelled back. The six of them dismounted and crouched down about a hundred yards away from the coppice. The dying campfire flickered, still casting enough light to indicate to the pursuers where their quarry were hiding.

Dr. Ben Wilson murmured something to Sim Borland, who shrugged and muttered back, "Well, it might work. If they give her up and make a break for it, then we can pick them off. We're not honor-bound when it comes to dealing with bank robbers and woman-snatchers." Cupping his hands to his mouth, he called out. "Send Mrs. Wilson back to us! You can keep the money and ride off. I'm deputy sheriff of Wichita, and I've got the same legal authority as the sheriff himself. What do you say?"

"You go to hell, mister!" Ed Magruder called back with a triumphant sneer. "You ain't got no good cards to bargain with. We've got the squaw and we've got the cash, and we're gonna keep 'em both. You just ride on back to Wichita nice 'n peaceful 'n maybe we'll let the squaw go when we've done with her."

"No!" Ben cried, and he started to run forward. Young Jimmy Felton leaped onto the unarmed man just as a shotgun roared, both its barrels discharged. As the two men fell to the ground, Jimmy's arm was grazed by one of the charges.

Elone uttered a stifled cry of horror as she peered into the darkness, praying that her husband was all right. She looked back to the outlaw crouching by her side, and saw Magruder reload the shotgun, level it, and squint to take careful aim. Suddenly she flung herself at him and pushed him to one side; the shotgun exploded, but the charge whistled harmlessly over the heads of her rescuers. A moment later, the bark of the posse's Colts responded, and Hank Everson uttered a strangled cry of pain as he put his hand to his left shoulder and found it bleeding from a crease.

"You goddamn bitch, you spoiled my aim! I'm gonna kill you for that," Ed Magruder swore as he turned toward Elone, cocking the lever of the shotgun to fire the second barrel. In desperation, the Indian woman crouched and flung herself forward, butting him in the abdomen and sending him sprawling. At the same time, Jack Marley, on one knee in the snow and squinting along the sight of his old Whitworth, pulled the trigger, and Magruder groaned as the bullet took him at the back of the neck. He reeled, reached back with one hand, his eyes rolling to the whites, then fell dead on his side before Elone.

110

"We give up, we give up," Bill Cruxhall cried. "Don't shoot no more!"

"All right, then, come out with your hands up. Mrs. Wilson, do you see the sack of money the men took from the bank?"

"Y—yes, I do," Elone tremulously called back.

"Bring it along, please. Thank God we came in time," Dallas Masterson called to her.

Elone stayed by the campfire just long enough to hurriedly dress, then, her eyes blinded with tears, ran frantically toward her husband, who embraced her. She then saw Jimmy Felton's bleeding shoulder, and quickly tore off a length of her petticoat to bind the injury. After being assured that it was just a flesh wound, she embraced the boy and praised him for his bravery.

Ben promised Jimmy he would take care of his shoulder as soon as they returned to Wichita; then, overcome by his joy at Elone's salvation, he knelt and wept.

Three days after Dr. Ben Wilson had brought his wife back to Wichita, there was a knock early in the morning at the door of his white frame house. He opened it to find a young cowhand, his Stetson twisted between his wiry, long fingers, who apologetically explained, "I'm sorry if I woke you up, Doc. Fact is, my boss, Dade Torrington, he's come down with a misery. Can't hardly breathe, and his face is turning a mite blue. He sent me off for the other doctor, but 'pears like he left town, from all I've heard tell. Could you come look at my boss?"

"I'll ride back with you in a moment. I just have to pack my medical bag with the tools and supplies I'll need," Ben explained anxiously.

A few minutes later, he mounted his horse and rode with the young cowhand back to Dade Torrington's large house on the outskirts of Wichita. The cowhand led him into the bedroom, where he found the middle-aged rancher lying with eyes closed, his face covered with sweat, his skin bluish, and a rasping sound coming from his throat.

Quickly, the Quaker doctor took Torrington's pulse, rolled back his eyelids, and then listened carefully to the wheezing sounds that emanated from the man's panting mouth.

"He's had a touch of diphtheria," Dr. Wilson said softly to the cowhand. "Go heat some water and get me plenty of

111

towels. I'm going to have to cut into his windpipe, or he'll die of suffocation—he can't breathe."

"I don't know, Doc—" the cowhand began dubiously.

"Do what I tell you to, if you want your boss to live!" Dr. Wilson snapped.

He stared at the gray-haired man in the bed, and shook his head and sighed. How well he remembered how Fleurette and Benjamin Hardesty—the owner of an iron mill and head of the general hospital where he had been employed—had both been stricken by diphtheria. He had performed a tracheotomy on each of them, and Hardesty had lived—but Fleurette had died.

The cowhand returned with the hot water and the towels. "Now, you'll have to hold his wrists above his head, and don't let him break away. He's in fever now, and he's not likely to feel too much. I have to do this, or he'll die right away."

"You do what you have to, Doc."

"Fine. Now I'm going to sterilize my scalpel, and then you can start holding him when I'm ready to cut," Ben Wilson ordered.

The cowhand had to close his eyes and turn away, nauseated by the sight as Dr. Ben Wilson expertly cut into the windpipe to relieve the congestion. Some time later, bandaged and sutured, Dade Torington lay quietly asleep.

"He's going to live. Now you stay with him all night, that's an order. If there's any sudden bleeding, or if he begins fighting for breath, send a messenger off to me, and I'll get back here in a jiffy."

"Bless you, Doc. He's a good man, good to work for, and he sure never figured to be laid low by something like this."

"I know what he was sick from. I ran into the same thing in Pittsburgh. Has he kept to himself while he's been sick?"

"Oh, sure, Doc! He took to his bed the first day he found it tough to breathe, only it got so bad, he just sent me over to find this Dr. Mannheimer."

"He's going to be fine. He hasn't lost too much blood, he's in good physical condition, and he's got a strong heart. You just watch over him all night and get back to me if there's any change. I'll be back out in a couple of days to see how he's doing. The stitches can't be removed for a week or so."

"Thanks again, Doc. I know he'll want to thank you, too, when he's well again."

The next afternoon, the same cowhand knocked at the door of Ben's house and this time handed him an envelope. Curious, the Quaker doctor opened it and then gasped at the sight of a bank draft for two thousand dollars. An enclosed letter read:

Dear Dr. Wilson:

I've known about you for some time, and I have to admit I didn't cotton to you because you married an Injun squaw. But I don't make a fuss about people I don't like; I just stay away from them.

Phil Casten—he's my handyman—says you saved my life. So I want to apologize for what I thought about you and your wife. I've heard about how you and the other men rode out to rescue her from those bank robbers. You've got guts, Dr. Wilson, and that appeals to me. I've heard tell that you'd like to have a hospital here in Wichita. This check is a contribution to help build it. And I'd like it a lot if you'd let me be a part of it once it's built, like maybe buy supplies or whatever else the hospital needs to keep folks well. As soon as I'm stronger and out of bed, I'm going to come over and apologize to you and your wife personally. I hope you won't hold it against me about what I thought before I knew better.

Your friend,
Dade Torrington

Dr. Ben Wilson turned to Elone and handed her the check, his homely face radiant with joy. "The bank paid a reward of two hundred and fifty dollars for the recovery of the money those men stole, my dear one," he told her, "and that will go into the school fund. But this check makes it possible for us to begin building our hospital before the year is over. Men of good works and good will appear when you least expect to find them. It is a lesson for us all to remember."

## Nine

On this bright February morning Judith Marquard thought fondly back to the happiest Christmas of her entire life. Her marriage to the devoted, gifted blind man, Bernard Marquard, had given her back all her self-esteem and her ability to love without fear of betrayal. Her past abuse by David Fales had been almost entirely erased from her memory—except she sometimes thought that perhaps, if it had not been for the effete Southerner's treacherous usage of her, she might never have known the joys of being either a mother or the wife of the kindest, most considerate man she had ever met. Moreover, at Christmas she had been able to tell Bernard that she had a very special gift for him: she was pregnant again. Their seven-month-old daughter Nancy, named after her dead mother, was thriving, and she secretly prayed this child would be another girl because she wished to name her Augusta, after Bernard's mother.

Judith also showered her affections on Rory, the English retriever that Jesse Jacklin, Bernard's former orderly, had purchased for her husband back in Virginia before their coming to New Orleans. Indeed, the quiet, friendly dog came to know her footsteps as well he he did those of his master, and would bark joyously when he heard her coming into the house.

Judith continued to work at the Brunton & Barntry Bank. Jason Barntry had visibly aged since his wife's death three years ago, and it had only been Lopasuta Bouchard's conveyance of Luke Bouchard's plea that had persuaded the bank manager to withdraw the resignation he had already tendered to Luke and Laure. He had engaged a housekeeper to look after his house and to cook his meals, for the thought of complete loneliness was anathema to him.

Nonetheless, in this February of 1879, Jason Barntry looked frail and ailing, much to Judith Marquard's concern.

By this time, thanks to the acumen and enthusiasm she had shown in her work since he had first engaged her, Judith performed many responsible tasks for the bank, one of which was visiting rival financial institutions and reporting on her observations of the type of customers they drew and what literature they issued concerning private or public stock. In addition, she often conferred with affluent factors, who dealt in sugarcane, molasses, cotton, and other profitable commodities, as well as with some of the foremost realtors of the Queen City. Jason Barntry had come to rely a good deal on her reports, and he had made considerable money for the bank by placing the capital into sound investments after he had read her analyses and talked with her to learn her reactions to the influential people she had met.

But just before the close of business on this Friday, Jason had called Judith into his private office. After having bidden her close the door, he gestured her to a seat and then folded his hands and stared at her for a long moment before speaking. "First, Judith, I want to tell you how valuable you've become to this bank. Your excellent work has had a great deal to do with a major part of the profits this bank has achieved in the past year or so."

"That's very kind of you to say, Mr. Barntry."

"No, not kind—just. I know how much you enjoy your work, even now that you're a wife and mother. My only question is whether you might not consider it prudent to give up your career in the bank to devote all of your time to your marriage and your children—no, I'm not especially discerning. You inadvertently told me last week you were going to have another child."

"Oh my goodness!" Judith blushed and looked away, sheepishly shaking her head. "But it's true. All the same, it won't keep me from working here, Mr. Barntry."

"I realize that. But I want to tell you something in all confidence. The fact is, Judith, I haven't been feeling well for some time now. I visited the doctor a few weeks ago, and he told me that I very well may have a touch of consumption—and that it would be wisest for me to give up my work entirely and perhaps even to move to a dryer climate."

"But you look fine to me, Mr. Barntry," Judith interposed.

"You're very flattering, my dear, and good for an old man's steadily decreasing ego. No, Judith, I've made my decision. Over the past week or two, I have been talking to the principal of a very stable bank here in New Orleans who would like to acquire my interest. It would be tantamount to a merger, and indeed it would strengthen the Brunton & Barntry Bank immeasurably, while bringing in much valuable new capital so that we could expand our investments."

"That would mean more work for the employees, wouldn't it?"

"I'm not so sure, my dear. Henry Kessling, the president of the New Orleans Alliance Bank, has indicated that he would like to bring in some of his own personnel for key positions—such as the one you have here with me now—so I can't guarantee you that, after I leave, Mr. Kessling might not replace you. Unfortunately, I do not think that, if he had so made up his mind, my urging him to let you continue your work would go heeded by him. So perhaps realistically, Judith dear, it would be best for you to think either of retiring or else, if you are determined to go on working, to look for something more stable. Rest assured, I'll give you every recommendation, if you should choose the latter course."

"I'm very appreciative of all you've done for me, Mr. Barntry. But I'm shocked to think of your leaving this bank and still more so of being replaced by a man who would make sweeping changes and perhaps alienate the loyal and faithful workers here."

"Nothing is definite yet, but I expect to work out the final decision shortly. I'm afraid that my doctor's opinion may override a good deal of sentimental idealism on my part. If I am ill, I certainly cannot carry forward the affairs of the bank with the same skill that I showed in the past and that has won me the trust of so many people like the Bouchards. As a matter of fact, I recently wrote to Mrs. Bouchard about this point, and she has just replied, reluctantly accepting whatever decision I feel I must make. I tell you this now, Judith, so that if this deal goes through and Mr. Kessling replaces you, you won't take it as a personal affront."

"Oh, I won't," the tall, lovely young woman avowed.

"But if it does happen, I'll certainly want to find another position. I want to be more than just a homemaker and mother."

"My dear girl," Jason Barntry shook his head with an amused little smile on his lips, "I confess I don't understand the modern generation at all. When I was a young man, it was a woman's whole life to marry and have children and devote herself entirely to them and to her husband."

"Yes, I understand that, and don't think I'm trying to shirk my responsibilities, Mr. Barntry," Judith gently assured him. "But we do have a housekeeper, and I can still spend plenty of time with Nancy when I come home and give Bernard all the attention that he needs. Yet at the same time, while I'm working and meeting different kinds of people, I'm learning more all the time, and it makes my communication with Bernard much richer. And also," she flashed Jason a winning smile, "there's a matter of a woman's keeping her attractiveness. It would be a great temptation not to watch my diet and not to care if every curl was in place and if I was dressed the way I should be, if I just stayed at home all the time. But this way, since I'm on public display, as you might say, I have to be personable and charming and well-groomed at all times. It's good for my morale."

"I give up," he laughed softly, and put up his hands in mock surrender. "But seriously, if I do decide to sell out to Mr. Kessling, I'll give you plenty of advance notice so that if he does make any drastic changes, you won't be displaced without warning."

"You've always been very good to me, Mr. Barntry, and I can't tell you how grateful I am—I value you as a friend even more than as an employer."

"That's very sweet of you, my dear. I'm touched. And now that I'm so lonely and feeling it more and more, what with my infirmities coming upon me, I do want always to stay in touch with you. Your bright face and your quick mind have helped me over many a rough spot these last few years since my wife died." He turned his face away.

Judith discreetly withdrew, murmuring, "Thank you, Mr. Barntry. I'll bring in that McKesson report after lunch, when you've time to look at it."

That evening Judith sat down to dinner with Bernard. Nancy was in her high chair, cooing and gurgling. As the housekeeper, a pleasant, middle-aged widow, brought in Nancy's meal first—warmed milk and a puree of beef, peas, and carrots—Judith smiled at her. "Thank you, Mrs. Rossiter. You always prepare the nicest dinners for us."

"It's my pleasure, Mrs. Marquard. I'll be in the kitchen, if you need me," the housekeeper replied genially.

As she spooned the baby's food, Judith said softly to her blind husband, "Jason Barntry had some distressing news for me today, darling. His doctor told him he ought to retire, and he's thinking of selling his stock to the head of another bank. That might mean I'd be replaced by the new president, since he'll probably have his own favorite for my job."

"That's not so distressing, really, my dearest." Bernard turned his sightless eyes toward the sound of her voice and smiled tenderly at his wife. "We've money enough, you know, so you don't have to work at all. And now that we're going to have another child, wouldn't it be sensible to stay home and devote all your time and energy to our family?"

"Darling, before we met and married, working was a financial necessity. However, it became more than that: it lifted my spirits, it has helped me meet some wonderful people—you, my love, being the prime example of that— and it has given me a feeling of worth that I never thought was possible. After meeting you and getting to know you as I did, I was enormously impressed by how you overcame your blindness with courage and determination, and I feel that, as your wife, I should have no less determination to make myself the best that I can. You see, my dear," she patted his hand, "your pluck had rubbed off on me, and I feel that I have to strive beyond what is considered the proper place for a woman—just being a wife and mother."

"I understand, Judith, and you make me extremely proud," Bernard assured her. "I understand, too—although you haven't mentioned it—that after so many years of penury, it is almost vital to you that you have your own, independent income so that you can never, under any circumstances, ever be left as penniless as you were after your parents died.

"I will respect your decision, my darling," he concluded, "and I want you to know that I think no other man in the world has a finer, more capable wife."

Tears sprang to Judith's dark blue eyes as she quickly rose, went over to him, and, putting her palm to his cheek, leaned forward to kiss him ardently. "And I can say the same thing about my husband—because I'm the luckiest woman in the world, Bernard. Thank you, honey, for understanding and approving of my decision."

"Since it means so much to you, then by all means do it, Judith. I want you to be happy." He reached for her and curved his arm around her waist, his face upturned to her. "I love you, Judith. You've made me happier that I ever thought I could be."

She kissed him again, and then, to dispel the emotionality of the moment, she said airily, as she went back to her seat, "I plan to make you happier still—and even then I'll not be able to catch up. May I pour you some of the Medoc, my darling?"

He chuckled happily. "Yes, please, Judith. I want to drink a toast to you and Nancy and the coming member of our very happy household."

Judith filled his glass with the vintage claret. "There, darling. And I'll drink to my wonderful, understanding husband."

In this first week of February 1879, a letter addressed to Lopasuta Bouchard had arrived from Leland Kenniston at his New York headquarters. It was all Geraldine could do to keep from opening it before her tall, handsome husband returned from his luncheon engagement with Andy Haskins.

The one-armed state senator had been extremely philosophical over their lunch at their favorite restaurant. "You know, Lopasuta, folks have been touting me up to run again next year—some of them even want me to line my sights on the governor's mansion. But to be honest with you, I don't think I have the chance of a snowball in hell. The South is going Democratic with a vengeance, and there are signs of it everywhere, even in our own senate. So I've decided to get out of politics and find something else that will keep me busy, something where I'll feel I'm still making a contribution to the people. Jessica understands, and she's all for it. I don't think she's ever liked my being in politics, if you want to know the truth, not after all that happened to us—you know, like that poor lunatic Darden who tried to kill Luke and me, and the shenanigans of that group of speculators who tried to blackmail me because I wouldn't go along with them. No, Lopasuta, I really don't have any further political ambitions, but I do want to serve people. All my life, people have helped me—like Luke, when he came to New Orleans right after the war and picked Joe Duvray and me off the wharf there to help him move on to Texas—and I'm going to try to pay back the debt. What're your plans, now that you're finally home?"

Lopasuta quickly outlined the story of his meeting with Leland Kenniston and the latter's offer. Andy Haskins nodded. "That sounds like a wonderful idea. I think Geraldine would welcome a respite from Montgomery—there's not much future for either of you here, if you want my opinion, where hidebound, narrow-minded people begrudge every success you make in court. At least in New Orleans, they're not all still fighting the Civil War."

"I know, and I feel the way you do. I'm just waiting for Mr. Kenniston to write me with an official offer. Then Geraldine and I will decide."

They parted amicably, and Lopasuta had gone home to be told that, indeed, just such a letter had arrived only this morning.

He opened it eagerly, and Geraldine impatiently waited for him to read it aloud:

Dear Lopasuta:

I spent only a week in New Orleans, but I had time enough to meet with Jason Barntry and to tell that I like him and find his bank extremely stable. He intimated to me that he himself may soon make a personal change, which may mean amalgamation with another bank of equally reputable solvency. That, if it goes through, would make doing business with the institution even more satisfying to me.

I have also engaged a Creole, a well-educated man who is wealthy enough in his own right so that I shan't have to worry too much about his trying to fleece me. He has done a good deal of traveling to Europe and even South America, he speaks several languages, and he knows a lot about the import and export business. Before the Civil War, his own father imported luxuries from Spain, Mexico City, France, and Belgium and was smart enough to convert his holdings into gold in a Parisian bank so that he could leave his son a considerable fortune when the war was over. His name is René Laurent, and he will act as my factor in the office I have engaged on Royal Street.

If you decide to work with me, I should like you to prepare to move to New Orleans as soon as you can to start studying for the Louisiana bar examination. You can, of course, already represent me in Alabama—which is excellent because as time goes by, I may do business in places like Montgomery, Birmingham, and Tuscaloosa.

I am prepared to pay you a retainer of three hundred dollars a month. I also will stand moving expenses for your family. Perhaps you would wish to rent a house initially—rather than purchase one—until you have taken the examination. Certainly after six months you will have been admitted to the bar, keen-witted as you are and already a top-notch lawyer. In the meantime, you'll work with René Laurent and understand what I'm trying to do in New Orleans.

Please wire me your answer as quickly as possible. As it turns out, I'll be able to get back to New Orleans either in February or early March, so you won't have to travel to New York. As you know, I'm counting on being introduced to your lovely wife. I'm sure that the two of you are happier than ever, and that what happenened to you in Hong Kong will remain only a very colorful memory.

My best wishes are to be extended to your charming Geraldine. I await your decision.

Your devoted friend and, I hope, employer.

Leland Kenniston

"Oh, darling, that sounds wonderful!" Geraldine exclaimed, after Lopasuta had lowered the letter and eyed her to see her reaction. "I think it will be so exciting for all of us!"

"You're quite sure? I hesitate only because it seems unfair to uproot you from your parents, just when everything is going so well between you and them," Lopasuta declared soberly.

"I want to tell you something very confidential, darling. Sit down and put your arm around me. That's wonderful." Geraldine snuggled up closer to him with a happy sigh. "You know how Mrs. Norton reconciled us—what you

121

don't know is that they've given me money to pay her wages, and also enough for Dennis and myself. Now, when I was a little girl, it was well and good for them to treat me as such; but even though I'm now a married woman, they *still* think of me as their little girl. And that's why I'll be ever so happy to start afresh in an exciting city like New Orleans. Mr. Kenniston sounds like an absolutely fascinating man; he's going to go places—and you'll go with him. And I know you'll do better as a lawyer in New Orleans than here."

"Yes, Geraldine," Lopasuta interposed. "As I've told you, Mr. Kenniston has agreed to my having time to do what he called clinical legal work, helping those who couldn't afford a lawyer to get justice."

"Of course, that's your nature. Don't forget, that's how we met, after you defended a poor black in the Montgomery court and I'd come up to compliment you."

"That was the luckiest day of my life, my sweetheart," he smiled, and reached over to kiss her very satisfactorily.

Geraldine giggled. "I'm very glad to see that, considering your exotic foreign adventures, you still seem to be very much interested in your wife—and I intend to make certain that you never lose that interest. Being in a place like New Orleans with all the cultural opportunities of that big city and all the different foreign elements is certain to broaden my mind; I can continue to be interesting to you, so that you won't ever want another woman."

"I never shall—you know that already."

"Silly; I was just teasing." She gently touched his mouth with her palm, then cupped his face and kissed him. "You are going to wire him, aren't you?"

"Right away, my darling."

Ten years ago, when Arabella Bouchard Hunter and her patient husband had a domestic spat whose amorous conclusion had led surprisingly to the birth of a daughter they appropriately named Joy, she had found that her life was very definitely not over at the mature age of forty-five. In this February of 1879, she was pleased to realize that, at an even more advanced age, she looked forward to her remaining years with a zest and eagerness she could not remember having, even when she had been a spoiled, flirtatious young girl on Windhaven Plantation.

To be sure, she missed James Hunter—who had died of

122

yellow fever two and a half years ago, but not before his having assured her that she had made him serenely happy and that, for all of her flightiness at times, he could not have hoped for a happier union. Just before his death, the reconciliation of her older daughter, Melinda, with Lawrence Davis, who had been carrying on a secret liaison with Marianne Valois, had gratified both her and James. Lawrence and Melinda were now certainly as devoted a young couple as could be found in all of Galveston, and the final proof of that was the birth of their fourth child, Arabella, two years ago. Her son, Andrew, now twenty-five, and his young wife, Della, had made a good marriage for themselves, too, and their two-year-old son, William, was a thoroughly delightful child. Even if Arabella were the type to look nostalgically back into the past, she would see only joyous memories.

After the Galveston hurricane in September 1877, Arabella had moved closer to the center of the city and purchased a one-story brick house with a charming little gazebo in the back in the middle of a flourishing garden —perfect for Joy, who loved flowers and the outdoors. Arabella thought to herself that she had never been so close to her two other children as she was to this precocious girl.

Nor did Arabella concern herself if a few of the socially snobbish ladies of Galveston, seeing her and her daughter at the theater or shopping, chose to think that Joy was her grandchild. Arabella thought that people who said that growing old was to be feared were foolish—or else, they didn't have a daughter like Joy around to make each new day full with unexpected laughter and love.

But that was only part of her life. Arabella was also devoting two days a week as a volunteer nurse at the Galveston General Hospital, and two days more at the Douglas Department Store.

Dr. Samuel Parmenter, the administrative director of the hospital, had paid her the great compliment of saying that, one day, she would be called the Florence Nightingale of Galveston for the courageous work she had done as a volunteer nurse during the yellow fever epidemic of April 1878. That admiration had turned, the last four or five months, to something more personal and quite pleasurable for Arabella Hunter. One day last fall, as she was concluding her work, Dr. Parmenter walked into the head nurse's office, where Arabella was discussing one of the patients she had been tending, and asked if he might have a moment of her time.

When she had taken her leave of Susan Enderby, the extremely efficient but hopelessly prim head nurse, Dr. Parmenter had unexpectedly asked, "I happen to have two tickets for the opera this evening, Mrs. Hunter, and I was wondering if you would like to have supper with me and then be my guest to hear *Faust*?"

She knew Dr. Parmenter to be a childless widower whose wife had died six years ago, when he plunged himself into administrative work to dull the sharp edge of his bereavement. She could understand that, for she had done as much in her own way when James had been taken from her. Dr. Parmenter was tall, gray haired, soft spoken, and reserved. He was also a gentleman of the old school in Arabella's book, gracious and courteous to women almost to a fault.

Surprised at this offer, Arabella had nonetheless agreed to share the evening with him. Away from the hospital, she discovered he was an exceptionally well-read and well-informed man, with a dry sense of humor. And when he finally told a very whimsical joke in which the head nurse figured, Arabella was convinced that she had quite misjudged him.

On impulse, a week later she invited Dr. Parmenter to her house and cooked dinner for him. She like the way he treated Joy as an adult, talking to her seriously and not being the slightest bit condescending. For her part, Joy was greatly impressed and, after he had gone, said to Arabella, "Mama, he's awfully nice! I learned a lot tonight about hospitals and all, and he didn't treat me as if I were a baby, either. You know what, Mama? I think maybe he would make an awfully nice daddy—that is, if you want to get married again."

Arabella had been overwhelmed by Joy's audacity, and in a flurried tone had exclaimed, "Joy, you just hush that sort of talk! What would you and I do with a man around the place, I ask you? I absolutely have no plans to marry anybody."

"But if you did," Joy had pursued with the ingenuous insistence of a child, "I think he would be just fine."

Arabella and Samuel Parmenter had a comfortable relationship now, and neither discussed the possibility of marriage. Rather, it was a supportive friendship, supper some-

124

times at a fashionable Galveston restaurant, or in her own house, and once he had surprised her by cooking a gourmet dinner by himself for Joy and her.

They liked books, the theater, music, and they enjoyed each other's company. Altogether, it was highly satisfying for a woman of fifty-five, who had really neither time nor inclination to think about her age.

## Ten

Last Christmas, the enterprising merchant Charles Douglas had given his red-haired wife, Laurette, a pearl necklace. After he had carefully hooked the necklace into place and received a prolonged and ardent kiss as his thanks, he said softly, "Laurette, sweetheart, what would you think if I told you I planned to open a store in New York City?"

"I'd say it's not entirely unexpected, Charles," she said playfully, putting her hand to his cheek and smiling. "You always did aim for the top—nobody can ever fault you for solid ambition. I, for one, hope you do it because, to tell you the truth, much as I enjoy visiting the Galveston and Houston stores and meeting with people like that marvelous Arabella Hunter, I'd much rather go to New York; it's so much more exciting. That Texas weather, especially in the summer, is absolutely withering."

"Well, my dear, I'm going to go down to Galveston at the end of February and talk to Alexander Gorth. He's done such a marvelous job of managing not only the store he acquired from Henry McNamara and then sold to me but also my big department store, that I'm going to give him a chance to see what he thinks of a really big town."

"You mean you'd let him manage your New York store, Charles? Do you think he's really ready for it?" Laurette was dubious.

"Well, that depends. First of all, I'd like him to bring his wife, Katie, along on this preliminary trip because I always believe in a woman's point of view. After all, a wife influences a man—just look at the changes for the better that you've wrought in me over the years, Laurette, honey."

"I know." She laughed, made a wry face at him, then kissed him quickly on the cheek. "I've had to save you from several designing women, but I really don't have the slightest worry about you on that score."

"Well, I like that!" Charles laughed with her. "I hope you don't put me down as an old fogy of forty-four who has given up any hope of kicking over the traces at this point?"

"Oh, no, I'm quite sure you can still kick up the traces, Charles—only I don't think you'd better. Just remember, red-haired wives have a lot more temper than the ordinary husband bargains for."

Charles gazed adoringly at his wife, who, though only two years his junior, looked at least ten years younger.

Charles Douglas had kept in constant touch with Arabella Hunter, and so, after he got off the train at Galveston, he paid a visit to her and Joy at their home before going into the department store to talk with his energetic young manager.

"I can't tell you, Arabella," he said as he sat on her couch, balancing a teacup and a china plate laden with a slice of homemade chocolate cake, "how valuable your association with my department store has been to me. You've helped bring in a great many customers, young Alexander Gorth tells me, and some of your merchandising suggestions,—particularly the display of perfumes, jewelry, and the like—have been extremely salesworthy. I've written to Max Steinfeldt in Houston who, as you know, is general merchandising manager for both the Houston and Galveston stores, to send you a check that represents your share of the profits I feel you've brought us over the last six months of last year."

"Oh, my gracious, Charles, you don't have to do that! Mr. Steinfeldt sends me a very generous check every month that more than covers the interest James had in the store plus the two days a week I put in," Aarbella protested.

"What you do in two days, Arabella, is more than a lot of clerks do in two or three months," he countered cheerfully. "You've earned that bonus, and I insist that you take it." He turned to smile at Joy, who was regarding him with admiration and not a little awe, because he was wearing the latest in men's winter fashions, a tweed suit with a heavy vest, and had presented himself at the door, which she had opened to his knock, in a new bowler hat.

"Well, Charles, I must say it's very kind of you. I do so enjoy my work. And do you know, once in a while Joy comes up with an advertising slogan for some of our new merchandise that I think might really have some merit. I shouldn't be surprised if, when she's a bit older, she'd be interested in being a copywriter. Maybe even for the Douglas Department Stores—what would you think of that?"

"Oh my goodness, Mama, you're embarrassing me," Joy gasped self-consciously, and looked away, her cheeks crimsoning prettily.

"On the contrary, Miss Hunter," Charles said graciously to Joy as if she were a grownup, "my experience is that a great deal of talent comes to light at a very early age. I think it's wonderful, and it's very likely that a few years from now I may be calling here again to ask you to formulate an entire advertising campaign. The fact is, my wife Laurette and I have often talked about creating a special line of goods, which only our department stores would have. It would be a kind of trademark, by which I mean that customers would identify those goods with the store and vice versa. So it's not quite so farfetched, Arabella, as you and Joy might think. Well now, I've got to be getting over to the store to see Alexander Gorth. He doesn't know I'm coming, so he'll be surprised."

"I'm so glad you decided to stop by this afternoon, Charles." Arabella Hunter glanced tenderly at Joy, who was still looking away. "And I appreciate what you said to Joy. I think she's very talented—but of course, being her mother, I'd naturally be prejudiced."

Charles finished his tea and rose, setting cake plate and teacup and saucer on a little tabouret near his chair.

"I'll get your greatcoat, Charles," Arabella offered, and returned with it, helping him on with it. "There now. I do hope before you leave Galveston you'll come back again, and this time for supper—Joy makes a simply heavenly chocolate pudding."

"Oh, my gracious, Mama!" Again Joy was blushing.

"That's one of my secret passions, Joy," Charles smilingly confided to the girl. "But I'm afraid I'll have to come some other time. You see, I'm leaving almost immediately for Chicago. Or actually, for New York."

"New York?" Arabella echoed, mystified.

"Yes, I haven't told anyone yet—actually, I was saving it for Alexander Gorth. I'm aiming for the top, Arabella. In New York, there's a famous 'Ladies' mile' along what they call Broadway. There are shops like Bonwit Teller, Lord & Taylor, and A. T. Stewart & Company that specialize in women's wear. It's very possible that some of your merchandising ideas could be put into practical use in the store I hope to open along that strip, if I can get a suitable location."

"That sounds absolutely thrilling! Do you know, I've never in my life seen New York, though of course I've read a great deal about it."

"Well, one thing that appeals to me, Arabella, is that with New York being the most important seaport on the Atlantic Ocean, I could less expensively import attractive demand merchandise—from, say, Paris—and, of course, convey it on from there to my stores in Chicago and Galveston and Houston. My personal feeling is that the country is on the threshold of a big industrial expansion, and I want to be in the foreground of it. Not just to make money—though, of course, I would do that, too—but to keep alert and alive and young. I don't want to sit back on my laurels because then my competition will get ahead of me.

"Anyway, I didn't mean to start talking shop. Thank you so much for your hospitality and that wonderful chocolate cake. And you, Joy, if I give your mother plenty of notice so that you can whip up that special chocolate pudding for my dessert, will you do it for me the next time I'm in Galveston?"

Joy giggled, blushed again, then shyly nodded. "You're nice; I like you," she frankly confided, and her mother and Charles Douglas exchanged an amused and indulgent look as he and Joy shook hands.

In six short years, the irresolute, self-conscious, pimply-faced clerk whom Henry McNamara had browbeaten and tyrannized to do the work of three men in his Galveston store at the skimpiest of wages had become, at thirty, a mature young man of quiet self-assurance and steadfast determination. Alexander Gorth attributed a major part of this to his good fortune in marrying saucy, red-haired Katie McGrew, with whom he had become infatuated when he would occasionally buy a few rolls or a loaf of bread at Gottlieb's Bakery, where she had worked. Now, at twenty-five, her sauciness had been tempered by a radiant glow which had come both with maturity and the knowledge that her husband adored her. Alexander had taken over Henry McNamara's store, cleaned it up, and stocked it with quality merchandise at fair prices to customers whom his unscrupulous boss had cheated on every possible occasion. When Charles Douglas had hurried to Galveston after the terrible hurricane had damaged his own larger department store and found that Alexander had helped save the lives of Arabella and Joy Hunter, he had asked the young store owner to become a junior partner. That association proved to Charles what business acumen Alexander had.

Charles walked into the department store about an hour after he had left Arabella and Joy Hunter. He made for the office where Alexander Gorth worked, and found his young partner in shirtsleeves, pouring over a pile of ledgers and pausing long enough to dictate a letter to a bespectacled, pleasant-featured woman in her early forties.

"I see you're always working, Alex," Charles Douglas pleasantly called out.

Alexander Gorth looked up, grinned, then turned to his secretary. "Mrs. Elders, that'll be all for now. You know how to finish the letter. Go ahead and sign it for me and please get it out, if you can, in the last post. Thank you." Then, he rose and held out his hand to Charles, who warmly shook it. "What a wonderful surprise! I hope you can come over this evening for dinner. Katie would just love to see you again. We've another baby now, you know; a boy, name of Patrick."

"I'll take you up on that. I've been traveling for the last ten days or so, and I haven't had a home-cooked meal since I left Chicago. Besides, I've a proposition for you, Alex. Do you think you can take off the rest of the afternoon so we can talk about it? Then, when we get to your house for dinner, you'll be able to tell Katie what I had in mind."

"It sounds mysterious, Mr. Douglas—"

"By now I think you can call me Charles, Alex. By the way, that profit statement you sent me the end of December pleased me a good deal."

"Thank you—it's very nice of you to say that—"

"But it's the truth! You've made money for me, and I'm grateful, Alex. In fact, I'd like to take you and Katie to New York with me."

"New York?"

"New York. I'm thinking of opening a department store there because it's the biggest city in the country, and it's growing bigger every day, Alex. Come on, let's get out of the store. Let's walk down a side street where there isn't much traffic, so we can take our time and talk."

A few moments later, the two men were walking down Sussex Street, a route only too well known to Alexander Gorth, for this was the street he used to take to Gottlieb's Bakery to catch a glimpse of that pretty redhead who was always so kind to him.

"You see, Alex," Charles Douglas explained, "I've a feeling that New York's going to be this country's biggest port. After all, most European merchandise, and especially Parisian styles and fashions, come directly to New York, so it makes sense to have a department store there. And to kill two birds with one stone, as it were, I'd like to take you and Katie to New York on a kind of vacation, a reward for all the fine work you've done for me the last year. Then you both could see what you think of the city and whether you and your children would like to live there. You see, if it all works out as I plan, I'd like you to run it. You'd have to get used to the idea that it's a great deal bigger than Galveston—a great deal more going on, too. And it gets cold in the winter—with snow and sleet—and it rains frequently the rest of the year. But after all, you went through a hurricane here, and sometimes the tropical heat is unbearable in the summer."

"My goodness! This is so totally unexpected! I'd have to discuss it with Katie, of course, Ch–Charles. Well, here we are at the house, and I'll bet she'll be even more surprised than I was when you walked into my office." With this, Alexander Gorth opened the door, and was instantly met by Katie, holding a two-month-old baby boy in her arms. She uttered a happy cry as she recognized Charles Douglas. "Well I'll be jiggered—fancy seeing you down here out of a clear blue sky, Mr. Douglas! Alex, it was wicked of you to bring him home like this without giving me fair warning!"

"It was my fault, Katie," Charles chuckled. "I practi-

130

cally invited myself over for dinner, but I really wanted to surprise you that way. You see, Katie, I've got something in mind for all of you—that is, if you're willing."

"Whatever in the world do you mean? But for heaven's sake, Alex, I'm ashamed of your manners! Offer Mr. Douglas a seat and don't have him stand there with his hat in his hands!" Katie said fiercely.

Alexander turned to his employer with a sheepish grin. "It's no wonder I'm crazy about her, Charles," he said.

"Don't think you can soft-soap me, Mr. Alexander Gorth," Katie sent back over her shoulder, as she carried her baby back to the kitchen. "I'm making Irish lamb stew—you'll just have to make do with it, I'm afraid, Mr. Douglas. If I had some advance notice, I could have given you a better meal—"

"Irish lamb stew sounds like just this side of heaven, Katie. Don't apologize for it. I just hope there's enough for a hungry traveler," Charles grinned.

Later, as they were enjoying a dessert of spice cake with raisins, Charles began to explain what he had in mind for both of them. Katie listened, her mouth agape, her eyes frequently shifting to regard her husband to see what his reaction was. As Charles regaled them with tales of all the wonders of the fascinating Eastern city, she finally shook her head and groaned with dismay, "Mr. Douglas, I certainly couldn't go now, even though I know you said you'd like to take us both on to New York. I have to take care of my kids. Patrick here is a whiner, and I've got to be up when he's hungry and get him regular enough so he'll keep on an even keel. But if you want to take Alex, that's all right with me."

"You really ought to have a maid, Katie," Charles suggested.

"No, thank you! I can shift for myself and my family very well. I'd get too lazy, and fat into the bargain!"

"There'd never be a chance of that, and you know it, Katie McGrew Gorth!" Alexander's tone was almost comically reproachful, and Charles had to hide his smile. But the look that Katie flashed the tall, dark-brown-haired young man reminded him of Laurette, and he told himself that a man who married a redhead was especially fortunate.

"Well, then, I will borrow Alex from you for a while,"

Charles declared. "I'd like him to look over New York and get the feel of it, see where the competition have their stores and what kind of merchandise they handle. Also, of course, to think over whether he wants to transplant you and the children."

"I do like Galveston a lot. It's homey, and there's no hustle and bustle—and we know most of our neighbors, and it's friendly-like," Katie spoke out slowly, airing her thoughts.

"That's all very true. But, you know, Katie, I was sort of small-town myself, because I started off in Tuscaloosa before the Civil War," Charles explained, "yet now I'd never want to go back to a small town, not after Chicago. And New York's even bigger and better in many ways. But let me reassure you that if Alex doesn't like it, I won't force him to take the job. To be sure, it will mean a promotion and a good deal more money for you both."

"Sometimes, Mr. Douglas, happiness and a home mean a lot more than money in the bank. Do you know what I'm saying?" Katie Gorth looked at him with a disarming smile.

"I know. So I'll let him be the judge, and I'm sure he'll make the right decision. And now that business matters are done with, would you think me a pig if I asked for another tiny slice of that wonderful spice cake, Katie?"

"Not at all. And you shall have a large piece, not a tiny slice!" Katie reached out for the carving knife and, with a flourish, cut an exceptionally large slice for Charles, who eyed Alexander and shook his head as he leaned over to whisper to his junior partner, "I think you're a very lucky man, Alex, and you should think very carefully about your decision. Don't agree to it unless you and Katie both feel that it's the best thing for all of you."

Two days after receiving Maxwell Grantham's wire offering to buy two thousand head of cattle from Windhaven Range, Lucien Edmond Bouchard and Lucas rode out after lunch to inspect the southeastern boundary of the ranch. One of the vaqueros had reported that while making an inspection tour that morning he had seen two large *jabalíes* race into a large thicket of mesquite not far from the Nueces River. Wild boar were always a cause of anxiety: if they wandered in among the cattle, they could very easily start a stampede.

Lucas and Lucien Edmond rode along on their geldings,

the high sun beating down on them. It was quite warm in this far southeastern part of Texas, even in February, a time when most of the country shivered under freezing winds and sleet and driving snow. "I'm glad you'll be coming along on this drive, Lucas. I know it will be difficult for Felicidad to spare you for so long, but we'll need all of our best men for a trip of this length," Lucien Edmond told his loyal friend.

"We'll be skipping the Kansas towns entirely, as I recall," Lucas remarked.

"That's right. In lawless, wide-open towns like Dodge, there's always the danger that the vaqueros will be insulted, or will run into some shoddy dance-hall girls who'll try to cheat them and start a fight. Besides, remember the trouble Ramón got into with that crooked Indian agent—what was his name—oh, yes, Jeb Cornish? This rancher, Grantham, will pay a far better price than any Kansas buyer would give us."

"Look out! Here comes one of those damn peccaries out of the thicket!" Lucas suddenly shouted, as he reached for his Spencer carbine, tugging it out of the saddle sheath.

Lucien Edmond's horse had gone a few paces ahead of Lucas's, and startled by the animal's sudden squeal, it reared up in the air and flung Lucien Edmond onto the ground. He uttered a cry of pain, and the peccary veered and ran back into the thicket from where it had appeared.

"Are you hurt bad, Lucien Edmond?" Lucas anxiously inquired as he steadied his own horse and then dismounted, running toward his boss.

"It's my leg—I don't think it's broken, but I can't move it—" Lucien Edmond panted hoarsely.

"Your horse ran off—but he'll just run himself out; he won't get lost. See if you can put your arm around my shoulders and get up," Lucas proposed as he squatted down and put an arm around Lucien Edmond's waist.

Lucien Edmond's face was pale and contorted with pain, and beads of sweat glistened on his forehead as he made an effort to rise, then winced and shook his head. "I think it's only badly sprained, but it's going to keep me out of that saddle for a while. Well, this certainly alters my plans! I obviously won't be able to go on the drive. I could ask Eddie to go, but Maria Elena will be giving birth soon, and I feel Eddie should be with her. There's Hugo to consider. . . . You see, Lucas, Hugo has been begging me

133

for the last couple of years to go on a drive, and I told him this time he could. But now . . ." He paused a moment, then asked, "Do you think you and Ramón could watch over him in my place?"

"Sure, we'll look after him. He's a mighty fine young man, and it's time he had some responsibility—begging your pardon for saying so, Lucien Edmond."

"You always speak your mind to me, Lucas. That's the way I want it. You're just like your father, Djamba. Wonderful men, both of you, without an ounce of deceit. I feel much better, knowing that you're going to be responsible for Hugo. Let me rest a moment, and then I'll try to get up again."

"You wait here, Lucien Edmond. I'll go back and get a litter to carry you—it'll be a mite easier."

Half an hour later, two of the vaqueros and Lucas gently carried Lucien Edmond into the living room of the hacienda. Maxine hurried to him with a cry of alarm. "Oh, God, darling, what happened?"

"We ran into a *jabalí* and my horse shied—my leg's badly sprained, I think."

"I know something about cracked bones, Lucien Edmond, so if you can bear to have me touch it, I'll tell you right off if it's broken or not," Lucas volunteered.

Lucien Edmond had a pillow under his right leg and lay back on the couch, closing his eyes. "Go ahead. I have to know one way or the other. But from the way it feels, I don't think I'll be going on that cattle drive to Colorado."

Lucas knelt down, took his clasp knife, and carefully cut down the top of Lucien Edmond's boot, so that he would draw the boot off without any agonizing pressure. Then, as carefully, he made a cut in the leg of his boss's breeches. "Now, I'm going to touch it very gently."

Maxine bent over the couch and took her husband's hands and squeezed them in hers, then kissed him and whispered, "I'm here; I'm with you, darling."

Lucien Edmond started convulsively as Lucas's gently probing fingers touched an extremely sensitive spot. "No, it doesn't appear to be broken, but I wouldn't be surprised if you've badly pulled a hamstring along with a severe sprain. I think we ought to soak it in hot water and salts, and then put a good, stiff splint on it, as tight as you can stand it. And then you'll stay in bed and rest up, Lucien Edmond," Lucas declared.

"I guess that does it, then. Maxine, Ramón and Lucas will both be on the drive to watch over Hugo. Maybe it's just as well. This way, he won't feel that his father's riding along, criticizing him at every turn, making notes of the mistakes he's bound to make. He's old enough to be his own man, and now he's going to get the chance."

## Eleven

Charles Douglas had induced Alexander Gorth to accompany him to New York the following afternoon. Katie had sent her young husband several appealing looks, while the Chicago merchant had intercepted. As a consequence, with a propitiatory smile, he had suddenly interposed, "Katie, I'm going to show him all the opportunities, then let him make his own decision. And if he thinks that New York is the place for you, I'll see to it that all your moving expenses are paid—and the profits would be far greater in New York, so Alex will be entitled to far more than he's earning here. Your husband has a future. He's an honest man, he's still young enough not to be afraid to merchandise and to do imaginative things to attract customers. Even when I was back in Tuscaloosa, Katie, I wasn't thinking small, and that's the way it should be with your husband: he's going to go forward, and not stay on the same level. I know it's easy to stay in a backwater town and tell yourself that you won't get into any trouble that way. But the fact is, it doesn't hurt to have money. And both you and Alexander, from what I know about your background, have known what it is to scrimp and go without. Just think of that, while I'm taking him off to New York."

"I'm thinking you must have kissed the Blarney Stone, Mr. Douglas," Katie irrepressibly broke out, and then giggled as she reached for Alexander's hand and squeezed it.

"I'll not stand in your way. If New York's what your heart's set on, Alex, honey, I'll follow you. I guess I would anyway, no matter where you wanted to go."

"Oh, my darlin' Katie McGrew Gorth," her husband replied in a good imitation of her lilting brogue as he leaned over and kissed her hard on the mouth.

"My gracious! What will Mr. Douglas think, an old married couple like us carrying on this way!" She pretended to be irate with him, but the loving look she sent him far belied that expression of indignation, and Charles chuckled to himself: more and more, Katie Gorth was reminding him of fiery Laurette.

"Now I'm going to do one more thing, Mrs. Gorth—"

"Oh, so now it's Mrs. Gorth, is it?" Katie spiritedly flung back at him, with a sly wink at her amused husband. "I can tell you're preparing to slip one over on me. But I'm wise to your tricks, Mr. Douglas. All right, let's hear it."

"But there are no tricks at all, Katie. I'm going to pay for a housekeeper for you, because you'll have your hands full while Alex is gone."

"That sounds very much like a bribe, Mr. Douglas." Katie eyed him suspiciously.

"But it's not. I just don't want Alex to worry, since you made it very clear that you want to stay at home with the children. And if he knows that there's someone to help out in case things start weighing down on you, I think he'll be able to approach this proposition with a clear mind and conscience.

"Really, I'd have preferred you to come along with us so you both could look the city over and do some comparing, but I can certainly understand that you wouldn't want to leave your infant son. However, I'm sure you'll be able to rely on Alex's judgment—his judgment doesn't seem to have let him down yet," Charles Douglas told her seriously.

"Well, Alex." Katie looked at him for a moment, and then declared, "If you decide that New York is what you want and you think we'll be happy there, of course I'll go with the idea. Do you think I'd hold back a wonderful husband like you—especially now that I've had a chance to smooth over a lot of your rough spots? Oh, no, Mr. Douglas," she turned back to the Chicago merchant, "I'm certainly not going to stand in Alex's way. If it's New York he wants, I'll be there with him, you can depend on that for certain." Then, turning to her husband, she shook her forefinger at him and sternly ordered, "You just bring back some photographs so I know what you're talking about when you start telling me all about New York, you hear?"

"Of course, honey. My gosh, Charles, I still can't believe it! New York—it's such a long way from Galveston—"

"It's up the ladder, Alex, and it's what you've earned—by your hard work and your honesty and your willingness to merchandise long-range—and not try for quick, greedy profits that only turn away customers in the long run—like your former employer, Henry McNamara," Charles declared. "Katie, might I trouble you for just another cup of coffee? Alex, in the meantime, you can get packed."

"How long do you think he'll be away from me, Mr. Douglas?" Katie wondered.

"Let's see now. We'll take the train back to New Orleans, then on to Chicago and from there to New York—that's about six or seven days. And then, say, ten days to two weeks in New York—a month, at the very most, my word of honor."

"Well, in that case," Katie mused aloud, "I'll just take you up on your offer to stand me a housekeeper with the children. If Alex is going to be amusing himself at those fancy restaurants and seeing all the sights, no reason why I shouldn't have some creature comforts, too."

"Now that's the spirit, Katie." Charles Douglas burst out laughing, as the lovely red-haired young woman reached for the coffeepot and filled his cup.

Alexander Gorth was wide-eyed with disbelief as he entered the ornately decorated, lushly carpeted railroad car. The black porter carried both their bags to the spacious compartment, fussed over them as a mother might over wayward children, and saw to it that they had pillows behind their heads for comfort. He informed them that luncheon would be served for another hour in the diner, and that the first dinner call would be at six.

When at last he had beamed a smile to them both and then closed the doors of the compartment, Alexander eyed his employer and shook his head. "Glory be, Charles, I never in all my born days saw a railroad car like this!"

"It's much better than going by steamboat, Alex. And it's faster, too. You know, railroad lines just about crisscross this big country of ours now, and it's much more scenic on a train than on a steamboat."

"I suppose you're right. Gosh, you probably do a lot of traveling!"

"Enough, and I like my comfort and luxury. You know, there's some interesting background to this car. It was made by a man named George Mortimer Pullman—I read about him in the Chicago newspapers just before I came out here. He's a man of forty-eight, and extremely ambitious and imaginative. He lives in Chicago, and he's a member of the Chicago Citizens' Law and Order League. During the railroad strike of two years ago, Mr. Pullman read in the papers stories about drunken youths fighting with the police, and workers in immigrant neighborhoods marching to demand higher salaries. So he's thinking next year of beginning the construction of a model town that would keep his plant and workers away from what he calls the 'evil influences' of the city and the rioting immigrant neighborhoods. His idea is that if you put good workers away from an atmosphere of discontent, they'll produce more for you, and you won't have any labor strikes to worry about to fulfill your contracts."

"You say he's going to build a town for his workers?" Alexander incredulously echoed.

"That's right. I only hope he doesn't exploit them and make them a sort of captive audience, if you know what I mean by that, Alex."

"I think I follow your drift, Mr. D—Charles." Alex grinned sheepishly at his slip.

"For God's sake, Alex, don't go back to calling me Mr. Douglas! I'm not that much older than you, you know, and we're friends. That's what counts most. But to go back to George Mortimer Pullman—he's a clever man, and I'll tell you why. He began his company under the name of the Pullman Palace Car Company, and he quickly took over plants and converted them so that he could manufacture his own wheels, glass, wood and metal parts, as well as fabrics. Best of all, so far as his profit scheme is concerned, he has a monopoly. He never sells sleeping cars like this, just leases them to the railroads. And he's made it compulsory for the railroads to use sleeping car porters and dining car waiters that he himself furnishes to the railroads through his own company. He's got offices in Italy, England, and France, and he's already supplied those countries with sleeping cars just as elegant as this one."

"Gosh all fishhooks," Alexander breathed, shaking his head. "I'd call him a man with plenty of vision."

"So would I, but I want to suspend judgment until I see how his model town works out. I hope his ambitious scheme doesn't become another new company store—an idea that's being used in the Deep South to keep menial laborers constantly in debt to the manufacturer or the land-owner. They never get a chance to get free of their bills and are forced to work, whether they want to or not, for the man who has the contract. If Pullman does that, then he'll be just another greedy capitalist in my book. I don't do business that way, and I never shall. But I have to hand it to him—he's organized this very skillfully so far."

"I have the feeling, Charles, that you think we're in for a business boom, and that's why you want to expand in New York," Alexander said as he leaned forward intently.

"Go to the head of the class, Alex. I knew I hadn't mis-judged you. You've got a lot of good business sense under that honest country face of yours. I sensed this when I first met you and I bought out your store to merge it with mine. I wanted to give you all the incentive I could, so that you could realize the potential inside of you. It's something that's born in a man, Alex, not learned and not made. It comes to you by a sort of instinct, and so far everything you've done for my store has worked out very well."

"But I'm only a small-town boy, Charles, and I can't hope to compete in New York on the same basis as high society muck-a-mucks," Alexander frankly confessed.

Charles laughed softly and patted him on the back. "I think you have a one-sided picture of New York. There are the well-to-do, to be sure, but you know, there are about twenty thousand tenements in New York City, and the ten-ants of those buildings number well over half a million."

"Good Lord almighty!" was all that Alexander could gasp.

"You'll see terrible slums, perhaps the worst in America, because these people have come from overseas in droves in the last few years. It's a kind of melting pot, with Irish, blacks, Slavic, and Germanic peoples, all fighting for an opportunity to carry on the way they want. You know, I'm hoping to hire some of these people, because they're very courageous and determined to succeed despite many hard-ships. I want to share my profits with good, imaginative

139

employees whose own personal growth will carry mine along with it and make my store a comer. That's how I was brought up as a boy by my folks, how I've always operated. And though I might get a few setbacks along the way, I can live with myself when I wake up and look at myself in the mirror."

"I can already see what you've done in Galveston and Houston, Charles."

"Yes, I've done very well in Galveston and Houston, and in Chicago, too, with the help of my partner who helped me rebuild after a fire eight years ago. But New York is the leading city in the country. If I can have a successful store there, it'll be the crowning glory of all that I've achieved so far. But that's enough shop talk for the time being, Alex. Let's sit back and enjoy the scenery. We'll have lunch served here—the porter will set up a table for us."

"My gosh!" Alexander was visibly impressed, and still more so, about fifteen minutes later, when the genial porter did indeed set up the table with fine silver and table linens, and brought each of them a tasty shrimp cocktail to start, then one of the best beefsteaks Alexander had ever eaten, with a baked potato, glazed carrots, a substantial salad, and, for dessert, an apple pie with sharp cheddar cheese as good as ever his Katie had baked for him, topped off with strong, rich coffee.

At the end of the luncheon, Charles Douglas took out two cigars and handed one to Alexander Gorth. "I'll have the porter bring a pony of Cusinier brandy. This is a memorable occasion for both of us, Alex—we'll drink a toast to a stronger and more profitable partnership than you and I have ever had before."

"Gosh," Alexander repeated wonderingly, "Katie won't believe all this. I know she won't!"

Alexander Gorth was even more impressed when the train they had boarded in Chicago pulled into the imposing new railroad depot straddling Park Avenue at Forty-second Street, which Commodore Vanderbilt had just built and optimistically called "Grand Central." He was awed by the great canopy of iron and glass vaulting fifty feet over the tracks which, as Charles knowledgeably told him, furnished a common terminal for many of the railroad lines entering New York City. As they entered the terminal itself, he was stunned by the varnished wood and superbly frescoed walls.

"New York is crowded and crammed, and you'll see taller buildings than you've ever imagined, Alex," Charles Douglas told his young manager, as he hailed a horse-drawn carriage. "We're going to stop at the Fifth Avenue Hotel, on Fifth Avenue between Twenty-third and Twenty-fourth streets. It has the first elevator any New York hotel ever had, and a very famous architect designed it. Everybody who is anybody stays at the Fifth Avenue, Alex."

"Goodness gracious," was all the young man could say. He glanced out the carriage window. "You know, Charles, I've never seen so many tall buildings. There's one that's— let's see now—three, four, five, six—wow! Seven stories! Katie just won't believe it!"

"There's a novelty shop in the hotel, Alex, where you can buy a set of photographs of New York's sights and you can mail them back to your sweet wife. That'll convince her. I think the Chinese have a proverb that a picture is worth a thousand words. And that'll certainly save you time writing long letters," Charles mischievously remarked. But secretly he was pleased at Alexander's utter naiveté: knowing how assiduous and enthusiastic Katie's husband was about his work, he believed that this excitement at seeing New York City for the first time was a fine omen. It would be a challenge for young Gorth, just as Chicago had been a great challenge for himself over the staid routine of a store in Tuscaloosa. "Matter of fact, I think we shouldn't do anything this afternoon other than have our driver take us on a tour of the better parts of the city. Then you'll get a fair idea of what it's like. Tomorrow, we'll really go out in earnest looking over the rival stores and deciding exactly where our own store should be." With this, he called out: "Driver, take us downtown—maybe as far as Fourteenth Street—then head back to the hotel. My partner here has never been to New York before."

"That a fact, mister?" The tophatted, bearded carriage driver turned back to scrutinize Alexander Gorth and tip his hat to him. "Well, then, sir, it'll be my pleasure and privilege to show a bit of it to you. You know, I was born here, gentlemen, and I wouldn't live anywhere else, I'll tell you that."

"Why not?" Charles Douglas wondered.

"Well, I don't want to bore you gentlemen, but the fact

141

is, exciting things are happening here all the time. For example, we got rid of Boss Tweed and pulled Tammany Hall down to size. Next year, we're going to have a real fine mayor, and he's going to bring even greater progress to New York City, you take it from me."

"Who might that be?" Charles was interested. If there was an honest and progressive administration, it could only help his new venture.

"Ever hear of William Russell Grace, mister?" The civic-minded carriage driver turned back to look down at his two passengers. After they both shook their heads, he went on, "Irish as Paddy's pig, but from a good family—you might say lace-curtain Irish. Anyway, he's going to run next year against Tammany, and he's going to be a reform mayor. One of his campaign promises is that he's going to reduce taxes, and all of us are for that, I can tell you!"

"Sounds like quite a man. And that's why you like New York?" Charles asked humorously.

"No, sir, that's not the half of it. First off, as I said, I was born here. My people are Irish, too, and here the Irish get a fair shake, living and working all around town. There's something for everybody in this town, whether you fancy the theater or sporting girls, or maybe even a good bare-knuckles bout at Madison Square Garden—it's diagonally across the park from your hotel. There's variety here that can't be found anywhere else, as far as I'm concerned."

"Well then, we certainly picked the right driver for your first tour of New York, didn't we, Alex?" Charles chuckled. "I like your spirit, driver. Just take us where you think we ought to go. My only other directive is that you take us to see what they call the 'Ladies' Mile'—can you do that?"

"Sure can, mister. Let's see, we're down to Thirty-fourth Street now—the 'Ladies' Mile' runs along Broadway from Twenty-third down to around Third Street, as you probably know, and you'll certainly want to see that huge A. T. Stewart store which takes up a whole block between Ninth and Tenth Streets."

"I've read about that back in Chicago—that's where I'm from, by the way. My name's Charles Douglas, and I've got department stores in Chicago, Houston, and Galveston. I'm thinking of opening one here."

"Waddya know? I've got a sister in Chicago—like as not,

142

she shops at your store. But you'll have to go some to beat the Stewart store. 'Course, old Stewart's dead now, died three years ago. He built a house on the northwest corner of Thirty-fourth Street and Fifth Avenue that looks like a white marble palace. Right next to old William B. Astor's fancy house. You know, next to Astor, Stewart owned about as much land as anybody else in New York. But the society swells put him down because of his trade, so all his money and all his brains didn't get him any friends at all, just two monuments—that house and that store."

"You're a most interesting and informative man. Let me ask you a personal question—how much do you make a week?" Charles had been mulling over some thoughts in his mind and now startled the carriage driver by this brusque, personal query.

"Well, good weeks, about thirteen dollars a week, mister."

"I really want to keep in touch with you—what's your name?"

"It's Patrick Keogh, Mr. Douglas."

"Glad to know you, Patrick. You married, with a family?"

"Yes, sir! My Molly and me've got three little ones, all boys—the pride of my life."

"When you drop us off at the hotel, Patrick, I want you to give me your address. When I get this store of mine started, I might just have a better job for you. And it would pay a lot more than thirteen dollars a week. You've given us quite an insight into New York; you might do very well as a floorwalker, or at the information desk of my new store. I'd probably pay about twenty dollars a week and a bonus."

"Glory be! You wouldn't be pulling my leg?"

"No, I mean what I say, Patrick Keogh. You'll be hearing from me. And now, let's complete our little tour."

For Alexander Gorth, it was an afternoon filled with incredible wonders. He found it hard to believe that there could be so much traffic in one place at one time: people clung precariously to horse-drawn trolleys racing up and down the avenues; carriages of every description clopped along, the hansom cabs among them picking up and discharging passengers at every corner; men and women rushed to and fro on foot, scurrying into and out of buildings the likes of which he had never seen. Most incredible

143

of all to Alex were the elevated railway lines that ran along Greenwich Street from Thirtieth Street down to the Battery and along Sixth Avenue, past the Croton Reservoir at Forty-second Street, and terminating at the Battery. The trains rushed along at the incredible rate of thirty miles an hour, their steam-powered engines belching sparks and smoke.

Again he breathlessly repeated to Charles, "Katie just won't believe this! I swear to heaven she won't, Charles!"

Finally, after traversing the city from uptown to downtown, east side to west, the personable carriage driver dropped them off at the Fifth Avenue Hotel, and Charles Douglas handed him a five-dollar bill. "Begging your pardon, Mr. Douglas, that's far too much," he protested.

"No, it's not—it was worth more. But I'll make it up to you once you start working for me. Of course, Patrick, that's going to take some time. First, I have to buy the site for my store, and then I have to construct it. But one of these days, before you know it, I'll be back here to hire you at that wage I promised. Good luck to you, and thanks for a most informative afternoon."

"God bless you, Mr. Douglas. Here—I'll write down my address for you. I'd be proud to work for a man like you. You're going to like New York—and New York's going to like you."

"Amen to that, Patrick. I'd hate to die friendless, the way poor old A. T. Stewart did. That's quite a store he has, and an even more imposing mausoleum."

"Amen to *that*, Mr. Douglas! Have a pleasant stay in the best city in the United States. Good day to both of you!"

"Now you see, Alex," Charles said as a bellboy hurried to take their satchels and escort them into the lobby, "that's how you learn things. We were lucky enough to pick a driver who took pride in his work—that's something I always notice, and that's the sort of man I always try to hire—who has loyalty and a good sense of humor.

"You know, what Patrick Keogh told me he made in a good week is just about what a restaurant cook gets here in New York City—a private cook can be hired for from eighteen to twenty dollars a month; a maid gets from twelve to fifteen a month, and a children's nurse about the same. That includes room and board, of course. Renting a house in a decent area in this town would cost you at least three hundred dollars a year."

"Holy Moses!" Alexander picturesquely exclaimed. He was not, as Charles had already noticed, given to blasphemous swearing, a welcome contrast from the lurid oaths to be heard on the prairies and the ranches and farms of this sprawling young country.

"You'd have to pay fifteen cents a pound for butter and the same for a dozen eggs, Alex," Charles continued. "Sugar goes for ten cents a pound, and you'd pay a quarter a pound for a roasting or frying chicken. You could buy the best beef there is to be found in all this town for about thirty cents a pound."

"I suppose that's because so much of it has to be brought into the city."

"Exactly. It's like I said: everything comes into New York—like Paris fashions—and I'll be right on the border of the Atlantic to get them when they come off the boat and be first to feature them in my inland stores. I can even foresee, Alex, that one day you and Katie might go to Paris, to find designers who will make lines of women's clothing just for me, and for no other merchant in all the United States. You see, Alex, you have to think big; then you have to back it up with hard work. And that's where both of us come in. Well now, how do you like our suite?"

"My gosh! It's wonderful—there isn't anything in Galveston like this." Alexander looked around at the draperies and the carpeting, and then at the elegant bathroom with its glistening white porcelain basin and tub. "And that elevator—that's something Katie isn't going to believe at all."

"We're going to have one in the Douglas Department Stores in Galveston and Houston by the end of next year—only I hope by then you'll be managing my store here. Now, I suggest we take a short nap to refresh ourselves. Then we'll have a bath, change into our evening clothes, and go down to Delmonico's restaurant. I've asked the desk clerk to reserve a table for us there for seven-thirty. You're going to eat high on the hog tonight, and that's something else you can tempt Katie with."

"I swear to heaven, Charles, I wish she'd have come along, even with the kids—she's not going to believe it from what I write her, or even from those photographs. And you're right about that nap. So much has happened in so short a time, I am a little tired at that."

"Well, dinner at Delmonico's will certainly wake you up. One of these days, Alex, you'll be taking your beautiful

145

wife there in a green velvet gown and all the men will be ogling her and envying you, and you'll be written up in the newspapers as the energetic young merchandising manager of the Douglas Department Store."

"It sounds too grand to be true, Charles," Alexander sighed as he eased off his shoes and then lay down on the bed. A few moments later, he was fast asleep. Charles chuckled to himself. "I think," he said to himself softly, "I will definitely have to find a capable man to replace Alex in Galveston—and that's not going to be easy. But it's going to be a lot of fun trying, all the same."

The next morning, after a leisurely breakfast in the hotel dining room, Charles Douglas and Alexander Gorth went out on foot to visit the "Ladies' Mile," despite the chilly weather and the threat of an oncoming snowstorm. "No doubt about it, Alex," the Chicago merchant cheerfully remarked as they walked briskly down the street from the hotel, "you and Katie will have to get used to a lot colder weather than you have in Galveston. And in summer, you might think you were back home in Texas because it gets hot and muggy."

"I don't mind cold weather at all, to tell you the truth, Charles," Alexander confided, smiling. "And Katie is used to hardships—she was orphaned early in life. But I'm just wondering if she'll like it."

"If you really want it for yourself, you'll have to sell her on the idea. But don't hide from her the bad as well as the good. Life in this city has its unpleasant side. As I told you, there are plenty of slums in New York, and the cost of living is much higher than it is in Galveston. On the other hand, once my store is ready—and here I am talking about a store when I don't even know what land is available, and I don't even know what contractor to sign up for building the store—I'll sit down with you and make you a profit-sharing offer that will more than compensate you for your move. If this New York store does what I think it can, Alex, I'd say you can count on—" he thought a moment and frowned, as he did some mental arithmetic, "—about two thousand dollars a year, plus an incentive bonus, depending on volume over a given estimate we'd both agree to, before we'd open the doors."

"That's just incredible, Charles!" Alexander let out a startled whistle of amazement at the mention of such a fabulous salary. "For that sort of money, I'd certainly be willing to risk it."

"Well, let's wait and see what we can accomplish this week. First, we're going to go into some of the stores, like Lord & Taylor's place at Twentieth Street. And I want to take a good look at Arnold Constable & Company in that white marble building of theirs two blocks away, at Eighteenth Street. You know, Broadway is a very important street up to around Thirty-fourth Street. But I'm told that if you were to go west of Broadway at that point, it's a sort of Barbary Coast. All sorts of places that a decent married man oughtn't to go to—saloons and restaurants, and really low dance halls that are already drawing attention in the papers around the country."

"Gosh! I wouldn't ever go to places like that," Alexander almost indignantly avowed.

Charles laughed and clapped him on the back. "Why should you, with a wife like that spunky Katie? But plenty of people do, and it's an area to stay out of at night. Well now, I noticed you giving the desk clerk a letter this morning—I'll bet it's to Katie."

"Yes, it is. I got a set of those photographs you mentioned, and I wrote her a quick note and told her that New York is more exciting than I'd ever imagined, and the buildings were the tallest in the whole, wide world."

"I'm not so sure of that, for the sake of accuracy, Alex, but maybe that will impress her. Well now, here we are at Lord & Taylor. Pay particular attention to the way they do their displays. I don't want to borrow a leaf from them—I want to set my own ideas into action—but when the time comes that a man can't learn from what his competition is doing, he ought to close his doors forever."

"Their windows are very exciting," Alexander Gorth confided.

"Yes, they are indeed. And that's something else. In a town like Galveston, you're catering to old-line families, sedate and traditional. There's a good deal of tradition here in New York, too, but there's a new, younger element coming into the city all the time, and you have to think of them for future business. At the same time, you can't offend your regular, old-time patrons by going off the deep end to cater to new trade. As I see it, a smart merchant has to walk a kind of tightrope and hope he doesn't stumble one way or the other. But anyway, let's go in and see how they're merchandising to attract the carriage trade. The carriage trade is where you make the most profits, obviously. On the other hand, if you want to run a middle-class department store, you'll go after volume and repeat business. You'll attract people who perhaps don't have the social background or the money either, but who are pretty stable customers and good to do business with on a steady basis. These are all facts you have to weigh when you come into a new city. That's why I want you to take some notes—good, I'm glad to see you brought along a pencil and some scribbling paper. We'll go over them at dinner tonight. This time, we'll have dinner at the Brunswick Hotel, just across the avenue from Delmonico's."

"Gosh, Charles, it can't be nearly so good as Delmonico's—nothing can. I was wishing Katie could have had supper with me last night. I felt like a pig fattened up for slaughter, I ate so much!"

"It was a pleasure to watch you enjoying yourself." Charles chuckled again and clapped Alexander on the back. "It's fun, when you travel, to treat yourself to famous restaurants. Then, when you go back home, you can lord it over the conversation and drop a few names and impress everybody."

"I'll remember that!" Alexander laughed as his employer halted at a counter where costume jewelry was being displayed.

"These are what I call gewgaws, Alex. But they bring in the women customers, and the women are the ones who make the men spend their money in your store, never forget that. The more you can do to attract the distaff side and convince them that you prize them and worship them and lean over backwards to make them feel at home, the more profits you're bound to make. If they call this the 'Ladies' Mile,' then they might as well call me the 'ladies' man,' because that's always been my motto, even when I was just a sales clerk back in Tuscaloosa. I sold to the woman, not the man. She was the one who would appreciate good values, and, even more, who would appreciate time-saving items that would ease her work in the kitchen and around the house."

At the end of the day, both men were exhausted, chilled almost to the bone, but Alexander Gorth had made copious notes of what he had seen, much to Charles Douglas's approval. As they hurried back to their hotel, they passed an

148

office building standing next to a vacant lot on Twenty-first Street and Broadway. Charles walked in to inquire of the uniformed building attendant if there was a real estate office nearby and was told there was an agent on the second floor of that very building.

Once inside the office, Charles Douglas introduced himself to a bluff, bearded man in his late forties, whose name was Daniel Terry. He was not only the agent for this building, but also for the lot next to it.

"Mr. Terry, I'm thinking of opening a department store here. I've got one in Chicago and two in Texas. I'll admit that, after my sort of crash tour of your fine city, I may have the feeling I'm about to bite off more than I can chew, but at least I want to try."

"You're frank about it, Mr. Douglas. I'll be just as frank with you. My partner and I are looking for at least a fifteen-year lease on that lot. If you opt for a longer lease, we can negotiate at a savings for you—but it's a very desirable piece of property."

"In other words, you won't sell it to me?"

"That's about the size of it, Mr. Douglas. Hope it doesn't frighten you off."

"Not till you tell me the price."

"I can see you're a man of acumen and decision. So I'll level with you. If you put a department store on that property, you'll be in competition with quite a few notables, as I'm sure I don't have to tell you."

"I know. I've seen a few of them already. But I'm still young enough to enjoy the challenge of trying to battle the big boys on even terms and doing things my way." Charles gave him a candid smile.

"Damn it all, Mr. Douglas, I like your spirit. My partner will, too. All right now, on the basis of a fifteen-year lease, I'm authorized to offer you a rental fee of five thousand dollars a year. The lease would have a few other stipulations—such as the quality of your building and the type of merchandise you will purvey, which must be approved by my partner and me. In this neighborhood, as you can appreciate, we don't want any fly-by-nights."

"Let me show you these letters of credit from banks in Chicago, Galveston, and Houston." Charles reached into his coat pocket and spread out the papers before the real estate agent.

Daniel Terry examined them, pursed his lips, and nodded. "I can see that you're not a beginner, and that you're highly thought of. I think we can do business, Mr. Douglas. And I'll let you in on a little secret: personally, my partner and I would be happy to see an outsider come in here and make a go of it."

"I'll tell you something else, Mr. Terry," Charles soberly averred. "You wouldn't have to worry about my coming to you and crying poor mouth. If I go into this venture, you'll never have to worry about your rent."

"Then of course, you're the sort of tenant we'd like to have occupy the property, Mr. Douglas."

"I wonder if you could put me in touch with a contractor who could build a store for me? I'd like to have it open by next Christmas. This young man—" he turned his head to nod at Alexander Gorth, who was standing respectfully behind him listening to the conversation, "—he's going to be the manager of the store, once I get it built."

"I'll give you the name of a very reputable one, Mr. Douglas. Matter of fact, he has an office on the floor just above us. His name is Jerry Stevenson."

"I'm obliged to you, Mr. Terry; we'll pay him a visit right now. And you'll be hearing from me soon." Charles shook hands with the real estate agent, and then he and Alexander climbed the stairway to the next floor.

They found Jerry Stevenson to be an affable, outspoken giant of a man at six feet seven inches in height, and a few minutes of conversation convinced Charles that here was a contractor who, like Max Steinfeldt, knew his business and could hire a hard-working crew who would take orders from him and carry them out promptly and correctly. After about half an hour's discussion, Charles shook hands with the contractor and exclaimed, "You draw up the specifications, Mr. Stevenson, and I'll come in to review them by the end of the week."

The contractor rose from his desk and followed them to the door. "I have a draftsman who's home with a cold today, but when he's back tomorrow, as I hope, I'll work with him on it. The design and cost estimates should be ready for you when you come in. It's a pleasure to meet a man like you, who knows his own mind and what he wants. I think I can get a store built for you even before the first of December this year."

"That's music to my ears, Mr. Stevenson! I'll see you again, and thanks for your interest and help."

As they left the building, Alexander turned to Charles and exclaimed, "Gosh, this is all happening so fast! I can't believe we've found the place so easily."

"It does seem too good to be true, doesn't it," Charles responded with a grin. "I must admit that although Mr. Terry seemed to be entirely trustworthy, I am a bit skeptical. Well, I'm not a babe in the woods, I assure you. As soon as we get back to the hotel, I'm going to wire my partner in Chicago, Lawrence Harding. Lawrence has many acquaintances here in New York, and I think it would be wise if they can make some inquiries about Mr. Terry and his firm."

"You seem to think of everything, Charles. I'm sure glad I've got a partner like you," Alexander stated.

Entering their hotel to freshen up before dinner at the Brunswick, Charles turned and said, "I'll let you in on a secret, but don't you dare tell anybody else. Chicago is a mere backwater town compared with New York, and I'm just a tiny bit terrified about this plan." Then he brightened. "But with you managing the store, Alex, I've got a feeling we can have a place that won't have to play second fiddle to anyone else, not even Lord & Taylor or A. T. Stewart & Company!" He grinned boyishly and slapped Alexander on the back. "Yes, Alex, I've got a feeling that, by next Christmas, you'll have earned a very substantial bonus for making a success of my New York branch!"

## Twelve

Lucien Edmond's accident considerably altered the plan for the drive. One of the nuns in the Catholic mission school over which old Friar Bartoloméo Alicante presided had worked briefly for a doctor before she had joined the order, and it was she who effectively applied a splint to Lucien Edmond's injured leg.

He made a bad patient, for he fretted and grumbled throughout his imposed bed rest while his leg healed, and Ramón and Lucas came frequently to confer with him. Maxine was secretly relieved that he would not go on the long drive. Even though she would be obliged to nurse him and to put up with his irritation at being so useless and helpless on the vast range, it would be a time for both of them to plan for the future of Hugo and Carla.

"If you take that trail," Lucien Edmond said to Ramón the day before the drive began toward the end of February, "it might not be a bad idea to add about five hundred steers. You'll be going past Fort Sumner and then Fort Bascom up in New Mexico, and from what Joseph McCoy told me, about thirteen years ago Charles Goodnight was paid a record eight cents a pound on the hoof for steers. He had to supply beef for several thousand starving Navahos whom the scout Kit Carson had brought to Fort Sumner for government supervision. That fort is still supervising the Navaho tribe, and my guess is that they'll need beef. We can pick up a few extra thousand dollars that way, and since Sumner is the larger of the two forts, you can probably sell most of those five hundred at your first stop."

"That makes sense, Lucien Edmond," the handsome Mexican emphatically nodded. "That'll mean twenty-five hundred head—plus, of course, the usual ten percent additional stock to make up for the inevitable losses along the way. So all told, we'll be driving just over twenty-seven hundred head of cattle. For that number, we ought to take about thirty vaqueros, well armed, and plenty of provisions. We can replenish some of these when we reach the forts, it's true, but I'd like to take along two chuck wagons. And we ought to carry as much ammunition for the Spencer carbines and rifles and some of the new Winchesters as we can spare from what you should keep on hand here. That should leave you with twenty vaqueros, Lucien Edmond."

"There's little danger of any attack here, so they should be more than adequate. Do you really feel you need to be so well armed?"

"Well, Lucien Edmond," Ramón stated, "don't forget we'll be going into rancher territory in parts of New Mexico, and we may have the same trouble we did back right after the Civil War, when the Sedalia citizens objected to our herd because they were afraid of Texas fever. And there's always the danger of rustlers and bushwhackers. I haven't forgotten the run-in we had with Jeb Cornish in Dodge City, and if I know that man right, he'll be looking for a way to pay us back—that's one reason I'm glad we're changing our route because we're not likely to run into him. But there are always plenty of others of his type around to watch out for."

"Yes, that's true." Lucien Edmond's brow furrowed. "I'm glad that both you and Lucas will be looking after Hugo. He's bound and determined to go on this drive, and I want him to. Either one day he's going to replace me as head of Windhaven Range, or he's going to decide on some new career which has nothing to do with cattle. The sooner he finds out which, the happier Maxine and I will be. Well, come see me before you leave. Damn, if I don't wish I were riding with you!"

"You won't have to worry about Hugo—I'll put him through the ropes, and I'll find out if he has any vaquero ability or not," Ramón replied. "And that's another reason I want to take all those armed men. I don't want your boy getting into any kind of range war his first time out. The better armed we are and the more watchful, the less danger there'll be of the kind of action where Hugo might get hurt."

"You've had him practicing with firearms, haven't you?"

"Yes, and he's reasonably good at it. He's young and energetic, with good reflexes. He's enthusiastic, but I've got the notion somewhere that maybe he doesn't know what he's getting into. He's talked himself into wanting to go because he wants to know exactly where he stands—and I certainly can't blame him for that; not at eighteen."

"You're absolutely right," Lucien Edmond agreed. "You say he's practiced with weapons, and you got him a good horse?"

"The best in the remuda, Lucien Edmond. You know, Easy, the six-year-old gelding that's been on three cattle drives already. He isn't skittish, and he's got stamina and heart. I've let Hugo ride him for the last couple of days, just to get used to him. They seem to hit it off pretty well together. The gelding gives a smooth ride, but he can go for a burst of speed when there's a stampede, or rounding up to be done. By the way, Hugo appears to have a natural aptitude for placing his shots on target. I think some of it's due to all his previous practice plus his understandable wish not to have to kill a man unnecessarily."

Lucien Edmond nodded, leaned back on his pillow, and uttered a weary sigh. "All right, then, you go right ahead. I suppose you've chosen the positions of your men?"

"Just about. I'll let Hugo ride drag for the first week, so he sees the worst of what a cattle drive can be, by getting all the dust from the herd into his face."

"Yes, you're right; that's what I would have done myself, if I'd ridden with you." Lucien Edmond Bouchard breathed another sigh and shook his head. "Well, Ramón, I have to give you credit. You've thought of everything. You'll be good for Hugo. I'll be anxious to know how he fares through the long weeks and months ahead. I want this to be a learning experience for him. That's one reason I overrode Maxine and allowed him to go this year." He extended his hand to Ramón, who shook it heartily.

"I'll say goodbye to you tomorrow before we leave, Lucien Edmond," Ramón told him. "And just relax. Everything's going to be fine. You know, although probably it's none of my business, you'll have more time with Carla, who's growing up to be a very beautiful young woman. Someday soon she'll want to marry and perhaps move away—"

"I've no doubt of that, Ramón," Lucien Edmond replied. "In fact, to give her the right start in life, Maxine and I have been thinking of sending her to a finishing school either in New Orleans, or in the East—maybe even in Europe. She should see something of the world before she settles down. Maxine and I will work that out. Well, good luck, brother-in-law. By the way, I haven't seen Mara in a week—"

"That's because she's been busy saying goodbye to me," Ramón grinned. "Don't worry, once I head out on the trail, she'll be over here drinking coffee with Maxine and bringing over the children and probably even helping Maxine out around the house. The best thing that ever happened to me was marrying your sister."

"It's the best thing that ever happened to her, so that makes you both even. Now get out of here, before I start feeling sorry for myself for not being able to ride along with you and Hugo."

\* \* \*

Ramón had estimated that, with the stops at the two army forts, the total route to the Arkansas River would be close to twelve hundred miles, and that four months would be required for a safe journey. Ramón said goodbye to Mara and his children, heartened by the fact that she would spend at least two afternoons a week teaching in the school run by the nuns. It would keep her from fretting too much about his prolonged absence, for this would be the longest trip that any Windhaven Range boss had undertaken since they had come to Carrizo Springs fourteen years ago. He bade farewell also to Eddie Gentry and Joe Duvray, and finally visited with Lucien Edmond. Maxine shook hands with him and wished him a safe journey, and added with a smile, "I know you'll have good luck, and I know that you'll look after Hugo."

"As if he were my own flesh and blood, be sure of that," Ramón assured her emphatically. Then, shaking hands with Lucien Edmond a last time, he said, "I've been thinking—although it's southeast from our destination in Colorado, I'd like to stop by the Creek reservation on the way back. I've checked the map, and it really won't add any additional traveling time. I could purchase some supplies for them in Wichita to leave with them."

"That's a wonderful idea! I should have thought of that." Lucien Edmond clapped his hand to his head. "Give my very best wishes to Sipanata and his people. Tell them that I'm with them in spirit and explain why I couldn't come myself. *Vaya con Dios, amigo.*"

Ramón grinned and nodded, then left the hacienda and mounted his horse. Hugo waited, tall and wiry in the saddle, wearing a sombrero, chaps, and new boots and breeches. He also wore a confident, almost swaggering smile. His mother had come out onto the porch of the hacienda to wave goodbye, and he self-consciously stiffened in the saddle, his shoulders straight, and waved nonchalantly to her, as if he had been doing this all his life. She was about to call to him to wrap himself up in his bedroll at night when the winds were cool, but refrained: she would sound like an overprotective mother who thought she still had a little boy as a son, and it would demean him in the eyes of the vaqueros. She contented herself with calling, "Just stay close to your Uncle Ramón; do what he says, and you won't go wrong, Hugo. I hope you'll have a fine time on the drive."

Lucas, seated on his piebald gelding, turned to grin at her and to call back, "We'll see he doesn't ride drag too often and get all the dust in his face, Mrs. Bouchard! He'll be just fine, don't you worry none about him! He rides a horse real good."

"Thank you, Lucas. And we'll look after Felicidad and your children while you're gone."

"I'm mighty grateful for that, Mrs. Bouchard. She gets a bit nervous when I'm away for a spell—and we're going to be gone longer than we've ever been. I'd appreciate it if you'd look after her extra-special."

"That goes without saying. Good luck, all of you." Maxine watched as Ramón, at the head of the drive, led them out. At the rear, the two large chuck wagons carried all the gear. Up front were the vaqueros' bedrolls and the tools needed on the range: axes, hammers, heavy shears in the event the men ran into unexpected stretches of barbed wire into which some of the strays might get entangled, long-handled mallets for driving tent stakes, and the like. Matéo Visanga, who had come to Windhaven Range eighteen months ago to join his cousin, Narciso Duarte, had been chosen to be the "Maria"—the cook—of the drive. He was personable, good-humored, short and plump, and had just turned thirty. He came by his cooking skill from several years of practice as a cook in a *posada* in Durango.

Hugo Bouchard had been instructed by Ramón to ride near the chuck wagon for the first few days, to get the feel of the drive. It was not just that Ramón wanted the youngster to have the unenviable post of bringing up the rear and getting the dust from the cattle hooves in his face, but also that it was well to break him in slowly, and not require too many tasks of him at the outset. Besides, as Ramón had shrewdly surmised, the ecstatic look on Hugo's handsome face indicated that he was already thrilled just at the prospect of being his own man and of sharing life under the stars with the vaqueros; he required no additional excitement. Everything was new and intoxicating to Hugo. In a word, he saw only the romantic adventure of the drive, and knew nothing of the dreary monotony and the unexpected dangers that beset any cattle drive—especially one of this magnitude and length.

For nearly two weeks, the drive followed the winding course of the Rio Grande in a northwesterly direction, until

156

at length the herd reached the mouth of the Pecos River, whose tortuous meanderings were cursed by cattlemen as the crookedest in the world. This treacherous six hundred-foot-wide stream started its life in the pure, cold mountains of northern New Mexico; but here, in its lower reaches, the water was highly alkaline and a turbid red color, the result of salts and clay picked up by the river in its journey through the plains lands. Lucien Edmond had warned Ramón and the vaqueros not to allow the cattle, the horses, or themselves to drink too deeply of these waters, or the result would be disastrous. Instead, they were to parallel the Pecos far enough to the east—so that neither cattle nor horses would smell the river—and to content themselves with watering the herd at various fresh creeks and springs dotting the trail until they were north of Pope's Crossing at the Texas-New Mexico border.

But still great care had to be taken, for many of these streams were reached only by steep, narrow trails. The cattle easily lost their footing on these banks, and occasionally, in their rush to reach the quenching waters, they stepped in too far and were caught by treacherous quicksand. The vaqueros tried as best they could to determine where this deadly mud lay, but still a number of steers, bulls, and cows were lost.

Because they were driving a mixed herd, it rapidly became apparent that, as best they could, the bulls would have to be kept separate from the cows: there were problems enough without infighting amongst the bulls attempting to determine a hierarchy within their ranks. And so each morning, after ascertaining the direction of the wind, Ramón would have the vaqueros put the bulls either at the head or the rear of the pack, whichever was the upwind position.

Ramón was determined to maintain a pace of twelve to fourteen miles each day, so long as the terrain remained relatively flat. As they trudged on, the dry country seemed interminable, and it wasn't until they finally reached Pope's Crossing that they felt any kind of goal had been reached.

Six hours passed before all the cattle were forded across, and Hugo Bouchard, despite his youth, felt the physical demands of the endless journey of plodding cattle, sullen skies, and tugging winds. He groaned inwardly when he realized that they had come a bare third of the way to their

157

final destination—and after that, there would still be the long, exhausting journey back.

He recalled how at the end of the first day—during which they had gone thirteen miles—he had scarcely eaten his ration of beans and salt pork with biscuits before flinging himself down on his bedroll, hugging it around himself, and rolling on his side, falling fast asleep. The shouts of the vaqueros at dawn had awakened him, and as he had tried to rise, he winced and groaned; the stress on his muscles from being in the saddle all day had been something he was not yet used to.

But by the end of the first week, out of dogged persistence, he had gotten his second wind, so to speak, and was more easily able to endure a full day's hard riding. Ramón, carefully observing him and noting his progress with satisfaction, gave him additional tasks, such as rounding up a stray. Hugo had learned to use a lariat with commendable skill, his horse was well trained to accommodate itself to its young and inexperienced handler, and now Ramón had no hesitation in assigning him temporary posts on all sides of the herd, though always accompanied by one or more of the vaqueros.

The days had been pleasantly warm, and the evenings mildly cool. For Hugo Bouchard, this new terrain was fascinating in its very grotesqueness: giant boulders and singular rock formations, as if eons ago a giant hand had taken reddish clay and capriciously shaped it, setting it down in the midst of uneven stretches of land that was partly covered with grass and partly with a thin, sandy topsoil. Here and there were giant cacti and huge clumps of brambles and mesquite.

One of the younger vaqueros, a man some two years older than Hugo, had observed how, although Hugo was by now readily accepted by the other men, he still kept mostly to himself, feeling very much a stranger in their midst. Early this morning, the vaquero rode over to Hugo—who had been placed near the end of the herd with little else to do except watch for wandering strays—and cheerfully accosted him: *"Buenos días, Señor Hugo. ¿Cómo está?"* Hugo gave him a feeble smile and intently glanced at the ambling heard over to his right, lest distraction cause him to overlook the task to which he had been assigned.

*"Muy bien, gracias."* Hugo gave him a feeble smile and

158

intently glanced at the ambling herd over to his right, lest distraction cause him to overlook the task to which he had been assigned.

"You know, Señor Hugo, if ever you should be in a desert where there are *saguaros* like that one you see over to your left, you would not starve or be thirsty."

"Oh?" Hugo eyed the young vaquero. "Why is that, señor—señor—"

*"Me llamo Tomás Maldero, Señor Hugo.* It is because if you cut it, and then suck or chew the piece you have cut, you will find *agua.* It is a good thing to know."

"Thank you, Señor Maldero." Hugo awkwardly nodded.

*"Pero no."* The Mexican laughingly shook his head. "Just call me Tomás. I am not yet old enough nor important enough to be called señor. And you see, this is only the second drive I have been on, and the others were to the forts of the *soldados* in Texas. So truly, you have as much experience as I, because you have ridden many times more around the ranch."

"Thank you. It's good of you to tell me this, Tomás."

The young man grinned and touched the brim of his sombrero. *"De nada,* Señor Hugo. I know why you are—how does one say in *inglés*—so *infeliz.* I mean, you look sad, and you feel that you are not one of us. But all of us wish you well, Señor Hugo, and think you have much *coraje."*

Hugo stared at the smiling man, little older than himself, and felt a lump in his throat. As much as he appreciated this offer of friendship, he wanted to hide his feelings, so he turned back to stare at the herd and saw that a yearling had ambled off and was trotting toward a stretch of thick grass. "Excuse me, Tomás, I have to get him back," he called, as he wheeled his horse toward the yearling and rode after it.

The Mexican watched Hugo wave his sombrero and shout at the yearling till it reluctantly trotted back to its proper place, and he then rode back to his own position farther ahead.

Ramón Hernandez had taken pains to draw up a comprehensive map of the route he intended to take to the meeting place with Maxwell Grantham. In making this map, Ramón had relied on some of the information sent to him by Joseph McCoy, which indicated that Fort Sumner,

159

where they hoped to sell some of the cattle, was now due north through what seemed unimpeded terrain.

That afternoon, as they came within a dozen miles of the fort, Hugo Bouchard was startled to see a dozen riders galloping toward them from the west, brandishing rifles. Alarmed at this ominous sight, he galloped his own mount up to Ramón, who rode at the head of the herd in his role as trail boss, and hastily reported what he had seen.

Ramón called an order to his men to have their weapons ready and, drawing his Spencer repeating rifle out of the saddle sheath, rode toward the oncoming horsemen. Hugo, tingling with excitement and yet feeling a tightening of his stomach muscles, put his hand on the butt of his carbine and followed his uncle. Ramón glanced back and frantically shook his head: he had no wish to involve an eighteen-year-old boy in what might prove to be an ugly confrontation. But Hugo thought that Ramón was only warning him not to draw the rifle out of the sheath, and so continued to ride behind.

"What the hell are you doing on our land, mister?" the foremost rider called, kicking his heels against his black gelding's belly and urging it to within fifty yards of Ramón. He drew it to a halt and leaned forward in his saddle, glaring at the handsome Mexican as Ramón approached him.

"Excuse me, señor, I didn't know it was private land," Ramón explained, as he drew alongside. "We're on our way to Fort Sumner. This is the Bouchard outfit of Windhaven Range in Texas. We have no wish to fight with you," Ramón declared propitiatingly.

"That so?" The rider was a grizzled, gray-bearded man in his late forties, his face weather-beaten, lean, and hard. His jaw jutted and his closely spaced, light blue eyes narrowed with suspicion. "You're on Mr. Ken Bassett's land, greaser," he glowered.

"In that case, I beg your pardon. I have a map of the trail we were taking, and I knew about the Goodnight Ranch at Bosque Grande, but I didn't know about Mr. Bassett's."

"Well, you know it now, greaser."

"There's no need to be offensive. My name is Ramón Hernandez, and I am the brother-in-law and partner of Lucien Edmond Bouchard."

At this point, Hugo could not restrain himself and burst

out with, "He's telling you the truth, mister! I'm Lucien Edmond's son, Hugo Bouchard."

The other riders had joined their belligerent spokesman, who turned to stare at Hugo and then guffawed. "Well now, sonny, you're a mite techy. And hardly out of swaddling clothes, yet on a drive like this."

"I'm old enough to handle a horse and a gun, mister!" Hugo hotly retorted, crimsoning at the ridicule.

"Quiet, Hugo, there's no need for that," Ramón interposed softly, then turned back to say, "We'll be off your land at once; there's no need for gun play."

"Mr. Bassett won't take it kindly that your damn herd is feeding itself on his good grass. I'm Dan Foster, Mr. Bassett's head honcho, and I'd say you owe us money for the grass your herd's eaten without permission."

"But that's highway robbery!" Hugo burst out again, unable to restrain himself.

"Shows how little you know about ranching, sonny," was Foster's contemptuous retort. "All right, then, Señor Hernandez, if you don't want trouble, you'll settle up. I'd say one hundred dollars would be a fair price."

"I'd say that was a little greedy, señor." Ramón was nettled and showed it.

Dan Foster leaned back in his saddle, then glanced around at his men, all of whom were armed with rifles, as well as holstered Colts at their belts. "Well, now, Señor Hernandez, if you want to argufy the matter, my boys here are pretty good shots—and we've got the drop on you. Like as not, apart from losing some of your vaqueros and maybe your own life, you might just lose a lot of your herd from a stampede over gunshots. I'd advise you to settle up and be peaceable."

"I've no wish to fight with you or your men—but I think you're a bit high-handed in setting a price like that. Very well, I will pay you, and I expect no more trouble till I reach Fort Sumner," Ramón angrily decided. He put his hand into the pocket of his windbreaker, drew out a wallet and counted out five twenty-dollar bills, then handed them to Dan Foster, who pocketed them.

"Now that's showing sense. All right, Señor Hernandez, now get your damn cattle out of here fast. If they stay any longer, they'll have eaten more grass than you've paid for, get me?"

Ramón curtly nodded, then wheeled his horse back and

shouted to his riders, "Drive them on! Make for Fort Sumner *muy pronto!*"

The Windhaven Range vaqueros rode up and down the long processional of the herd, waving their sombreros and shouting, till at last the placid animals began to move forward in that inexorably slow surge of an orderly drive. Ramón gestured toward the herd, as he said to Foster, "Now take your men and those rifles away from our outfit. We'll be in Fort Sumner by tomorrow, and we probably won't ever pass by this stretch again."

"If you do, Señor Hernandez, you've got a pretty good idea what'll happen to you. Mr. Bassett doesn't take kindly to other ranchers using his land to fatten up their cattle. Thanks for the hundred." Foster uttered a sarcastic laugh. He turned his horse and rode back westward, his men following him.

Ramón exhaled a sigh of relief, then took out his bandanna and mopped his forehead. "That was a bit too close for comfort. And you, nephew, you were a little hotblooded there, and I thought we might have some trouble."

"I'm sorry, Uncle Ramon, but I couldn't sit there and let him call you a greaser and talk to you the way he did." Hugo's face was crimson with discomfort.

"I know that. What mistakes you've made have been understandable ones, and they're far outweighed by the assistance you've given us. You're a fast learner, and you will surely be a good vaquero. As for the one or two mistakes along the way—you've learned from them so you won't repeat them. That's all anybody can ask of a man these days. Now let's get back and find a camp for our cattle where we can bed them down and have ourselves a good, hot meal before we go into Sumner tomorrow. Come along, *mi compañero.*"

This time, Hugo flushed with pride as he followed his uncle back to the herd.

## Thirteen

Ramón's praise had so exhilarated young Hugo Bouchard that, when it was time for supper, he volunteered to help Matéo Visanga, who had his hands full cooking meals for so many men. The unusual length of the drive to Colorado had necessitated taking along far more provisions than would ordinarily have been carried if the drive had been simply to one of the Kansas cow towns. Fortunately, the two chuck wagons were compact and versatile, which greatly facilitated the preparation of meals for thirty hungry vaqueros.

At the rear of each wagon, there was a box for storing tin dishes, a Dutch oven, frying pans, kettles, and sturdy coffee pots. Each wagon contained standard staples like green-berry coffee, salt pork, cornmeal, flour, and beans. There was a folding leg attached to each chuck box lid to form a table when lowered, so that the cook might readily prepare breakfast, noon, and evening meals.

In the front of each chuck wagon, there was a securely fixed water barrel, with a handy spigot running through the side of the wagon. Beneath the wagon bed itself, there was a cowhide sling to hold dry wood, kindling, or buffalo chips, so that a fire might be started swiftly. Finally, under the drivers' seats, there were special boxes that contained axes, hammers, and spades, as well as several revolvers and extra ammunition, in the event of a surprise attack.

Matéo Visanga drove one wagon, and Francisco Lorcado, a man of twenty-nine from San Luis Potosí and another newcomer to Windhaven Range, drove the other. Lorcado acted more as a helper, since he had whimsically confessed that all he could make was coffee, but he more than made up for his lack of knowledge by improvisation and swift, hard work. So when Hugo Bouchard volunteered to help out this evening, Francisco Lorcado was only too happy, since he much preferred to have some time to play his guitar and sing sad mariachi songs. He had chosen a brown-and-white cow to symbolize a girl he called Dolores who, he claimed, had jilted him back in San Luis Potosi for a man twice his age who owned land, a house, and many *pesos*.

"You see how it is with poor Francisco, Señor Hugo," Matéo told him with an expressive jerk of his thumb. Francisco was already hastening off with his guitar to seat himself near a gnarled scrub tree and serenade the cow, much as Don Quixote might have addressed a rhapsodic poem to his Dulcinea, pretending that a tavern wench was that unattainable inamorata of his dreams. "But with you, it will be much different, *no es verdad?* First of all, you are young, you are much better looking than poor Francisco, and you will have your pick of all the señoritas because you are the son of the *patrón*."

Hugo crimsoned, for, to tell the truth, he had until now thought very little about the opposite sex; it was true that there were a number of attractive young Mexican girls and women on Windhaven Range, but the urgency that he had felt these past few years had been that of discovering his own identity, rather than an awareness of his developing sexual feelings. He mumbled something and began, at the cook's polite suggestion, to cut up some onions for the stew. As he did so, Hugo glanced over to the tree where Francisco was still serenading the cow. Yes, he thought, perhaps as the *patrón*'s son, he would have more opportunity to court a young lady of his choice than poor Francisco; nevertheless, he felt a bond with the lonely vaquero. How often, during these long weeks of struggling to become used to the rigors of the trail, had he himself been lonely, just as Francisco was now. Not for a girl, perhaps— it was not yet time for that—but for the solace of his home and family. All at once Hugo had an overwhelming sense of oneness and comradeship with Francisco—in fact, with all the vaqueros who stolidly and devotedly pursued the duties of the trail, far from the comforts of loved ones. They were partners in a great enterprise, and Hugo felt lucky to be one of them.

Back in Carrizo Springs, Lucien Edmond, his wife Maxine, and their daughters had just finished dinner, and Lucien Edmond had decided to go for a short stroll near the creek. His leg had responded nicely to proper treatment and by now had almost healed. Pablo Casares had made a crutch for him, and he used this for support and to keep his weight off the lame leg. But already he was telling Maxine that within another week or two, he could easily be back in the saddle supervising the activities of the ranch.

Just before leaving the hacienda for his walk, he had been conversing with Maxine, telling her that as soon as he could, he would like to drive a few hundred head of cattle to Santa Fe, or perhaps even New Orleans. To this, Maxine had gently parried, "Lucien Edmond, it's high time you learned how to take a good long vacation so that we can look around and see what we've missed the last few years. Why shouldn't you and I go to New Orleans or to Santa Fe, just to see the sights and enjoy each other's company away from the responsibilities of the ranch?"

And he had lowered his eyes and finally, with an apologetic little laugh, declared, "Of course, you're right, my darling. I guess I've been letting myself be too busy, and taking you for granted—which isn't at all saying that I don't love you as much as when I saw you that first day when you'd come from Baltimore, but simply that it's true that I've concentrated all my energy into building Windhaven Range so that our children will one day enjoy all its benefits."

"So far as money is concerned, dear Lucien Edmond," Maxine gently responded, "we have all we need. And Joe and Eddie could handle the ranch if you really decided one day to retire and simply be a gentleman of leisure and catch up on what we've missed, like opera and the theater and travel. And by the way, while we're thinking of the future, we really must spend more time discussing what Hugo and Carla are going to do one day."

"I suspect Hugo is going to go a long way toward finding himself by the time he returns with Ramón," Lucien Edmond avowed. "He was so eager to go on the drive, that I'm sure when he comes back he'll tell me that he's ready to handle more responsibility here, whenever I'm ready to give it to him."

"I wouldn't be so sure, dear Lucien Edmond." Maxine smiled knowingly.

He shrugged philosophically. Maxine was in one of her romantic moods, and he knew better than to try to inject

165

his own thoughts at such a time. Instead, he hobbled off for his stroll to the creek and back.

Maxine sat down at the spinet and, closing her eyes for a moment, decided what she would play. She chose a Chopin nocturne, for it was poetic and wistful, and there was a kind of bittersweet loveliness to it—a perfect complement to her mood.

From the nocturne, she turned to two of the same composer's Preludes, and then, with a sigh, as if admitting that she had plunged herself too far into pensiveness, she played a cheerful Haydn sonata, and finally a sonata by Domenico Scarlatti, originally written for the harpsichord.

She was so absorbed in her music that she was not aware that lovely Carla had come into the living room and stood beside the door, transfixed by the music and not making a sound.

When at last Maxine drew back her hands and sighed again, Carla exclaimed, "Mama, that was just wonderful! I've never heard you play more beautifully!"

"Carla—I didn't know you were here—"

"I know, Mama. I didn't want to spoil it. You know, Mama, the way you were playing just now, you could have been on the concert stage, or even perform in Europe."

Maxine turned to face her daughter with a warm smile. She patted the place on the bench beside her and murmured, "Come sit down beside me, Carla."

Carla did as she was bidden and impulsively kissed her mother affectionately and gave her a hug.

"Thank you, my dearest, that was very sweet. And that was a very pretty compliment you paid me—but you see, Carla, I'm quite content with my life."

"But didn't you ever really want to travel and be famous, Mama?"

"No, not really. It's only because you haven't heard any music except what I play here that you think I have anything more than just a superficial talent, Carla. No, don't look at me like that, it's quite true. There must be thousands of people all over the world who play just as well as I do and a great deal better. And yet they aren't on concert stages, either. No, Carla, I loved your father as dearly as I do now, and so I was very content to marry him, to give him children, to follow him here to Texas, and to help build a home. And now he has achieved something that will live long after both of us, that is to say, Lucien Edmond and myself—and it will be a legacy to all of you children."

"You shouldn't talk like that, Mama! You're going to live an awfully long time; you're still so young and beautiful—"

"And that's a lovely compliment, too, dear Carla." Maxine hugged Carla and kissed her, and then, her face sobering, added, "But you're a very different woman from me. At nineteen, an age when many girls are already married and even have their first child, you've never really been away from Windhaven Range. Decidedly, your father and I are going to have to plan to send you somewhere where you can find your truest potential. And we also want you to make a wonderfully happy marriage. But here there's no one—and we've no neighbors with eligible sons who might be worthy of you. What would you think, Carla, of going to New Orleans, either to a college or perhaps to a finishing school that specializes in art?"

"I'd like it very much, Mama."

"Well now, I think that Lucien Edmond and I will talk it over and see that, come fall, you will have your chance."

"I'd miss being away from you and Papa, of course," Carla said wistfully.

"But you'd be so busy with new friends and your studies that you really wouldn't be homesick. And you wouldn't be all that far away. I'll send a letter to Hollis Minton, Laure Bouchard's New Orleans lawyer, and ask him to investigate some schools there."

"I'm so grateful to you, Mama. And now won't you please play some more for me?" Carla put her arm around her mother's waist and gave her a hug and a kiss, then rose and sat down on the plush sofa. She wondered if Hugo was enjoying himself outdoors with all the men—riding horseback, eating whenever he liked, swapping stories, and making friends with the vaqueros. It was a lot easier for a man than for a woman, she told herself. It was true that there were times when she felt very lonely, even though her mother and father and brother and sisters were here and they all loved her. She had often dreamed she would like to have her own chance at finding out what she could do best and what was in store for her—and now it seemed her dream would come true.

167

## Fourteen

They reached Fort Sumner a little after noon the following day. Ramón halted the herd near the fort and beckoned to Hugo. "You might as well start learning how cattle are sold, nephew," he remarked. "I'm going to see Major Donahue. Your father and I found out from the commander of Fort Inge that this Donahue likes good beef and will pay a fair price—at least six cents a pound for steers that have had plenty of grazing last fall to put fat on their bones."

"That's very interesting, Uncle Ramón," Hugo replied. But his answer was more automatic than sincere.

By now, Hugo was sporting a blond stubble, his attempt at growing a beard like many of the other vaqueros and thus trying to appear older. Ramón pretended not to notice, but gently suggested, "Before we ride into the fort, nephew, pour some water from your canteen onto your bandanna, then rub it into your chin and cheeks. There's dusty grime on your face, and we heard this Major Donahue is a stickler for neatness."

Greatly abashed, Hugo obeyed, and then followed Ramón as the handsome Mexican rode toward the gate of the fort. The corporal of the guard led them to the major's office, where Ramón met a lanky, rawboned man in his mid-forties with a russet spade beard and sideburns. He rose from his desk to greet his visitors, sharply eyed Hugo—who stared down at his boots and momentarily wished he was back in the saddle—then brusquely declared, "I've heard about you from Fort Inge, Hernandez. So you've brought along some steers in the hope you could sell me some beef, have you?"

"Precisely, Major Donahue. I've all of four hundred and fifty fattened head—not counting those few for our use on the trail."

"You can probably sell some of those to Fort Bascom, if you're going along the Goodnight-Loving Trail, as I suspect you are."

"That's what we're going to do this year, Major Donahue. No fear of hostile Indians along that way."

"No, they're a thing of the past, and I don't mind telling you that I'm glad of it; I don't enjoy killing Indians who just want to hunt their buffalo. But to get to the point, I'll take three hundred of your steers. Does six-and-a-half cents a pound suit you?"

"I'll settle for that. But you'll have to accept my tally and weight."

"Windhaven's reputation for honesty has preceded you, Heranadez. The commander of Fort Inge reported that you're the finest outfit he ever did business with. I'll take your tally. I'll have my Sergeant Mallory get a detail of men to help you drive the cattle into the pen at the other end of the fort. Will you and your friend here take supper with me?"

"It would be our pleasure, Major Donahue."

"Good. Now, to conclude our business, Señor Hernandez, the paymaster was here just last week, so I can either pay you in greenbacks or, if you prefer, a sight draft."

"The draft will be fine, Major Donahue," Ramón declared. These drafts, which could be redeemed at any federal bank, were actually preferred by trail drivers. In the event of an attack by rustlers or bushwhackers, a draft could be hidden with ease, whereas the more obvious greenbacks could readily be stolen.

"That's settled, then. Incidentally, give my regards to Colonel Emerson when you get to Bascom. Well, see you at supper—we've got a pretty good officer's mess here. Sergeant Mallory shot a deer for us yesterday, so we might have some venison tonight."

"I'm looking forward to it. Thank you again, Major Donahue. Incidentally, let me introduce Hugo Bouchard to you. He is the son of Lucien Edmond Bouchard, who runs Windhaven Range."

"Well now, youngster, you do look like a Bouchard at that, from all I've heard of Lucien Edmond—tall and blond. Getting good experience, is he, Hernandez?" Major Donahue gave Hugo Bouchard another sharp look, but there was a twinkle in his gray-blue eyes, and Hugo managed a feeble smile at the major's remarks.

169

"Well, it's his first drive, but I'd say he's learned a great deal already. The first thing was not getting saddle sores," Ramón quipped.

Now Hugo wished the floor would open up and swallow him, for Major Donahue uttered a short bark of a laugh as he responded, "I learned that when I was a plebe at West Point. Well now, Bouchard, if you don't care for being a cowhand, you could always join the army. I could use a good subaltern here, and I'd even start you off as a corporal."

"No—no thank you, s–sir," Hugo quavered, clearing his throat and looking more uncomfortable than ever.

"See you at supper then, Major Donahue. Come along, Hugo." Ramón extricated his nephew from what he understood was a trying situation. As they went out onto the parade grounds in search of Sergeant Mallory, Ramón grinned and nudged Hugo in the ribs. "You took that very well. I purposely didn't introduce you right off, because I wanted to see what mood Major Donahue was in. But at least you'll get a good supper tonight, a lot better than beans and biscuits and salt pork or jerky. Now let's go see about getting those three hundred head into the pen."

Lucas and the other vaqueros made camp, bedding down the herd about a mile from the fort, and the genial Mexican cook had begun preparations for a hearty supper. By way of propitiating his outfit for their not being able to share the major's hospitality, Ramón had given orders that two of the steers be slaughtered and the meat prepared for meals for the next few days. Lucas, who had been appointed assistant trail boss, understood only too well why he had not been invited to parley with the commanding officer of the fort: more than likely, he would not have been invited to have supper with the major and his subordinate officers because he was black. One reason Ramón had taken young Hugo Bouchard with him was in the event that Major Donahue had any aversion to Mexicans.

Shortly after sundown, as the vaqueros were enjoying a supper of steak and beans and biscuits, a rider on a black gelding approached the camp. He was stocky, his thick black beard was flecked with gray and exaggerated his bulbous nose, and he wore a black patch over his left eye, with an ugly, purplish scar running from the edge of the eye

170

socket down almost to his jaw—the mark of a hunting knife.

He did not dismount, for it was the code of the range that a stranger must be invited to do so when he came upon an outfit. It was Lucas who hailed him. "Looking for someone, stranger?"

The one-eyed rider nodded. "My name's Jack Hayes, mister. Rode down from Dodge City to see the major. I work for a cattleman who sells some of his beef to the army."

"You might be a bit late, Mr. Hayes," Lucas cheerfully responded. "We just sold three hundred head to him this afternoon."

"Well, no harm trying. Say, that chow smells mighty good. Think your cookie might have some to spare?"

"Sure. We killed two steers a couple of hours ago, so there's bound to be plenty left. Tie up your horse and step up to the chuck wagon, Mr. Hayes."

"That's mighty kind of you, mister." The black-bearded man dismounted and tied the reins of his black gelding to a nearby tent stake. "And that fire feels good, too, on a nippy night like this. Say, what's your outfit?"

"It's the WR, out of Carrizo Springs. Ramón Hernandez is our trail boss," Lucas told him.

"Sure. I heard tell of the WR—that's for Windhaven Range, ain't it?"

"That's right, Mr. Hayes. Go get yourself some grub and come sit yourself down by this fire. You're welcome to bed down for the night."

"No, I'll go on into the fort and finish up my business. My boss won't take it kindly when he finds out you beat me to a sale. Still, he'd expect me to make a try at it."

"Sounds reasonable."

Jack Hayes ambled over to the chuck wagon and soon returned with his tin plate piled high with steak, beans, biscuits, and a tin mug of coffee. Sitting down tailor-fashion opposite Lucas, he wolfed down his food, devoting all his attention to his meal. When he finished, he belched, shook his head, and declared, "Damn good chow. I'm grateful to you, mister."

"My name's Lucas."

"Glad to know you, Lucas. By the way, I'm a Union man—guess you could tell! If I'd worn a Reb's uniform, I

171

wouldn't be sitting here talking to you right friendly-like, now, would I?"

Lucas eyed him and tried not to show his rancor at the thinly veiled insult. Casually, he replied, "No, I guess you wouldn't." Then, by way of making a joke to ease the tension of that slurring remark, he offered, "I've worked on the range so long my color could come from the sun, you know."

"Guess it could at that. Guess the Texas sun turns everything dark, don't it? Well now, I think I'll have me another mug of coffee. Your cookie makes the best coffee I've had in a long spell."

Lucas watched the one-eyed man walk back over to the chuck wagon with his empty mug, then shrugged. He didn't much cotton to Jack Hayes, and he wished he hadn't been so free to converse with the man. Still, there was probably no harm done. Just the same, this Hayes was probably a brawler, the scar showed that up, and he had two holstered Colts at his belt with the holsters pared down for a quick draw. He thought to himself that perhaps he'd tell Ramón about Hayes. Maybe Ramón would recognize a description of the man. For himself, it was the first time he'd ever seen the man before, and he didn't care if he ever saw him again.

Jack Hayes sauntered over with his coffee, seated himself next to Lucas again, and adopted a confidential, friendly tone, as he leaned toward him and nonchalantly asked, "Where are you bound from here, Lucas?"

"Oh, Fort Bascom, and then Forts Elliot and Belknap on the way back," Lucas replied blandly. Growing suspicious of this stranger, he thus intimated that the outfit would make a circular trail to Fort Sumner, head back to Kansas, and thence to Windhaven Range itself. If by any chance Hayes happened to be a bushwhacker, the knowledge that the Bouchard outfit was going from one army fort to another should frighten off would-be cattle thieves, since it was well known that army patrols regularly rode out at a distance beyond their forts to make sure that the territory was clear of hostiles and outlaws. Before the drive set off, Lucien Edmond and Ramón had discussed the growing menace of outlaws from the Neutral Ground, bases of operation from where they would steal horses and rustle cattle in quick forays against the smaller, isolated ranches.

172

"Well, thanks for the chow, and tell your cookie he makes terrific coffee. Maybe I'll be seeing you again—only next time, I'll try to sell my boss's cattle before you get to the forts." Hayes rose and stretched with a yawn. "Good to meet you, Lucas. Wish you good luck on the trail."

"Thanks. You, too."

Jack Hayes walked over to the tent stake, unknotted the reins of his placid, patient gelding, mounted it, and rode off toward the fort. Lucas eyed him for a moment, then shrugged and dismissed him from his mind.

He might have been more concerned if he had watched longer. The night was dark, and as Hayes reached the gate of the fort, he veered his gelding northward and began to gallop. He had news for Jeb Cornish, and it was a little more than two hundred and fifty miles northeast to Dodge City. Cornish would want to know the whereabouts of that damned greaser who had killed Jeb's partner in Dodge.

Jeb Cornish, though an accredited government agent—whose lawless tactics had not yet been discovered by his federal employers—had organized a gang of bushwhackers who kept tabs on Texas cattle shipments bound for Dodge and beyond. It had been nearly two years since Frank Thompson had died when, at Jeb Cornish's orders, he had tried to fleece Ramón Hernandez out of the money Cornish had paid Ramón for the Bouchard herd by involving him with a dance-hall girl. The fat Indian agent—whose federal post authorized him to purchase cattle for Indian reservations, as well as for nearby army forts—had sworn to get even with "that sly greaser, the next time I hear he's out on the range with a herd of cattle."

As he rode through the night, grinning at his own cleverness and enjoying the sensation of his well-filled belly, Jack Hayes laughed aloud. It had been like taking candy from a baby. That damn-fool nigger—Jesus, it had nearly made his chow stick in his craw to have to palaver with a nigger!—had tried to be real clever when he'd said that the Bouchard outfit was going on to Fort Bascom and then the Kansas forts. Anybody who knew cattle knew damn well three small army forts couldn't buy what he had quickly gauged to be well over two thousand head. Nope, if they were heading for Fort Bascom next, it could only mean they were following the Goodnight-Loving Trail north and bypassing Kansas.

173

Well, he should reach Jeb Cornish in several days, and the Bouchard outfit shouldn't be too far from this fort by then. Unless he missed his guess—and he was sure that Jeb would agree with him in spades—they'd be heading on up to Colorado. There'd be plenty of time to waylay them on the trail before they reached either Pueblo or Denver and to get their cattle off on the Atchison, Topeka & Santa Fe. By God, Jeb would give him a bonus for locating the damned greaser! He leaned back in his saddle and chuckled reflectively. There ought to be an even bigger bonus if he personally gunned down the greaser. He'd mention that to Jeb. If the price was high enough, he'd ask for the job.

He broke out into a braying laughter at the thought. If there was anything he couldn't stand, it was these sons o' bitches who thought they could outsmart Jeb Cornish or himself, Jack Hayes. There was a fellow lying in an unmarked grave outside Abilene, who had thought he was a mite smarter than Jack Hayes about five years ago. That fellow hadn't taken it kindly when Hayes accused him of cheating at cards—which he'd done—and the man had had two of his buddies hold Hayes down, while he took a knife and gouged Hayes's cheek, leaving this scar he'd carry to his grave.

But a couple of weeks later, Hayes had caught the bastard in an alley without his bully boys around, and knocked him unconscious with the butt of his Colt before dragging him into an abandoned shed, gagging him, and working him over with his knife the way an Injun would. That had been sheer pleasure. And profitable too: the guy had a wallet with seven hundred dollars in it. Maybe Jeb Cornish would pay him that much to do the same thing to Ramón Hernandez.

## *Fifteen*

They had traveled at least eight hundred miles. Though it often followed the course of the winding rivers, the trail was, fortunately, easy to follow. By now Hugo Bouchard had begun to realize that his glorious dream of freedom in the outdoors, of being his own man without the supervision of his father and overly solicitous mother, was illusory. Young as he was, he vaguely began to understand that the pleasures of anticipation are not, alas, always those of realization.

There were long hours in the saddle, and although his young, resilient muscles had toughened after the first few weeks, there were still many nights when he flung himself down on his bedroll, too exhausted to eat much more than a spoonful or two of beans and a bite of meat. And it seemed that no sooner had he fallen asleep than the lowing of the cattle and the noisy orders of the vaqueros beginning to shape them up again imperiously summoned him from dreamless, vitally needed sleep.

Ramón and Lucas watched him carefully all the time and often conferred as to his progress. Halfway to Fort Bascom, Lucas said to Ramón, "You know, Ramón, he's hankering so awful much to be a man, you have to admire him for it. But he's not having the good time he thought he would when he started off with us."

"I expected as much. And you'll notice I've kept off his back by not giving him too much work to do—just enough to keep out of mischief and concentrate on what's expected of him. Doing it will satisfy his own need as a man to know that he can stand up to a job that has to be done, and not beg off or expect special privileges because he's Lucien Edmond's son. The vaqueros think he's done very well for a *niño*—but of course, if he heard them say that, he would

175

be furious, both with them and with himself. No, they have to call him *compañero* and *hombre* and mean it from the heart, before Hugo Bouchard will count himself full-grown."

"He's not bad at roping, and he rides well," Lucas conceded, as he rolled a cigarette with one hand, put it to his mouth, then thrust a small mesquite branch into the nearby campfire and lit it. "And he's killed many rabbits for us and an occasional deer now and again. So he's doing his share."

"That's true. But he still keeps to himself a good deal at mealtimes, and he doesn't join in with the vaqueros when they sing, or make small talk with them about what they hope to do when the drive's over," Ramón pointed out. "I suppose he doesn't feel he's been accepted by the outfit. Something has got to happen to make him feel just that before we get back, or he'll always be wondering. But my feeling is that he's not really cut out for a rancher's life and that if you sat down with him and asked him to talk right from the heart, he'd tell you he couldn't see doing this for the rest of his life."

"I think you're right, Ramón," Lucas agreed as he took a puff at his cigarette. He was silent for a moment, then he said, "I've been figuring the time it's going to take us to swing around from Fort Sumner on to Colorado where this Grantham fellow is going to take over the herd. Do you think we'll make the date agreed on?"

"Oh, yes, unless we run into a severe storm or a bad stampede, or a bushwhacking raid, we'll make it and with time to spare. We've run into some pretty good patches of grazing land thus far, and I've heard there are a few near Fort Bascom—which we should reach in about a week. That'll fatten our stock and make a good impression on Grantham, which may mean a great deal of business in the years ahead, if he's satisfied with what we sell him the first time. So I don't want to push this particular herd. You know, the days go by so slowly, I think that's getting under Hugo's skin, too. When you only drive at most fifteen miles from sunup to sunset—well, he's itching for action, I can tell. I just hope he'll get it without having to use his carbine—except to kill us some fresh meat for our supper every now and again."

"I think," Lucas said thoughtfully, "he's been growing up on the ranch without having much to do, and now all of a sudden he's grown up and feels that everybody expects him to be just like his father. Maybe he should go away to a college, or something like that, just to see other places and learn new things."

"I think you're right about that, Lucas. For people like you and me, the ranch is our life; it's good and it's satisfying—besides, we've both got families. Poor Hugo is on the edge of growing out of his boyhood and getting ready for manhood, but he's neither fish nor fowl. Well, we'll just keep watching over him. I've caught him looking my way several times when he's been riding for hours without doing anything more than just watching the cattle plod along— I've the feeling he wants to tell me how he feels, but he's scared that maybe I'll laugh at him. But I'll never do that." Ramón uttered a sigh. "We'll just have to see how things work out for him. And maybe, if he doesn't like it enough, he'll decide what he really wants to do—and then it's between him and his father."

Lucas kicked at a stone and sent it flying with his boot out toward the west. He squinted, a hand over his eyes, and then mused, "I guess you figure we'll need extra time because of the forts and the different trail we're taking, isn't that right?"

"That's basically it, Lucas. The terrain from New Mexico on up to Colorado is something we've never crossed before—there are mountainous regions we'll have to get through—so I want to allow all the time that's necessary, without running the cattle ragged. However, I also want to open up a few more army markets for Windhaven Range cattle, and Lucien Edmond agreed with me. The money we made selling those three hundred head to Major Donahue proves the point I made to Lucien Edmond. If we can get enough new buyers who will stay with us over the next few years, one day we won't have to make these drives. It won't be much longer, Lucas, before the railroads send feeder lines down to the big ranches—yes, like ours. Then all we do is brand them and disinfect them and make them walk right into the cattle cars and do all the work themselves."

"That would be something to see! Do you really think it will happen?" Lucas demanded.

"I don't think there's going to be much open range left five or six years from now, Lucas; that's my honest opinion. Well," Ramón said with a yawn, "we'd better get our rest while we can. We've had an easy go of it; everything

177

has been in our favor, weather and grazing grass and no interruptions. It's almost too good to be true."

With each new day, Hugo Bouchard became more restless and disenchanted. It was an entirely physical life, one which demanded constant vigilance and stamina. He had begun to think of himself as a kind of alien among all these cowhands. Even though they were pleasant to him and he, in his turn, to them, he felt himself to be an outsider who would never quite be accepted by them as an equal.

He also discovered that there was nothing romantic about riding miles in pursuit of a runaway steer, heifer, or bull, then bolting down a meal whose monotonous regularity had already caused him to yearn for the lavish table he had enjoyed at home. And since he was more than nominally fastidious, it often irked him that he could not take a daily bath and scrub himself down with soap. When they had finally crossed the Alamagordo Arroyo north of Fort Sumner, he had taken an improvised bath, and the vaqueros had teased him. But to take a quick plunge in a muddy stream was hardly the same thing as luxuriating in a bath to cleanse all grime and dust and then toweling oneself vigorously.

Nevertheless, he doggedly kept his feelings to himself, and he did what work was assigned to him with a steadfast determination: at least it would not be said of him that he was a shirker. Ramon and Lucas noticed this and secretly commended him for it. But both men had already decided that if Lucien Edmond Bouchard should want a frank appraisal of his son's potential as a rancher, they would urge him to let Hugo select the kind of career in which his mind would play more of a role.

Just before they reached Fort Bascom, Hugo ate a hasty breakfast of flapjacks with corn syrup, bacon, and coffee, then mounted his horse and, at Lucas's carefully phrased suggestion, went off toward the northeast to drive a dozen straying cows back into the herd. They had apparently wandered off in search of a stretch of blue grama grass that was particularly tasty. Whenever Ramón transmitted an order to him to be given to Hugo, Lucas had taken particular pains to make it sound like a suggestion, rather than a direct command, so that the sensitive youth would not take umbrage and feel that he was being tyrannized.

178

Hugo rode off, caught up with the errant cows, and, shouting and waving his sombrero, directed them back toward the main stream of the plodding herd. Suddenly his horse whinnied and pawed the air with its front hooves. The unexpected maneuver nearly unseated him, and as he tried to control the frightened horse, he caught sight of a lizard nearly two feet long off to the right, about a dozen feet from the horse. Its skin was studded with orange and black beadlike tubercles, and a sibilant hiss emerged from its open mouth, making visible its flittering, pointed tongue. Grimacing, Hugo instinctively reached for his carbine and, holding it at the hip, fired a round to destroy the lizard.

His revulsion and startled fear had made him thoughtless. To the south, Ramón cursed in violently profane Spanish as the herd, frightened by the sudden explosive sound of the carbine, began to run. He swiftly directed the vaqueros to ride after the cattle and to soothe them as best they could before they ran too far and exhausted themselves, with a subsequent loss in weight.

Meanwhile, Hugo wheeled his still-trembling horse back toward the others, but as he sheathed the carbine, he uttered a dismayed cry to see what his impulsive action had done. "My God, I've made them stampede! I forgot all about what Uncle Ramón told me," he said to himself, his face taut with contrition.

When Ramón saw Hugo ride up, he shouted to him, "Keep away! You're not experienced enough to handle a stampede! If you get too close, your horse might get knocked down and throw you under the hooves!"

"I—I'm sorry, Uncle Ramón—I didn't think—it was horrible! A big lizard that was orange and black, and making a hissing sound—"

"That's a Gila monster, Hugo. Next time, just ride your horse as fast and as far away from it as you can, but don't shoot it unless it's going to attack you. More men can get hurt in a stampede than ever could from the bite of one of those ugly lizards," Ramón told him, with a friendly smile to soften the implied rebuke.

Hugo nodded, flushing hotly, pulled his sombrero down over one side of his face, and trotted off, keeping well out of the way of the vaqueros who were chasing the fleeing herd.

It took almost till sundown before the skillful vaqueros

179

managed to subdue the frightened cattle and finally bring them to a halt, seven miles east of the trail toward Fort Bascom.

After they had bedded down the herd, the vaqueros were impatient for their supper, for the exhausting work of quelling the stampede had made them ravenously hungry. Hugo stayed at the back of the camp, eating by himself and feeling more out of place than ever. Ramón and Lucas, sitting near the campfire, glanced back at the solitary figure obscured by the darkness of the night, and Ramón murmured, "*Pobrecito.* But I haven't got the heart to say anything more about his firing the carbine. Now, if he'd been a vaquero, he'd have made a game of it, taken his knife and killed it with a quick, quiet throw. But you can't expect someone his age who's never been out on the range before to know all these things. I just hope he doesn't become too unhappy with himself. He's been brooding all day."

"I think, Ramón," Lucas rejoined politely, "that one of these days Hugo will have a chance to prove himself."

"I certainly hope so. Well, this is why I've allowed extra time to reach Grantham—because here we lost a day, and we'll lose another half-day getting back to where we started from, just before he fired at that lizard. Still in all, there's no harm really done. I thank the good *Señor Dios* that no one was hurt in the stampede."

"Amen to that," Lucas nodded. Then, glancing back at Hugo again, he shook his head. "He's really done very well for his first time, you have to admit that. And I still think he's going to show the real stuff he's made of before this drive is over."

## Sixteen

It had taken Jack Hayes just under a week to ride the two
hundred and fifty miles from Fort Sumner to Dodge City
and to report to Jeb Cornish that, quite by chance, he had
run into a herd from Windhaven Range headed up by
Ramón Hernandez. Just as the outlaw had surmised, the
unscrupulous Indian agent chuckled and said, "That means
he's bound for either Colorado or Wyoming, up the
Goodnight-Loving Trail. I told you he was a goddamned
sly greaser—he knows better than to try to come back to
Dodge, after what he did to poor Frank Thompson."

"I thought you'd be glad to know that I found him for
you," Hayes boasted. "And seeing as how I can guarantee
you that just say the word and he's a dead man, I want a
good price for my services."

"You'll get it. It's worth five hundred to me—"

"Jeez, I'd kill President Hayes himself for that much, so
help me!" the scar-faced, bearded ruffian swore greedily.

"No need, he won't get a second term. He and Lemon-
ade Lucy have just about got this country fed up with his
holier-than-thou Bible-spouting." Jeb Cornish sighed nostalgically. "Boy, what I wouldn't give to see old Ulysses
Simpson Grant back in office, when there were cigars and
whiskey galore, and people could make deals without some
righteous, church-going snooper ratting on them!" Then his
face twisted into a grimace of hate and he brusquely went
on, "If Hernandez is heading that way, and I'm sure he is,
that'll give us time to meet him just beyond the Colorado
River crossing. He'd be heading up in the direction of
Pueblo, unless I miss my guess. How many head of cattle
would you say he had along with him?"

"Best as I could make out, Jeb, I'd say two thousand or
so. And they're good stock; I'd say they're mostly yearling

and two-year-old breeding bulls and cows. They'll take prime prices anywhere we sell them, whether it's to a rancher, an army fort, or an Injun reservation."

"Damn! That herd ought to be worth thirty thousand, give or take a couple of thousand. Look, you'll find the men holing up in Abilene. Round them up, get plenty of supplies and a good, sturdy wagon, and pack it with guns and ammo. Let's see, now—" Cornish abruptly rose from his desk and waddled over to a colored map on the wall. Squinting and tracing on it with a stubby forefinger, he stated, "I've heard that many times those big ranchers in Colorado or Wyoming come down to meet trail drives and take the herds off their hands. So I don't want you going over to Colorado, because any outfit that would meet Hernandez's would put the odds in the damn greaser's favor a lot more than I want."

"So what do I do, Jeb?"

Cornish turned back to the map and squinted at it for a long moment. Finally he said, "I'd say that damn greaser'll be getting to this here Trinchera Pass—that's right on Goodnight's old trail—long about the middle of June. Just before the pass, the country turns rugged. There're large rock outcroppings the drive will have to pass through that would be ideal places for an ambush. So you've got plenty of time to round up my crew of bushwhackers and be there waiting for them, get me?"

"Sure, Jeb. I'd say he's got about thirty cowhands with him. But I'll tell you this, I saw a lot of Spencer carbines and rifles."

"If you get yourself thirty good men, we'll have enough guns to wipe them out, especially if we take them by ambush. Don't forget—I want that greaser killed, and then I want those cattle driven to the edge of Indian Territory. When you've done the job, you'll send a rider on ahead to me here in Dodge, and I'll send a roundup crew. They'll be cowhands, not bushwhackers, so our branding should be done before they get there so they won't be suspicious. You'll have to see to it, Jack. You line up the men who know how to kill quick and brand quick."

"Don't you worry none, Jeb. Anyhow, I'm going to handle the greaser myself with my knife." Jack Hayes grinned crookedly as he touched the sharp hunting knife in a sheath at his belt; the bone handle had seven notches. "It'll be eight notches when I get back. And, if you want real proof, I'll even bring you his scalp, Injun-style."

"That won't be necessary. Now get out of here, and I don't want to see you back here till you come in with the news that you've got a herd and that damned greaser's planted six feet under without a marker."

"I could use the cash you owe me for this scouting trip, Jeb," Hayes whined.

The fat Indian agent glowered at the outlaw, then took out a wallet and grudgingly extricated several bills and tossed them into the air. Hayes deftly caught them, thumbed them, and then grunted, "That'll do. But don't forget, you'll owe me the five hundred when the rustling job's done."

"Don't you worry about that. Now get out of here. Some small Texas rancher is coming in today with about three hundred head he couldn't sell anywhere else, and you know what I'm going to tell him? He's got the wrong time, and the market's gone to hell—so he won't get much more than what I just paid you. Beat it now!"

## Seventeen

It was the second week of June, more than enough time to make the rendezvous with Grantham by mid-July. Yet toward the end of the trail there would be rough going through hazardous mountain passes. On the other hand, if all went smoothly and they found themselves there two weeks ahead of the appointed time, the stock could be put to graze, and the vaqueros given a chance to mend their equipment, to hunt and fish to replenish their store of provisions, and to get much-needed rest after the arduous journey they had made.

Coming back, Ramón estimated, allowing for a stop at the Creek reservation to bring Sipanata supplies which he would first procure in Wichita, it would mean about eleven hundred miles all told—shorter than the route out because it was less circuitous. But they could easily average twenty-five to thirty miles a day returning, which would mean about a month and a half—so certainly by the first week of September they should all be back.

Before they had left Fort Bascom, where another hundred and fifty steers had been sold, Ramón had done a little bargaining with the quartermaster, who sold him some bacon and salt pork and told him that they had more flour than they needed. Ramón had bought a hundred fifty-pound sacks, after having first inspected a few token sacks to make certain that the flour was of good quality and not full of weevils. At eight dollars a sack, it came to about sixteen cents a pound, less than the army had paid for it, according to the quartermaster who had sworn Ramón to secrecy about that information. "That's what comes of having damn bureaucrats way off in Washington while we're out here, Mr. Hernandez," the bespectacled, middle-aged quartermaster had told him.

They had stopped just outside Fort Bascom for two days so the herd was rested as were the vaqueros. There was now a strong camaraderie between them all—even with Hugo Bouchard, Ramón had gratefully noticed. They wouldn't be pushing hard from here on out because both cattle and men would need all their stamina when they reached the higher ground of Colorado and the mountain range. When Joseph McCoy's courier had originally brought the news of the Colorado rancher, he had given Lucien Edmond a map of this territory, showing the next phase of the trail leading to the Trinchera Pass: the drive would go up a mesa—Goodnight Hill—then north to Blake Lake, Carrizo, Palo Blanco Arroyo, then west of the Capulin Peak to the Cimarron River, and then over the Trinchera Pass. Ramón thought to himself that it was a good thing there were plenty of watering and feeding places before the pass, because once they started climbing into the higher elevations, the cattle would need all the strength they could muster.

The final leg of the journey would be tricky, more so than anything they had yet encountered. True, the trail was broad enough and would accommodate a herd of cattle—if it were capably handled so that the animals would not take fright—but all the same, Ramón thought, it would be the first time he had ever had such difficulties to meet. He knew the importance of this drive: the money from Maxwell Grantham would give Lucien Edmond freedom to expand Windhaven Range, and Ramón's own share would let him build a larger house for Mara and the children, and give her a much-needed vacation—perhaps to New Orleans or to New York.

Ramón would spend some of his own profit to buy supplies and clothing for the abandoned Creeks in Indian Territory. He knew how much they meant to Lucien Edmond and to Lucien Edmond's martyred father, Luke. Lucien Edmond had told him how, long ago, the first Bouchard to come to the *Estados Unidos* had been befriended by the Creeks in their original home of Econchate, in Alabama, where Windhaven Plantation had been the preface to Windhaven Range. It still amazed him that he was a part of this family, united in marriage and, through his children, in blood. He had been a homeless, penniless Mexican who had been betrayed by a ruthless opportunist. Instead of patriotically fighting for his country's freedom, the man had shot him in the back and left him for dead because he refused to raid a church. Well, Ramón mused, he still loved his native country, but now his heart was inextricably tied to his beloved Mara and his new home.

During the noon meal, Ramón again consulted the map and estimated that they were now about sixty miles from the Cimarron River that flowed about twenty miles south of the pass. Since they were well ahead of schedule, he would allow them a week to reach the river and let the cattle drink their fill and graze on the plentiful grass. All in all, Ramón concluded, things were going extremely well.

But that evening, as they bedded down the cattle and prepared for dinner, there was a sudden howling of wind and a brief sandstorm. The cattle became restless, and about two hundred head ran off helter-skelter. Ramón sent a dozen of his best vaqueros, including Narciso Duarte and Felipe Sanchez, after them. It was not till midnight that the vaqueros returned, reporting that ten more heifers had been lost. Ramón swore under his breath. He hated to lose cattle, even though they allowed extra head for the inevitable losses, and he had hoped to give any of the extra head to the Creeks. Still, there was no help for it, and in the morning they would continue their journey even if the heifers were still missing.

By the next morning, the sky was clear with no sign that there had ever been a whirling, howling sandstorm. Ramón counted them lucky in not having had more of the herd stampede. Fortunately, his vaqueros were well trained and experienced, and they had kept the herd from getting too skittish. But Ramón shuddered to think that if there had been thunder and lightning, it might have been a far different story.

By the sixteenth of June they were within sight of the Cimarron River. The water was low and easy to ford, and Ramón gave the signal to begin the crossing. He could see the wide stretch of dark-green grass along the bank and for some miles beyond to the north. He could just make out, to the north, sitting like mighty sentinels, two huge outcrops of rock through which the trail passed. They seemed to act as a giant doorway to the really difficult part of the drive: the gradual ascent through winding canyons and on to the lower mountain range which would lead to Trinchera Pass. They might do well to spend three or four days here watering and grazing this prime stock before proceeding, as well as letting the men rest for the next leg of the trip. He knew from having consulted the map that about twelve miles beyond the stretch of grass, the terrain began to ascend through harsh rock formations. And on mountain ranges, there was always the danger of a boulder suddenly dislodging, which might cause an avalanche and, in turn, instigate an extremely dangerous stampede. The vaqueros would have to be their fittest and sharpest in such an event.

By midafternoon of the twenty-first of June, after Ramón and his men had let the cattle rest and water and graze to their hearts' content for four days, they had advanced another seven miles and leisurely began to seek a site for the night camp, since sunset was only a few hours off. About three miles to the northeast Ramón could clearly see the outlines of the stark precipice of rock and, just to this side of it, a forest of fir, spruce, and birch trees. If there were a storm; or a hard wind blowing down from the mountains, those trees would offer a helpful shield for the herd.

Hugo Bouchard hadn't been feeling quite as lonely, thanks to the friendship of young Tomás Maldero. Nonetheless, he had never been so bone-weary in all his young life. The shouts of Ramón and Lucas shortly after dawn to

186

waken the outfit and get them ready for breakfast and the continuation of the drive still made him groan as he opened his eyes and realized that yet another monotonous day in the saddle awaited him.

By now, he knew that he did not want to do this for the rest of his life. Yes, it was good to be accepted by the men, and not to have made too many mistakes—and better still, not to have been scolded like a baby for that stupid blunder he had made in shooting at the Gila monster. But all the same, he knew that when he returned with Ramón and Lucas, he would ask his father to let him go away to a college where he could acquire a skill, where perhaps his interest in books and languages might be turned to a profession in which he could use his inquisitive mind and his energy. Besides, he remembered how his father had spoken to Ramón of how, one day soon, there would be railroad feeder lines down into the southeastern part of Texas, so that there would no longer be any need for long, exhausting cattle drives like this one. Raising cattle, branding them, tallying them, driving them into chutes to ascend into cattle cars to be taken to the east or the west as meat for the cities and towns was definitely not an exciting profession to him, though he admitted how vital it was to the well-being of the country. He did not yet know what he wanted most to do, but what he did know most definitely was that it would not be this.

It was just after sunset; the evening was quiet, there was hardly any wind; an evening star had appeared and a bright half-moon was starting to rise in the east. Ramón had ordered his men to bed down the cattle near the trees and post six guards near them, while the cook and Francisco Lorcado hurriedly prepared supper.

Hugo Bouchard was restless. The pace today had been slow, purposely so, he understood. Ramón had gone off to confer with Lucas on how to proceed, now that they were about to travel through the rough, rugged territory that marked the beginning of the ascent through the mountain pass on their way to the rendezvous. Hugo thought glumly that it would be nearly another month before the delivery would take place, and then, even granting that the return home would be much swifter, it would certainly not be until early September that he saw his father, mother, and sisters again.

187

Today he had ridden stolidly on his docile, obedient horse, with little to do except wave his sombrero and shout at some of the more restive cattle toward the back of the large herd. Since dinner was at least half an hour away, and twilight lasted longer in this clear air, he thought that he would take a short walk through the forest. Perhaps he might find some wild berries; by now, Hugo was heartily sick of the sight of beans and bacon, salt pork and biscuits. He shouldered his carbine, thinking that perhaps he might come across a deer or a rabbit—that would certainly improve the fare. Rabbit stew or venison would be mighty appealing. After the meal, as always, there would be idle conversation, the sound of guitar music—which some of the vaqueros played to keep the herd from stirring restlessly through the night—and then exhausted sleep and a swift reveille in the morning, when the pattern of drudgery and monotony would recommence.

He walked slowly, absorbed in his own thoughts, out of sorts yet not wanting to complain to Ramón. At least he had made no more mistakes lately, but he was very lonely and still felt himself to be an outsider. He could sense the loneliness of the vaqueros around the campfire—when he overheard their conversations, talking of sweethearts or wives and their hopes and dreams for the future; but there was no consolation in it, and he refused to intrude himself: he sensed that if he did, they would listen respectfully— since he was the son of their *patrón*—but it would not be genuine, wholehearted enthusiasm. He was certain that some of them had already discussed him and hinted that the only reason a raw recruit like himself came along on this, the longest of all the Windhaven Range cattle drives, was exactly because he was Lucien Edmond Bouchard's only son.

He thought of Carla, who was a year older than himself and now really very lovely; his younger sisters, Edwina, Diane, and Gloria, promised to be equally attractive. Ruth was still an infant, but undoubtedly she too would be a beauty. It would be easy for them, even Carla; they could always marry and have families of their own. But for him, it was enervating to be out here near the boundary between New Mexico and Colorado and to know that what awaited him in the future was succeeding his father as head of Windhaven Range. He did not want it, and yet he despondently knew that he might well end up inheriting the responsibilities of the ranch from his father by virtue of the fact that he was the only son.

Distractedly, he kicked a rock in his path, and then he squatted down, his eyes wide and surprised, looking at an empty bean can. There was still some sauce inside the can, indicating that it had been opened not very long ago. That would mean that others had camped here. He thought it was important enough to tell Ramón, and so, picking up the can, he retraced his footsteps back to where his uncle stood with Lucas at the chuck wagon.

"Uncle Ramón, I found something—I thought maybe you should have a look at it," Hugo exclaimed.

"What's this, now?" Ramón turned away from Lucas and stared at the can. "That is strange, indeed. Where did you find it?"

"Just inside those trees—I went for a walk, you see. From the way it looks, Uncle Ramón," Hugo's voice firmed with his growing assurance that he had found something significant, "I'd say it was recently used, wouldn't you?"

"Why, yes" Ramón turned it over and over, examining it.

"My God!" Lucas suddenly exclaimed, slapping his palm against his forehead. "I meant to tell you, Ramón, but it seemed so insignificant at the time—"

"Tell me what, Lucas?" Ramón demanded.

"When you and Hugo were negotiating the cattle deal at Fort Sumner, a rider came into camp saying that he had come to the fort to see about trading cattle for his boss. There was something about the man that I didn't like, so I sort of suggested that we'd be going on a different route than the one we've actually taken. Like I said, I had thought of mentioning it to you, but it completely slipped my mind—"

"Never mind, Lucas. One lone rider would hardly seem threatening to anyone. Besides, we can't be sure that he has anything to do with this," Ramón placatingly told his friend. Lowering his voice, he murmured, "Hugo, go a little ways farther among the trees and see what else you can find. If there are people hiding there—no, what am I thinking of? I'll not use you as bait for a bushwhacker!"

"Do you think that's what it is, Uncle Ramón?"

"It could be, Hugo. Tell you what: Lucas, you go tell Narciso what we've been talking about. Hugo, I'll go in

189

there while you cover me. Crouch down out of sight, just beyond the trees where I go in, and keep your carbine ready to fire. In this darkness, if anyone else fires, you'll see the light from the explosion, and you can have a target to fire at and probably hit someone who's trying to kill us. I'm going to walk there very casually now, and you do the same in a moment, once you see me go in—*comprendes?*"

"Yes, Uncle Ramón." Hugo felt himself tingle with excitement as he watched the handsome Mexican leisurely walk over toward the grove of trees, and enter exactly where he had entered, for Ramón could make out the marks of his boots by the moonlight. As Ramón disappeared, Hugo walked slowly after him, then crouched down on the ground with his carbine at his shoulder and his eyes squinting along the sights.

A few moments later, Ramón came back and, a finger to his lips, gestured for his nephew to follow him back to the campfire.

"You're right about that; there've been quite a few men camping there, and not too long ago, either, judging by the horse droppings. But there aren't any signs of cattle hooves, and that means the men who camped there weren't driving cattle but were after something else. It might be us, Hugo."

"Do you—do you really think so?" Hugo's voice trembled, and a sudden apprehension mingled with his excitement at having been the one to discover the telltale can.

"It's very likely. Do you see that outcrop beyond? We're supposed to go through that gorge tomorrow. It would be a fine place for an ambush—that is, if any bushwackers are hiding up there. If that is their plan, they'll have seen us coming from a good distance; that would give them time enough to move their horses around to the other side of the gorge, where we'd not see them, and then climb the nearer side of the ridge and lie in wait for us."

"Gosh—you can tell all that?"

"Nephew," Ramón tartly muttered back, "when you've been on as many drives as I have, you learn to expect trouble and prepare for it in advance. If it doesn't happen, you thank *el Señor Dios*—if it does, then you're not taken by surprise and can defend yourself properly. I'm going to have a talk with Lucas and Narciso."

\* \* \*

On the top of the western wall of the steep precipice, a burly, red-bearded man knelt beside Jack Hayes, a telescope gripped in his pudgy hands, and squinted through it. "Tarnation!" he growled, "there's enough light by the moon to see that greaser you and Jeb want so bad—he went into the woods there, right after that tall blond kid came out of there and handed him something."

Hayes snarled, eyeing a slender, beardless brown-haired man in his late twenties. "You stupid son of a bitch! I told you to clear up all our traces! I'll bet you left an empty can lying there. Now we've tipped our hand—and like as not, that greaser'll bypass this trail and take the Raton Pass to the west. There's no help for it—what do you see there, Reuben?"

Forty-year-old Reuben Huntley, the man who was squinting through the telescope, had a price on his head in three states—Missouri, Kansas, and Nebraska—for the murder and robbery of settlers driving their wagons westward. He turned to Hayes and murmured, "The greaser's gone over to the fire, and he's talking with a nigger and one of the Mexes. They've got the wind up, no two ways about it, Jack."

"Just what I thought. All because that nosey young squirt took a notion to go into the woods there and see what he could find. Well, there's only one thing to do. They're within range, even from this distance. We'll wait a bit longer, and then we'll sling some lead at them. For sure that'll stampede the herd, and then we can pick them off as we want. Now keep down. And you, Reuben, pass the word to the others."

Ramón had had Lucas spread the news around the camp that they might be under surveillance by a band of bushwhackers, and without seeming to be alarmed, they were to get their weapons and be ready for an attack, which could come at any moment. Ramón swore under his breath: if there really was to be an ambush, the sound of gunfire would create a far worse stampede than poor Hugo's forgetful single shot. This was something he had not in the least expected on this route. He thought it strange that Joseph McCoy had not warned them of the possibility of rustlers; he knew how fiercely McCoy detested the thieves and marauders who would try to profit by violence and bloodshed against honest ranchers who had spent long months of work preparing cattle for the drive.

At that very moment, Reuben Huntley lifted his Whitworth, squinted along the sights, and pulled the trigger. Hugo Bouchard uttered a cry; only by at that same instant having leaned to one side to talk to his friend, Tomás Maldero, he had not been killed. He saw the flash and heard the whistle of the bullet. Remembering Ramón's advice, he knelt down, lifted up his carbine, and triggered it. He fired seven rounds, and a howl of pain answered that volley. One of the bullets had wounded the ruffian who had left the empty can in the woods, though it was only a minor shoulder wound, but the element of surprise was over now, and the advantage would swing to the Windhaven men.

"Take cover, vaqueros!" Ramón cried as he flung himself under one of the chuck wagons and lifted his Spencer repeating rifle. Lucas lay beside him, while Narciso and Felipe, experienced vaqueros who had gone through several attacks and did not make the mistake of panicking, placed themselves under the other chuck wagon. By tilting up their rifles, they could easily reach the top of the ridge with their superior weapons, and they waited now for the bushwhackers to reveal themselves.

Jack Hayes swore violently, as he turned to Reuben Huntley. "Of all the goddamned bad luck I ought to put that stupid bastard for leaving that can back there in the woods. Now we're stuck up here, and we can't get down."

"Take it easy, Jack. The moon gives us pretty good light, and we can pick them off. Remember how much Jeb Cornish wants that herd and the greaser's scalp," the red-bearded outlaw counseled him. Then, leaning forward, peering just over the rim of a boulder at the top of the outcrop, he triggered four shots down toward the vaqueros, in the vicinity of the campfire, which still burned brightly.

The crashing sounds of rifle and carbine fire, reverberating within the gorge itself, aroused the drowsing cattle, and the high-pitched bellows punctuated the sound of further gunfire, as the bushwhackers poured down a furious fire at their intended victims. Now the herd began to run pell-mell in every direction, lowing and bleating till the night was filled with the sounds cowhands dread the most: that of a herd in frenzy. One of the yearlings went down, a stray bullet from the top of the canyon wounding it. Its companions, hardly noticing, trampled over its shuddering body as they rushed onward through the night.

"There goes a week's worth at least," Ramón muttered to Lucas, "and you can add as much time to that as it'll take us to beat off this attack. Who the devil are these men? I've heard about outlaws in the Panhandle, but I hadn't thought we'd find them so near Colorado." Then, a sudden thought assailed him: "Where's Hugo?" Cupping one hand to his mouth, he called out, "Hugo, get down beside me under the wagon, *pronto!*"

Hugo Bouchard had crouched beside the nearest wagon wheel; he now scrambled toward his uncle and flattened himself alongside Ramón, his heart pounding wildly as he reloaded his carbine.

"I think you hit one of them, Hugo. Good man! That showed them we were ready for them."

"I—I've never shot a man before, Uncle Ramón. I—I hope I didn't kill him—" Hugo quavered, suddenly feeling queasy in the pit of his stomach.

"You can't think about such things, Hugo," Ramón instantly reproved him. "You certainly don't think it bothers them if they shoot and kill you, do you? There is no law out here to guard us. We are out in land where no one patrols except the vaqueros of the owner, as happened with that rancher who had us driven off his property. Those men would have thought nothing of shooting first and asking questions later. We were lucky. Just keep down and don't show anything of yourself, Hugo."

"The cattle—" the youth began.

The whine of a rifle bullet as it dug into the ground near Ramón interrupted his answer to his nephew. Seeing the flash above, he aimed his carbine and squeezed the trigger. There was a wild yell, as one of the outlaws straightened, then pitched forward, falling into the bottom of the gorge three hundred fifty feet below. "The cattle, *amigo*," Ramón muttered, "will have to wait until we settle this matter. *Madre de Dios*, I think there are as many of them as there are of us, and they have good guns, too. It's a good thing you found that can and told me about it, or many of our vaqueros might have been killed before we had a chance to defend ourselves."

"Th—thanks, Uncle Ramón," Hugo murmured as he huddled himself under the wagon.

The Windhaven Range vaqueros had taken what cover

they could, piling their bedrolls and blankets into makeshift parapets in front of them. Crouching behind them with their rifles and carbines pressed along the top, they waited for further gunfire from the top of the canyon before returning fire. The cook and Francisco Lorcado lay under the other chuck wagon, with Tomás Maldero, Hugo's friend, beside them. They all depended on the directions they would receive from Narciso and Felipe, for none of the three had ever experienced an attack on the trail. By now there was no sign of the herd, which had scattered in every direction after the first volleys. Then a sudden gusting wind stirred the gritty soil, and some of the vaqueros turned their faces away and closed their eyes, remembering the violent sandstorm they had earlier encountered.

High on the top of the ridge Jack Hayes muttered to Reuben Huntley, "This is a Mex standoff, seems like to me. Look, the moon is getting hidden by those clouds blowing in from the northwest. Whyn't we have some of the boys scoot down to their horses and charge the damn greaser and his cowhands?"

"Not a bad idea, Jack. Might take them by surprise. I'll go talk to Nate Tandy—he bosses about a dozen of Jeb's reg'lars. If he thinks it's all right, we'll try it. Us and the others, we'll cover them by rapid gunfire down on those bastards!" With this, Huntley carefully rose to his feet and, stooping so as to minimize himself as a target from below, scudded along the ledge of the summit, and bent to a heavy-set, brown-bearded man in his mid-thirties, whose squinty-eyed image graced many a sketched "wanted" poster in the offices of sheriffs and postmasters throughout Kansas and Nebraska. "Nate, how'd it be if you took your boys in on horseback and went in shooting? Jack and the rest of us, we'll keep them busy dodging the lead we'll sling down at 'em."

"Sounds good to me—I want some action. Otherwise, we'll be the targets up here, come dawn. We've lost two men already, you know. Damn good men—and damn lucky shooting, I'd say. But I think we've at least evened the score down below, with all the lead we've been sending them! Okay, then. Just you have Jack and the rest of the gang primed and ready the minute we come out on horseback 'round the side."

"Good as done, Nate."

During this discussion between the outlaw leaders, the

194

firing of their men from the top of the plateau had slackened, and Ramón murmured to Lucas, "They're up to something, sure as you're born. I'm sure they're going to try a sudden attack to take us by surprise."

"How do you think they will do that?" Lucas queried.

"They must have their horses around the east side of the gorge, which we can't see from here," Ramón speculated. "My guess is that some of their men will climb down to their horses and come charging us. Can you get word to Narciso? He'll pass it along to the others."

"Right away," Lucas nodded, and began to crawl slowly out from his shelter and toward the other chuck wagon. Lucas scrambled behind it and quickly relayed Ramón's message. Narciso nodded, and then called softly in Spanish to about a dozen of the vaqueros who were over to his left, crouching behind their piled bedrolls and blankets: "Be ready, *amigos*! I think they're going to charge us! Don't waste ammunition. Let them come as close as they can, and then *muerte a los bandidos—todos!*"

A dozen of the outlaws had reached their horses on the other side of the rocky spire; mounted, armed with rifles and carbines and crouching low, riding Indian style, they awaited Nate Tandy's signal. He raised his arm, and the dozen riders swept forward in a galloping arc toward the campsite.

The moon, which had been completely obscured for the last half hour, suddenly broke through its shield of clouds, just as the bushwhackers reached the fringe of the campsite. They fired at whatever targets they could see, but hardly had they triggered their first shots when a withering volley from behind the impoverished parapets answered them. Four of the men tumbled off their horses and lay sprawled, dead, while another, mortally wounded, pitched from his saddle with his foot caught in the stirrup. Dragged by his frenzied mustang, he expired a few moments later. Two others of that dozen were wounded, but managed to gallop their horses past the camp.

Yet in return, three of the vaqueros were left dead or dying, including Tomás Maldero. The young vaquero had moved out from under the chuck wagon as the riders swept by and had shot down one of them, when a companion, seeing the flash of the carbine, aimed his own rifle and took Tomás squarely in the forehead with his bullet.

Hugo Bouchard—trembling with mingled fear and ex-

citement as the riders swept down on the waiting camp—
heard the thunder of gunfire next to him and beyond him,
and warily peered out from under the chuck wagon, trig-
gering his carbine. The light of the moon allowed him to
see a squat rider stiffen in the saddle, throw his hands in
the air, dropping his rifle to the ground, roll over once, and
lay still. He did not know that this was the bushwhacker
who had just ended the life of his friend, Tomás Maldero—yet he did know that this time he had killed a man.
He uttered a heartfelt groan, closed his eyes, turned his
head to one side, and retched. But the battle continued to
rage around him; the spang of a rifle bullet that thudded
against the rim of the chuck wagon a few inches above his
head abruptly recalled him to the terrifying reality in
which he was unwillingly involved.

At the top of the canyon the remaining bushwhackers,
forsaking caution, rose to their full height and, peering
down, aimed their rifles and carbines at the dark piles of
bedrolls and blankets that the vaqueros had put up for protection. Ramón caught one clearly in the sights of his Spencer rifle and squeezed the trigger. The man fell backwards
and disappeared, and Ramón sniggered grimly as he
turned to Lucas and muttered, "I shall say my prayers of
thanks to *el Señor Dios* for making the moon bright when
they came down upon us. Even so, I'm afraid we lost some
good vaqueros whom we shall mourn for a long time." And
then, as a bullet bit into the base of the chuck wagon above
his own head, he ducked, uttering a Spanish profanity.

Five riders out of the dozen who had circled the other
side of the canyon on horseback and attacked had survived
the accurate fire of the vaqueros. These included Nate
Tandy himself, who reined in his foaming horse well beyond the camp, deep inside the ravine. He glowered up at
his companions ensconced at the peak, then shook his rifle
at them. The other four men clustered around him, soothing their frightened horses, swearing volubly under their
breaths. One of them was a hunchback named Alejandro
Bensares, who had murdered his faithless sweetheart in
Durango, and then killed one of the *federales* sent to fetch
him to prison. Fleeing across the border, he had made his
way to Dodge City to join Jeb Cornish's renegade band.
Now he leaned toward Nate Tandy and swore, "*Por los
cojones del diablo,* where did those *gringos* learn to shoot
like that?"

"They're vaqueros, and many of them are greasers," Tandy growled back, at which the hunchback's eyes angrily narrowed, and he vituperatively retorted, "Say that again to me, Señor Tandy, and I'll cut off your *cojones* with my knife—I swear it by the Virgin of Guadalupe!"

"Shut your mouth, Alejandro, there's work to be done. Are we going to let these cowhands get away from us? Don't forget all the *dinero* Jeb Cornish promised," Tandy replied.

"It is not enough for which to sacrifice our lives, Señor Tandy! I for one have had enough. We came upon them at point-blank range, and yet they killed more of us than we did of them. *La suerte es mala*, I say, and I ride back to Dodge!" With this, he wheeled his mustang eastward and began to ride off from the battle scene. With a sadistic grimace, Tandy steadied his horse, squinted along his rifle, and pulled the trigger. The hunchback bent forward over the neck of his mustang, his own gun dropping to the ground. As the horse began to bolt, his body slipped to one side and fell, sprawled on the ground.

"Ain't no cowards in my outfit, boys. Now how do you feel about it? Do we go back and finish them off?" he demanded of the other three unscathed bandits. They eyed one another, philosophically shrugged, and then one of them reluctantly muttered, "It's worth a try, Nate. If we give up, we'll have nothing to show for all this except a damn long ride, the waiting, and our dead pals."

"Right. You follow me and we'll use up all our ammo—taking some of them to hell with us!" Tandy exclaimed defiantly. He leaned over the neck of his horse and patted it, then he nodded to the trio. Spurring their horses, they rode back Indian style, directing their horses with their knees. While one of them drew out his two holstered Colts and began to empty them at what targets he could see, each of his two companions fired a rifle with one hand and a Colt revolver with the other; Tandy contented himself with his repeating rifle.

Two vaqueros went down before this stubborn attack, but the man with the two Colts was hit almost as he fired his first rounds, a mortal wound in the chest, and he fell off his horse and lay groaning with agony as the three other men rode back toward the mouth of the ravine.

Nate Tandy's rifle accounted for still another vaquero, before Lucas's well-aimed shot took him at the base of the spine and left him sprawled over his horse's neck, paralyzed, dying. The two other bushwhackers kept firing till their ammunition was exhausted. One of them nearly hit Felipe; he could feel the wind from the bullet as it whizzed past his left ear, but he stood his ground, coolly leveled his Spencer carbine and killed the man who had almost killed him. Narciso shot down the other.

Now there was a silence around the campsite and from the pass. High above, the survivors, led by Jack Hayes and Reuben Huntley, swore furiously. "We're done for!" Hayes panted as he reloaded his weapon. "We've gotta get back to Jeb. Maybe he'll send us back with more men to take care of that goddamned lucky greaser. We had them right in our trap, and we let them get away. Hell's fire, Reuben, let's get down to our horses and head for Dodge, before they take a notion to ride after us."

"Damn right, Jack." Huntley turned and gestured to the other men crouching behind boulders at the peak. "Let's get out of here!"

They scrambled down, ran toward their waiting horses tethered far to the east of the pass, mounted, and rode off.

Ramón waited, till the stillness grew oppressive. "Wait," he cautioned Lucas, "it might be a trap. But I think they've lost too many men, and they've probably decided that we're too strong for them. Let's hope so, anyway."

"Well, we'll wait till you give the word, but we'd best have the men start after those cattle, I'm thinking," Lucas rseponded glumly.

"You know, I completely forgot about them the last half hour." Ramón Hernandez uttered a dry chuckle. "But you're right—the work of getting them back is going to be much more of a problem than fighting off these thieves. I still wish I knew who they were."

Then he turned to Hugo Bouchard, who lay trembling, pale, and spent. Ramón reached out to put an arm around the youth's shoulders. *"Bueno, hombre,"* he muttered. "Your father would be proud of you. I saw you bring down that one rider after he'd fired at us."

Lucas had crawled toward the other chuck wagon and learned from Francisco Lorcado the tragic news of young Tomás's death. He moved closer to Ramón and whispered in the latter's ear. Lucien Edmond's brother-in-law stifled a groan, then turned to Hugo: "I have bad news for you, *mi compañero*. The young vaquero, Tomás, was killed when

198

those men rode on us. Rest assured, he died bravely and without pain. He died fighting for you and for me, Hugo. I know how much you liked him. Lucas and I will help you bury him while most of the men go round up the cattle. And you'll go along, too—"

"Oh, my God, no, Uncle Ramón, don't make me! I—I—oh, God—he was so young—so kind and friendly—oh, my God—" Hugo burst into hysterical sobs and covered his face with his hands.

Ramón said nothing, but put his arm around the youth's shoulders and tightened his grip. Finally, he said softly, "Yes, you'll ride after the cattle, Hugo. It'll be good for you. Go ahead and cry. You are not less of a man because you do—not when you mourn a friend."

"But—but why couldn't anyone do anything for him—Uncle Ramón?"

"There was no time to do anything except survive. You will remember only that when you were with Tomás, it was good. That is the way it was meant to be between men who meet driving cattle to market. Come on, stand up. Go have some coffee—there's still some left, and it's bitter enough to wake you up. And don't feel sorry for yourself, or for Tomás. He had no pain, and he died knowing you were friends fighting together."

Hugo took a handkerchief and loudly blew his nose. Then he stared deliberately at Ramón and finally blurted, "I'm glad you let me come with you on this drive, Uncle Ramón."

"I know, nephew. But I've a feeling you won't be on any more. Now go drink that coffee, and then go with Narciso and Felipe and the others while we begin the very sad duty of burying our comrades. There's nothing like doing a job when it has to be done—even when your guts tell you you don't want to do it—to make you forget about Tomás."

## Eighteen

The toll was heavy in the victory over Jeb Cornish's bush-whackers: six Windhaven Range vaqueros had been killed and three wounded, one of them having taken a bullet deep in the shoulder. Ramón improvised a bed in one of the chuck wagons for the badly wounded man, and applied a tourniquet to stop the bleeding.

Ramón, Lucas, and three other vaqueros buried the men who had given their lives to protect the herd, and left markers with their names cut into the wood. Because the cook had been killed, the easygoing Francisco Lorcado was pressed into service to replace him, and, though grumbling, he swiftly prepared a breakfast of flapjacks, bacon, and coffee. Several of the vaqueros had already ridden back with a few hundred head of the stampeded herd that they had found only a few miles away.

These men reported that the rest of the herd seemed to have scattered many miles in several directions, and Ramón sighed heavily, realizing that it might take at least a week before most of the cattle could be rounded up to be driven on to the rendezvous with Maxwell Grantham.

Although convinced that the rest of the bushwhackers had long since ridden off, Ramón armed himself with a loaded Spencer repeating rifle and warily rode around the base of the outcropping. The marks of many horses' hooves told him what he had already suspected. In the ravine it-self, he could see the bodies of three dead bushwhackers who had fallen from the peak to the dusty ground. Having already counted the bodies of those who had ridden against the camp, he estimated that these would-be cattle thieves had lost at least fifteen men; perhaps a few more bodies were up on the ledge, and probably several of the survivors had been wounded.

The sun was out, the sky was cloudless, and there was a gentle stillness to this arena of death and violence. As he rode back and stared at the markers of those loyal men whom he had counted as friends as much as *trabajadores,* he reverently crossed himself and sadly thought that he would much rather have had not a single vaquero killed: it was a hollow victory indeed. The men from Windhaven Range had loyally followed him all the way from the Nueces River to find dusty graves here, far from their original homes and from the camaraderie of the Windhaven Range bunkhouses, where they had forged lasting friendships with compassionate understanding of one another.

Disconsolately, he rode back to the chuck wagon where Francisco Lorcado was feverishly putting more flapjacks on the stove and heating more bacon in the skillet. Lucas was standing by, eating a quick breakfast with his fingers from a tin plate.

"Well, Lucas, we might as well prepare to move out and go slowly, till the other men catch up with us with the rest of the herd," Ramón wearily declared.

"Yes. I suppose so, Ramón. What about Manuel Olivera?" Lucas glanced over at the chuck wagon in which the wounded vaquero lay.

"I know. That bullet has to come out. It may have shattered the bone. But I'll need help, and besides, the bleeding has stopped for the time being. I don't want to hurry the business of digging out that bullet."

"Yes, that's true, Ramón." Lucas shook his head and took a swig of his coffee. "You must realize, I'm sure, that those men were lying in wait for us."

"I've figured that already. The question is, who they were and who sent them."

"Maybe," Lucas shrewdly hazarded, "it was somebody you riled in Dodge the last time we drove cattle to Kansas."

"*Por Dios,* that may be it indeed! *Sí, por supuesto—*" Ramón clapped a hand to his forehead and shook his head. "That agent for the *indios,* that fat man who began by calling me a greaser—it very well might be him. Remember that business in the saloon, when that *gringa linda* came to me with a story that her *patrón* was cruel to her and that she wished help? It begins to make sense, Lucas. Of course, there's no proof; I looked at the men we killed, and I don't recognize a single one of them. But it would be easy

201

enough to hire a gang. All the same, it's a long shot—how would they have known we were going up to Colorado this way instead of to the usual Kansas markets? Unless, of course, that rider you mentioned works for Cornish. Oh, well—anything is possible, I suppose."

Lucas glumly shook his head and finished his coffee. Ramón turned, hearing the sound of horses' hooves, and brightened. "It's Hugo and some of the other vaqueros! And they've got some more of the cattle!" He hurried out to meet the riders.

Young Hugo Bouchard's face was begrimed, and lines of fatigue made him look far older than his eighteen years. His shoulders slumped as he sat in the saddle, and he was breathing hard. Narciso, who had ridden with him, energetically exclaimed, "*Patrón, este vaquero joven es muy bueno*. He rode ahead of us, and he saw many of the yearlings off to the west and pointed them out to us. Some vaqueros are going north and others east, for that is where the rest of the herd ran to. They have gained many miles through *la noche,* of course, but we will find them, do not fear, *patrón*."

"That's good news; *gracias,* Narciso. Come get some breakfast, you and your men. Lucas, I'd be obliged if you'd round those cattle they brought back into the line with the others and soothe them as much as you can—though I think by now they're too worn out to want to run off again," Ramón instructed.

As Hugo slowly and laboriously eased down from his saddle and stood leaning a moment against his horse, fatigue written in every slumping part of his body and on his haggard, dirty face, Ramón came to him and squeezed his hand in a hard grip. "I'm proud of you, nephew. Come get some breakfast now—and then you're to ride in the chuck wagon with Manuel Olivera. He had bad luck—he took a bullet in the shoulder, and it must come out when we've time."

"I—I'll be glad to help him all I can. And—and I'd like to help—that is, when you're ready to take the bullet out, Uncle Ramón," Hugo volunteered.

"I'll hold you to that, *mi compañero.* Now you go get some breakfast, and that's an order!"

"Yes, Uncle Ramón." Hugo tried to straighten his shoulders. He looked at the handsome Mexican trail boss and then, his eyes suddenly filling with tears, stammered, "I—I want to help Manuel. I want to do it for Tomás. Do you understand that, Uncle Ramón?"

"Yes, *mi compañero,* I understand it very well, and your father would understand it, too. As Narciso said, you are now a vaquero. You have earned your spurs. No one in my hearing will ever say that you are too young, or because you are the son of *el gran patrón* you are being given favors." Then, in a gentler tone and with a smile, "But you know, a vaquero must obey the trail boss. Go to the chuck wagon and eat well, then sit with Manuel and comfort him."

Three days later, a dozen of the Windhaven Range vaqueros caught up with the drive, herding some eleven hundred head out of the stampeded herd. The other *trabajadores* were still in pursuit of the rest, fulfilling Ramón's gloomy prediction that it would take at least a week to reassemble the stock destined for sale to the Wyoming rancher.

By evening of the third day, Manuel Olivera was feverish from his shoulder wound, and Ramón decided that the removal of the bullet could wait no longer. He and Lucas clambered into the chuck wagon and knelt beside the wounded vaquero, who lay with two heavy blankets under him to ease the hardness of the wooden floor and the wooden pallet.

"It's time, Manuel," Ramón said in Spanish. "If I don't take the bullet out now, your fever will get worse. We need you back with us, my friend."

Manuel lifted his head and faintly murmured, "*Comprendo, patrón.* I am ready. Let me say a prayer first, that I will live to see my sweetheart in Chihuahua once again."

"You will do better than that, *amigo,*" Ramón smilingly responded. "When we get back, we will send for her, and then Friar Bartoloméo will marry you both in our church."

A wan smile curved the vaquero's trembling, cracked lips, and his eyes brightened. Then he lay back and closed them, murmuring, "I am ready. I will pray while you take the bullet out. Do you think it will hurt very much?"

"Yes, *amigo,* but you will drink all the tequila you can to deaden the pain." Ramón turned to Lucas and said, "In my saddlebag you will find a bottle of tequila. Please bring it to me."

Ramón had already sterilized his sharp hunting knife by

holding the blade over the noontime cooking fire. He eyed Hugo. "This will not be a pleasant sight, *mi sobrino*. I will understand if you do not wish to watch this."

"But I do, Uncle Ramón," Hugo protested. "I want to help. I told you I want to do it because of my friend Tomás."

"Very well." Ramón gave him an admiring smile. "Then you will do exactly what I tell you to do. Ah, here is the tequila. Now then, Manuel, I will pour it into a cup, and Hugo will put his arm around your shoulders and lift you up gently so that you may drink your fill."

Manuel sighed and nodded. Hugo knelt beside the wounded man and, an arm around his shoulders, gently lifted him up as Ramón held the cup to his lips. The vaquero drank thirstily, then smacked his lips. *"Es bueno, muy bueno; gracias."*

"You will need more than that. Drink, *amigo*," Ramón urged.

After four cupfuls, Manuel's eyes blinked and then drowsily closed, and he began to mumble incoherent words. Ramón shot Hugo a pleased look. "That's exactly what I wanted. Now then, Hugo, can you take hold of his wrists and hold them very tightly? He must not break away from you, *comprendes?*" The youth nodded. "Lucas, once I have removed the bullet, the wound will need cauterizing. Run out to the campfire and—here, take this skillet. Put a burning twig into it so I can heat my knife." Lucas did as he was told and then Ramón directed him to hold the numbed man's legs. "It is all we have here; we cannot wait for any *médico* to tell me if I have done right or wrong."

Hugo took the wounded man's wrists in his strong young hands and gripped them firmly. Very gently, Ramón lifted away the temporary bandage he had applied, exposing the ugly wound. He took a deep breath, murmured a silent prayer, and then began to probe for the bullet. The vaquero arched and shuddered, moaning, *"Jesús María,"* but the tequila had deadened his nerves, so that his struggles were feeble. Suddenly his head turned to one side and he lay still. Ramón anxiously felt for his heartbeat, then sighed with relief. *"Bueno.* He has fainted. It is the best thing for him. And I can see the bullet. Manuel will live to marry his sweetheart in the blessed church at Windhaven Range, I am quite certain, if the help of the good God will keep me from blundering now!"

"Uncle Ramón," Hugo broke in, "shouldn't you make some sutures with a needle and thread? That will keep the wound from reopening and bleeding and also speed the healing process."

The handsome Mexican gave his nephew a startled look. *"Por Dios,"* he ejaculated. "How do you know that, *amigo?"*

"Because I've read all the books in Pa's library, and some of them are about medicine and operations. Why don't I get a needle and a spool of thread and bring it to you now? You will see what to do. Maybe I can help a little."

"That's a good idea. All right, then. Lucas, you don't have to hold his legs anymore, he's fainted. So stanch the flow of blood with those clothes you have there—ah, I have got hold of the bullet. Hurry, Hugo!"

The youth scrambled out of the chuck wagon, hurried to his horse, and rifled through his saddlebag. Before he had left, Maxine had given him a sewing kit, telling him, as a solicitous mother might well do, "In case you have to do any patching of your britches or your coat, you'll find some very strong, coarse thread in there, and it will hold till you can get back."

He hurried back with a spool of thick black thread and a needle and handed them to Ramón. *"Gracias, mi compañero.* Here is the bullet—it is good luck for Manuel that it did not shatter the bone. It lodged very close to it, but the danger is now over, so far as I can tell. Still, he has lost a lot of blood. Now then, Lucas, hand me the skillet." The smell of burning flesh filled the chuckwagon, and Lucas had to fight to keep from retching. He quickly threaded the needle and handed it to Ramón.

*"¡Bueno!* Now, since you have become a self-appointed *médico,* Hugo, you will please tell me what I should do now?" Ramón directed.

"Of course. Right there, do you see that strip of mangled flesh near the bone? Sew it to the other part—there," Hugo pointed with his forefinger, and Ramón nodded.

Fifteen minutes later, Ramón had finished closing the wound. Manuel Olivera, though still unconscious, uttered a faint moan.

"He will have a bad scar, but to be sure, it is a lot better than losing his arm or dying." Ramón sighed exhaustedly. "You will stay with him, Hugo?"

"Of course. And, when he comes to, maybe Francisco can make a strong broth. If there's any stew left, the juices of that—"

"¡Caramba!" Ramón admiringly chuckled. "All of a sudden we have a doctor in our midst." His face sobered. "But that is very good. And Manuel will be the first to thank you. Considering that there is no hospital around here for who knows how many miles, it is fortunate that you remembered something out of all your reading, my nephew."

"I—I'm glad I could be of some use. I only wish—I wish poor Tomás were still alive." Hugo's voice was unsteady and he looked away, blinking his eyes to clear them of the sudden tears.

"His spirit knows how you valued his friendship, my nephew." Ramón's voice was strangely tender. "I think that, in spite of our bad luck with the stampede and the loss of those good men, we have gained something very valuable in you. Truly you are *mi compañero*. I salute you."

Despite Ramón's optimistic hope that the rest of the stampeded herd would be recovered within a week, it was actually ten days after the attack by Jack Hayes and his bushwhackers that the exhausted vaqueros drove back the last of the equally exhausted cattle. When a final tally was made, Ramón was distressed to find that two hundred fifty-three bulls and cows were missing. His riders had pointed out that it would be well-nigh futile to continue searching for them, for they had had too good a start. Besides, many might have actually died if, as was suspected, they had veered west and found themselves in higher, rocky terrain with little water.

Disconsolately, Ramón ordered the drive to be contin-ued. The worst part of the trail now lay ahead of them: the ascent across the lofty and dangerous Trinchera Pass. Thereafter, the trail would descend, as they traveled north-ward toward their rendezvous with Maxwell Grantham at the fork of the Apishapa and Arkansas rivers, about forty miles east of Pueblo.

Grantham's telegraph wire to Lucien Edmond Bouchard had proposed that the rendezvous take place in July—but it had not specified an actual date. Ramón estimated that with good luck, which included stable weather, he and his

206

men could still reach the appointed meeting place by about the twentieth of the month. "This is what we'll aim for, *hombres*," he told his vaqueros when they had made camp that next evening and awaited the evening meal. "It's slower going from here on for the cattle, yet we still must try to get from eight to ten miles a day, without pushing them too hard. There won't be much grazing grass or water along the trail. Trinchera Pass will take some doing, but if we can manage it, we'll have a rich reward for all of you and for the *patrón*."

Francisco Lorcado, now pressed into constant service as the "Maria" of the outfit, had swiftly adapted himself to necessity—as well as to the stern discipline Ramón imposed in his capacity as trail boss. Lucien Edmond's brother-in-law, still mourning the death of his vaqueros, was in no mood to tolerate excuses or complaints about the extra amount of work the assistant cook was obliged to do because his predecessor had unluckily taken a bullet during the attack. Lucas, however, volunteered to help the amiable, easygoing Mexican, and between the efforts of the two of them, the vaqueros were well fed. Lucas himself shot a mountain goat and ordered the men to slaughter the last two steers, so their diet was enhanced with fresh meat—a well-deserved and much-needed supplement after the exhausting ordeal they had been through. One noon when they paused for lunch, two of the vaqueros came across patches of wild blackberries, and Francisco was able to bake tasty pies that night, which cheered the spirits of the exhausted crew.

Hugo had remained all this time with Manuel Olivera in the improvised hospital wagon, but by the time the vaqueros had caught up and they reassembled the herd, Manuel was up and about and riding his horse to ascertain the degree of convalescence. To his great delight, the vaquero found that he could move his arm without excessive pain and that, apart from loss of weight and understandable weakness after receiving his wound and after the crude operation Ramón had performed, he was in excellent health.

On the night when Francisco served the blackberry pies, Manuel strode up to the chuck wagon and blusteringly demanded a whole pie. "You're out of your mind, *hombre*," the cook indignantly told him. "Just because you rode in my wagon like a millionaire who takes one of those newfangled trains, you have no right to be so greedy. Shame on

207

you, Manuel Olivera! If I give you a whole pie, many of your *compañeros* will go without it."

"Oh, no, *amigo*," the vaquero grinned. "It's not for me—I wish to give most of it to our young *médico*. I know that it was he who helped save my life, and I wish before all the vaqueros to express my thanks and also to say that he is *muy macho*. He is not a boy now, he is a man. And if it had not been for him, I might not be here to ask this pie of you, Francisco Lorcado."

Some of the nearby vaqueros who had heard this interchange began to laugh and then to cheer and to echo in chorus, "Give the pie to the son of the *patrón. ¡Es muy macho, gran vaquero!*" At last, Francisco capitulated, shrugging and rolling his eyes heavenwards to indicate that he was helpless before such acclamation.

Manuel took the pie and strode to where young Hugo Bouchard was sitting beside his bedroll, finishing his beef and beans. "I have brought you a present, Señor Hugo," Manuel declared, as he squatted down and handed the pie to the startled youth. "All of us wish to thank you for the help you have been to us on this drive, and I especially, whose life you saved."

"But I only did what had to be done. I don't need any thanks—I can't eat all this pie, either," he laughed. "Please, Manuel, you have to share this with me and with your friends, as well."

"Very well, then, but you shall have the biggest piece. Here, I will cut it and put it on your plate—there you are! And now, if I may have the privilege of sitting next to the *médico joven*, I shall enjoy the pie even more!"

Ramón had watched this badinage with growing amusement and, at the same time, great pleasure in knowing that his young nephew was being so enthusiastically accepted by these weather-beaten, hardworking vaqueros. He could sense, too, how lonely Hugo Bouchard had been during his formative years, having had few close friends. For the children of the vaqueros, knowing the status of their parents as *trabajadores,* did not dream of socializing with the son of the *patrón.* Even though Lucien Edmond openly encouraged a warm friendship between his family and the *trabajadores,* the men had been inhibited by centuries of tradition into "knowing their place," and did not take the *patrón* completely at his word. That was why, in Ramón's opinion, Hugo's experiences on the drive would be of inestimable value in helping him find himself and be able to relate to others from vastly different circumstances than his own, enabling him to channel his abilities and natural attributes into the life that was truly destined for him.

Hugo had felt exhilarated by having his rudimentary medical skills be of such aid to the genial vaquero, and it had eased his grief over the loss of his friend, Tomás. He had also asked Ramón to let him help Francisco, and his uncle readily gave him permission. The men they had lost could not be replaced now, which meant that those who were left had extra chores to assume. And teamwork was now more vital than ever, if they were not to risk reaching the appointed rendezvous late and perhaps finding that Maxwell Grantham had given up and gone back to Wyoming.

Hugo realized that the contrast between the monotony of the drive and the excitement he felt when he took part in the battle against the bushwhackers and then helped with Manuel Olivera's operation had become enormously emphasized. He knew with a mature finality now that, when he got back to Windhaven Range, he would tell his father that he did not want to inherit the range, or to do what Ramón did. Yet conversely, he had come to admire his uncle even more: realizing the thousand and one details for which Ramón was responsible and seeing the handsome Mexican's patience and common sense displayed during the most adverse circumstances had shown Hugo a side of his uncle that he had not actually realized during his time on Windhaven Range. How far all this was from the studies he had pursued in the books in his father's library! And yet, he was grateful for it: without having come on this drive, his values and his judgments of people would have been simply book values and judgments, without real substance. Now he began to learn for himself how to think and how to appraise. He felt very grateful and, at the same time, very humble.

## Nineteen

On the first of July, the Bouchard outfit reached the Trinchera Pass, the highest elevation on the trail. The weather was warm, but the evenings were cool because of the increased altitude. There had been no further trouble, and Ramón had seen no sign of any other riders since the bushwhacking.

Negotiating the mountain trail required experience and patience, for the cattle were obliged to pass in double file, rather than in their customary mass. The lead vaqueros rode the most surefooted horses out of the remuda, ones Ramón himself knew and recommended to them, mature horses that had been on several previous drives and could be relied upon for steadiness. If a horse grew skittish here on this narrow pass and veered too far to the right, he could unseat his rider and send him hurtling down to the rocks below.

Manuel Olivera sought to prove to his comrades that the time he had been forced to spend convalescing from his wound while the others toiled from sunup to sundown in no way lessened his skill as a handler of cattle. Hugo, with Ramón's approval, stayed with the chuck wagon to help Francisco Lorcado. There was no need to venture the youth's safety—inexperienced as he was—on a narrow mountain pass where there was room at most for two riders and two head of cattle abreast at one time. Toward the end, the trail would broaden, but they would still be miles away from completing the hazardous transition from mountain pass to level ground. Then the trail would take them northward across the Purgatoire River and past the famous Apishapa Ranch. After that, it would be a matter of a week at most to reach the rendezvous agreed upon by Maxwell Grantham.

On the next to the last day through the pass, the morning showed a sullen, darkening sky, which caused Ramón no little perturbation. So far, they had been fortunate that the weather had been clear, with no outbursts of rain or wind. Even so, knowing that a sudden and unexpected noise, like the breaking of a tree branch, or the clanging of Francisco Lorcado's skillet could set the entire herd into maddened, unreasoning flight, Ramón invariably said silent prayers that all would continue to go well.

He was first at the chuck wagon to hurry his breakfast of bacon and biscuits and coffee, and turned to Lucas, who stood beside him. "We'd best have the men eat as quickly as possible, Lucas—I don't like the looks of that sky. I pray *el Señor Dios* will not send lightning and thunder, or at least He will wait till we reach the end of the pass and come down to broad stretches of ground. I do not want to lose any more of this herd, or Señor Grantham will think that Lucien Edmond Bouchard is not a good businessman and cannot be relied upon to keep a contract."

"If this Mr. Grantham is a working rancher, Ramón," Lucas assured him, "he'll understand what we've been through. Myself, I think we were awfully lucky not to lose more head then we did after that bushwhacker attack. And what we've got left has grazed and watered very well; the animals are fat and in good spirits and very strong. If he knows ranching, he'll recognize prime quality."

"I say that to myself, Lucas," Ramón wryly responded. "All the same, I shall be much happier by tomorrow night, when we can make camp—if God so wills—on level ground, without worrying about falling off the cliffs in our sleep."

The vaqueros took only a few minutes for a token breakfast, and then began to move the herd. Waving their sombreros, calling out gently but not urgently, they set the huge processional in its ponderous, inexorable move forward. In double file, the herd moved onward in a slow, measured gait while the vaqueros nervously glanced up at the sky and muttered prayers under their breath. Francisco Lorcado drove the lead chuck wagon, while Hugo rode in the second. The lumbering wagons were sent on ahead of the herd to find a spot to make camp and set up the makeshift rope corral of the remuda.

By noon, it seemed to brighten somewhat, but by two

o'clock in the afternoon, the sky grew darker than ever, and there was the sudden rush of oncoming wind. Ramón swore under his breath and crossed himself, looking back to see how the herd was following. Narciso Duarte and Felipe Sanchez, riding point on each side behind him, came up at his signal to confer.

"I can only hope there won't be thunder, *amigo*," Ramón told them. "Somehow we'll have to keep them from sharply turning to the right and keep them away from the edge. Look down below—there's nothing but a wide, deep ravine. If a man should fall, all the trees and shrubbery in the way would save his life—but that wouldn't help the *ganado*. Keep them moving, and gentle them all you can. If we can only have another two or three hours before the storm—there's sure to be a wider stretch up ahead on that hilly spot. Do you see it, where those pine trees are?"

"That's four miles away at least, *patrón*," Narciso replied as he peered northward, cupping a hand over his eyes and squinting. "The air is so pure, it might even be farther than that. But as you say, if we can get the herd there in time and make camp, all will be well."

They moved on another hour, and then, without warning, there was a sudden peal of thunder, and the sky grew darker still. The cattle began to low and to mill nervously, those behind the leaders nudging forward, trying to quicken their footsteps, fearful of the wind and of the sound of thunder.

"Careful now!" Ramón shouted to his vaqueros. "Gentle them, ease them, talk to them—anything! We're in for a storm. May the good God save us all and guide us for just a little longer, I ask only that!"

There was another clap of thunder and the wind suddenly swirled, blowing dust into the riders' eyes. They hastily donned their bandannas as masks over their noses and mouths, blinking their eyes repeatedly to clear them, and continued to call out in soothing tones to the restless herd.

The wind grew louder, with a mournful, keening sound. Ramón, ahead of all of them and coming to a sudden broadening at the right of the trail, rode his horse onto that vantage point so that he could supervise the movement of the cattle and, at the same time, be out of their way. Narciso and Felipe rode quickly up ahead to take his place, going about five yards ahead of the lead bull.

There was a third, prolonged rumble of thunder; the

212

lead bull bolted forward, and the two behind it followed suit. Narciso and Felipe waved their sombreros at the fleeing animals and called out reassuring phrases, but already the rows behind the vanguard had begun to press forward. All through the herd the sounds of snorting and lowing and the sight of tossing horns and rolling eyes bespoke the nervous agitation that this coming storm evoked among the lumbering cattle.

They came to a winding turn of the pass, the most narrow and dangerous of all, Narciso and Felipe saw. At once they decided on a heroic attempt to prevent the precipitate rush by the lead bulls whose fear was spreading like a contagious epidemic that would soon affect the entire herd.

The pass turned now to the west by some thirty degrees; where it turned, it became a somewhat broader shoulder allowing perhaps six cattle abreast at its widest point. Two sturdy scrub trees grew along the edge of the cliff, and Narciso and Felipe, swiftly dismounting, tethered their horses to these trees. They stood with their sombreros, waving the herd toward the left, to indicate to the animals that they must turn and not go straight on, or they would plunge over the cliff into the ravine far below.

The lead bull came upon them, lowering his head, his horns gleaming with the sudden rain that had begun to fall. Gesturing wildly, the two vaqueros swung their sombreros and shouted, *"¡Vamos! ¡Vamos!"*

The bull, hearing their voices, lifted its head and then turned to the left. Ramón, watching from his somewhat elevated place above the trail, breathed a sigh of relief and crossed himself in grateful thanksgiving. The two bulls loping behind the leader followed the latter's direction, and it seemed the worst was over. Tirelessly, Felipe and Narciso kept directing the milling cattle to make the turn of the pass. Then, one of the yearlings slipped and lost its balance and fell against Felipe, flinging the vaquero against the tree to which his horse was tethered; only clutching the tree with all his strength saved him from falling over the cliff and into the ravine below. He disengaged himself from the tree and stepped back onto the trail just as the fallen bull rose to its feet, and he leaned toward it with his sombrero waving toward the right. But still shaken by his narrow escape, Felipe lost his balance and stumbled forward. The bull's horn gored him in the side, and he fell to all fours with an agonized groan of pain.

213

Narciso seized Felipe's fallen sombrero and waved both of them at the oncoming cattle to direct them. Meanwhile, he called out words of encouragement to Felipe, "Be calm, *amigo!* They will soon pass, and then I will help you with your wound! Have courage, *mi compañero!*"

Felipe crawled feebly over toward the sheltering scrub tree and, pulling off his bandanna, clapped it against his bleeding side. The wound was only about an inch deep, but it was bleeding badly.

Narciso cupped his hands and called out to Ramón, "Felipe's hurt! He was gored and he is bleeding out his life—is there a vaquero who can help us? I must stay here and direct the *ganado!*"

"Tell him to keep the bandanna pressed against the wound as tight as he can! I'll ride up ahead to Hugo and bring him back."

So saying, Ramón leaned forward and urged his mount to trot along the shoulder at the right of the trail, which followed the arc of the mountain. His superb horsemanship guided the animal safely along the edge, until he passed the lead bull and galloped after the two lumbering chuck wagons and the spare horses of the remuda tethered to the backs of the wagons.

"Hugo! Hugo!" Ramón cried at the top of his voice, "Felipe's been gored! Can you ride back with me and help? Bring your needle and thread!"

Hugo heard his uncle and called back, "I'll get them right away, Uncle Ramón! I'll ride back behind you on your horse—it's too narrow a trail to try anything else."

"I know, nephew! Hurry!"

Hugo had found the needle and thread and cut some clean strips from a spare bedroll. Ramón guided his horse skillfully along the again narrowing trail till he was directly alongside the chuck wagon, and then reached out with one hand and called, "Hugo, take my hand and see if you can swing yourself up behind me—that's it; good man!" Ramón nimbly wheeled the horse's head around and returned along the shoulder by which he had come, riding back toward the bend in the pass.

Narciso was still waving both sombreros, his voice hoarse now from shouting. But the danger was over—the storm had subsided, and the herd was turning obediently to the left and away from the treacherous edge of the cliff.

Ramón realized that they could not get across to help Felipe, and if Hugo tried it by foot, it would be even more dangerous. There was no help for it: Hugo would have to wait until the last of the cattle had passed.

Hugo dismounted and waited, while Ramón rode off toward the head of the drive. Observing the constant and now orderly progression of the cattle by pairs, much as the animals marched into Noah's Ark, Hugo thought it would be a good hour before the last of the herd passed and he could get across the trail to the wounded vaquero. "Felipe, are you all right? Are you holding the bandanna against your wound to stop the blood?" he called.

"*Pero sí*, S–Señor Hugo," Felipe feebly called back, gritting his teeth. The wadded bandanna was soaked with blood, but the worst of the bleeding was over. Yet his face was pale and contorted with pain, and his strength had begun to wane.

When finally the last of the cattle had passed, Hugo hurried across the trail to aid the wounded vaquero. Narciso was kneeling beside him, one arm around Felipe's shoulders, his other hand pressing his own bandanna against the wound.

"Have you any brandy—I mean, *aguardiente*?" Hugo asked Narciso.

"*Sí*, Señor Hugo. I have some in my canteen."

"Get your canteen, then, Narciso, and pour some on the wound. It will burn, but it will help cleanse it against infection. Then I will sew it up. After that, we must find a way of moving him without straining any of the muscles of his side, or it might start the bleeding again."

Narciso nodded, hurried to his horse and took his leather canteen out of his saddlebag, then knelt down beside Felipe again and gently drew the wounded vaquero's hand away from the wound. He grimaced at the sight of it. "It is raw, but it does not seem too deep. I will pour the *aguardiente* on it, as you say."

"*Bueno*. And then let him have as much as he can to drink. It will be like the operation for Manuel, you understand, and when I sew up the wound, he will feel a great deal of pain. If we can put him to sleep with the *aguardiente*, so much the better," Hugo explained.

Narciso nodded eagerly. "*Sí, comprendo*." Supporting his friend with his left arm under Felipe's shoulders, Narciso tilted the canteen and Felipe drank thirstily, emitting a sigh as the fiery brandy began to dull the pain of his wound.

"Is there more left?" Hugo asked. Narciso nodded and again tilted the canteen to Felipe's lips. By the time it was emptied, Felipe was drowsy, and his eyelids began to droop. As Narciso gently let him lie back down on the ground, he vouchsafed, "He is going to sleep, Señor Hugo."

Hugo knelt beside the vaquero to examine Felipe's wound. "I'm going to try to make this as quick as I can. It's not a very deep wound, and that's why I think he'll be all right if we can get him to camp without making him get on a horse," Hugo declared.

"I am grateful that you have come with us, Señor Hugo," Narciso murmured. "You have already saved Manuel's life, and now you will save that of my good friend, Felipe. For one so young, you already have the blessed skill of healing. Perhaps this is why the good God had you come with us, that He might show you what is truly in you."

Hugo stared wonderingly at the genial, mature vaquero. His eyes widened, and then he nodded to himself. Indeed, this was a confirmation of what he had somehow instinctively felt, even when for the past several years he had begged his father to let him come along with the men. It was not driving cattle Hugo Bouchard sought, but rather his own identity, that he might be his own man and discover his own best attributes. And now, thanks to the vagaries of chance, he understood what was intended for him, and he felt a great eagerness to return to Windhaven Range and to tell his parents that he intended to go to medical school.

Hugo worked quickly, wanting to make the ordeal as short as possible. The coarse black thread held, and in a short time he had sewn the puckered edges of the perforation together. Then he took a clean cloth and wrapped it around Felipe's side, just above the hip, and made it as tight as he could. "Now, how do we get him to camp?" he asked Narciso.

"If we could make a litter, it would be the best way, Señor Hugo," Narciso volunteered, doffing his sombrero and scratching his head, as he looked around him.

"But we don't have ropes or enough wood to make one," Hugo countered. "The horses can go ahead, can't they?"

*"Por supuesto,"* Narciso agreed.

"Well, then we will carry him on foot between the two of us. It is the best we can do. It will not jostle him and make the wound reopen. It will take a long time to reach camp, but it will be worth it."

"That is very true. I am grateful to you, Señor Hugo. You know what to do, and I will follow your advice."

"I do not have that much skill, Narciso. I have been lucky, and perhaps if I did this correctly, it will not take long for Felipe to heal. Now, Narciso, if you will hold him under the shoulders, I will take his ankles."

Narciso nodded. Untethering the horses, he smacked them on the rump and sent them off along the trail. Then, stooping, he very gently lifted Felipe while Hugo grasped the vaquero's ankles. Thus, slowly, holding him between them, they set out to find Ramón and the others.

On the nineteenth day of July, Ramón and the Windhaven Range outfit drove their herd to the grassy plain at the juncture of the Apishapa and Arkansas rivers. Reaching the site, they perceived a camp already set up, and a tall, gray-haired man in a white Stetson and gleaming black boots gesturing at them.

"I was beginning to worry a little," the man said affably, as Ramón dismounted and came toward him. "I'm Maxwell Grantham."

"I hope we did not delay you, Señor Grantham," Ramón apologized, "but we had some bad luck. We were attacked by bushwhackers, and the herd stampeded. Alas, I bring you only about nineteen hundred—but those are in prime condition, I assure you."

"Never mind, I certainly can't fault you for being only a hundred short after such trouble. You and your men must be exhausted. Set up your camp alongside mine; my cook is already preparing steaks and biscuits and beans. After we eat, we'll talk business."

"You are very kind, Señor Grantham. Oh—forgive me! I am Ramón Hernandez, Lucien Edmond Bouchard's brother-in-law and partner."

"I've heard about you, and how you've handled yourself in some of the Kansas markets, Señor Hernandez. Well, I can see that you've kept the cattle in fine shape." He turned to watch Ramón's vaqueros drive the herd into the

217

encampment. "I like a man who keeps his word, no matter what the difficulties are, Señor Hernandez. It's very likely that I'll continue to do a good deal of business with you and your brother-in-law. Now come along while I extend my hospitality to you all."

## Twenty

Andy Haskins had continued to mull over his feeling that there would be no purpose in pursuing a political career now that the Democrats were solidly in power. Politics were very much on his mind one evening when he and his wife, Jessica, had Dalbert and Mitzi Sattersfield to dinner. The two men had a great deal in common: each of them had lost an arm in the Civil War, and each of them had begun life all over again, to rise high in their fields of endeavor, thanks to the help of loyal friends and even more loyal wives.

Mitzi Sattersfield, who had once been a maid in Laure Bouchard's first husband's bordello—which cleverly camouflaged from Union soldiers the operation's real function, that of a bank—was now a respected and devoted wife and mother. She had in many ways been responsible for Dalbert Sattersfield's present position as mayor of Lowndesboro. Adoring her older husband, she had had the temerity to write Governor Houston to ask him to champion the one-armed store-keeper; and Dalbert had been elected.

Andy Haskins, along with Joe Duvray, had been working as a stevedore in New Orleans to keep alive after the war. Luke Bouchard and his family had come to New Orleans to seek a new home in Texas, and Luke, in a chance meeting, had perceived the integrity and decency of these two friends. Joe was now a partner at Windhaven Range; Andy—who had gone there as well—had come back to Alabama nine years ago on a visit. He had stayed on to help neighbors of Luke's, Horatio Bambach and his daughter,

218

Jessica, and after marrying Jessica, Andy was asked by Luke to supervise Lucy Bouchard's four hundred acres along with the Bambach land that Andy and Jessica had inherited. Luke subsequently deeded the tract to Andy, and now his holdings along the Alabama River were substantial. From the life of a successful farmer, Andy had entered politics, being elected first to the Alabama House of Representatives and then to the Senate.

Now at dinner, Andy and his guest, Dalbert, sorrowfully recalled how, through the ironic circumstances of fate, both of them had been involved in the heroic death of their benefactor, Luke Bouchard.

"You won't have any trouble being reelected as mayor, Dalbert," he now told the former storekeeper. "This is a small town, where everybody knows you, and where it doesn't matter what your political party is. You treated people decently when you sold goods to them, and you're still doing it. But with me it's different. The Democrats have such a grip on this state and most all the Southern states that it's pretty hard for any Republican to get elected. I'm not even going to try to run for reelection next year."

"But I'd say the same about you, Andy," Dalbert protested, and Mitzi nodded her own enthusiastic agreement. "When you were in the House of Representatives, people tried to bribe you and then blackmail you, and you showed what you were made of, by rejecting and exposing the perpetrators. I'd say you might be wrong about not running again, Andy."

Andy Haskins turned to Jessica. She was somewhat pale and drawn, a condition which had persisted after the birth of her last child, Margaret, five months ago, longer than Andy believed it should have. Indeed, just before the Sattersfields and their children had arrived at the Haskins's house, Andy had told Jessica, "Honey, after the doctor's seen you next week, you and I are going to take a little vacation and rest up. I'll hire a nurse for the children, and we'll just go off by ourselves and have a sort of second honeymoon."

Andy turned back to Dalbert and pursued: "You see, Dalbert, you're already in your second term as mayor, and as far as Lowndesboro is concerned, as long as you're able to hold office, they won't even look for anyone else. But that's not typical of the whole state. This is a small, rural

219

village, and here folks just get on with the business of living; they don't have time for or care about grand schemes. But the politicians in the cities like Birmingham, Selma, Tuscaloosa, and Montgomery, they've got axes to grind. And they're mainly Democratic, and I'm a Republican and will be till my last breath. No, Dalbert, after Jessica and I take a vacation, I'll think of something else for myself to do—something that I can be proud of doing and that will give me something to get my teeth into. I really don't want any more to do with politics. There's other work to be done. Maybe like helping the handicapped, or the poor."

"Then I take it," Dalbert Sattersfield said, "that you're not looking forward to settling down as a gentleman farmer—not entirely, at any rate?"

"There's no reason why I should. Besides, you know that Burt Coleman is handling my land and even making money for me, without my having to do anything. That alone would make me feel sloppy and lazy, so I just have to get into something else that has meaning to it."

"I'm glad things are going well for Burt," Dalbert commented. "He was in such despair after his first wife died, and having to raise his first two sons all alone. But Amelia and Burt seem to have a good marriage, and they're about to have a child—Amelia's first and Burt's third."

"Yes, they're the salt of the earth. So you see, Dalbert, the future of my farm is all set. And your future is, too. If anything, Mitzi will light a fire under you and try to get you to go on from being mayor to maybe even senator like me, or governor," Andy teased, laughing as Mitzi blushed hotly and looked to Jessica for help.

The latter sympathetically rejoined, "Now, Andy, that's not fair. I think it was just wonderful that Mitzi had gumption enough to write Governor Houston to come speak at her husband's rally."

"Yes, of course it was, dear," Andy said softly, and then eyed Dalbert. Both men were silent, for that remark had once again reminded them how Luke Bouchard, in trying to wrest away the derringer from an assailant, had taken the bullet meant for the governor.

"Well, this has been a wonderful dinner," Dalbert now turned his attention to Jessica Haskins, "but I do wish you hadn't gone to all this trouble. You shouldn't be spending all that time in the kitchen, not when you've had such a long recovery."

220

Mitzi nodded, and said to Jessica, "I agree. You and Andy ought to take a nice long vacation and rest up. And maybe during that time Andy will find what he really wants to do, if he isn't going to stay in the political arena."

"I'd like that very much," Jessica responded. "I have perfect confidence in Andy, and I know that whatever he chooses, it will be the right thing for him; and if he'll be happy in it, it will make me happy, too. I certainly respect his judgment, and I never try to influence him one way or another."

"Now there is a considerate wife—just like you, Mitzi." Dalbert touched his napkin to his mouth. "And now I think it's high time we make our way home. Jessica, could I help with the dishes before we go?"

"Now, Dalbert, what sort of hostess do you think I'd be if I allowed you to do that? Andy and I can manage very nicely."

"It was just a wonderful supper, and I appreciate your preparing for the children, too." The one-armed storekeeper rose to help Mitzi gather their brood.

After the Sattersfields had taken a cordial leave, with effusive thanks from both Mitzi and Dalbert, Andy took charge of his own children and saw that they were safely in bed. He cradled little Margaret in his one arm, while Jessica put the dishes to soak. "No need to finish them tonight, honey," he urged. "And you remember to see Dr. Kennery next week. I don't like the fact that you haven't got your strength back in all this time."

"I'll see him, of course, dearest."

"And after that," Andy firmly declared, "you and I will go away and have that rest. Fact is, I could use a little myself."

Two days later, Laure Bouchard was having breakfast with Lucien and Paul, now twelve and ten respectively, with seven-year-old Celestine and six-year-old Clarissa, and with her last-born, John, nearly two, cooing in his high chair. Marius Thornton entered the dining room with a letter that had just come by post and apologized for the interruption. "Sorry to break in on you like this, Miz Laure," he explained, "but I thought you'd like to see this. It's from Tuscaloosa."

"Thank you, Marius. Tuscaloosa—I must confess—wait, I think I know whom it's from."

Marius smiled at the children, realizing that their up-bringing depended on Laure alone. Last night, he and Clemmie had speculated that it would be a good thing if Laure got remarried to a good, dependable man, who would act as father to these growing children and relieve her of the weighty responsibility she had been compelled to assume.

He nodded and went out, while Laure slowly opened the letter. "Who is it from, Mother?" young Lucien asked. Laure turned back to him, her eyes warm and tender. Per-haps of all her children, she loved Lucien the best, for it was he who represented her beginnings with her beloved husband.

How well she remembered Luke when he had first come to New Orleans, still married to his sweet, demure wife Lucy—who was soon tragically killed. She recalled how she herself had been engaged to the good and honorable John Brunton who, to protect her, had made her a host-ess at the Union House—and yet, despite her loyalty and affection for him, she had been drawn passionately to Luke from the first. She had found herself pregnant, and after John's death, and that of Lucy, Luke had come back to New Orleans to woo her. Although believing that the child was indeed Luke's, she had resisted him, saying even if the child were truly his, it was not reason enough for her to marry him. But his courage and integrity eventu-ally won her over, convincing her of his love.

The honor, spirit, goodness, and love of both of these men had seemed to be bequeathed to her fine, intelligent boy just on the threshold of manhood. In him were the memories of both Luke and John, memories she would cherish to her dying day.

"Read us the letter, Mummy!" Clarissa eagerly ex-claimed, and Celestine added her own voice to the demand.

"I will, children—wait till I open it first. And you know, if it's very personal, I shan't be able to read it all to you." Laure had from the very start treated her children as if they were reasonable adults, believing that, by appealing to logic and by explaining things candidly to them, they would not grow up pampered and demanding. More than Marius Thornton realized, Laure Bouchard was well aware of the burden of widowed motherhood: if there were flaws in any of her children, they would be attributed solely to her. She would persevere to make certain that none should be shown favoritism or special privileges, so that all of them might grow up together in a companionable harmony, which would develop their potential talents to the fullest.

She opened the letter and quickly scanned it to learn that it was from Edmond Philippet. He had been a non-secessionist and landholder who had freed his slaves and taken little part on either side in the Civil War. He had been looked upon as a traitor and a scalawag by his fellow townsmen, and when his wife had eventually died of pneumonia after a long illness, it had been said by malicious neighbors that she had wasted away because she did not share her husband's uncommon views. Despite all this, Edmond Philippet had been vindicated, was now looked upon as one of the most respected men in the entire state, and gave a great deal of money to charity.

After a deranged, former Confederate captain, William Darden, had tried to kill both Andy Haskins and Luke Bouchard at the instigation of unscrupulous land speculators who used the poor man's paranoia to get back at Andy and Luke for exposing their scheme, Philippet arranged to have Darden cared for at a private sanatorium he had subsidized.

The doctor who had been head of the sanatorium had died of a heart attack in the fall of 1878, and Philippet had reluctantly assumed charge of the institution. All this was in her mind as Laure read the letter to herself.

Dear Mrs. Bouchard:

Never having had the privilege of meeting you personally, I know of you only through my association with your late husband. I mourn for him, because the world can ill afford to lose greathearted men like him. When William Darden was committed to my sanatorium, and I learned what motivated Mr. Bouchard's involvement with this tragically unbalanced man and found, moreover, that he proposed to pay for Darden's expenses, I was struck with admiration for him. I hope you will forgive me for my very belated condolences.

I come to you now with a problem as I would have come to your husband, knowing instinctively that a man like Luke Bouchard would choose for his wife a woman of warmth and intelligence. My physician tells me that I should go to a drier climate, perhaps Ari-

223

zona or New Mexico. I am reluctant to do this, for this sanatorium has been a dedicated commitment for me since my own wife's death nearly a decade ago. I will do it only if I can find someone who would qualify for the directorship by having the same humanitarian ideals that characterized your husband.

This is why I now ask you if you have in your circle of friends anyone whom you think might be a suitable candidate. To be sure, there would be a generous salary attached to the position, since I have been extremely fortunate in material affairs and been able to endow the institution to a degree of long-range solvency. My wife and I were childless, and perhaps this is why the sanatorium means so much to me. It represents an achievement and a contribution to society, as well, by providing service to those who most urgently require it and yet who may be without means to afford it.

I beg you to forgive me if I have in any way distressed you with this letter, for it was surely not my intention. However, if you should know of someone, please have him communicate with me as soon as possible.

I have promised myself that, when I finally turn it over to a worthy successor, I shall ask your indulgence to allow me to pay you a visit and to express in person the respect and admiration which the name of Luke Bouchard will always evoke within me.

I have the honor to be your most devoted servant.
Edmond Philippet

"But what does it say, Mummy?" Clarissa again demanded.

Laure blinked her eyes quickly to clear them of the sudden tears that this touching letter had evoked, and airily replied, "It's a letter, dear, from one of your father's old friends. He says that he would like to come to visit someday soon and also that he would like me to find someone to run his sanatorium, so that he may go out West for his health."

"What's a sanatorium, Mummy?" the irrepressible Clarissa again piped up.

"It's a kind of hospital, dear, where they take care of people who are sick. Not physically sick, you understand, but sick in the mind from terrible sorrows or sufferings that are too strong for them to endure." Then, brightening, and to change the subject swiftly, so that the children would not draw it out to an unbearable degree, she proposed, "This evening, if it isn't too cool, how would all of you like a picnic supper? You know what a wonderful cook Amelia is; perhaps she can prepare something for us over an open fire."

"That would be fun, Mother," Lucien enthusiastically agreed, then looked up at the clock. "Come on, Paul, you and I have to go to school now."

The two boys attended the rural school near Lowndesboro, and Marius Thornton drove them over and then picked them up at the conclusion of the day. For some time, Laure Bouchard had been thinking of finding more comprehensive schooling for her two sons: there would be a limit to what they could possibly learn at the rural institution, and since both boys were almost as omnivorous as their father in reading whatever they could find, it was her feeling that it might greatly benefit them to go away to a private school, perhaps even abroad.

As she went to take John out of his high chair and back to the nursery, Laure reminded herself that, since Luke's death, she had been remiss in some of her maternal duties. There was no doubt that Luke's death had dazed her and left her so vulnerable that she had very nearly succumbed to the insidious machinations of William Brickley. That had very nearly spelled disaster for Windhaven Plantation, as for herself. Now, thank God, the Bouchard affairs were in excellent order, and there was no excuse for her procrastinating any further over deciding what future the children would have and how best to arrange for it.

Lopasuta had mentioned that as lawyer for the Bouchard family—"I hope that I shall still be retained in that capacity, even though I have been decidedly absent from Bouchard affairs due to circumstances beyond my control," as he had banteringly phrased it—he was of the opinion that Laure should seriously think about finding a better educational institution for Lucien. Lucien was the heir to Windhaven Plantation—Lucien Edmond having been bequeathed all of Luke's interest in Windhaven Range—and he should be groomed for that responsibility. Legally, even if the boy did not choose to live upon the land, he would one day still be obliged to determine how it would be run. He would be responsible as she was now for the lives of those who worked upon the land, which the original Lucien Bouchard had been given by the Creeks of Econchate.

That was why she was grateful for Edmond Philippet's letter, even though it had saddened her. For this letter had compelled her to look into herself and to find that she had neglected more than she had realized when she had been preoccupied with her bereavement.

Accordingly, as Marius came to take Lucien and Paul to the rural school, she said to him, "Marius, would you do me a great favor? After you've left the boys, would you stop at Andy Haskins's place and ask him and Jessica if they could have dinner with me this evening? Tell them I've something very important to discuss with them."

"Of course, Miz Laure, be glad to."

## Twenty-one

To Laure's great delight, Marius Thornton informed her that Andy and Jessica Haskins had accepted her supper invitation and expected to arrive at the red-brick chateau at seven that evening. It turned out she could not keep her promise to the children for an outdoor picnic, since it had begun to rain, so to compensate, she asked Amelia Coleman to make a special cake with gumdrops of which the children were inordinately fond. She asked Lucien and Paul to help and to serve supper on a table set up in Lucien's room for the children, and Clarabelle Hendry would prepare John's supper. Laure fervently promised them that the very next clement evening, they would have their picnic.

Andy and Jessica came with only their newest baby, while the other children were supervised at home by the wife of one of Andy's tenant farmers. Laure was glad to have this opportunity for a private *tête-à-tête* with the one-armed senator and his gentle wife.

As they were finishing their coffee, Laure leaned forward and earnestly declared, "Andy, I had a special purpose for asking you and Jessica here tonight. You remember William Darden?"

"I do indeed." Andy sadly shook his head. "How could I ever forget that poor, tortured soul? But why do you ask that now?"

"Because I've had a letter from Edmond Philippet, Andy. He took over supervision of the Tuscaloosa Sanatorium, but he wrote me that he's quite ill. His doctor has recommended that he move to a drier climate in the West, and he asked me if I knew anyone I could recommend to replace him."

"Yes, Luke told me all about Edmond Philippet," Andy replied slowly. "He's been doing wonderful work at that hospital of his. You know, Laure, for the most part in this country, the senile and the mentally disturbed are still being treated the way the English used to treat them at Bedlam—locking them up in chains, as if they were dangerous monsters. A private institution, run the way Philippet has done, is a blessed salvation. I only wish there were more such institutions."

"I knew you would feel like that, Andy. You've become the stronger because of your handicap, but a man like Captain Darden—broken, defeated by life, and robbed of everything he held dear through the circumstances of war—couldn't survive, and his mind gave way. You would understand people like that—and you'd be perfect for that job. I propose you apply for the post of director. I know you've said that you feel the Republicans won't have a chance in next year's election, and that you're thinking of withdrawing from politics. Well, this would give you something rewarding to do."

"Andy, that's a simply wonderful idea!" Jessica's eyes were shining as she turned to her husband. "You're so kind and thoughtful and compassionate, just as Laure says. You'd be the ideal director of that place. And your reputation for honesty and achievement as a representative and senator would certainly enable you to get many contributions from the wealthy and the influential people of this state. I think you ought to write that letter, Andy."

"Do you, honey?" He put his arm around her and leaned

227

forward to kiss her on the cheek. "Then I'll do just that. I can gradually ease out of my work as state senator because, actually, we don't have much on the agenda for the rest of the session, and in the fall, after summer recess, everybody'll be getting ready for next year's election. Yes, I think I'll write that letter as soon as we get home."

"That's just wonderful!" Laure exclaimed happily. "When it comes to looking for donors, Andy, you can put me down at the top of your list. I'd be very happy to make a substantial contribution to such a worthy cause, particularly if a man like you will be in charge of it."

Having clearly set her mind on those plans that she regarded as being of immediate necessity, Laure Bouchard felt exhilarated for the first time since the death of her husband. For now she was beginning to cope with the realities of her life, and doing so without feverish anxieties and agonized emotions.

Two days after the supper with Andy and Jessica Haskins, Laure sent Marius Thornton to Lopasuta Bouchard's Montgomery house with a message couched in the insouciant diction of her youthful days, when she had so outrageously flirted with Luke Bouchard: "May your adoptive mother presume upon your fondness for her by inviting herself to supper?" And to be sure, the answer had come back that he and Geraldine would be overjoyed to see her.

She was welcomed by Mei Luong (who had very rapidly expanded her English vocabulary) and was shown into the parlor, where Lopasuta and Geraldine were waiting. After greeting her, Geraldine broke out, "We're just about ready to go to New Orleans, Laure—Lopasuta has accepted the position with Mr. Kenniston. We've both decided not to give up this house, but rather we'll go down there and temporarily rent until we see how things work out. When Lopasuta passes the bar examination and can take over Mr. Kenniston's legal affairs in New Orleans, then we'll think about selling it, or renting it, or whatever."

"How wonderful! Well, darling, if you're going to New Orleans, I can give you a list of the many sights you'll want to see and the fine restaurants, the theater, and the opera you can enjoy. And speaking of plans, I invited myself over for supper to talk to Lopasuta about Lucien's future."

"I'd be delighted to make some suggestions, Laure," Lopasuta declared.

She touched his arm and smiled as she said, "It's the matter of his school, and Paul's as well. You see, Lopasuta, the Lowndesboro school is limited in scope. I'd say it can offer at most another year for Lucien, and I consider that he'll end up with only a smattering of education out of the whole time he's spent there."

"That's true. A private school, of course, is always a good idea. And you know that there's money enough available in the estate to send both the boys to the finest European schools, such as in France, or Switzerland, or even England."

"I've thought of that, too. That's why I wanted to come over this evening and ask your advice."

"I am happy to say, supper now is ready," Mei Luong suddenly broke in, in her sweet, charmingly accented voice. Geraldine had shown her how to cook many of Lopasuta's favorite dishes, to augment the Chinese recipes which both of them found a delightful change from the usual American fare.

Midway through supper, Lopasuta clapped his hand to his forehead and exclaimed, "I should have thought of it earlier, Laure! Mr. Kenniston might be able to give you even better ideas about an education abroad. I think I told you that he's a self-taught man, but he's had extensive dealings in England and Ireland for his importing and exporting firm. He's very intelligent, and very candid and honest. That's why I haven't the slightest hesitation in going to work for him in a strange city."

"Why, that sounds like a wonderful idea! Will you let me know when you'll be seeing him?"

"Well, after I'd sent him the wire accepting his terms, I got one back from him only yesterday saying that he'll be in New Orleans at the very end of this month, but only for a day or two—just long enough to formalize our arrangements. However, he'll be back perhaps two months later, and he plans to stay for a week or two then—that would give you enough time to meet him and to talk at length about such matters," Lopasuta proposed.

"It couldn't be better. As a matter of fact, I confess I've had a longing to see the city of my birth, and it'll be a welcome change. Also, I'm worried about Jason Barntry. Hollis Minton, the lawyer who's handling the bank's dealings with the gambling casino, wrote me recently that Jason's health seems to be failing, and he's already discussed

229

with Mr. Minton the possibility of selling his shares and retiring. I know that he kept on after his wife's death out of sheer loyalty to dear Luke, and I wouldn't think of asking him to make any further sacrifice, certainly not at the cost of his health. He's earned his retirement."

"Well then, we'll plan on having you stay with us—we'll surely have a house by then—as soon as Mr. Kenniston comes to New Orleans for his more extended visit," Lopasuta avowed.

"I'm so glad I invited myself over this evening. My! Everybody's so busy making new plans and getting involved with new ideas! And that reminds me—last week, I had a letter from Dr. Ben Wilson. Do you know that he and his Elone are embracing the movement for women's suffrage?"

Geraldine's eyes widened, and she leaned forward with an undisguised interest in this new topic of conversation.

Noting his wife's eagerness, Lopasuta declared with a laugh, "I think you may have started something, Laure—something that neither one of us will be able to control!"

Geraldine turned to him, and in a voice of playful sarcasm she retorted, "My darling, if you'll remember, when I took my marriage vows to you, I promised to love and honor you—*not* be controlled by you!"

"I shouldn't think of ever doing that, my darling," Lopasuta protested, and the woebegone expression on his face made Geraldine giggle. Turning to Laure, she said, "Do give me Dr. Wilson's address before you leave tonight. I want to write him, and I want to introduce myself to Elone by mail." Then she turned back to Lopasuta and fervently declared, "Don't you see? It's all the same, Lopasuta: the poor people whom you represent are fighting for their rights as citizens. Well, it's about time we women fight for *our* rights, too! Why, do you realize that the lowest, most conniving man in this country—like that awful Mr. Brickley who had you kidnapped to Hong Kong—has more privileges than either Laure or I?"

"Yes, that's true," Lopasuta solemnly agreed. "I, for one, agree that women should have the right to vote and shouldn't be drudges or slaves to their husbands."

"Well, now, Laure, you heard that. So, if you ever see me shackled to the stove, you'll know that my husband didn't keep his word," Geraldine laughingly countered.

"I'll wager this Mr. Kenniston of yours will be able to

230

give you a little history of the attempt to get equality for women in Europe, where they're still in the Middle Ages," Laure said.

"I'm sure that's true," Lopasuta nodded. "In my studies, I've found that in many of the European countries, the very traditions of their cultures impose an inferiority upon the female. The man may cast his wife aside or divorce her, and she has no appeal."

"Well, don't forget," Geraldine interposed, "that here in this country there's many a man married twenty years or so who suddenly sees a young girl and decides that he wants to start life all over again, so he tries to cast his wife aside. The male always has the upper hand in just about every country, and it's high time it stopped."

"I think," Lopasuta put in, "that all this is very true, but I do not think that we'll see, in our lifetime, women holding high public office to right these wrongs."

"And I hope, my dear husband," again Geraldine's tone was one of bantering sarcasm, "that you don't hold the view that a man's brain must necessarily be superior to a woman's?"

"Never! Look how smart you are! You took me back— and that's why I'll always love you," was Lopasuta's quick reply, which earned him a hug and a kiss and made Laure laugh till the tears came to her eyes.

"I want to compliment you, Mei Luong, on this lovely dinner," Geraldine said as coffee was being served, and she looked up and smiled at the young Chinese woman. "We enjoyed it very much; thank you a thousand times."

"It is my duty. Is a joy to do things for nice people," Mei Luong replied in her much improved English.

When she had gone back to the kitchen, Lopasuta said, "You know, when Mr. Kenniston and I reached San Francisco, before we boarded the train back, we got an inkling of the harsh treatment the Chinese receive here just from the way poor Mei Luong was treated when we went to a restaurant. I understand there's a bill now in Congress to restrict Chinese immigration; I hope that President Hayes will veto it as a violation of the Burlingame Treaty of 1868. For if it should be passed, then gracious, good-hearted women like Mei Luong would be denied the chance to come to this country for a freedom they cannot know in their own male-dominated country."

"Hear, hear!" Geraldine gleefully clapped her hands at this. "There's hope for my husband yet, I do believe."

"I frankly expected Lopasuta to take such a stand, because it's in keeping with his whole philosophy of life—to be on the side of the underdog," was Laure's merry riposte.

Showing her mercurial nature, Geraldine turned back to her husband with a tender smile and look that quite belied the flippant sarcasm she had affected. She said very gently, "I know. But it's good for a woman to hear every now and then from the man she loves and respects that he shares her convictions. I think it will strengthen our marriage."

"I think it already has," Laure murmured.

Andy Haskins wired Edmond Philippet that Laure Bouchard had suggested he confer with the ailing sanatorium director. Now, a week later, he made a visit to Tuscaloosa and spent a full day with the gentle, elderly philanthropist. At the conclusion of their meeting, Philippet engaged Andy as director of the institution. He would instruct his board of directors to honor the contract to be drawn up between them and that Andy would begin his official tenure the following January, when his term in the senate would be formally ended. In the meantime, both men agreed, Andy would spend what time he had free from the legislature in acquainting himself with the activities and facilities of the sanatorium and having supervisory control over all decisions that would affect its future.

Jessica Haskins would willingly move to Tuscaloosa next year when her husband fully took over his new duties. The thriving University of Alabama, founded in 1831, burned by Broxton's Union raid in the last year of the Civil War, had reopened eight years ago. Awarded a grant of over 46,000 acres of public land, the school had sold most of it for $90,000, the money being used in construction of new buildings. The noted scientist, Nathaniel Thomas Lupton, was its president, and he had attracted an able faculty and drawn a roster of outstanding students. Such an atmosphere, Jessica was certain, would be an ideal one in which to bring up their children, who one day might attend this highly accredited scholastic institution. And since Burt Coleman was supervising Andy's acreage so capably, there would be a continued income which would supplement her husband's earnings; thus they could amply provide for their family's continued welfare.

At the end of the same week, Lopasuta Bouchard and Geraldine, together with Mei Luong and Dennis and Luke, left for New Orleans. They would see Leland Kenniston for a day or two, rent temporary living quarters, and Lopasuta would begin his studies for the bar examination of the State of Louisiana. Laure saw them off, and reminded them to let her know when Leland would return for a lengthier time to New Orleans, so that she might meet him and discuss with him the future schooling of her two boys. She was radiant and vivacious, her mind teeming with optimistic hopes and plans for the future. It was not that she no longer thought of Luke—for often, of an evening, she looked up at the towering bluff where he was buried beside his imperishable grandfather and Dimarte. It was more that she had learned to reconcile the past and look forward to the future, for this truly was the Bouchard credo, one which had strengthened the family through its worst tribulations, one which had deepened its loyalty in far-flung locales of this growing young country, and one which, so long as the name of Bouchard existed, would weld them together in an increasingly stronger and triumphant bond of love and purposeful achievement.

## Twenty-two

For the first time in several years, Lucien Edmond Bouchard found himself obliged to take his ease in the hacienda of Windhaven Range. To be sure, he had the utmost confidence in Ramón, and in one sense, he was almost grateful that he had been compelled to stay home and at the same time give Hugo the chance to prove himself. Maxine was ecstatic over having her husband with her, giving them the opportunity to discuss at length the future of

233

their children, as well as the seemingly unimportant details of daily domestic living with which he had rarely had to occupy himself. But these, as Maxine quickly made him see, were part and parcel of their marriage; they made up the warp and the woof of everyday living, and by understanding them, Lucien Edmond would better understand her own motivations. Although he had once twitted her, when she had come with her uncle from Baltimore to visit Windhaven Plantation, over being a "blue-stocking"—by which he meant primarily a female intellectual—he never had reason to feel uneasy with her intelligence: Maxine Bouchard had the rare gift of being able to express her fine intellect in such a way that it blended harmoniously with Lucien Edmond's own desires. And though he led an outdoor life and was not scholarly as his father had been, Lucien Edmond was not unaware of this adroit balancing of the marital scales, and appreciated Maxine all the more.

At any rate, all that annoyed him was the lessened activity he was obliged to endure until his leg strengthened. The pain had gone, but he was not yet certain that he should trust himself to the saddle. As it was, he spent much of his time in reflecting over the future of the vast acreage of their sprawling ranch and its diverse facilities, which he intended to add to before he had finished his stewardship of this rich, fertile land. The church and the school were progressing beautifully: the gentle nuns provided an excellent education, and old Friar Bartoloméo Alicante was serenely enjoying what he called his "spiritual retreat, although this does not mean that I have retired from active communication of our dear Lord's faith in his creation, man. It means only that you have graciously welcomed me to rest among you, and in return for my bread and my shelter, to sing His Praises for you and your workers and all those of you who humbly believe in His divine teachings."

Now at the end of March, Lucien Edmond had decided that it was time to send his annual gift of cattle to the village of the great Comanche chief, Sangrodo. The Indians were now led by Kitante, the dead *jefe*'s oldest son and the stepson of Catayuna. Once a captive and then the wife of Sangrodo, Catayuna diligently supervised the education of the children she had given Sangrodo and was one of the most enthusiastic teachers in the school at Windhaven Range. It gratified her, and it gave her a purpose and a reason for living. For just as Laure Bouchard realized how much she had lost at Luke's death, so Catayuna looked back often to the idyllic times she and Sangrodo had had together in a union that at first had seemed bizarre and ill-fated.

Friar Bartoloméo Alicante, now nearly sixty-six, had been in poor health ever since he had been brutally tarred and feathered by Comancheros. After having recovered from that harrowing experience, he had gone to Sangrodo's stronghold just across the Mexican border, for there were many Christianized members of that now-peaceful Comanche tribe. He had come to Windhaven Range after urging his bishop in Sante Fe to appoint a successor to him who would further the conversion of Sangrodo's villagers, most of whom had married Mexican women. Their own Comanche wives had been slaughtered by Captain George Munson of Fort Inge when their stronghold was still in Texas, not far from Windhaven Range. The bishop had responded to Friar Bartoloméo's request for a successor by appointing Friar Jorge Mendoza, a younger man full of enthusiasm and who shared his older colleague's admiration for these Indians, who had once been the most feared of the plains.

Though he was now far from the stronghold, one of the pleasures which Friar Bartoloméo most enjoyed was receiving long, cheerful letters from Friar Mendoza, filled with anecdotes and good news about his former flock.

On this March day, a courier arrived with a letter for the old priest. He eagerly opened it and read it, and, after he had done so, turned to Lucien Edmond, who was sitting beside him on the veranda enjoying the warm sun, and exclaimed, "When you send your gift of cattle to young Kitante, perhaps your vaqueros could do a great favor and a good Christian deed at the same time. This letter from Friar Mendoza tells of a most unusual young woman. It may be that, in the kindness of your heart—and you have done so much already—you may see fit to bring her here to the school, which the good sisters and Catayuna manage so ably."

"I'd certainly like to know about such a person, Friar Bartoloméo. Why don't you read me what Friar Mendoza has to say about her?" Lucien Edmond pleasantly offered.

"Indeed I will, my son. Here is what he says:

My dear brother in Christ:

There is a young Mexican woman from a neighboring village whom I have taken under my wing. You see, her village is extremely poor—there are only a few small farms there and last year the crops were very disappointing, so the poverty has increased. Since I am allowed funds by the bishop for such purposes, I have contributed money now and again to buy food and clothing for these unfortunate people.

One of the farms is owned by the maiden aunt of this young woman, who took over its management when her brother died two years ago. Since it is almost impossible for two women to run a farm alone without help—and especially when the crops are bad—I went there to see if I might be of service. That was how I met Carmen Rodago.

She is twenty-two years old and has shown a tremendous desire to educate herself. The *alcalde* of this little village had some books and lent them to her, and by her own perseverance and determination, she taught herself how to read and also how to write simple letters.

I hope you will forgive me, but I could not help telling her about the wonderful school you and the sisters have started. Señorita Rodago begged me to write you, hoping that you would be willing—in exchange for her working in the school with the children—to take her in and give her the further education she so merits. You will understand that my duties do not permit me to spend further time teaching her myself, nor is it within my own abilities to do so.

She expressed to me the hope that one day she could be a teacher herself, perhaps returning to her own village where she could educate the poor children there and in the surrounding communities. Myself, I do not hold much hope for any success in this village, and already many of the younger people are thinking of leaving and moving elsewhere where the land is more fertile and rewarding. Yet, I should hate to see this gifted young woman cast aside and her talents wasted. If it is at all possible, could you write me and tell me whether such an arrangement could be worked out?

Yours in Christ, and wishing you long, happy years, I am,

Friar Jorge Mendoza

"I agree with Friar Mendoza that a young woman like that should be given every opportunity to better herself. If she has a gift for teaching, I'm sure it can be utilized," Lucien Edmond Bouchard declared.

"Perhaps, then, the vaqueros, when they take the cattle to Kitante, could get word to Friar Mendoza of your feeling—and when they return, they could bring Señorita Rodago with them?"

"Of course that could be done. And if this young woman should feel that she is being given charity, I'm certain that she can further help out with the cooking or sewing for the vaqueros in the bunkhouses—anything that will make her feel that she is earning what she is given, so she won't feel out of place."

"You are indeed a kind man, my son. I shall write a letter to Friar Mendoza, which your vaqueros can deliver to him. It will serve as an authorization for him to send Señorita Rodago back with your men."

"By all means. I'm going to have Nacio Lorcas and Eddie Gentry be in charge of this short expedition. Because Eddie was about to become a father again, I didn't want to send him on that long drive to Colorado. And as for Nacio, he has been with me almost from the very start and is one of the most loyal workers I have ever known. It will be a pleasant diversion for him to see his native land again, and particularly to go on a journey on which there will certainly be no hardships or dangers," Lucien Edmond declared with a smile.

And so, the next afternoon, together with four other vaqueros, Eddie Gentry and Nacio Lorcas set out with a hundred head of cattle, and in Nacio's saddlebag was a letter, which Friar Bartoloméo Alicante had penned to Friar Mendoza. It would not take them much more than a week, so they took only a small supply wagon filled with provisions and a few cooking utensils.

Eddie and Nacio had found each other sympathetic friends ever since the Mexican had come to Windhaven Range. Nacio, like all the other vaqueros, knew that Eddie's fiancée had died tragically young, giving up her life to save that of a child about to be run down by a carriage. When the news had reached Eddie, he had been agonized but, happily, fate had consoled him through the opportunity to save Maria Elena Romero, who had been sold by her impoverished Mexican father to a saloonkeeper to serve as a dance-hall girl and prostitute. Eddie Gentry had been forced to kill the saloonkeeper in self-defense, and he had taken Maria Elena Romero back to Windhaven Range, learned that she had fallen in love with him, and now they were happily married, with a five-year-old son, Peter, a two-year-old, Douglas, and their newborn daughter, Eva.

Because of his hard work and skill, Eddie had been given some valuable Windhaven Range acreage by Lucien Edmond and, in a sense, was as much a partner as Joe Duvray. Eddie did not hold himself above the vaqueros, but acted exactly as if they were his equals and had made friends with all of them. Easygoing, likable, hardworking, he had purposely taken a course in Spanish from the nuns this last winter, so that he could speak Spanish more fluently, an act which further pleased the vaqueros, who appreciated his interest in them.

Nacio Lorcas, now thirty-four, had originally been hired by Ramón Hernandez, along with his good friend, Santiago Miraflores, when Ramón had gone to Nuevo Laredo looking for men who were good with horses and who did not wish to be *peones*. Santiago, while acting as a night guard on a cattle drive, had been knifed by cattle thieves who had planned to ambush and kill the entire Bouchard outfit. Eddie Gentry had valiantly acquitted himself during that battle, and Nacio, who mourned his murdered companion, had thanked the young Texan for having helped him avenge his dead friend.

On their first night out on this drive, after they had had their simple supper, the two men sat side by side by the campfire. Nacio was sturdy, almost as tall as Eddie, with black hair and a small but very neat mustache of which he was very proud, and though he was softspoken by nature, there was a lively streak in him. At times, when he was in a particularly good humor, he would make disconcerting jokes about his fellow vaqueros, who sometimes thought that he was singling them out for derision. But then, as quickly, he would turn a joke against himself, and they would laugh and know that he was only trying to enliven their spirits during the monotony of a cattle drive. "It is good, this chance we have to ride together as vaqueros again, Señor Eddie," he said softly. "And I am very happy that you have a family, and that Maria Elena makes you such a fine wife—you have earned it, after you lost poor Señorita Polly."

"Yes, Nacio," Eddie uttered a nostalgic sigh, "I've been a very lucky man. Polly would have made me a wonderful wife, and I'll always remember her, but no one could be sweeter than Maria Elena. So it's as you say, *el Señor Dios* looked after me. But you, Nacio, you're not married. Aren't there any señoritas you fancy?"

"Ah, *pero no*, Señor Eddie," Nacio shrugged. "It is not that I do not want an *esposa*, but you know yourself that all the señoritas on Windhaven Range now are señoras. My *compañeros* have seen to that. Oh yes, perhaps I might wait for some of the girl-children to come out of school and to grow up and be old enough to marry, but then I would be *viejo*, and they would laugh at me." He shrugged again. "But then, Señor Eddie, I am used to getting along with very little. That was the way I grew up. You see, Santiago and I lived outside a tiny village where our fathers each had so little land that it was hardly worth calling a farm, to be honest with you—just enough food so we did not starve, but not enough so that we could ever have a second helping. I have two brothers and a sister, and they left the village before I did. My mother was old and sick, my father was already dead, and there was no work in Nuevo Laredo. Santiago was almost twenty years older than me, and he was a kind of uncle to me all my life. That is why when Santiago heard that Señor Hernandez was in town and looking for vaqueros, Santiago took me along to seek him out. We told him that we would do any work in the world, if he would only give us a chance in *Los Estados Unidos*. And the very first thing he did was to give me an advance on my wages, Señor Eddie, so I could buy medicine and food for my poor mother—may the saints watch over her dear soul in heaven, for she died two months after I came here to work for the *patrón*."

Eddie Gentry put a hand on Nacio's arm, deeply moved by what the vaquero had told him. He could understand the hardships this cheerful, hardworking, usually self-effacing man had endured without complaint. Now, the wry smile on Nacio's face showed that he was making light of his own lack, and he expected no more. "Never mind,

239

Nacio; one of these days you'll find a wife who'll see right away that you're *un hombre bueno*," he consoled his friend.

"Señor Eddie, perhaps it is well that a man cannot look into the future and see what is in store for him, or he might give up hope. So you see, if it is meant to be for me, it will happen. And besides, I am glad that I work for the *patrón*, because he is a good man, and you are my good friend, and it is pleasant this evening to sit and talk like this. And now we shall get some sleep, *no es verdad?*"

### Twenty-three

Shortly after noon a week after their departure from Windhaven Range, Eddie Gentry, Nacio Lorcas, and their four companions drove the hundred head of cattle into a large wooden-fenced pen, which Kitante's braves had built beside their new stronghold. Kitante came out of his teepee with his Carmencita, who held their year-old son, Egorde, the Comanche name for Smiling Deer. Their second child was so named because, almost from birth, he had been active and happy, with no tendency to cry or whine. Kitante was inordinately proud of Egorde and his elder son, Kwaku-h, and prouder still of his young Mexican wife, who had run away from a bandit camp ruled by her tyrannical father and stepmother to entreat his aid.

On the other side of the stronghold there was a small wooden church, another proof of the peaceful new life of these Comanche Wanderers. They had once been regarded as the scourge of the Southwest, but only because their lands had been stolen from them and their buffalo herds slaughtered so that they would be forced to go far to the north to enable the railroads to extend the white man's settlements.

Kitante himself was a devout Catholic, and Carmencita had been brought up in that faith. She had been horrified

240

when, as her mother lay dying, her father had ruthlessly forced her to leave with him and a coarse, sensual woman named Juana. He had forced a priest, at gunpoint, to marry him and Juana, and Carmencita had abhorred this sacrilege. And when her stepmother later told her that Carmencita was pledged to the most vicious bandit of them all, she had fled and met Kitante near the stronghold. He had been challenged to a duel with knives by her father's chief lieutenant, yet Kitante had found the strength and courage to kill him, and thus win Carmencita as his wife. They had been closely bound by these events, and Carmencita was now happier than she had ever been before.

Friar Mendoza came out of his church, having heard the calls of the vaqueros as they drove the cattle into the pen. Eddie and Nacio dismounted and shook hands with Kitante, then turned to the Franciscan friar, who made the sign of the cross over them and smilingly declared, "I am surprised to see you, for I have not yet heard from my dear old friend and colleague, Friar Bartoloméo."

"He is well, *mi padre*," Nacio replied as he reached into his saddlebag, "and he has sent this letter to you. He has told Señor Bouchard about Señorita Rodago. Our *patrón* says in the letter that there will be a place for her in the school, and that we are to bring her back."

"Your *patrón* will be blessed for his act of good will and kindness to this devout young woman, who is eager for knowledge so that she may have a worthy place in society," the friar beamed. "Kitante's people have been most gracious to her. They have made her a teepee for herself, and she has spent much time with their children, doing what she can by way of thanking them for their hospitality."

He took the letter from Nacio, opened it, and read it, nodding approval, and then, pocketing it, averred, "Señorita Rodago is teaching the children now. When she has finished, I will introduce you to her, and you will see for yourselves how well intentioned she is, and how gracious and yet humble. This is a good thing your *patrón* has done, yes, for of course she could not hope to have a permanent life here in the village with the *indios*. Also, her aunt was taken ill just a few days ago and because she is so old, I do not believe that she will recover. I am going over to visit with her this afternoon, to see how she is. It is a sad thing, for if she dies, Carmen Rodago will be all alone— and that, too, is a reason I am anxious to see her have an opportunity with your *patrón*. Friar Bartoloméo has told me so many things about the hacienda which is called Windhaven, and I have told Carmen Rodago how the wife of Kitante's father, the Beloved Woman Catayuna, lives there now and teaches school with the holy sisters."

Friar Mendoza turned to Kitante and said, "I must go now to Portafila. Tell Señorita Rodago that I will return for her tomorrow. I promised her that I would take her to say goodbye to her *tía,* just before she leaves for Texas."

"*Mi padre,*" Kitante told him, "while you are gone, I shall prepare a place for these good men who have brought the cattle to my people, and Carmencita and I will introduce these two men to Señorita Rodago."

He turned back to Eddie Gentry and Nacio Lorcas, "One day soon, Carmencita and I wish to take our sons with us to visit the Beloved Woman, if it is permitted."

"You needn't wait for an invitation, Kitante," Eddie chuckled. "You'll be welcome any time. Perhaps you'd like to go back with us when we leave?"

"I would like to, but we are to have a tribal council next week over which I must preside. You understand, as *jefe* I may not think of myself alone, nor even of my Carmencita and our child. I must follow in the footsteps of him whose name we no longer speak, but which is in my heart and will be until with my last breath I am taken by the Great Spirit."

"His name is still remembered with great honor and admiration at Windhaven Range, Kitante, be sure of that," Eddie Gentry told him.

"It is good to hear such words from a *wasichu.*" The young chief gripped the Texan's shoulder, and the two men stood looking at each other, each respecting and admiring the other. Carmencita, cradling her infant son in her arms, watched with a radiant face. One of the elderly women in the village had told her only this morning that her husband, young though he was, had already shown great ability as a leader and that one day his name would be celebrated in the lore and songs of the Wanderers.

"I think often of him who sired me," Kitante continued. "You must know from our custom, Señor Gentry, that we do not speak the name of one who has gone to the Great Spirit. It is said to bring bad luck. But I will tell you that, as *jefe,* I think always of my father and of the wisdom he helped place within my mind, so I might be worthy now to

242

replace him. I know how often he said that it was men like your *patrón*, the Señor Bouchard, who would stand beside *los indios*, when all others wished them killed like mad dogs. And from the news I have had from runners who come across the border, Señor Gentry, I am glad that my father did not live to see what happens in your *Estados Unidos*, when one of your best leaders says for all to hear that he believes that the only good Indians are dead ones. And when the Sioux and the Cheyenne defeated your General Custer at Little Big Horn, many *wasichus* rejoiced and said that soon there would be no more Indians because the soldiers would pay them back for General Custer."

"I am sorry that there have been those of my people who say such evil things, Kitante," Eddie apologetically retorted. "It is not the way I think."

"This I know already. But now you shall meet the *mujer joven* of whom the *padre* speaks," Kitante said. "At the end of the village the braves have made a low circular fence around a small clearing to be a playground and also a schoolroom; you will see her there with the children. They love her, and she has already learned much of our language during the short time she has been here."

Nacio Lorcas and Eddie Gentry followed the tall young Comanche chief to the back of the village. There, just as he had described, was a large, low circle of wooden fencing, no higher than the knees of a full-grown man. Inside, about thirty children sat cross-legged, listening intently to an attractive young woman whose black hair tumbled to her shoulder blades and dropped tangled curls at her cheekbones. Her face was heart shaped, and her eyes were wide and of a very dark brown under thick, expressively arching brows. Her mouth was firm and full, her chin rounded and dimpled. She was of medium height, and she wore a buckskin jacket and leggings.

She spoke in a sweet, clear voice, and she used many Comanche words in translating her story, which Eddie recognized as being an adaptation of one of Aesop's Fables. It was a story of the ant and the grasshopper, and how the industry of the ant won out over the carefree, hedonistic life of the grasshopper. "This is why, children," she said to them in mixed Spanish and Comanche, "your mothers and fathers lay away stores of food, so when there is little hunting, you will always have enough to eat. They are like the ants. But there are those who would like only to go to war

243

so they can count coup over their enemies; they have nothing to show for what they have done except perhaps a few scalps. They are the grasshoppers. But here in this village, because of your fine *jefe*, I have seen no grasshoppers."

There was a cheer from the older children, and several of them began to ply the young Mexican woman with questions, which she answered thoughtfully. "Tomorrow, when the sun is high in the sky, I will see you all again. Remember what I have told you today. When you are older, when you have horses and bows and lances, remember to be like the ant, and never like the grasshopper," she concluded with a smile.

Nacio stood entranced, holding his sombrero with both hands pressed against his lean waist. He turned his head toward Eddie Gentry and whispered, "*¡Por Dios! ¡La señorita es muy linda!*"

Eddie eyed his companion, and then knowingly chuckled as he said softly, "Do you know what I think, Nacio? I think that Cupid has shot you with an arrow."

"Señor Eddie," Nacio affected a look and tone of incredulous astonishment, "how can you say a thing like this? It is only the first time I have seen her." Then, with a nostalgic sigh, he murmured almost to himself. "Yet she is still *muy guapa*. She reminds me of a girl I once knew in Nuevo Laredo, the daughter of a *hacendado*. I was too poor, too worthless for her even to look at me, but, *caramba*, how I wanted her! And there is something of her in this young woman."

"That's exactly why I said that Cupid was aiming his arrow at you and hit you square, Nacio," Eddie playfully joked.

Nacio blushed under his weather-beaten tan, shifted his feet on the loamy soil, and looked discomfited as he strove for a reply. Finally, lamely, he retorted, "There is no law against looking at her."

"Not at all, else we'd all be in jail—in the *calabozo*," Eddie chuckled.

"I know what you are saying and what you think, *amigo*," Kitante teased, his dark eyes dancing with merriment, while Nacio shifted from foot to foot and looked embarrassed. Raising his voice, Kitante called, "Señorita Rodago, I wish you to meet these two men, who have just brought cattle to feed my people. They come from Señor

244

Bouchard and from my friend, Padre Bartoloméo. I think they have good news for you."

"But that is wonderful!" the young woman joyously exclaimed. "Padre Mendoza told me about Windhaven Range, señores. Is it true, is it possible that your *patrón* will take me in there and let me learn as well as go on teaching?"

"Yes, ma'am," Eddie said as he shuffled his sombrero between his hands. Carmen was as lovely as his own Maria Elena, and there was more of a determined spirit in her eyes and in her poise and bearing, as if she were waiting for the summons to prove herself.

"It is true, señorita. Friar Bartoloméo received the letter from Friar Mendoza and talked with Señor Lucien Edmond Bouchard about your coming to Windhaven Range," Nacio explained without taking his eyes off the lovely black-haired young woman.

"Everyone is so kind to me," she impulsively replied.

Nacio now stared at her so openly and admiringly that she could not help blushing and looking down at her feet. Aware that he had embarrassed her, he hastily sought to make amends. "But how could one not be kind to you, Señorita Rodago? I saw you there, talking to those *niños*, and I said to myself, 'Nacio, I am glad that we came here to fetch this woman to our hacienda.' It is all arranged."

"And how long will the journey take, Señor Nacio?"

"It is Nacio Lorcas, *servidor de usted,*" the vaquero declared emphatically. Then, in a softer tone, he added, "It is not too long a journey, Señorita Rodago. It took us seven days and nights, but that was because we were driving *los ganados,* you understand. I promise you we shall be back within four days at the most. That reminds me—is it possible that you can ride a horse, señorita?"

"Alas, I cannot—I wish I could. And I hope this will not change your mind about taking me back with you," Carmen Rodago earnestly responded. "It is like a dream come true! Even though I admire the Comanche and I know that many of them have become *católico,* I wish to learn more so that I shall always be able to earn my bread without being dependent upon others."

Nacio declared, "I have learned something today, señorita." And when she stared quizzically back at him, her eyes widening, he pursued, "It is that I had not known

245

before that a woman could be so beautiful and, at the same time, so wise."

At this, Carmen blushed furiously and lowered her eyes, while Eddie Gentry gave his companion a swift, searching look. He realized from the look on Nacio's face that his friend was in no way being sarcastic, but rather eminently sincere. Eddie smiled happily. As sometimes happens between two persons who have never before met, there is a sudden kindling of interest that makes it seem as if that moment of meeting had been fated from the very start.

At last, somewhat regaining her poise, the young brunette replied in a noncommittal tone, "You are much too kind, señor."

"To my friends, I'm called just Nacio."

"*Gracias,* S-Señor Lorcas," she faltered, not yet able to bring herself to address him so intimately at first meeting.

Eddie thought it was wise at this point to intervene. "Kitante has invited us to a feast this evening, and we plan to leave for Windhaven Range tomorrow around noon, if that is satisfactory with you?"

"Oh, yes, señor!" She uttered a deprecatory laugh. "I have very little to take along, except the clothes I am wearing. My old aunt is very poor, you see. I hope it is not too much trouble for you to wait until I have said my farewell to her."

"Of course not," Eddie assured her. "Certainly, a day or two more doesn't matter. There is no hurry whatsoever about our returning. Señor Lucien Edmond Bouchard appointed us to bring these cattle as a gift for the young chief of the Comanche. It goes back, you see, Señorita Rodago, to the time when Señor Bouchard's father saved Kitante when he was a boy from dying of the bite of a rattlesnake. Sangrodo, Kitante's father, and Luke Bouchard became good friends, and Lucien Edmond Bouchard continues that friendship. Indeed, it was a brotherhood of the blood, which the Comanche practice with those they respect."

"Yes, I know of this custom. So that is how it was. Padre Mendoza told me only a little, and I thought it strange that the Comanche tribe should have such friendship for a *gringo.* But now I understand it."

"Exactly, Señorita Rodago," Eddie nodded.

"Oh please, both of you, you must call me Carmen. After all, I am no one of importance, nothing more than a very poor orphan from a very poor village."

"You are much more than that, Carmen, if I may be so bold as to say so," Nacio almost fiercely put in, and then it was his turn to grow red in the face and to turn suddenly to see where he had tethered his mustang.

That evening, at Kitante's order, there was a convivial feast to welcome the Windhaven vaqueros, in acknowledgment of the prized gift of cattle for the villagers. There was dancing, too, with the Mexican wives of the Comanche braves wearing their most colorful *serapes*, followed by the tribal dance of the warriors themselves. But they were no longer warriors—rather, peaceful farmers who had broken and buried the war arrow since Sangrodo had led them across the Rio Grande to this, their new stronghold, a sanctuary from the punitive raids that soldiers would have made upon them if they had remained in Texas.

And finally, to Carmen's delight, there was even a dance by the children in their tribal costumes, generating much merriment and laughter.

There was sorrow also: Friar Jorge Mendoza had ridden back from the nearby village with the news that Carmen's aunt had died just after he had arrived. He comforted the religious young woman with the news that he had had time to shrive her aunt, so she had passed from this life to the next free of guilt and sin. He handed Carmen her aunt's final and only gift, a silver crucifix, which had been given to her by her father half a century ago.

Carmen kissed the crucifix and then wept silently, while Nacio Lorcas, his heart in his eyes, stared longingly at her. Nacio told himself that, in his prayers, he would thank *Nuestro Padre* for having been chosen by the *patrón* to come to the Comanche village, giving him the chance to meet Carmen Rodago.

When it was time to leave the next day, Carmen again ruefully reminded Eddie and Nacio that she had never learned to ride a horse. Nacio told her that she could ride in the supply wagon and boldly proposed further, "If you will permit me, Carmen, I will drive the buggy and one of the other vaqueros can take my horse. Thus, I will drive the horse, and you will sit beside me. I will also avoid the ruts in the road, so you will not be bumped, and your journey will be the easier."

"That is very kind of you, Señor Nacio," Carmen shyly

247

thanked him. At this, the mature vaquero brightened, for at least Carmen had come partway to acknowledging him by his first name, even if she had tacked a "señor" in front of it. And the look of ineffable happiness he shot Eddie Gentry made his friend turn away, lest he laugh out loud and thus offend his companion.

Eddie estimated that, riding slowly, they would reach Windhaven Range on the morning of the fifth day. There was no need to hurry and to discommode the young woman, who had never before made so long a journey.

Kitante had insisted that the Windhaven men take a side of beef left over from the feast the night before, to use as provision on the trail. Carmen insisted on being the cook, and on the first evening of the journey she set about making *bistec asado* over the smoldering campfire. When it was finished, she brought some on a tin plate to Nacio Lorcas and, her eyes lowered and blushing, stammered, "I do not know if it is very good, Señor Nacio, but I should like your opinion."

Nacio tasted it, lifted his face skyward, and uttered a rhapsodic sigh. "I have never tasted anything more delicious, I swear it on my hope of salvation, Carmen! If, when a rogue like me dies, I am permitted to enter paradise, I only pray I may have heavenly *comida* like this."

"Oh, you are teasing me! It is not fair." She drew back, a disappointed look on her lovely face.

"I swear to you, as surely as my name is Nacio Lorcas, that I do not poke fun at you." He took a generous bite of the meat, chewed it and swallowed it, then uttered another rapturous sigh. "You may ask my friend, Señor Eddie, if I ever lie."

"It's true, Carmen, I've never heard him tell a lie in the years he's been with us," Eddie Gentry told her with a smile. "And besides, to settle the matter, let me have some of that, too." He ladled a portion onto his plate, bit into it, chewed it and swallowed it, and then nodded. "It's wonderful, Carmen."

"Do you—do you really think so? It is kind of you to say that. *Gracias*. I will give the other men theirs." She hurried back to the cooking fire, only to turn and send Nacio Lorcas a long, grateful look.

It was the fourth and last evening of the return journey. Nacio and the others might easily have made it back to

Windhaven Range by that very evening—but the genial vaquero had no wish to hurry. Seated beside Carmen Rodago, feeling the pressure of her body when at times the swiftly trotting horse, obedient to Nacio's expert direction, veered to one side to avoid a mudhole or a shallow gully and shifted the young woman against him, he actually wished that this journey might never end. She was still shy with him, but there were sidelong glances now, and stammered words that often trailed off into silence when she felt herself overwhelmed by the new emotions beginning to rise within her.

Yet though he was longing to tell her that he was already in love with her, Nacio angrily rebuked himself. He told himself that it was only because he was so lonely and because she was the first attractive young woman he had known in longer than he cared to remember that he was feeling this way. Besides, he chided himself almost indignantly, by what right did he, a humble vaquero, have to pay court to such a charming young woman whose proximity to him was simply because of her circumstances?

The four vaqueros and Eddie Gentry understood very well what was happening between these two, but tactfully took no notice of the growing infatuation between Carmen Rodago and Nacio Lorcas. They wished him well, for they liked and admired him. He was a trustworthy companion and a man to be relied on when danger threatened.

They made camp about eighteen miles southwest of the Nueces River, on a slightly elevated grassy knoll not far from a freshwater stream, one of the many tributaries of the river itself. Carmen volunteered to fetch water for the evening meal, and took a bucket and walked toward the stream. The men busied themselves making a campfire and taking out what supplies they would need for supper. Eddie Gentry leisurely stood guard, his Spencer carbine at the ready, though in this area there really was no danger of attack by either bandits or Indians. Nonetheless, it was an instinctive precaution, better taken than neglected, as many a frontiersman had learned to his sorrow.

Night was coming on quickly, and from the west there was the faint rumble of thunder. Suddenly there was a shrill cry of terror and Nacio Lorcas straightened, uttered an echoing cry of apprehension, and ran toward the sound.

In the twilight gloom, Carmen had failed to notice a rift in the ground, and her step precipitated her headlong into a

249

crevice. As she dropped the bucket, she reached out with both hands and seized a small dwarf tree growing out of the side of the narrow ravine, which was at least twenty feet deep.

"I'm coming, Carmen, I'm coming!" Nacio shouted as he hurried toward the area.

Carmen desperately held on to the tree with both hands, but her weight was beginning to draw upon the sturdy, deep roots of the scrub tree, and she hysterically called out, "Hurry! It's going to tear away—oh, please help me!"

Guided by her cries, Nacio reached the ravine and peered down. "Hold on and don't move! I'll get you out safely *querida!*" he shouted. He ran back as fast as he could to his horse, grabbed the lariat from the saddlehorn, and ran back to the rift. Squatting down, he looked into her tearstained and contorted face. Clumps of earth were tumbling down, dislodged as the tree's roots gave way. "I'm going to let down my lasso, Carmen," he shouted. "Catch it and loop it under your left arm, then grab on to the rope with both hands—as you do, I'll pull you out! Are you ready?"

"Oh, yes, but do please hurry, the tree is going to give way at any moment—" she sobbed.

The loop of the lariat descended just past her shoulders. Gritting her teeth and taking a firmer hold of the tree with her right hand, Carmen swiftly grasped the lariat with her other hand and slipped it under her arm, then held on tightly to it while she let go of the tree with her right. Hardly had she done so when the tree completely dislodged and tumbled to the bottom of the ravine. Nacio tugged on the lariat, calling words of encouragement to the terrified young woman, until at last he had drawn her clear of the rift.

Kneeling down beside her, he eased the lariat and drew it from her, and then solicitously demanded, "Are you all right, *querida?*"

"Oh, yes—thanks to you! You saved me, Nacio! I was so afraid!"

"There is no need to be afraid anymore, *querida*. Rest a little. Supper can wait. When I heard you cry out for help, I thought I'd lost you forever—"

She lifted her tearstained face and stared at him. "Did you—did you truly feel that, Nacio?"

"*¡Sí!* And that is because—I will not hide it any longer, and I do not care if you think me a stupid man for saving it—I'm in love with you, Carmen, *mi corazón*. I would be honored if you would marry me, and I would work hard all of my life to make you happy."

Her eyes were bright with tears, but her lips were curved in a tremulous smile as she stammered faintly, "I—I feel about you the same way, *mi* Nacio. We have known each other only a very short time, but I already see what a kind, good, brave man you are."

"And I, what a beautiful, wise, and sweet *mujer* you are. I did not dream that the good *Señor Dios* would take pity on my loneliness and let me find such a one as you, Carmen."

He bent his head and put his hands to her shoulders, and they exchanged their first kiss. She gave him her lips trustingly, and her arms linked around his shoulders as the kiss was prolonged. Nacio believed that he had been transported to paradise, and his heart was wildly pounding when at last the kiss was ended. "Oh, *querida*, I am speechless— I—I—will you—do me the honor—say you will marry me, *querida*!" he hoarsely urged. "There is a church at Windhaven Range, and the old Padre Bartoloméo, who is a good friend of your Padre Mendoza, can marry us there, if you wish it."

"Yes, I do. With all my heart and soul, *mi* Nacio. You will not mind, though, if I study with the sisters so that I can become even wiser and more helpful to you in building our home and then, in time, our family?" She blushed at these last words and lowered her eyes. Nacio could not speak, for his heart was too full. At last, he regained control enough to say, in an unsteady voice, "That would please me greatly, dear Carmen."

When they arrived at Windhaven Range the following afternoon, Nacio Lorcas took Carmen's hand in his when he and Eddie went to the hacienda to report to Lucien Edmond and Maxine Bouchard. As it happened, old Friar Bartoloméo Alicante was conversing with them, and when he saw the vaquero and the demure young woman, he rose with alacrity and came to her, his arms open, his face beaming, as he declared, "Friar Mendoza has answered my letter in the best of all possible ways!"

251

"You are too kind to me, *mi padre*," Carmen self-effacingly murmured, and lowered her eyes as she saw Maxine and Lucien Edmond smilingly regard her.

Nacio, who found his sombrero an encumbrance between his suddenly awkward fingers, could no longer contain himself. "I beg your pardon, *patrón*, but Carmen and I have something to say, if I may be permitted?"

"By all means," Lucien Edmond approved.

"We have fallen in love, and we wish to be married. Perhaps Friar Bartoloméo will do us this great service?"

"My children, what you have said to me fills my heart to overflowing." The old priest embraced Carmen, then turned to Nacio. "By all means, I shall gladly perform the ceremony which unites you. Dear Señorita Rodago, you will begin a new life here as Señora Lorcas. Oh, this is a happy day indeed!"

"Nacio, you certainly have my blessing, and you have earned your right to happiness," Lucien Edmond avowed. "Let us have a great *fiesta* tomorrow evening, with dancing and singing. It will give all of us here a chance to salute you, Nacio, as a *gran vaquero*, and to welcome Carmen into our community."

"I should like to be best man," Eddie Gentry spoke up.

"You are very kind, Señor Eddie." Nacio was very near tears, so moved was he by the rush of happiness that surged through him at this reception. His free hand continued to cling to Carmen's as if afraid that someone would suddenly separate them. "There is none better to stand for me at my *día de boda!*"

The next afternoon, in the diminutive church crowded with Nacio Lorcas's companions, who had bathed and dressed in their very best for the occasion, the old Franciscan friar united Nacio and Carmen in holy matrimony. Eddie Gentry nervously fingered the ring, which Lucien Edmond had bestowed on the newlyweds as his gift. Eddie was staring intently at his friend when the doors of the church opened and admitted the bride. In his turn, Nacio Lorcas stood spellbound, staring at the young woman. Her beaming face was framed by a white lace mantilla, and her gown would not have been out of place if the wedding had occurred at the Escorial in Madrid. Carla had generously offered Carmen this dress, one which she had worn to a ball in Galveston a year before.

252

The *fiesta* was joyous, and the evening was pleasant, with breezes from the river fast relieving the oppressive heat of the day. As the vaqueros and their families made their way to the tables piled high with food, they noticed what looked like hundreds of fireflies ringing the area. Drawing closer, the glinting lights became dozens of paper lanterns strung on wires and hanging on the branches of trees. Some of the men played their guitars, others violins and concertinas, as they sang old Mexican songs and danced. By acclamation, Nacio was called upon to do the Mexican hat dance, and he acquitted himself with éclat. Then, as midnight neared, the musicians played a dreamy waltz, and Nacio took Carmen into his arms, and the two of them danced alone as all applauded.

Carla stood between her mother and father, entranced by this heartwarming scene. "One day, dearest Carla," Maxine murmured to her, "you may paint that from memory and give us a memento of this wonderful evening."

"I must apologize to you, dear Carla," Lucien Edmond whispered to his daughter. "When Joe Duvray went into San Antonio some weeks ago to visit the bank and to purchase supplies, I asked him to buy a ring as a gift for you for your forthcoming birthday. But I gave it to Nacio and Carmen, for it would never do for them to marry without a proper ring. However, you shall have something even better: the opportunity to go off to school."

"Oh, Father, you're so good, I love you so! You know how happy I've been, growing up out here on this wonderful ranch. But it will be wonderful, too, to have the chance to go to school in a city! I'll make you proud of me, you and Mother both, I promise!" She embraced him, tears glistening in her dark eyes. And then, as a kind of afterthought, she wistfully murmured, "I do hope Hugo will give up the idea of being a rancher—maybe he'll join me in college, studying something he will find more rewarding than riding horses and driving cattle."

Lucien Edmond looked over at his wife and chuckled. "I'm beginning to suspect that the two of you are conspiring to keep Hugo from staying on Windhaven Range! But I have to confess that I, too, have been seriously reconsidering Hugo's future. It appears that at this point, none of us feels certain that Hugo should take over this ranch. I wonder what Hugo has decided by now. Well, not having him take over from me isn't really important. We've Eddie and Joe and Ramón—among the three of them, they'll keep it going when I decide to stop ranching, if it turns out that Hugo has discovered he wants to do something else with his life."

The hour was very late. The musicians were winding down, playing the last set of dances, and Nacio and Carmen had already slipped away unnoticed to their cottage, one of several that the vaqueros had built near the bunkhouses two years ago. Lucien Edmond turned to his wife and said, "May a doting husband have the honor and pleasure of this last dance, dearest Maxine?"

### Twenty-four

During the first week of May, Robert Markey, followed by the faithful mongrel, had crossed over into Texas and was steadfastly heading south in the hope of finding Windhaven Range. That hope alone had given him the strength to doggedly continue toward the compassionate Mexican trail boss, the one person who had shown kindness to him since he had gone out from Indiana to Kansas as a homesteader.

He had been haunted all these months by the memory of how his wife and child had died in the blizzard, despite all his efforts to save their lives. He had ridden along on the young mare that Ramón had given him, weighted down by the imponderable guilt, which he could not efface, that somehow his ineptitude as a farmer had cost the lives of his wife and child.

Now, aside from his mare, Jenny, the dog was his only friend. There were times—as he trekked from one farm to another to earn money to buy food that would enable him to reach his final destination—when he talked to the animal as if it were human and could understand and sympathize with him, condone his faults, and pardon his transgressions.

Undaunted by his bleak, condemnatory rejection from the sanctimonious Jed Bowland, he had stopped frequently along the way to ask for work. He had occasionally come across somewhat larger farms, and the reception in these places had been kinder. One of the jobs had lasted from mid-February till the end of April. But as he moved farther south, he found more ranches than farms, and there his luck was virtually nil.

Just over the border of Indian Territory, in northwest Texas, he had stopped at a prosperous-looking frame house, with a barn and a small bunkhouse. Robert Markey had tethered his horse to the wooden fence a hundred yards away from the house, and, turning to the mongrel he had named Tramp, urged the dog to stay there. "They might not like dogs, Tramp, so you let me go ahead and find a job, and then I'll be able to get meat for you. My God, but you're thin—I'll help put some more fat on your bones. Just stay with me, Tramp. But be good now and don't bark, please. They might take offense at it."

He hunkered down, cupped the muzzle of the dog between his palms, and petted its face earnestly. The mongrel had uttered a low whine, and Robert chuckled and nodded as he straightened. What a comfort it was to have this dog along with him! There had been long, lonely nights, when he had thought he would be crushed by the fears and doubts and guilt that swirled inside of him. If it hadn't been for this four-footed companion and his mare— between the two of them, he'd known deeper friendship than he'd ever made, either back in Indiana, or on that ill-fated Kansas farm.

As he straightened up to walk to the house, he thought wryly that the only compensation for all these unremitting months of effort was the physical change that effort had wrought: he was leaner now, wirier, for he endured more exertion in a concentrated period of time than ever before, and yet to almost no avail. After that comparatively long-term job on a farm where the elderly owner and his wife had been grateful for even his amateurish help, Robert had found little work to keep him going. He had come to this small ranch hoping almost against hope that they would take him on.

His knock at the door was answered by the ranch owner, a Dutchman who had moved out to Texas from the East. Robert had been given a meal with four other cowhands in

255

the kitchen, all of whom looked at him contemptuously. One of them had muttered to his companion, "He's got the look of a sodbuster, if I ever saw one."

And then, after lunch, the rancher ordered him to try his hand at breaking a wild mustang. It had tossed him twice, and the Dutchman had sneered, spat on the ground, and said, "*Ich denke nicht, mein Herr*—you can't do me any good. When I hire a man for *Arbeit*, it is not for to make me *lachen. Auf Wiedersehen.*"

Wearily, Robert had mounted his mare and ridden off, the hooted jeers of the four cowhands ringing in his ears.

There were very few farms here in Texas, and the next ranch owners were even less sympathetic than the Dutchman had been. One was a shriveled old man with sparse gray hair. His brother, some five years younger, was fat and bald; both were bachelors. They had a comely Mexican housekeeper, a dozen ranch hands, and four hundred head of cattle. The younger brother gruffly asked him to go out and help the hands brand some of the cattle he intended to sell in Fort Worth. Borrowing a lariat from one of the hands, Robert had missed two calves as they trotted away from the two men around the fire with the branding iron. The rancher had followed him and stood looking over the corral fence. After the second calf had gone by, he had bawled out, "That's all, mister. Better be on your way. Next time, don't come asking for work under false pretenses. You didn't even earn the meal you got."

Once again, he had heard some of the hands sneeringly call him a "dumb sodbuster. He can't rope a calf any ten-year-old kid could handle." By now he was inured to this derision and rejection. He only hoped that as he continued to head south, somewhere he would find Ramón Hernandez and Windhaven Range. And maybe, if he told Ramón how bad his luck had been, maybe there'd be some sort of chance for him, even if it were only washing dishes in the bunkhouse kitchen.

By now, he had made his way past San Antonio, and the much-traveled trail he followed took him toward the southwest. It was midafternoon when suddenly the sky turned dark. The wind began to howl, and the next thing he knew, his eyes were nearly blinded with swirling sand. Dismounting, one hand over his eyes, the other gripping the reins of the mare, he stumbled blindly onward, hoping to find a

256

clump of mesquite or a group of boulders to provide shelter.

The wind seemed to increase its ferocity just as he reached a group of gnarled trees. He had enough presence of mind to make his mare lie down, coaxing her and finally shoving her, and then he lay beside her, waiting for the storm to abate.

Groping for his bandanna and spitting on it, he rubbed his eyes to clear them of the gritty sand clinging to his eyelids. Then, suddenly, he realized that Tramp was not with him. He raised his head to try to spot the dog, but the biting sand forced him back down almost immediately.

Two hours later the wind began to die down and the sunless sky lightened. He stumbled to his feet and urged the mare up, tethering the reins to one of the trees. He was frantic at the thought of having lost such a faithful companion. He ought to have made sure that the dog was beside him when the storm started. Yes, what the cowhands said about him was true; he was just a stupid sodbuster, after all. He couldn't even keep a mongrel dog safe from harm.

He began walking in all directions, calling out as loudly as he could, "Tramp—here, boy! Where are you? Tramp, here I am—come on, boy, that's a good boy!" until his throat was hoarse. But there was no sign of the dog. His head bowed, his shoulders slumped, he stumbled back through the sandy soil to where he had left the docile mare. He untied the reins and, aching with fatigue, mounted her. Then he rode slowly southward, seeking Windhaven Range. With the kind of luck he had had already, he wasn't even certain that this long quest would be successful. He didn't want to think about what would happen if he couldn't find the man who had been so kind to him.

As he sat astride the mare, he kept looking back, hoping against hope that Tramp would suddenly materialize. But it was growing darker now, and night would soon be upon him—time to find someplace to camp. He didn't have many provisions left. Yesterday, at the last ranch when he'd had lunch, he'd managed to sneak a few pieces of bread and a piece of stringy boiled beef brisket into the pocket of his britches. In his saddlebag there was only a little flour, just enough coffee for a final pot, and a piece of sharp cheese, as big as his fist, which a sympathetic cook had given him about a week ago. He really didn't feel like eating, not with Tramp gone. His aching heart reminded him how much the dog had meant to him during this long trek. When he confided his innermost fears and dreams to the dog, Tramp had seemed to understand exactly what he was saying, and would sometimes nudge him with his muzzle and whine as if empathizing.

He let the mare amble onward along the trail. The sandstorm had covered many of the old tracks now, but there was still a faint outline to follow. Maybe the next rancher would know exactly where Windhaven Range was.

He rode another two miles, and then decided he had had enough for the day. He saw a small stream and a stretch of sparsely grassed land over to his right, and decided that this was as good a campsite as any. As he dismounted, he thought to himself that, at the moment, the prospect of getting on the mare again and riding on was unbearable—yet it had to be done.

And that reminded him that he didn't have much to offer the mare, either. A couple of handfuls of oats in the other section of the saddlebag, that was about all. Well, at least she could graze on the grass. She deserved a lot more, but he just didn't have it. He tied the mare's reins to a lone, twisted scrub tree surrounded by bushes, plunged his hands into the side of the saddlebag, held out his palms filled with the oats and let the mare eat that way. He repeated this until all the oats were gone. Then he untied the reins and walked with her to the stream. He watched her dip her muzzle into the water and drink, until he thought she had had enough, and then jerked up the reins gently, saying, "That's enough now; that's enough, girl."

He led her back to the tree and tied her and then began to prepare his meager supper. There was plenty of dry wood around, dead branches from the tree broken off by the storm, and he soon had a small, cheerful fire going. It gave him the illusion of being safe and at peace. He took out the bread and the meat and made a sandwich, and listlessly began to chew. The bread was stale by now, and the beef was stringier than ever, but at least it was nourishment.

The sky had cleared, and stars and a quarter moon had come out. He locked his arms around his knees and looked up at the stars. Suppose they turned him down at Windhaven—where would he go then? What would he do? He'd have to find that man, Ramón Hernandez, and make a clean breast of what a mess he'd made of his life, ask for a chance to prove he had something in him. After all, Ramón had saved his life, and he remembered that the Mexicans had a proverb that, if a man saved your life, you owned him a debt you had to repay by being of service in turn.

Suddenly he heard a noise, off in a clump of bushes to the left. His heart began to beat rapidly, and he moved cautiously back to the mare and pulled his rifle out of the saddle sheath. It could be a wolf—then again, it might be one of those jackrabbits. Food for tomorrow, at least.

He aimed the rifle at the rustling sound, cocked it—then uttered an incredulous cry and dropped the rifle. Out of the bushes, its tail wagging furiously, came the mongrel.

"Tramp—oh, thank God! Tramp, boy, I thought you were lost forever! Oh, Tramp, come here to me!" he sobbed, as he sank down on his knees and held his arms out to the dog. It whined, then barked and came to him, its tail wagging faster than ever. Robert Markey hugged the dog close to him, buried his face in the animal's thickly furred neck, and sobbed unabashedly.

Finally, he rose to his feet. It was an omen of some kind. It had strengthened him, and he thought that he could face the future now with a little less bleakness.

### Twenty-five

Heartened by his reunion with Tramp, Robert Markey rode with a new determination toward his goal. That morning, he stopped by a small ranch and managed to earn his lunch and some extra food to take with him by helping fork piles of hay into the barn for the cattle and horses. He was told by the bluff, middle-aged rancher that the Bouchard spread was about forty-five miles due west. And this time, because Robert had been given a simple chore with which, as a farmer, he was thoroughly familiar, his energetic work at last earned him a commendation: "Windhaven's a pretty big spread, mister, but all they raise is cattle there. Me, I've got a few crops besides needing hay for my horses and cattle, and I like your style. You gave an honest couple of hours for the grub I gave you, so if you don't make out there, come on back. Maybe I can use you for harvesting in the fall. Mind you, I'm not promising much, but at least you'll have food and a place to sleep."

"I—I'm grateful to you, Mr. Ellison," Robert stammered at the unaccustomed praise. "But I have to see a certain man there. I owe him a debt, and I'm hoping to pay it back and earn a place there."

The rancher gave him a quizzical look. "Well now, if you mean what you say, you'll be the first fellow I've met in a long time who feels he has to settle his accounts. Good luck to you—and don't forget what I told you: if there's nothing for you there, you come back here, and I'll find something for you. I like a man who's straightforward with me and pitches in when he's given something to do."

So Robert mounted his mare and rode on toward Windhaven Range with renewed spirit. Tramp trotted along, looking up occasionally to bark and to wag his tail, and Robert smiled and then chuckled, and it was the first time he had been happy since the tragic death of his wife and child.

Now that he knew he was near Windhaven Range, it was as if an elixir of life had been imbued into his very pores. He made camp for what he hoped would be the last time, and slept soundly through the night. When dawn broke, he finished the last of his provisions, sharing them with Tramp. He picked up the small sack of hay the farmer had given him and dumped it on the ground for the mare. Then, after washing himself off in the small stream a few yards off, he stretched out on his blanket and slept for about two hours. He woke to the bright sun and the feel of Tramp's warm tongue licking his cheek to waken him.

Hugging the dog, he frolicked with it for a few moments, till Tramp backed up and indignantly barked at him. Robert laughed till there were tears in his eyes. It was a kind of catharsis after the long days and nights of utter misery. Just before he mounted the mare, he bent down and told the mongrel, "I've got a good feeling about where we're going this time, Tramp, boy. Maybe they need another watchdog—maybe they don't even have one, and you'll do just fine. So now let's go and find a new home for both of us—yes, and for you, too," he said to the mare as he straightened up. The horse pricked up its ears and snorted, sounding remarkably like a dubious human.

This set him laughing all over again, an almost hysterical laughter. If a stranger had passed him at this moment, he would have deemed the young farmer utterly mad—and yet, Robert Markey had never been saner in all his life. The guilt had been purged away, and now there was only a furious desire to start life again on terms with which he could cope and by which he could prove himself to be of worth.

It was just past noon when at last he saw the sprawling hacienda, the bunkhouses, the church, the school building, and, to the west, the houses and cottages of all the families living at Windhaven Range. Vast, rich grass stretched farther than the eye could see, and cattle grazed peacefully almost to the horizon. Here and there, a vaquero placidly rode his horse, watching over the herd and making certain that all was well. The sun shone, the air was warm, and the sky was dotted with fleecy clouds that intensified its dazzling blue. And what struck Robert most was the utter serenity and peacefulness of this setting; it was kind of symbolic assurance to him that he at last had come out of the storm and stress of the bitter elements and his own personal tragedy into an aura of well-being and hope.

He rode up slowly toward the hacienda, and some of the vaqueros coming out of one of the bunkhouses stared curiously at him, and even more at the mongrel trotting alongside the docile, weary mare. Reaching the house, he dismounted with a long sigh of relief, then tied the reins to the hitching post. He squatted down and cupped the dog's muzzle, saying, "Now you stay put, Tramp, okay?" To this, the dog gave an answering bark and then sat down, his tongue lolling between his jaws as he watched his master walk toward the door of the ranch house.

When he knocked, it was Maxine who opened to him and smilingly asked, "May I help you?"

He courteously removed his battered hat before replying, "Excuse me, ma'am, I—well, my name's Robert Markey, and I'm looking for Ramón Hernandez."

"I'm so sorry," she told him, "but Señor Hernandez is

261

away on a drive. I'm Mrs. Bouchard—perhaps my husband could help."

"Yes—I—I'd like to talk to your husband, if I may—if I'm not disturbing him."

"Not at all. Come in." And then, seeing how exhausted the stranger was, Maxine solicitously added, "You look very tired—you must have come a long way. Perhaps you'd like to have a bite of lunch? It would be no trouble at all."

"That's very kind of you, Mrs. Bouchard," Robert uttered a bit nervously. "Truth is, I'm plumb out of food." He then added, as if it would explain his dilemma, "I've come all the way from Kansas."

"Good heavens! Come in here with me; I'll introduce you to my husband right away."

"Thank you, you're very kind."

She led him into the dining room, where Lucien Edmond Bouchard had just finished his lunch and was sipping coffee. He was reading the San Antonio newspaper, which his men had picked up two weeks ago when they had gone there to bring back supplies for the ranch.

"Don't get up, dear. I've asked this young man to have a bite of lunch. His name is Robert Markey, and he says he's come all the way from Kansas to see Ramón."

Lucien Edmond genially nodded to the newcomer and gestured toward the chair opposite him. "Sit down, by all means. As my wife undoubtedly must have told you, Ramón's away on a drive. You say you came from Kansas?"

"I'll go out to the kitchen and get you some hot food, Mr. Markey," Maxine softly interposed, then left the room.

"Yes, you've certainly come a long way," Lucien Edmond resumed. "Did you meet Ramón in Newton or perhaps Abilene on an earlier drive?"

"I—I might as well tell you the whole story, Mr. Bouchard." Robert Markey fidgeted nervously in his chair; he looked down at his hat that he had put in his lap, and then set it on the floor. The pause gave him time to recollect his thoughts. "Well, Mr. Bouchard, it's like this. The summer before last, Ramón Hernandez and his men were driving a herd to Dodge."

"Yes, I remember it very well—he had some, well, problems in that town. That's where you met him?"

Maxine now returned with a bowl of stew, biscuits, and a cup of coffee, which she set before young Markey. He looked up and, his face filled with gratitude, thanked her. Then he turned back to Lucien Edmond. "Not—not exactly, Mr. Bouchard. You see, I'm a farmer. Two years before I met him, I came out from Indiana with my wife, Marcy, and we'd just had a baby the month before I met him. I wasn't doing very well—in fact, the land wouldn't raise anything; not wheat, nor rye, nor barley—and we were just about starving. I was riding out looking for—I really don't know what—and I saw the herd, and there was a stray steer and I—well, Mr. Bouchard, I cut it out."

"Oh?" Lucien Edmond regarded his visitor with widened, startled eyes, leaning forward to listen.

"They—they were going to lynch me. They said I was a rustler. And then—and then Mr. Hernandez came by and made them let me go—and he gave me the steer and some supplies, too. Then—well, we had a terrible blizzard in Kansas this past January. My wife and child died and I didn't have anything left, except my horse, my rifle, and a bit of food—and I—I went off searching for Windhaven Range and Ramón Hernandez. I wanted to tell him what happened and pay him back—I was hoping I could do it by working." Robert leaned back and closed his eyes, his forehead damp with perspiration.

Lucien Edmond stared at the young farmer, then sympathetically shook his head and gently suggested, "You'd best eat your lunch before it gets cold, Mr. Markey. It took a lot of courage for you to tell me this, I know. I think you're a very honest man. I'd never fault anyone if he were driven to rustling because his family was starving. I'm glad Ramón didn't let the vaqueros hurt you."

"It's—it's damned decent of you to say that to me, Mr. Bouchard, when it was one of your own steers."

"I've lost many more than one steer on the trail, and I don't think twice about it. This one went for a good cause. Now eat your lunch, and then we can talk. I don't think that Ramón will be back much before early fall. You see, he went to Colorado to meet a Wyoming rancher who wanted to buy stock. And he'll probably swing back over and pay a visit to the Creek reservation in Indian Territory before he returns."

The savory smell of the food made the famished man attack it with gusto, and Lucien Edmond smiled again as he leaned back in his chair. Tentatively, he flexed the muscles of his leg and was pleased to find that the stiffness

263

was just about gone. Very soon he could be in the saddle again. It was all very well to be coddled by Maxine—he certainly enjoyed it, and they had been drawn closer together because of it—but all the same, a man wanted to make do for himself and not feel pampered, at least not on a ranch.

"How about seconds?" he offered, after Robert had polished his plate clean.

"I feel like a pig—but it's so very good—"

"Then seconds you shall have," Lucien Edmond said with a grin. Raising his voice, he called, and Maxine came in from the kitchen. She took Robert's plate back to the kitchen to refill it, returned it to him, then poured more coffee into his empty cup. She then went back to the kitchen, tactfully leaving the two men to talk alone.

When Robert had finally finished his lunch, Lucien Edmond leaned back and declared, "If all my vaqueros had your appetite, I'd be eaten out of house and home!" He chuckled and assured the young man, "I'm joking, of course. Now, what can I do for you?"

"I—I'd very much like to work for you, Mr. Bouchard. I'll tell you the truth, I'm not very good at anything except being a farmer, and the way the land turned out for me the last two years, I'm beginning to wonder if I'm even a good farmer. But I'm not afraid of work; I'll do what I'm told and I'll try to learn and earn my keep."

"That's a good attitude. You're young and strong and intelligent, and you've got a real motive. Yes, I think I might find a place for you here. But I promise you that you would indeed have to earn your keep. Sentiment is fine and I'll help you all I can, but if you're of no use to my operation here, you can't expect a job long-range."

"I'll take my chances on that, Mr. Bouchard."

"Fair enough. Tell you what, Mr. Markey, go over to the larger, main bunkhouse and ask the vaqueros where you can find Eddie Gentry—he acts as foreman here when Ramón's gone. He'll give you a bunk and a bedroll. You have a horse, you say?"

"A mare. She's tuckered out from all she's been through, and I am, too, for that matter." Robert Markey gave a faint smile and chuckle.

"I shouldn't wonder. Well, we've plenty of horses in our remuda, and the vaqueros go out and rope wild mustangs whenever they see a herd so there's no shortage of horses.

Anyway, have Eddie take you to meet Walter Catlin. I think it would be good for the two of you to work together—you've both had some hard times and unhappy experiences. I think he'll show more interest in you than the average vaquero, just because of what he's been through."

"I'm grateful, Mr. Bouchard. You won't be sorry you gave me this chance, I swear to you, you won't. And—and would you thank your wife for the wonderful lunch?"

"My pleasure. Well, then, Mr. Markey, I'll be seeing you in the next few days to find out how you like us and how we like you."

After settling his exhausted mare in the stable, where he put a generous amount of hay down for her to eat, he unhitched his saddle, removed the saddlebags, and flung them over his shoulder. He sauntered over to the big bunkhouse, with Tramp following closely on his heels, and explained to the vaquero sitting on the porch who he was and why he was there.

The man indicated an empty bunk, with its foot locker for his meager possessions, then directed Robert to Eddie Gentry's house.

"I'm obliged to you," he told the vaquero. "I hope you don't mind if my dog stays here while I seek out Mr. Gentry."

"It is no problem at all, señor," the genial man replied. "I am very fond of dogs—I used to have one much like this one when I was a boy. He was very smart and very brave. And I am thinking that your dog is like that, too, *sí?*" He ruffled the dog's fur and frowned. "I am also thinking that this *perro* is much too thin! *Con su permiso, señor,* I will take this little one to the kitchen and find him a good, meaty bone."

"That would be very nice of you," Robert beamed. "By the way, I don't even know your name."

*"Me llamo Carlos, señor,"* the vaquero replied.

"Nice to meet you, Carlos. And please call me Robert." He bent down to his faithful companion and grinned. "Well, Tramp, looks like both of us have made friends already. Now, you be a good boy, and do exactly what Carlos tells you to do while I go off and see about earning our keep."

He found Eddie Gentry planting a small vegetable garden at the rear of his house, and after hearing Lucien Edmond's instructions, the genial Texan escorted Robert Markey to one of the cattle pens where Walter Catlin was supervising the branding.

Walter introduced himself, then declared, "Fact is, I remember you, because I was in that outfit heading to Dodge when Felipe and Narciso wanted to string you up."

The young farmer turned scarlet with mortification and looked down at his shoes. Walter gently prompted, "I didn't say that to make you uncomfortable, Markey. I'm glad Ramón did what he did for you."

The young farmer then told Walter all that had happened to him since his meeting with Ramón, and why it was that he had come to Windhaven Range.

"Damn, I'm sorry to hear that. You know, I was going to Dodge on unfinished business and I thought about you when I got there, wondering if you'd make out. Well, I guess our paths are crossing again. My luck has sure changed for the better—I married a sweet girl here, Connie Belcher, and we've already got a son—so maybe yours will change, too."

"I'm glad for you, Mr. Catlin."

"No need for the 'mister,' Markey," Walter Catlin dryly chuckled. "The only difference between us is that I've got some experience on Windhaven Range under my belt, and you're just a tyro. Well, we'll get started in a nice, easygoing way. I don't want you to get the feeling that I'm like a schoolteacher standing over you with a ruler, or anything like that."

"Thanks for talking to me this way, I appreciate it. Would it be—is it all right if I call you Walter?"

"Sure you can. Matter of fact, it'll give you the feeling you've got a friend here on the ranch—you'd go about your work with a little more interest that way. And I'll call you by your first name."

"I'm glad Mr. Bouchard picked you to supervise me, I truly am. And I'm going to make good, you watch and see."

"I hope you do. I have a lot of sympathy for you, Robert. I think we'll get along just fine."

"Thanks again. Well, I guess we'd better get started. What do you want me to do first?"

"Well," Walter suggested, "let's see how much you know about roping a steer, or, to start you off easy, a calf."

Robert Markey suppressed a dismayed sigh, and followed his new mentor to the smaller cattle pen used for branding calves and yearlings. At Walter's gesture, a grinning vaquero opened the small gate and let out a calf that trotted placidly out into the center of the pen and stood blinking its eyes. Robert deftly caught the lariat which Walter tossed and essayed casting it out, but it fell short.

"No, that's not right. You've got to make a wide loop and fling it with some speed, then yank at it as it goes over the calf's head. Let me show you," Walter proposed.

Robert stood attentively watching as the older man expertly roped the calf. "Then you hog-tie him and get him down for branding, pushing him over to the side like this— you see? Then shorten your lariat and take a hold of the rear legs, so he won't kick too much when he feels the brand. Everybody has his own way of doing it, Robert, but the first thing is of course to get your lariat over your animal's head so you'll have control. All right, now you try it."

Thus began a series of arduous training sessions for the young farmer. Lucien Edmond had told Walter that Robert Markey was to be shown no favoritism, but rather given as many strict tests as possible to see what his stamina might be and his attitude in responding. Because the young farmer was eager to earn his place on Windhaven Range, he doggedly persisted until after about a week he could throw a lariat with a reasonable degree of accuracy.

Next came the breaking-in of wild mustangs, a task at which Robert inwardly cringed. After his docile mare, some of the mustangs he had seen kicking up their heels and snorting in a nearby corral made him wonder if he could ever master them.

Again, Walter Catlin was infinitely patient. He showed him how to lasso the mustang, draw him to a halt, put a saddle on him, and then quickly mount and use the single end of the lariat as a rein and also a choke, if the horse proved intractable.

Robert worked out for a week in an otherwise empty corral. He was thrown several times each day, ending the afternoon bruised and exhausted. Though he winced when he went after the rebellious mustang again and again, he showed no cowardice, and Walter made a mental note that, at least, the young farmer was stubbornly determined to persevere.

"I think I'll let the big boss take a look at what you've learned so far, Robert," Walter finally decided at the end of the second week. "He's the one who decides whether you've got a job here or not, you know. I think you've shown a lot of guts, and I know exactly what you've been thinking and feeling, but tomorrow we'll find out just what his answer is."

Because of his past sorrow and long years of tracking down the man who he believed had been directly responsible for the death of his wife and child, Walter had more indulgence for Robert Markey than his often noncommittal attitude showed toward the younger man. He also hoped that Robert's luck would change as his own had. Walter Catlin and Connie could not have been happier, and the son they had named Henry, after Connie's father, had delighted the elderly man as well as her stepmother, Maybelle.

On Saturday afternoon, the end of Robert Markey's second week of grueling apprenticeship, Lucien Edmond Bouchard walked out to the corral. He leaned against the fence, his hands gripping the top rail on either side, his eyes intently narrowed as he watched Walter open the gate and admit a spirited mustang. Seeing Robert in the pen, the roan mustang reared, its front hooves flailing the air as it snorted angrily. The young man warily circled the rebellious mustang, a lariat in his right hand and a saddle on the ground near his feet. With an expert throw, he took the mustang around the neck and yanked it forward, tying the rope to a fence rail. He swiftly stooped to retrieve the saddle and flung it on the horse's back, but before he could draw the cinch strap to secure the saddle, the roan angrily whinnied and kicked out at him, grazing his shin.

Robert swore under his breath, and Lucien Edmond hid a smile with his palm. He exchanged a knowing look with Walter Catlin, who stood opposite him outside the pen, and nodded as if to say, "Let's see what he does now, after that rebuff."

By now, some of the others had come out to watch the apprentice show the *patrón* what he had learned, including Eddie Gentry and Nacio Lorcas. These two men had chatted a good deal with Robert Markey during the past two weeks and admired his determined spirit after the bereavement he had so cruelly suffered. Now, as they came up to join Walter and Lucien Edmond, they watched with sympathetic interest.

The saddle had been flung to the ground in the mustang's violent movements. Setting his teeth, Robert retrieved the saddle and, warily avoiding the mustang's kicks with its rear legs, flung the saddle over the horse and drew the cinch strap tight. Then, lunging quickly forward, he loosened the lariat from the rail, hurried back, and putting a foot into the left stirrup, vaulted himself into the saddle.

Furious, the roan tried to unsaddle him, bucking and kicking wildly, and twice Robert was thrown. Bruised and aching each time, he stumbled to his feet, hurried after the mustang, and avoiding its kicks, again mounted. The third time, he defied its attempts to unseat him until at last, snorting and whinnying, the roan lowered its head and acknowledged defeat.

Wearily, Robert Markey dismounted, and Walter Catlin entered the pen to lead the mustang away. Lucien Edmond called to him: "Good work, Markey!"

The vaqueros who had watched now applauded, calling out, *"¡Gran vaquero!"* and Nacio and Eddie cheered and waved their sombreros.

The young farmer turned to face Lucien Edmond. "I gave it my best, Mr. Bouchard," he said, saluting Lucien Edmond by touching his forehead with his right forefinger. "Thanks for the chance you gave me."

"You're talking as if everything were over and you were on your way out. Quite the contrary, Markey, quite the contrary. You've got a job here. That wasn't the most elegant way I've seen of breaking in a mustang, but you stuck with it and did it. That's what counts. And you'll get smarter as you have more opportunity to learn under Walter's training. I'll sign you at thirty-five dollars a month and found. And that's just to start."

"I'm very grateful, Mr. Bouchard."

"You earned it." Lucien Edmond waved a hand to return the salute, then walked back to the hacienda.

Walter, Nacio, and Eddie came forward to congratulate the novice. They shook hands with him and clapped him on the back. Eddie looked at the others, and then remarked, "We'll have to take Bob here under our wing, *amigos,* otherwise he'll get himself kicked to death by some of those old mustangs. They're really ornery, and they don't know a *gran vaquero* when they see one. But you'll show them, won't you, Bob, boy?"

"Sure. Thanks, Eddie. And you, too, Nacio and Walter." Robert reached for his bandanna and wiped the sweat off his forehead. "It's good to have friends like you. It's good to have a job, too."

"What you need now is to rub some liniment where that mustang kicked you, or your leg'll be stiff as a board by tomorrow morning," Eddie volunteered. "A medicine show came through last summer, and darned if old Nacio here didn't buy a couple of bottles—he thought it was for drinking, to make señoritas go wild over him." He laughed, slapping his thigh. "It was a lousy love potion, but it's a pretty good liniment."

"Now that is not a nice thing to say, Señor Eddie," Nacio quipped while making a long face and pretending to be irritated. "But on second thought, maybe it *did* work! I now am married to my beautiful Carmen, am I not?"

"Maybe you're right after all," Eddie chuckled, and clapped Nacio on the back. "Come on Bob, he'll give you the bottle and you can rub plenty on. Then it'll be just about time for lunch. Bet you've worked up an appetite!"

"I sure did. You're real pals," Robert hoarsely declared.

And so they indeed had become. So much so, a month later, that Lucien Edmond Bouchard, discussing them over the dinner table with Maxine and his daughters, whimsically referred to them as the "Four Musketeers."

## Twenty-six

Leland Kenniston had sent Lopasuta Bouchard a telegraph wire a week before his expected arrival in New Orleans, telling the Comanche lawyer that he looked forward to at last meeting Geraldine. Although Leland would be in the Queen City for only two days, this trip would mark the beginning of the young couple's life in New Orleans.

Geraldine and he had decided to keep the house on Montgomery Street, which Jedidiah Danforth had bequeathed to Lopasuta. As Geraldine had wisely pointed

270

out, when they finally made their stay in New Orleans a permanent one, the house could be rented and thus provide useful income to be put aside for the children. Accordingly, she had gone across the street to Elizabeth Steers, the elderly widow who had at first made trouble for the young couple, but ended up becoming a good friend.

Mrs. Steers now welcomed their friendship and, on several occasions when Emily Norton had been ill or unable to act as nurse while Lopasuta was still missing, had herself volunteered to substitute. So Geraldine gave Mrs. Steers the news that she and Lopasuta were temporarily moving to New Orleans and that as soon as Lopasuta was admitted to the Louisiana bar, they would be putting their house up for rent.

Lopasuta, Geraldine, Mei Luong, Dennis, and Luke boarded the steamboat *Belle of the River*. As they boarded, Lopasuta thought of the irony in taking this boat: the last time he had sailed her, it was toward his meeting with William Brickley. What an ill-fated journey *that* had turned into, he thought with a rueful grimace.

They had made reservations by wire at the St. Charles Hotel, located in the American Quarter on St. Charles Avenue at Common Street. It had first been opened on Washington's birthday in 1837 and boasted an immense dome, Corinthian portico, and a famous gold service valued at at least twenty thousand dollars. During the Civil War the hotel had been the headquarters of the detested General Benjamin Butler, commander of the Union troops occupying New Orleans.

Geraldine had wanted to stay in the French Quarter at the City Exchange, which had been famous for its social activities like fashionable balls and masquerades, but Lopasuta informed her that in 1874, the hotel had been sold to the state of Louisiana and was currently being used as the state capitol. It had been the scene of the meetings of the infamous "black-and-tan" legislature, as well as of the disturbances which had punctuated the attempts of the White League to overthrow carpetbagger rule and regain control of the state government. At the present time, there was a considerable amount of speculation that the capital would be transferred to Baton Rouge.

Mei Luong was fascinated by the lush scenery as the boat steamed along the Alabama River; when the steamboat neared Mobile, the landscape became almost tropical.

271

Watching at the rail, Lopasuta told Geraldine, "Just think, my darling, it was ninety years ago when Lucien Bouchard—then still a young man—followed the trail by pack mule along this river. And that was where he began his dynasty, of which I am a humble and very grateful part."

When they reached the great levee of New Orleans, Lopasuta quickly engaged a carriage to drive them to the St. Charles Hotel. He was happy to find that there was no animosity toward the young Chinese nurse here, as there had been in San Francisco. He would have been indignant if he had known that the state of California had recently proposed a new constitutional amendment at its convention which was to forbid the employment of Chinese in the state; two months later, popular vote would endorse this prohibitive ruling.

Leland Kenniston was waiting for them in the lobby of the hotel, where he himself had engaged one of the largest rooms. When he saw them enter the hotel, he quickly came forward and shook their hands.

"What a pleasure it is to see you again, Lopasuta—and you, too, Mei Luong," he exclaimed, "and what a delight it is to make your acquaintance at last, Mrs. Bouchard." Then, turning to Lopasuta, he added, in a confidential tone: "You see, my good fellow, I did not think you would have much cause for concern. Obviously, I'd say, you've been reinstated. And your wife—"with this Leland raised his voice slightly—"is truly one of the loveliest women I've ever seen."

Geraldine blushed becomingly and stammered a token phrase of thanks. "You'll all be my guests at Antoine's tonight," he went on. "It's unquestionably the finest restaurant in New Orleans—indeed, it has a reputation of being one of the very best in this country. It's unsurpassed for the treatment of fish, especially pompano; for Creole gumbo, or bouillabaisse, Antoine's is assuredly the place." Seeing that Mei Luong looked mystified, he explained, "Bouillabaisse is a soup or stew with several kinds of fish and shellfish, cooked with tomatoes, olive oil, and saffron. If you like fish, you must certainly try it." The young Chinese nurse looked modestly down at her feet, astonished that this illustrious man should pay her such regard.

Dinner at Antoine's was indeed memorable. Leland was a splendid host, and saw to it that the finest wine was served to his guests. He had engaged a private room so that if the boys should cry, they would not disturb the other patrons, and once again Lopasuta was impressed by the solicitude of the energetic Irishman.

When they had finished dessert, Leland had ordered liqueurs, with a brandy for himself and a cigar to accompany it—after considerately asking Geraldine and Mei Luong if they would find the smell of tobacco offensive. He turned to Geraldine and declared, "I'm glad I had this chance to talk with you, Mrs. Bouchard. When I return here—probably in June—I hope we'll spend a good deal of time together. Your husband has undoubtedly told you of the proposal I made to him."

"Oh, yes. It's certainly very generous, Mr. Kenniston."

"Not really. It's no more than Lopasuta will soon deserve once he passes the bar examination. And, of course, I'm going to stand your moving expenses. Are you planning on selling your present house?" Leland inquired.

"We've decided to keep our Montgomery house for the time being, Mr. Kenniston," Geraldine explained. "We can rent it while we're here—or go back to it, should things not work out."

"That's a very shrewd idea, and I compliment you for it. You're a very practical young woman, just exactly the sort of wife I imagined Lopasuta would marry."

Again Geraldine could not help blushing at such warm praise, and Leland chuckled and turned to the Comanche lawyer. "I'll just have time, before I take the steamboat back to New York, to take you over to meet René Laurent, who is acting *pro tem* as my office manager. As I've previously mentioned, he'll be handling all of the business affairs. He'll bring you up to date very quickly on the economics as well as the politics of New Orleans; he'll acquaint you with the intended scope of my importing and exporting firm—specifically as regards this Louisiana office—but the rest of the time he'll be aware that you'll be studying for your bar examination."

"Yes, Leland, I look forward to meeting him tomorrow."

Leland turned to Geraldine. "I was convinced that here was a fine man who had a great future and could be of inestimable help to me the moment I met him. And he told me all about you and how much he loved you. I presume you have no lingering doubts on that score, Mrs. Bouchard."

For the third time, Geraldine could not help blushing,

but the look she gave Leland defied her discomfort. "Of course I know that he was true to me, Mr. Kenniston. However, if you were worrying about my approving my husband's working for you, your charm would make me force him to say yes, even if he hadn't wanted to."

Leland Kenniston burst out laughing and, lifting his brandy snifter, made a toast to the élan of women—and Geraldine Bouchard in particular.

After breakfast the next morning, Lopasuta kissed Geraldine and told her that he was off to spend a few hours with René Laurent and Leland Kenniston. He took a calash to the office, where the genial Irishman had already preceded him. He found the Creole affable, personable, and extremely gracious, and the three men spent about two hours in conference, discussing the economic trend in New Orleans and the South in general, shipping costs, and potential future investments. At the conclusion of the meeting, Leland declared, "At the end of August, I hope to go to Ireland. It will be for two reasons: one sentimental and the other practical. The former, because it's where I was born, and the latter, because I'm most interested in the importation of finely woven linens. In the Irish countryside, some of the most beautiful tablecloths, napkins, and even fine bedsheets are being woven, and they are superior to any other I've ever seen. And of course, the Irish are world renowned for their whiskey, and I propose to import quite a few hogsheads of that national product. But as I said, I expect to come back here before then, Lopasuta, and find that you've passed the bar, and also, René, to learn how our new office is doing."

"I'd like it very much if, at that time, you'll give me advance notice, Leland," the young Comanche lawyer eagerly interposed, "so you may meet my adoptive mother, Mrs. Laure Bouchard. Her oldest son, Lucien, is in his teens and we've discussed the possibility of his continuing and furthering his education in Europe."

"We have some schools in Dublin which would be excellent for him, especially if he's a gifted student," Leland avowed. "I'd certainly like to meet Mrs. Bouchard. I promise to let you know well in advance so you can make arrangements with her to visit while I'm here."

"She's a beautiful, sensitive woman, Leland, and she's

also outstanding in business. I'd say her judgment is second to none."

"She sounds a rare phenomenon, Lopasuta, and that increases my interest in meeting her. Well then, gentlemen, I think we've just about discussed everything on the agenda today. My steamboat lifts anchor at three this afternoon, so let's have a quick lunch at one of those delightful Creole restaurants nearby, and then I'll take my leave of you both."

As they finished their lunch, Leland turned to Lopasuta and told him, "I've arranged for you to study with Judge Eustace Pompfert. He's semiretired now, but in his day he was one of the finest and busiest trial lawyers in Louisiana; he was appointed to the highest court of this state. He stepped down from the bench two years ago, and the opinion of the reliable sources I've asked is that you'll not find anyone who knows the law better than Judge Pompfert. I had lunch with him yesterday and arranged for you to work part-time in his office while you read for the Louisiana state bar examination. He'll act as your personal professor, Lopasuta. If you're rusty in anything, he'll brush you up and bring you up to date. Pay particular attention to contracts: when this office expands, there'll be many contracts with suppliers, and I want to be sure that when you handle my business affairs, you'll draw up agreements that pinpoint what I'm to do and what my supplier must do to make the contract valid."

"I look forward to meeting the judge. I'll call on him this afternoon."

"Excellent!" Leland Kenniston rose and the trio walked out of the restaurant. As they walked up the street, Leland put his arm around Lopasuta's shoulders and explained, "I've had a busy time of it, but sometimes that's the way I like to work best. When there's a deadline, I try to get as much done as I can to make the trip worthwhile—and I certainly have. By the way," he took a wallet from his coat pocket, "here is a bank draft—your retainer for the first three months plus moving expenses. By that time, I should certainly be back here for at least a week or so, and we can go over everything. By then, too, I'll expect good reports about you from Judge Pompfert. Oh, incidentally, on your recommendation, I opened an account at the Brunton &

Barntry Bank when I was here in January. I met Jason Barntry, and I thought very highly of him. When I hired René, he confirmed your assessment that it's an extremely solvent bank, and their impending merger will make it — even more useful to me. It's as I've said—you've already proven your worth to me, and this retainer is merely the beginning of a lucrative relationship for both of us."

"This is very generous of you." Lopasuta pocketed the draft and shook his employer's hand. "With this, Geraldine and I should easily find a comfortable place to live."

"As to that," René Laurent broke in, "I may be of some small service. I know of a property on Greenley Street—a very charming old, but still sturdy, two-story house, with a beautiful wrought-iron balcony overlooking the street. As a matter of fact, it's very near the Brunton & Barntry Bank. The broker is a friend of mine, and he mentioned that the rent is very reasonable—seventy dollars a month, which includes the furnishings. It's part of an estate; the owner and his wife died last year, and the son is in Europe—I believe studying painting in Paris. He's willing to rent it or, if the right price is offered, sell it. I imagine you could take a six-month lease on it, if you like it."

"That sounds wonderful! I'm much obliged, M'sieu Laurent. If you'll give me the name and address of your friend's office, I'll go there with Geraldine first thing tomorrow. Well, Leland, now that I'm actually here, I'm really excited about the opportunity you've offered me. And I'll certainly study hard and pass that bar examination."

"I'm counting on you to do it, Lopasuta. Judge Pompfert tells me that, with your background, you should be able to take it early in June. I'll time my visit here about then, because I'll be eager to spend the autumn in Ireland and then some time in London and Paris looking after my business. So good luck to you and your family. Please tell Geraldine I look forward to knowing her better—she's a marvelous woman, and I can see why you were so concerned about her feelings toward you. You make good on this deal, Lopasuta, and the two of you will have every comfort that you've ever dreamed of. Well, I'd best get back to my hotel, check out, and get over to the dock to board my ship." He shook hands with René Laurent and Lopasuta Bouchard in a final farewell.

* * *

Judge Eustace Pompfert reminded Lopasuta of Jedidiah Danforth. He had a leonine head of pure white hair, and although quite tall, age had made him stoop-shouldered. His pedantic seriousness hid an underlying vein of wry, sarcastic humor—often at his own expense. The young Comanche lawyer warmed to him almost from the first hour of their initial meeting. "I'm seventy, Lopasuta," he intoned, his pince-nez slipping as he spoke, "and I was born here, which gives me several advantages over you to begin with: knowledge of the locale in which you'll be practicing—if you pass your examination—plus a reasonably good recall of the machinations and outrageous illegalities that have gone on here since I was a young man. I've seen every form of legal chicanery known, and quite a few others that haven't yet been included in the statutes. So I'll be able to point out the pitfalls of our Louisiana legal system better than just about anyone else of whom you might inquire. So much for that. I expect you to tell me all about yourself, the bad as well as the good."

Lopasuta was already smiling after such an introduction. He was certain that this man would draw from him the very best he had to give and, without any false praise, give an impartial critique of his shortcomings as well as his assets.

Lopasuta left with the promise to return the next afternoon, indicating that his first order of business was to find a place for his wife and children to live.

"Very sensible," Judge Pompfert announced. "And a word of advice—try to avoid the fleshpots in which this fascinating, colorful city abounds. Oh, I know you're a married man with two children, but New Orleans has temptations that have undermined many a steadfast character. I'll see you tomorrow, two sharp. Be prepared for an oral test on all you know about torts. From there, we can go on to specifics on how Louisiana contract law differs from what you learned under that able teacher you had back in Montgomery. Oh, yes, I knew Jedidiah Danforth; salt of the earth. You have an excellent foundation, young man. Now be off with you and find a comfortable abode!" the old judge briskly dismissed him.

Before meeting Geraldine for lunch, Lopasuta Bouchard went to the Brunton & Barntry Bank. Tall, blond Judith Marquard ushered him into old Jason Barntry's office; Lopasuta was shocked to see how listless and pale the banker

277

had become in the nearly two years since their last meeting, just before William Brickley had kidnapped him and sent him off to Hong Kong.

"How good it is to see you, Mr. Bouchard." The old man made an effort to rise, but Lopasuta shook his head. "Please don't get up, Mr. Barntry. I just wanted to tell you that I shall be living here in New Orleans. You've met a Mr. Leland Kenniston, who has just opened a branch of his importing and exporting firm here. He wants me to pass the Louisiana bar examination so that I can represent him legally, particularly in contracts. Geraldine and I are down here looking for a residence, and I've a house on Greenley Street to see with her tomorrow morning."

"Well, I'm delighted to hear that, young man!" the old banker declared effusively. "It sounds very much as though your career has taken a definite turn for the better. You and your lovely wife will like New Orleans, I'm sure. But I'm afraid our association will be coming to an end. You see, I will be retiring shortly."

"So Laure Bouchard informed me," Lopasuta said. "I understand that you will be merging this bank with another—I presume it's for health reasons."

"That's what my physician keeps telling me," Jason Barntry said with a faint smile. "Apparently if I wish to remain on this earth, I must take what is left of my body off to a drier climate like Arizona or New Mexico. Therefore, in about two weeks, I shall officially sell my stock to Henry Kessling, who is the president of the New Orleans Alliance Bank. I must say, though, I find it difficult to think about retiring and doing nothing after all these years. . . ." The ailing banker trailed off his words.

Lopasuta courteously remained silent for a few moments before continuing. "You know, Mr. Barntry, I'm sorry that Leland Kenniston won't have your expertise to rely on much longer. I'm sure he told you that he has a good deal of capital, and he's expanding his New York home office with a branch here and, eventually, one in San Francisco as well. It's your acumen that prompted me to recommend this bank to Mr. Kenniston."

"I'm very grateful for your thoughtfulness." Jason sighed. "I only wish something could be done for that charming young woman—Judith Marquard. I'm afraid she won't be working here once Mr. Kessling takes over. He's indicated to me that he wants to bring in his own specially trained personnel. You see, he's more involved in speculations of land and buildings than I myself have been of late, and that will change the operation considerably. Judith is a very capable young woman, very gifted and devoted to her work, and I should very much like to see her situated before I leave."

"Mr. Barntry, I've been thinking that when I pass the bar, I'll need someone to help me—initially to be a stenographer, but eventually there'd be more responsibility than that. Perhaps Mrs. Marquard would be interested."

"She may very well be." Jason nodded his head admiringly. "She has a little girl, and she's going to have another child rather soon, yet she wants to go on working. I really do admire her and respect her a great deal. Her desire to work is motivated by something in her background—nothing at all to her discredit, I assure you! I'd call it a kind of determination to prove to herself that she's much more capable than others used to think her."

"I'll talk to her, of course. Thank you for telling me. I do hope Geraldine and I will be able to dine with you before you leave, Mr. Barntry. And before I forget, I am to convey to you Laure Bouchard's warmest greetings and good wishes."

"That's very kind of her. Ah, I shall never forget her kindness, nor Luke's. To have known such people as friends all these years is undoubtedly one reason I've been so reluctant to give up my post at this bank. But I mustn't keep you. It was good to see you again, Lopasuta—please let an old man call you by your first name."

"Of course, Mr. Barntry. God bless you."

As he walked slowly toward the entrance of the bank, Lopasuta paused and stepped over to Judith Marquard at her desk. "He looks very ill, Mrs. Marquard," he said softly.

"Oh, yes; it worries me so. He's such a fine, good man. He was wonderful to me, when I came here from Alabama, when I didn't think I'd ever lead a proper life again. And thanks to his giving me my job in this bank, I met my husband, Bernard."

"Mr. Barntry just confirmed that he is planning to sell the bank. I suppose that means that there'll be some changes?"

"Oh, yes," Judith nodded. "I'm afraid that's true. I can anticipate that the new president won't want to keep me on. And you know, even if he were to offer to keep me, it just wouldn't be the same working here without dear Mr. Barntry. However, I do want to keep on working, so I guess I'll look elsewhere. Of course I'm going to have another child in August as you may be able to tell," she declared with a quick smile. "But a few months after the child is born, I'll want to go back to work again. Bernard doesn't object—he's so kind and understanding of my reasons for wanting to go on working, even though he has money enough to keep me home as just a wife and mother."

"I think that's very commendable. But I was about to say, Mrs. Marquard, you undoubtedly have seen some of my correspondence from Montgomery and know that I am a legal representative."

"Yes, I do know that."

"Well, through a long set of circumstances I won't bore you with, I met a New York businessman who's started an office here, and he wants me to represent him here in Louisiana. I hope to be accredited by early June, and what I was thinking—well, once I start handling cases, I shall need an assistant. You could be invaluable to me. Of course, I'd get Mr. Kenniston's permission to engage you, and I'd make sure that you'd get a decent salary."

"I think I'd like that very much. You're very kind to concern yourself with my personal problem, Mr. Bouchard."

"Not at all. Mr. Barntry speaks so highly of you that even if I didn't know you personally, it would be recommendation enough. I'll be in touch with you again, Mrs. Marquard, as soon as I pass the bar examination."

Geraldine, Mei Luong, and the two boys had come over from the St. Charles Hotel to meet Lopasuta at the Greenley Street address. He, meanwhile, had made a brief stop at the realty office to tell the broker of his interest in the property, and to acquire the key.

When Lopasuta arrived at the house, the others were already there, walking around the charming two-story building, admiring it. As René Laurent had mentioned, a wrought-iron balcony overlooked the street, its ornamental grillwork softening the brick. Around the back was a small garden, which, though it needed tending, showed great promise: an enormous magnolia towered over the site and masses of bougainvillea twined over an intimate gazebo. Geraldine thought to herself that it would make a delightful spot to sit with her husband on warm evenings, and during the day it would make an excellent playhouse for the boys.

Lopasuta opened the main door with one of the keys on the ring, and stood transfixed. To one side was a salon, ornately furnished, with magnificent plastered cornices. The obverse of this was a dining room, also beautifully decorated. A winding stairway ascended to the second floor. As Mei Luong went to inspect the kitchen, Lopasuta beckoned to Geraldine. "It's charming! I'm told that it's quite an old house with a long tradition to it," he told his lovely young wife.

After Geraldine had inspected both floors, she pronounced it eminently satisfactory. "The rent is certainly reasonable, isn't it, Lopasuta?" she remarked, as any practical housewife might.

"Yes—I think we can afford it on the retainer Leland gave me, darling," he quipped. "We won't even have to touch the money I saved from my law practice in Montgomery—it's still in the bank and getting interest, too. We aren't exactly poor—even though I was gone from you over a year."

"Yes, my darling," she said softly. "Not only wouldn't I have dreamed of touching the money you'd saved in your account, you know perfectly well that, legally, only you are entitled to dispose of it."

He eyed her for a moment, then burst out laughing. "I see where all this leads to, Geraldine. You definitely are in favor of women's rights, including not only the right to vote, but the right to spend a husband's money."

"And why not, sir?" she answered him in a mock-indignant tone, her arms akimbo. "Here you went traipsing around the world, off without so much as a fare-thee-well, leaving me in a dreary little town to fend for myself as best I could!" She laughed gaily at his look of consternation. "But seriously, this house is just wonderful!"

"I agree."

"It will be just perfect. The large room with the connecting room, at the back of this floor, will do beautifully as bedrooms for Mei Luong and the children. And we can have the entire second floor to ourselves."

"Yes, that library on the second floor will make a perfect sanctuary where I can lock myself up with my law books and study to pass the bar examination." Lopasuta was not to be outdone.

"Good!" Geraldine declared, her eyes sparkling with mischief. "Then I'll know exactly where you are all the time, and I shan't have to worry about your flirting with one of those Creole beauties!" Again he burst out laughing, and then they embraced.

Mei Luong entered the salon, smiled, and shook her head. It was true that she still had a great deal to learn about this strange new country, but she could easily understand why this pretty girl loved the handsome *wai kuo jen*. And she could understand, too, why Lu Choy must have loved him. Perhaps, if the gods were kind, she, too—alone in this strange country—might one day find a man who would be as tender and loving as her employer was to his American wife.

Lopasuta arranged with the broker to rent the house and thanked him for his help and courtesy. It was not far from the very house that Luke Bouchard had rented when he had left Windhaven Range to return to New Orleans and ask Laure Prindeville Brunton to be his wife. And now so similar a house would shelter their adoptive son, the off-spring of a Comanche brave and Mexican mother, and a courageous young woman who had defied convention and the will of her parents to merge her life inseparably with his. Theirs was a love in its way as strong as that which nearly ninety years before, a Creek girl had nurtured for a Frenchman who had come to a strange new world to begin his dynasty.

## Twenty-seven

Over the next few months, Lopasuta Bouchard worked as if he were the only pupil in a new and strange school, spending endless mornings, as well as afternoons, in the office of Judge Eustace Pompfert. The white-haired jurist reviewed what seemed to Lopasuta everything he had ever learned over these long years. Sometimes the dryly caustic judge would send him into the huge library to take a case from the law books and work up sufficient statute references to win it in open court. Then, after Lopasuta had done intensive groundwork, Judge Pompfert would dissect Lopasuta's findings and unexpectedly counter the Comanche lawyer's conclusions with obscure references that would hypothetically turn the verdict against him.

Or again, he would casually bid Lopasuta to assume that he was representing Leland Kenniston's importing and exporting firm and to draw up a valid contract between Kenniston and an imaginary supplier. After examining Lopasuta's longhand commentaries, he would light a cheroot, lean back, and adjusting his pince-nez, drawl, "Why didn't you insert a clause to indemnify Mr. Kenniston against an act of God, such as the supplier's death, or perhaps bankruptcy through flood or hurricane or plague? What would happen to Mr. Kenniston in the event those things occurred? You haven't protected your client sufficiently, Mr. Bouchard. Now get back into the study and bone up, if you hope to pass the examination."

On such occasions, Lopasuta felt like a chastised little boy, but he grimly nodded and, without a word, went back to his diligent studies. He admired Judge Pompfert, who more and more reminded him of Jedidiah Danforth, and he knew very well that without the older man's counseling, he could not hope to achieve the future that he so eagerly planned for Geraldine, Dennis, and Luke.

As for Geraldine, she had never shown herself to be more sympathetic than during this arduous phase of her husband's life. There was no opportunity for him to socialize or to make new friends: all his time was devoted to cramming his mind with *obiter dicta*, Circuit and Appellate Court decisions and reversals, and obscure footnotes, which seemed to alter and paradoxically reshape a judgment that he had believed unshakable. Throughout it all, he admired Judge Pompfert's wily method of forcing him to use every facet of his mind, so that what he learned was not simply parroting, not simply memorizing facts to be able to gush them forth before the state examiners. Each day, Judge Pompfert would, without warning, suddenly pose probing questions on this or that case. And he had learned enough of his mentor's personality by now to feel heartened when the old man exhibited a quick, faint smile—his expression of accolade.

Geraldine saw to it that Lopasuta was well fed, and that a minimum amount of time—but nonetheless warm and companionable—was spent with her and his two young sons so that he did not lose sight of what he meant to her and to the children. When he came home at night, mentally as well as physically exhausted, she would kiss him tenderly, urge him to take a bath while supper was being prepared, and then would herself wait upon him. She refrained from asking him about his progress, for she could comprehend well enough from his demeanor when he came back to the brick house on Greenley Street how well or how badly he thought he had done that day. She went out of her way to cheer him in many little ways, by telling him how much she loved him and how happy she was here in New Orleans. Sometimes, when he was in a more relaxed mood, she would tell him how she and Mei Luong and the boys went down Royal or Chartres streets to the fine shops and what they had seen in them.

Before he knew it, the first week of June was upon him, and Judge Pompfert declared, "I'd say you are certainly well versed in Louisiana law, especially torts and contracts, Lopasuta. You'll find the examiners fair, but inclined to be tricky at times. That's why I've played the role of devil's advocate, to put you in mind of what you may be expected unexpectedly to know when they question you. And if you find 'expect unexpectedly' a strange phrase, I advise you to read Alfred Lord Tennyson, whose *Idylls of the King* abound in that sort of paradoxical construction. Well, sir, good luck to you; come back and tell me how you fared."

Lopasuta appeared before the state board of examiners the next morning, a Friday. After the examination, composed of both oral and written questions, he was given an hour for a late lunch. When he returned, at four in the afternoon, the pompous vice-president of the Louisiana State Bar Association looked at his two colleagues and permitted himself a condescending smile as, clearing his throat, he declared, "My colleagues and I consider you a worthy addition to the legal profession in Louisiana, Mr. Bouchard. You will receive formal written confirmation of our findings within the week. You certainly came well prepared. My congratulations, sir!"

Lopasuta felt his legs tremble as he rose. He exhaled a sigh, and then his lips curved in a delighted smile. "I—I'm most grateful to all of you. Thank you. I assure you I shall do my best to justify your confidence in me, gentlemen," he finally declared, hoping his tone nearly matched his inquisitor's in pomposity.

He inclined his head respectfully toward the three examiners, and though every impulse in him urged him to run down the stairs to hail the nearest calash and be taken home to Geraldine to tell her the wonderful news, he forced himself to walk slowly and solemnly out of the examination room.

Once on the sidewalk, glancing around and seeing that no policeman was in sight, he let out a resounding whoop. And then, as quickly, he compressed his lips and stood placidly so that the passersby saw no one at all who might have been responsible for it.

At last he saw a calash coming, hailed the driver, and after he had given the driver the address, leaned back and closed his eyes. A warm, triumphant glow surged through him. Now he was on the threshold of a new life, one which he promised would make up to his dear Geraldine for the privations she had suffered during his unplanned absence. As fervently, he pledged that he would never forget his origin, never forget the Wanderers from whose tribe he had come all this long way into a white man's world. To this end, he would devote a fair part of his life to upholding the pursuit of justice for the oppressed, the poor, and the needy. Only thus, he knew, could he prove himself worthy of the illustrious name of Bouchard, which martyred Luke Bouchard had been generous enough to bequeath him.

When he arrived home, his face radiant, to tell Geraldine that he had successfully passed the examination, she hugged and kissed him and then exclaimed, "Darling, I have a secret longing I've never told you about, but now is the time. I've always been intrigued by games of chance, so let's celebrate your success and indulge my curiosity! Why don't we go to Laure's famous gambling casino, have dinner there, and if you'll be a generous darling and give me a few dollars, I'll see what kind of luck I have. How about it?"

Lopasuta stared blankly at her for a moment, then took her in his arms and murmured, "Geraldine, you are full of surprises; there is always something new and fascinating about you."

"And I shall stay that way until you no longer have the vitality to look at any other attractive woman, I promise you," was her teasing, whispered answer, as she returned his kiss with ardor.

When Milo Brutus Henson had first seen Lopasuta Bouchard descend from the train at the Montgomery railroad station, he had been frightened out of his wits. During the months since that fateful day he spent considerable time taking stock of the situation. It would prove intolerable if Lopasuta ever found out that he, Milo Brutus Henson, had had a hand in the plot to send him off to Hong Kong.

There were, to be sure, a few wealthy carpetbaggers still left in Montgomery who had no love for the tall young Comanche lawyer. At first, Henson had believed that, now that he was back in practicing law, Lopasuta Bouchard would eventually so antagonize one or another of these men that they would be willing to go to extreme measures to eliminate him from the local scene.

But as time passed and there was no news in the *Montgomery Advertiser* of Lopasuta's appearing in court, Henson began to make cautious inquiries around town. All that he heard was that Lopasuta seemed to be quite content to be reunited with his wife and child. At the same time, no one seemed to know where he had been for so long a time, but no one seemed concerned enough about it to try to find the answer.

At last, his fear, hatred, and impatience could no longer be kept in check, and so, about the middle of April, Henson had driven his buggy down the street on which Lopasuta's house stood and, drawing in the reins, got down from the buggy, tied the reins to a hitching post at the curb, and then walked along the opposite side of the street from Lopasuta's house. After he passed, he covertly looked back. But he saw no signs of life. The front-room curtains were drawn, but there was no light anywhere, although it was already twilight.

Nonplussed, he had retraced his footsteps and finally took up enough courage to cross boldly to the house, and even to go up to the porch.

At that moment, Elizabeth Steers had opened the door of her house across the street and came out onto the sidewalk. Observing Henson standing there staring at Lopasuta's house, she called to him, "Sir, maybe I could help you—whom are you looking for?"

"Oh—" He whirled, then doffed his bowler hat and affected an unctuous smile. "You startled me, madam. A friend of mine told me to look up Mr. Bouchard, as I am in need of the services of a good attorney."

"Well, sir, your friend was right in telling you that Mr. Bouchard is a very able attorney. However, he isn't at home, and he won't be for some time," Mrs. Steers volunteered.

"Oh? What a pity! I was so looking forward to meeting him. Perhaps you could tell me where he's gone? I travel on business constantly, you see," he improvised, "and it's just possible that I might be going to where he is now, and then I could look him up, you see."

"Well, he's in New Orleans. That's all I really can tell you—or should tell you, since I don't know you, sir." Though she wished to be helpful, Mrs. Steers was not particularly impressed by the ingratiatingly oily look on Milo Brutus Henson's face, nor by the way he had stared so long at Lopasuta's house.

"Well, then—as it happens, I shall be there on business soon. Perhaps I'll find him there. Thank you, madam. You've been most kind and helpful."

With this, Henson had climbed back into his buggy and drove back to his house, in better humor than he had been since January when the deal with his friend, Albert Saw-

287

yer, in buying up some parcels of land near Tuskeegee had worked out exceedingly favorably.

As he let himself into his house, he thought once more that he could hire a ruffian to take care of Lopasuta. He knew of several reliable men in New Orleans who would commit almost anything from mayhem to murder for a price. It might be an excellent idea to contact one of those men to see if they would undertake tracking down Lopasuta Bouchard to put him out of the way once and for all. Only this time, Henson told himself, he would demand proof before final payment. He did not particularly care to see ghosts, especially not of a man who he had been assured would never be seen in Montgomery again.

As he came in, Elaine Fairfield, his blond, ripely contoured mistress, hurried to greet him. "Milo, darling, I'm so glad you're home."

"My dear," he beamed, and patted her behind, "put on your best dress. We're going to have dinner at the State House Restaurant. It's just about the best food in town, and I feel like celebrating tonight."

Elaine had kept her tenure as mistress longer than her predecessors, one reason being that she did not pry into her lover's affairs. Nor did she on this occasion. "I'll be ready in a jiffy, Milo darling. It's sweet of you to take me out. I'll repay you when we get back home—I promise." With one arm around his back, she slid her other hand down to brush against his loins in wordless intimation of how she meant to gratify him. He shuddered and flushed, licked his lips, then hoarsely muttered, "All right then, honey—go get dressed in your purtiest. And I'm going to hold you to what you just promised, Laney."

On this warm June evening, full of anticipation for their night of celebration, Lopasuta and Geraldine took a *fiacre* and ordered the driver to take them to La Maison de Bonne Chance. The gambling casino, on Esplanade Avenue, was that with which the late William Brickley had ingeniously involved the unsuspecting Laure Bouchard into a partnership, intending solely to bankrupt her and bring opprobrium upon the Bouchard name. With his death and the discovery of his machinations against her and Lopasuta, Hollis Minton, the bank attorney, had legally transferred the casino to Laure with full and unencumbered title. She, in turn, had appointed Bernard Marquard's former orderly, Jesse Jacklin, to manage the enterprise. She had given strict orders that the utmost honesty was to be practiced at all times: New Orleans residents and tourists alike would find La Maison de Bonne Chance a convivial place of entertainment, where they might gamble with the certainty that the outcome would depend entirely upon luck and skill, and where also they might have the finest food available in New Orleans, as well as good wines and liqueurs.

Remembering how she had had to preside as hostess at the Union House, where it was absolutely essential that young women sell their sexual favors in order to ingratiate the Union officers who tyrannically ruled the Queen City during the Civil War, Laure had told Jacklin that there would be no prostitution whatsoever allowed at the casino. "There are houses on Rampart Street to satisfy those seeking lustful pleasure, Jesse. I'm certainly not a moralist, but I do not care to make a profit by selling flesh, particularly when it is that of unfortunate young women who may well have no choice in leading such a life."

Jesse Jacklin, resplendent in white linen frock coat and matching trousers, with a flowery cravat, stationed himself in the foyer of the establishment to welcome his guests. Two years ago, Jacklin had married an attractive forty-year-old widow, and they reside in a house just a block away from Bernard and Judith Marquard. About a year ago, Edith Jacklin had told Jesse, "Now that I know you're running an honest house and there aren't any fancy women to take into guest rooms, I think it's high time I occupied myself with something more than looking after our house. If you've no objection, dear, I'd like to supervise your staff, to insure that your guests are always treated properly and with respect." And so Jesse had good-naturedly allowed his attractive wife to work with him, a decision that had made their marriage even more companionable.

When Lopasuta and Geraldine entered, Jesse enthusiastically greeted them and personally escorted them upstairs. He sat them at a table near a shuttered window, and consulted with them on the choices of entree that evening. Geraldine's eyes sparkled with delight at being treated with such solicitous attention, and she happily declared, "I just love New Orleans! Isn't this wonderful? Such an elegant, beautifully furnished house is like something you read about in one of Sir Walter Scott's romantic novels."

"Not quite, darling," Lopasuta chuckled. "Have you forgotten that *Ivanhoe* has to do with castles and Normans and Saxons?"

"Oh, you're such a stickler, Lopasuta!" Geraldine bantered. "Save 'the whole truth and nothing but the truth' for the judges of the court and talk to me the way you would to your wife and sweetheart."

"Who, of course, are one and the same," was his immediate reply.

"They had better be," she shot back with a soft laugh.

An hour later, after a delightful dinner of baked crayfish, chicken *cordon bleu*, and asparagus hollandaise—served with a superb Chablis—then finishing with a mouth-watering trifle for dessert, Geraldine and Lopasuta went into one of the gaming rooms to try their luck. "I'm going to try *vingt-et-un*," she confided to her husband, "if you've no objection."

"Not in the least. But take a table where you play only with the dealer. Then I'd say you'll have a fifty-fifty chance," Lopasuta encouraged her.

"Well, my love, you're not the backward reservation Comanche some people might take you for, are you now?" she twitted him. Lopasuta laughed exuberantly. Never had he felt so happy, so at peace and so full of hope for the future. Reunited with his lovely, ardent wife, partaking of her zestful spirit, which strengthened his own and kept him from brooding over the past, he felt a new life was about to begin for both of them. Somewhat to his surprise, she had shown uninhibited fondness for Luke and treated Mei Luong with such graciousness that he often told himself he was a most fortunate man in having a wife understanding and compassionate enough not to be swayed by jealousies. Many a woman, he knew, might have railed against his infidelity with poor Lu Choy, yet never once had Geraldine alluded to that liaison. On the evening before they left for New Orleans, her arms around him, her eyes steadfastly looking into his, she had said something he would never forget: "My sweet husband, I can understand how Lu Choy couldn't help being smitten by you, and from all you've told me, she was a fine, deserving woman. I'm happy that she was able to console you a little for being away from me. I'll always remember her, and I pray that her soul is at rest."

Geraldine now walked toward a table where a tall, slim

290

dealer in his early thirties sat. As she seated herself across from him, the dealer respectfully murmured, *"Bon soir, mam'selle."* His stylish black goatee bobbed as he continued, "My name is Eugène D'Onorio, *à votre service."*

"My gracious," Geraldine giggled, "how very charming! I should like to try my luck with you, m'sieu."

"That is what I am here for, mam'selle."

"It is madame—Madame Bouchard," Geraldine confided, glancing back at her admiring husband, who had come up behind her and who returned her tender look.

"Bouchard? An honored name in this house. But you are far too young to be 'madame.' "

"Careful, M'sieu D'Onorio; this is my husband, and I warn you that his forebears, the Comanche warriors, were the most feared in all of the Southwest at one time," Geraldine gaily informed the dealer.

"Please believe, m'sieu," Eugène D'Onorio looked apologetically up at Lopasuta, "I meant my remark only as a compliment."

"And I took it as such, M'sieu D'Onorio. My wife has an impetuous sense of humor."

Geraldine again smiled at her husband. Then, leaning back, she expectantly awaited the deal. Eugène D'Onorio drew the first card from the shoe and turned it up for her—a queen. Next followed one turned down for himself, and then an ace dealt for Geraldine. "I've won!" she exultantly exclaimed. The goateed dealer indulgently smiled, turned up his card, without expression, then dealt himself his second one, a ten. This done, he smiled and shoved the chips toward her. "You did indeed win, madame, for I have only twenty. I am delighted that such a beautiful woman has such good fortune on her first play."

"There, Lopasuta," Geraldine turned to smile back at her husband, "in the event that you ever become infatuated with one of those famous belles of New Orleans, I shall know where to turn. M'sieu D'Onorio is handsome enough to turn any young lady's head."

"You do me too much honor, madame." The dealer inclined his head, trying to conceal a wry smile on his face.

Geraldine lost the next hand, but won the next three. She declared herself delighted, and handed a chip to the dealer. *"C'est comme pourboire,"* she explained.

*"Je vous remercie, madame. Et je vous souhaite bonne chance toujours."*

"I've already had it—the casino is very appropriately named, I'd say." Geraldine rose from the table with a pretty little curtsy. "Lopasuta, why don't you try your luck with this charming gentleman? That will prove whether he was giving me an advantage simply because I happen to be an attractive female."

"Oh, no, madame," Eugène D'Onorio protested in an almost anguished tone, "such a thing dare not happen in this house!"

"I'm only teasing, m'sieu. I know how honest the casino is, because Mr. Jacklin, the manager, was appointed by my dear friend, Laure Bouchard," Geraldine explained.

Lopasuta, with a philosophical shrug, seated himself, and the dealer shuffled the cards and put them into the shoe. Lopasuta put up a five-dollar stake from his hundred-dollar pile of chips. Geraldine, leaning behind him with her hands gripping the top of the tall straight-backed chair in which he sat, watched intently.

Much to Geraldine's surprise, Lopasuta seemed to be acquainted with the game. When the dealer dealt himself an ace and eyed Lopasuta to ask, *"Est-ce que m'sieu désire l'insurance?"* the young Comanche lawyer nodded and put two five-dollar chips out to his right side on the green baize cloth on the table.

Indeed, the dealer had twenty-one, and although he thus surpassed Lopasuta's hand, the latter nevertheless received one-and-a-half times his insurance stake.

Geraldine was profoundly impressed. She whispered, "I thought you were an absolute tyro, Lopasuta. When in the world did you ever learn anything about cards?"

"In the stronghold, my mother played monte with my father and she taught me, as well. And besides," he grinned, "I found a pamphlet on gambling games when we first came to New Orleans, and to take my mind off my law books, I read it."

When eleven o'clock neared, Lopasuta rose. He had won four hundred dollars. It was more than a month's retainer from Leland Kenniston, and after giving Eugène D'Onorio a tip of forty dollars, he handed one hundred to Geraldine and said, "Spend this on whatever you like, my dearest one. But now, the stress and excitement of this long day have caught up with me, and I think it's time for us to go back home."

As they went back down to the foyer, Geraldine's arm

linked with Lopasuta's, Jesse Jacklin met them at the door. "I'm told that you had good luck, Mr. Bouchard," he genially greeted the Comanche.

"Indeed, and it's a very good omen for the future. But I shall be careful not to come here too often lest I delude myself with the notion that I might be able to earn my living playing cards," Lopasuta responded with a grin.

## Twenty-eight

That memorable night of celebration had yet to conclude for Lopasuta. When he and Geraldine were preparing to return shortly before midnight, she turned to him, her arms around his neck, and whispered, "It's been the most glorious evening, my dear one! And aside from celebrating your passing the Louisiana bar, I have another reason for wanting to celebrate. You see, Lopasuta, I'm pregnant again. I've known for a few months, but I didn't want this news to be an additional burden for you while you were struggling with your studies. Our child should be born by early December, darling."

Lopasuta was speechless with delight. Holding her closely, kissing her forehead and hair and ears, he avowed how much he adored her and how grateful he was at having been restored to her. And then, befitting a night of such joyous excitement, they made love with abandoned passion, each knowing the other's moods and ardors as if they had never been parted from each other since their wedding night.

Leland Kenniston had kept in close touch by telegraph wire with Lopasuta throughout the latter's diligent pursuit of a license to practice law in Louisiana. When the Irishman heard that Lopasuta would be finished by the end of the first week in June—a fact he had learned from old

Judge Pompfert, who had assured him that "my prize pupil is as certain to be admitted as death and taxes affect every citizen in this republic"—he had wired the Comanche lawyer that he planned to arrive in New Orleans on the tenth of June and stay for ten days to two weeks. As soon as he had received this telegram, Lopasuta sent one of his own to Laure Bouchard, urging her to meet the man who might well guide Laure into selecting the best possible schooling for her oldest son, Lucien. He then informed Leland of this plan, expressing his delight that the two of them would finally meet.

Leland Kenniston arrived in New Orleans on Wednesday of the following week, taking a suite at the St. Charles Hotel. Laure Bouchard, having received Lopasuta's wire informing her of his employer's imminent visit, also reached the Queen City that day. At Geraldine's invitation, Laure took a calash out to the house on Greenley Street. "Laure will be quite comfortable in the guest room on the second floor, darling," Geraldine had told her husband. "We certainly can't have family staying in some impersonal hotel."

"I wouldn't have it any other way, my love," was Lopasuta's reply.

Lopasuta then kissed his wife and left for the office to meet his employer. Accordingly, Geraldine alone welcomed Laure when she alighted from the calash. The gracious old Creole driver descended to help her step down and then took her two valises to the house, where Geraldine stood waiting in the doorway. The two women embraced effusively, and then Laure stepped back, her hands on Geraldine's shoulders, and merrily declared, "I do believe you're pregnant, my dear—either that, or you've been indulging in too much rich Creole food!"

"You're right the first time," Geraldine laughed. "Oh, Laure, it's so good to see you again!"

"Geraldine!" Laure exclaimed as they entered the parlor. "This house is wonderful! Now, you're quite sure I won't be putting you out at all?"

"Absolutely not! There's a guest room on the second floor, and what are guest rooms for if not for guests—especially a guest who is also my dear friend," Geraldine assured her.

Laure smiled fondly at Geraldine. "All right—you've

294

convinced me. I must confess that I'm looking forward to some woman-to-woman chats. I get rather lonely sometimes."

The two women went up the stairs to the guest room where Mei Luong took Laure's luggage and proceeded to unpack the bags.

For this important trip, Laure Bouchard had bedecked herself in a traveling costume as seen in the pages of her favorite magazine, *Harper's Bazaar*. Of a dark green grosgrain trimmed in velvet of the same shade, the skirt had two *tabliers* covered by deep pleatings, and the back panel was heavily draped and poufed. Above the skirt was a deeply pointed basque with a tightly nipped waist. The double row of buttons terminated in a lacy spill of her jabot, with the lace of her guimpe—a waist-length blouse—showing through at the cuffs of the three-quarter sleeves. Laure removed the bodice as the warmth of the room enveloped her, then unbuttoned the jabot, leaving her in the sheer cotton guimpe. She placed her matching parasol on the bed and removed her flowered-and-feathered straw bonnet, exposing the glory of her golden chignon. Looking as stately as a *grande dame,* she was nonetheless youthful enough at thirty-eight to attract a discerning man who would cherish mature beauty, and not have his head turned merely by a young face and nubile figure.

Leland Kenniston was in excellent spirits. He gripped Lopasuta's hand and shook it warmly, declaring, "Good work—though there wasn't a single doubt in my mind you'd make it! And now you can really go to work for me. You see, we already have a case to take to court. I had my lawyer in New York draw up a contract with a man who runs a conveyor business here in New Orleans. This man has his stevedores meet ships docking at the wharf; then they transport the goods to a central warehouse, which he owns, and from there, he delivers the goods to specified locations. René was able to buy one hundred cases of excellent Bordeaux wines, fifty white and fifty red, which arrived last week. Unfortunately, the conveyor claims that he wasn't apprised of what the shipment was and, in the process of hauling it from the ship to his warehouse, smashed the bottles in forty cases. Now he claims that I'm liable because I didn't inform him that the merchandise was fragile; however, my New York attorney dispatched a letter to him with the contract, advising him of what the shipment would consist. You, Lopasuta, will take the letter, a copy of which my New York attorney gave me just before I left to come here, plus the contract itself, and file suit against this idiot in the Circuit Court of Louisiana. Here are the documents you'll need. My New York attorney respectfully submits that you serve the man with a subpoena, informing him that he is liable for legal action."

"I'll attend to that this very afternoon, Leland."

"Excellent! Incidentally, I presume that Mrs. Bouchard has come to town, and she has decided to take advantage of my offer to help her son with his future schooling?"

"She has indeed. She arrived today, and she's staying at our house, Leland."

"Marvelous!" The Irishman's eyes glowed with pleasure. "I want you all to have dinner with me, at Antoine's. I'll reserve a private room so we can be to ourselves and talk to our heart's content."

"That sounds delightful, Leland," Lopasuta assured him. He looked down at his feet for a moment, hesitating before speaking again. "Do you know, Leland, after the shock of Luke Bouchard's death wore off somewhat, I confess I started thinking that a man like you might very well be able to bring Laure out of herself a bit. She's had a great burden on her ever since Luke's death, and although she's learned a great deal about running her own business affairs, she feels the responsibility of her children now as never before. It would be nice for her to enjoy life more and feel happiness for a change."

"From all you've told me, I absolutely agree with you. Let's just see what happens. Now then, back to business. Next week, René is going to open a very elegant shop for us. We will display the most attractive items of cargo that I am buying abroad, part of which I intend to have transported here. It will be René's duty to keep abreast of what New Orleans people are buying and want to buy, and that, in turn, will guide me to making judicious purchases."

"That sounds like an excellent plan, Leland."

"I'm glad you agree! I'm going to count on you for ever-increasing observations in the months ahead, Lopasuta, and I know you won't let me down. Now, I think it's time that we both go freshen up for dinner. Shall we say Antoine's at seven?"

* * *

Leland Kenniston, dressed in a frock coat, vest, and trousers, with a full cravat, top hat, and walking stick, arrived at the famous New Orleans restaurant at six forty-five. The maître d', remembering him as an important, as well as affluent, customer, solicitously escorted Leland to the private room he had engaged. Leland proceeded to order a dinner worthy of a connoisseur. He specified that there should be no more than two waiters, and that there should be ample time between the service of courses to give his guests and himself opportunity to renew their acquaintance.

Leland now sat waiting in the elegant room for his guests to arrive. Consulting his gold pocket watch, he nervously fumbled with the chain as he replaced it in the watch pocket of his vest. He laughed at his own apprehension, telling himself that here he was, a man of the world, feeling as awkward as a schoolboy over the forthcoming meeting with Laure Bouchard. When he probed his emotions to ascertain the origin of his anxiety, he finally had to admit to himself that indeed, for all his financial success, his life was lacking that one element that spelled true happiness: the love of a woman. And from all that Lopasuta had told him of Laure, she sounded as though she might be, at last, the ideal woman for him. Oh, to be sure, he had had many brief romantic liaisons, but they had either occurred at times in his life when ambition superceded affection, or they had been with women for whom he could never feel anything more than just a passing fancy.

His musing was interrupted suddenly when the door of the private room was opened by the maître d' who ushered in Lopasuta, Geraldine, and Laure. Quickly rising to his feet, Leland made his way around the table to wait for the formal introductions.

Lopasuta shook hands with his employer, and then, taking Laure by the arm, he smiled and announced, "Laure, I would like to introduce Leland Kenniston, of whom you have heard so much. Leland, this is my adoptive mother, Laure Bouchard."

Leland took her proffered hand in his for just a moment, but that brief moment sent a sensation through him as though he had been shocked. His eyes were wide with admiration, for he was enchanted by the beautiful woman standing before him. Laure, in her turn, found this tall, black-haired Irishman quite fascinating. His friendly blue eyes twinkled merrily over an aquiline nose, sensual mouth, and firm jaw. From the way he comported himself, Laure was certain that here was a man who, though he might lack traditional background, was nevertheless gallant, self-assured, and forceful. She found herself wondering for a fleeting moment if this captivating man might not prove to be hazardous, one who would expose her vulnerability and her loneliness that she had finally managed to repress, laying her open to heartbreak.

The mutual spell was broken as Leland finally uttered, "It is a great pleasure for me to finally meet you, Mrs. Bouchard. Lopasuta has told me so much about you."

"Thank you, Mr. Kenniston—and thank you for inviting me to dinner with you. I have always loved Antoine's, and it has been far too long since I last partook of their exceptional fare."

"I trust you won't be disappointed by what I have taken the liberty of ordering," Leland declared, as he sat Laure in the chair to his right. Lopasuta suggested that Geraldine sit to Leland's left, while he himself took the seat between the two women across from Leland.

The maître d' hovered solicitously until Leland announced, "I believe we're ready now, Armand. You may bring us the wine and the first course."

"Oui, M'sieu Kenniston," he effusively declared. "I guarantee that you and your guests will have no cause for disappointment." With a slight bow, he turned smartly and withdrew from the room.

As the waiters brought in the wine and the appetizers, Leland surreptitiously glanced at Laure. From Lopasuta's praise of Laure Bouchard, he had conjured up a vision of her—and yet he had not been prepared for her stunning beauty. Instinctively, Leland knew that to be overly aggressive at their first meeting, to let her sense how incredibly desirable he found her, would be a fatal error; indeed, it would more swiftly drive her from him than would any other method of wooing he might use. Therefore, he constrained himself toward behaving with an easygoing, casual attitude, though inwardly every fiber of his being was whetted by her loveliness. That she was a widow also imposed a moral constriction upon him: how obvious it would be to confront her with the stereotypical argument that she had previously been happy with a man—therefore, now that she was bereaved, all the more reason to take another to console herself! That attitude of a swaggering, conceited male who viewed himself as the panacea for all female wants, needs, and ills was one that would instantly drive away a woman like Laure Bouchard.

Dinner began with a superb vichyssoise, moderately warmed and garnished with chopped chives. There followed a salad of asparagus, beefsteak tomatoes, romaine lettuce, watercress, and sliced mushrooms, with a subtle vinaigrette dressing. Then came pheasant under glass, with tiny roasted potatoes and small fresh peas, accompanied by a delicate Médoc. For dessert, there was a *bombe surprise*, and, to accompany, a Chateau Climens, one of the great dessert wines. Dinner was finished with a rich, marvelously aromatic Creole coffee, with apricot cordial for the ladies and Cusinier brandy for the men.

The waiters had appeared at discreet intervals, working with swift and silent efficiency, thereby giving the quartet ample opportunity to talk and to become better acquainted with one another. Laure mentioned that she had visited the bank and met Henry Kessling, who had taken over Jason Barntry's stock and post. Jason had already left for Tucson and the bank would now be called the Brunton & Alliance Bank of New Orleans, which Laure believed was an equitable nomenclature.

Lopasuta mentioned that Judith Marquard had resigned the week that Jason Barntry had left for Arizona. "I talked to her when I began my studies for the bar," Lopasuta remarked, "and I told her that it was quite likely I would eventually need someone of her ability."

"That's an excellent idea, Lopasuta," Leland Kenniston interposed. "Besides secretarial work, she can research city and county records on some of the history of New Orleans that may be valuable to you, as well as sound out other financial institutions, realtors, and speculators—much as she did at the bank. I foresee, Lopasuta, that within the next year your duties will go far beyond the courtroom."

Laure eyed the Irishman as he spoke to her adoptive son, and was quite favorably impressed by the respect and warmth he conveyed. She observed that he was extremely personable, without that overbearing quality which many successful and self-made men seemed to emanate. He was decidedly virile and forthright, characteristics she admired; his words sounded sincere, not glib or contrived for the sake of effect on his listeners. These excellent signs gave her confidence in Lopasuta's future under such an employer.

As they were finishing their coffee, Lopasuta casually remarked, "Leland, I mentioned to you that Mrs. Bouchard is most interested in finding a really outstanding school for young Lucien. He's thirteen now, a highly formative age, and if he's well placed in a progressive institution, his mind can be challenged and expanded to reach his true potential."

"Oh, yes," Laure quickly spoke up, with a gracious smile at the black-haired Irishman across the table from her. "What Lopasuta says is true. There are, of course, good schools here in this country, but perhaps by sending Lucien abroad, we would expose him to a more cosmopolitan background and imagination as well. I am certainly as patriotic as anyone, and I dearly love my country; still, our schools, for the most part, are backward, especially here in the South—a natural result of the tragic war between the states."

"I agree with you, Mrs. Bouchard," Leland replied with an emphatic nod and a pleasant smile. "I don't know how much Lopasuta has told you about me, but my father and mother were immigrants out of County Mayo in Ireland, poor as church mice with no book learning other than what they were able to teach themselves. Yet at the same time, they saw very clearly the necessity of a sound education, and it was thanks to the determination of my parents to get me some schooling—we emigrated here when I was very young—that I managed to amount to something."

"I like the respect and admiration in your voice when you speak about your parents, Mr. Kenniston," Laure told him. "Because I'm a widow now, I'm all the more concerned about Lucien and engendering his respect for me. When a woman has to be both father and mother to an adolescent boy, she can't always be certain that her personal judgment is best for his progress. That's why I'd be very grateful for any suggestions you might care to give me."

"I'm most honored that you seek my advice, Mrs. Bouchard," he thoughtfully replied. "Am I correct in assuming that you yourself are Catholic, as was your husband?"

"That is correct, Mr. Kenniston. Unfortunately, in Alabama there are only one or two churches of that faith, and they are far distant from Montgomery. So Luke and I did our best to instill the basic convictions of Catholicism in our children ourselves."

"Quite admirable. Now, I may say I am reasonably familiar with England—though I must admit, Mrs. Bouchard, that most Irishmen have a rather prejudicial view of that little island."

She smiled and nodded, acknowledging his quip. He went on: "There are, of course, superb schools in England, such as Eton and Harrow. However, as a Catholic in a Protestant country, your son might not get the reception to which he is entitled by merit and background. That is why I should propose one of the better schools in Dublin.

"Father Patrick O'Mara, headmaster of the Academy of St. Timothy's, is a personal friend of mine. He's renowned throughout the British Isles as an eminent teacher and theologian, and if you have no objection, I'd be very happy to write him a letter introducing you and your son to him and indicating that you will contact him personally. At St. Timothy's, not only will Lucien receive a fine European education, but also his spiritual needs will be cared for. As it happens, I plan to take a trip back to my homeland in August, both for business and for sentimental purposes, and it would be a pleasure and an honor to escort your son on the voyage."

"That's most generous of you, Mr. Kenniston!" Laure exclaimed, with a delighted glance at both Geraldine and Lopasuta. "I would like to have him enrolled by the time the fall term opens, and this would give me just enough time to make the necessary plans."

"I have a further proposal in this regard. Since I should like Lopasuta and Geraldine to see my New York headquarters, once you have made the necessary arrangements with Father O'Mara, perhaps you would like to travel with them with your son to New York, enabling me to extend my hospitality to you as well until it's time for Lucien to sail."

"That's really an overwhelmingly generous offer, Mr. Kenniston. I may just take you up on it!" Laure exclaimed. "I really can't thank you enough. Incidentally, my second son, Paul, who will be eleven in December, is soon going to need just such an educational program as Lucien. Perhaps in two years' time, Paul could join Lucien at St. Timothy's, if Lucien does well and is happy at this school."

"The boys are not coddled there, I will tell you that sincerely, Mrs. Bouchard," Leland candidly replied. "That is to say, they're not made to feel that they are the elite and privileged and, therefore, immune from all discipline if they are lazy or amoral or rowdy. But for a boy with a keen, quick mind who is eager to learn, this school offers the most hospitable of welcomes, and the instructors concern themselves very personally with each of their charges. You might say that the faculty is a kind of family *in absentia*, and that, of course, helps allay the pangs of homesickness. There are many outings into the countryside, for instance, and sports competitions that teach the values of honor and teamwork and the like."

"Your description gets better and better, Mr. Kenniston," Laure declared with a smile. "I shall certainly write Father O'Mara at once."

"Without seeking to flatter you, Mrs. Bouchard, I should say that your children are exceptionally fortunate in having so concerned and far-seeing a mother." At this, Laure could not help blushing and looking away, but almost at once her eyes returned to the magnetic man across the table from her. Already, she had the stirrings of more than mild interest in him; yet, remembering how swiftly William Brickley had insinuated himself into her attentions, she at once began to put up mental barriers. This, like the other experience, was much too swift, much too opportunistic. She would wait—but there was no denying that Leland Kenniston was a fascinating man and that, when he spoke, it was with an appealing sincerity. She knew that she wanted neither a dandy nor a ghost-image of her beloved Luke. And she told herself once again that smooth talk often concealed hidden pitfalls, and that she would be wary.

As the waiters entered to clear away the last of the dinner dishes, Leland asked one of them to bring the maître d'. When Armand entered, Leland commended him without ostentatious show, which pleased Laure. "My compliments to your staff, and above all to your chef. An incomparable dinner, and the presentation by your waiters was exactly what we hoped for. Please distribute this *pourboire* to the staff, and thank you again for making this such a memorable occasion."

Lopasuta rose and drew back Geraldine's chair, and Leland quickly and gently murmured, "May I, Mrs. Bouchard?"

Laure glanced up at him. A warm flush suffused her heart-shaped face, much as if she had been a schoolgirl, and she murmured back, "Thank you very much, Mr. Kenniston," as she allowed him to draw back the chair.

As they emerged, the maître d' followed Leland and asked if he might be permitted to call a carriage. "Oh, no, let's walk a bit," Geraldine eagerly put in. "I just love New Orleans at night. The gaslights at the corners, and the facades of the shops, and the old homes and the apartments with their iron balconies—it's so very romantic!"

"You see, Leland," Lopasuta explained, "Geraldine and I spent our honeymoon here, and so she's understandably fond of this city."

"And you, Lopasuta, now that you are away from Montgomery with the prospect of remaining here for a few years, how do you feel about it?" the Irishman earnestly demanded.

"I like it very much. To be sure, the intensely humid summer and the ever-present danger of yellow fever are definitely drawbacks, but in the main, I think there are great opportunities here. And as you've said yourself, Leland, the port continues to grow in importance and traffic."

"Precisely. Well, at any rate, I'm happy that I was instrumental in reacquainting you two lovebirds with a city that means so much to you both," Leland concluded with a smile.

A cooling breeze had come in from the levee, which justified Geraldine's impulsive suggestion that they walk for a while and see New Orleans at night. On the main thoroughfares, the civil guards, the equivalent of policeman, were stationed in plain view. It was only if one wandered off toward Galatin Street, or near the wharf at night, or perhaps on the outskirts toward the south, that there was real danger. To be sure, at the lower end of Rampart Street, expecially around midnight, there were occasional drunken brawls and sometimes even stabbings. But as a rule, New Orleans residents went about freely at night to gambling salons, the theater and opera, or sometimes, and more daringly, in carriage parties to see the cockfights or the outlawed combat between fighting hounds and bears in a carnival tent.

Geraldine and Lopasuta were walking slightly ahead, and so Laure found herself paired with Leland. She turned to him to say, "I'm most grateful to you for your suggestions about my son Lucien, for a very delightful evening, and for your very generous hospitality. It was a superb dinner."

"It was my great pleasure, Mrs. Bouchard. Do you plan to stay in New Orleans long?"

"I—" She hesitated, not wanting so swiftly to let him know that she had come solely to meet him and to discuss her son. She admitted to herself that she was exceedingly curious about this man whom Lopasuta had praised to the skies—determined to find out what kind of man Leland Kenniston really was—but she would not admit this to him, and so she finished, "It has been some time since I visited my casino, and this seemed an excellent opportunity to kill two birds with one stone, as they say, Mr. Kenniston. I also wanted to visit with Geraldine and Lopasuta and see their new house. It's absolutely charming."

The memories of Luke's own similar house crowded in upon her at this moment, and she found herself somewhat confused. Tonight, she knew, she had felt liberated from her reclusive mourning, and she had enjoyed the supper and the conversation, as well as Leland's courtly treatment, as if she had been young again and unpledged to any man. And yet, once again she had to caution herself not to be taken in by the romantic setting, or the memories, or even by Leland's apparently guileless and friendly nature. Oh, yes, how easy it would be to succumb to the moment, to all its allure. Even this first time, he had already unconsciously signaled his interest in her—she could sense it, and sense also that it was not pretense on his part. And that made her warier than ever.

What few people knew about Laure Bouchard was that there was to her nature a sensuality hidden well beneath the poised image by which most observers saw and judged her. Luke Bouchard had roused it, and during their marriage, he had been inspired by the passionate ardor of which he knew her capable to bring her again and again to the heights of physical passion and total fulfillment as a woman.

But this sensuality extended well beyond the act of love: it was reflected in Laure's enjoyment of good food and wine—but always without excess—her love of music and the other fine arts, and her pleasure in such simple things as the sunset, flowers, the soft flowing sound of a river, and the calls of birds. To her, the world was a multiplicity of sensory delights, each to be savored for its own sake and yet which would complement her nature as a woman for whom love was a consummation and distillation of all the emotions in life.

Laure airily concluded by saying, "I certainly shan't stay longer than a week, but long before the end of my stay, I shall write Father O'Mara at your very kind suggestion."

"Oh, yes—I've written the name and address on this slip of paper so you won't have to trust your memory, Mrs. Bouchard." He stopped as they reached the corner and drew a folded piece of paper out of his coat pocket. "Instead of writing him, I shall send off a transatlantic cable informing him of your interest and telling him to anticipate your inquiry. It should take no more than a matter of weeks to conclude all the arrangements."

"Thank you again, Mr. Kenniston."

While they further paused at this intersection of Royal and Endicott, to let a hansom cab go past, Laure suddenly heard a plaintive meow. She turned and saw a gray cat, looking lost and distraught, in the middle of the street. A carriage was bearing down on it from her right, and Laure uttered a stifled cry as she put her hand over her mouth.

Leland Kenniston saw the cat and, heedless of danger to himself, raced into the middle of the street, scooped up the cat in his arms, and hurried across to the other side, just as the carriage thundered by.

"Oh, God, he might have been killed!" Laure breathed, aghast. Her eyes fixed on him, and she saw him stroking the cat's head and murmuring to it and heard the plaintive, answering meow. He recrossed to her, still holding the cat in his arms.

"How brave you were—to risk your life over a cat," she said in an unsteady voice.

"We Irish have a fondness for cats, Mrs. Bouchard. When I was a very little boy, my grandmother once told me that we should always be kind to animals because it might just be true, as some folks say, that we come back to life in animal form. I've read that there are those who believe that we originally descended from the apes—though I don't exactly hold with that," he said, making light of it. "My, my," he exclaimed, "this cat isn't mangy at all, and—look here—it has a collar. The poor thing must have

305

strayed away from its home and found itself out in unfamiliar territory, terrified by the horses and the carriages."

"You are very kindhearted, Mr. Kenniston." Laure was still shaken by what had happened.

Lopasuta and Geraldine had witnessed this event and came rushing back across the intersection. After determining that Leland was unhurt, Geraldine fussed over the cat still cradled in his arms.

"Allow me to convey you all back to your house," Leland offered, "and then I'll see to it about returning this cat to its owner."

"There's a carriage," Lopasuta called, and hailed it. Lopasuta opened the carriage door and ushered in first Laure and then his wife. Then he clambered in the rear seat and Leland sat beside him as Lopasuta gave the coachman the address.

When they arrived at Greenley Street, the Irishman got out, still holding the cat in his arms and talking to it soothingly. After Lopasuta had emerged, he extended one hand to help Laure and Geraldine to the safety of the curb.

"It's been a perfectly wonderful evening, Mr. Kenniston. I am so pleased that we've finally met," Laure told him. Her green eyes fixed on his handsome face, and she found herself incalculably drawn to him. Here was a man of courage and inner strength who did not flaunt his wealth. The social grace he had acquired seemed almost instinctive with him, an integral part of his being without affectation or posing. She felt that with this man she might trust her instincts somewhat more than she had immediately after Luke's death.

"Perhaps we may have dinner again in a few days, if all of you are free?" he proposed as he got back into the carriage.

"That would be very nice," the three of them chorused. "Thank you again for a lovely evening," Laure called after him.

He nodded, tipped his hat, and then, ascertaining the name and address of the owner from the tag on the cat's collar, gave the coachman the address. The carriage rolled off into the night.

Laure stood a moment transfixed, while Lopasuta and Geraldine watched her, exchanging a knowing glance. Geraldine put a finger to her lips and Lopasuta nodded. He would make no comment, but he was very happy that

Laure had found Leland Kenniston to her liking. As for himself, long ago he had decided that he could well stake his future on this man's judgment and friendship and, most specifically, on his employment.

## Twenty-nine

Milo Brutus Henson had invited Carleton Ivers to have dinner at his house to discuss Lopasuta Bouchard, and the tall, bony-faced man readily accepted. Now sixty-four, his sparse hair was white, above dark-blue, greedy little eyes and a small, lecherously ripe mouth. Carleton Ivers had never forgiven Lopasuta Bouchard for having intervened in the banker's coarse treatment of Amelia McAdams—now Amelia Coleman—at Lopasuta's favorite Montgomery restaurant. Because Amelia's father had embezzled five thousand dollars of Ivers's money, the banker had forced the attractive young woman to act as his housekeeper and to oblige him sexually when he demanded it. Lopasuta had overheard Ivers threaten Amelia with a whipping, and he had then and there offered her a job as cook at Windhaven Plantation and marched her out of the restaurant, to Ivers's unconcealed fury.

"Good to see you again, Carleton, boy," Milo Brutus Henson chuckled. He gestured to his acquiescent mistress, Elaine. "Fill Carleton's glass with the best bourbon in the house, Laney, honey. You be awful nice to this man; he's real important here in Montgomery. Lent me a lot of money to help me out once, he did, and there's nothing I wouldn't do for him. And don't be put off by how old he looks—he's still damn good in bed, and I think I might just let him prove that with you tonight."

"Oh, Milo, honey, please, do I have to?" she murmured for only her protector to hear; "protector" was the euphe-

307

mistic title Henson had awarded himself to justify his ruthless exploitation of helpless young women.

"You damn well have to, bitch," he whispered back.
"Don't put up a squawk, or I'll take it out of your hide."
Then, aloud, "She's bashful, Carleton. You see, I'm the
only man she's been to bed with all these months, so she'll
take a little coaxing. But come bedtime, I'll send her to
your room, and once she's peeled down, she'll shed all her
shyness, along with her duds—you'll see if she doesn't, ha,
ha!"

"Mightly friendly of you, Milo," Carleton Ivers purred
as the young woman brought the decanter of bourbon to
him, and filled his glass to the brim. "Whoa, now, honey!
Want to get me so drunk I won't know how to take care of
a right purty piece like you? You just leave the decanter
here—that's fine, thank you. Your name's Laney?"

"Her name's Elaine," Henson interjected, "but her bed
name's Laney. Maybe you'll invent another name for her
once you try her out. But let's get down to business. You
want to know the real reason I invited you over?"

"For another loan, maybe?" Ivers speculated.

"Not hardly. I did pretty well with my partner from St.
Louis a couple of months back. No, I'm not pining for
money. But I'm scared, and I'm mad."

"That's sort of like double talk, Milo. What are you getting at exactly?"

The land speculator leaned forward across the table, his
face contorted with anger. "Maybe you don't know it, but
that goddamned Injun lawyer got back alive."

"You're joking!"

"No, I'm not. You stay in your bank all the time, or in
your house with some of those sluts you have sent up from
New Orleans or Natchez, so you don't know what's going
on. But I saw him. Months ago, at the railroad station,
when I was waiting for my St. Louis partner. Plain as day,
plain as the nose on your face, Carleton. He was getting
off, with some Chinee girl and the girl was carrying a
baby—looked part Chinee to me, but I didn't want to get
too much in sight so he'd see me. And that white wife of
his—that shameless hussy who ought to be tarred and
feathered and ridden out of town on a rail for mating up
with that son of a bitch—she and that Laure Bouchard
were there to meet him. I tell you, he must have more lives

308

than a cat. I thought William Brickley took good care of him."

"So did I. And Brickley's dead now."

Henson replenished his glass with bourbon, and after swigging down a quarter of it, he set the glass down on the table and belched. "Look, like I said, you've been stuck at your bank or in your house fooling around with your girls, but I've done some groundwork on this. I finally went to his house, and spoke with an old gossipy fool of a woman living across the street. She let out that he and his wife and their kids and that Chinee girl had left town. I told her that I had some legal business I wanted him to help me with, and would she please give me his address. She wouldn't give me his exact address, but she did say they'd gone to New Orleans."

"That was smart," Carleton Ivers said admiringly. He turned to eye the attractive young woman who, at Milo's gesture, had sat down at the table, but this time in a chair next to Ivers. Permitting himself a lengthy, appraising look and then smirking at her, Ivers reached over and pinched her thigh.

"Oh, please, Mr. Ivers, you're too strong," she protested, and then giggled with a mischievous smile.

"You're quite a piece, honey," Ivers declared. "I'm surely looking forward to taking Milo up on his offer." He turned back to Henson and demanded, "Anyway, so what are you getting at? You found out where that Injun lawyer moved to, but at least he's out of our way."

"You've still got a score to settle with him for taking that octoroon away from you, don't you, Carleton? And I don't want any further chance of him sticking his nose in my legal affairs as he did in the past. Brickley did all he could to get rid of him—only it didn't work. So I've decided to handle things myself, and that's what I've just about done."

"Now you're talking in riddles. You mean you're going down to New Orleans and get rid of him yourself? You haven't got the guts for it, Milo, with all due respect," Ivers contemptuously declared, then reached over and gave Elaine another sly pinch, which made her giggle again and send him a dewy-eyed look that promised him everything if only he'd be patient.

"That's not what I mean, Carleton," Henson irritatedly snapped. "But I'll tell you something—though if you ever breathe it to a soul, I'll deny it and call you a liar in the

309

*Advertiser*. I once did take a shot at him, but I missed, more's the pity! I'd have saved myself all this aggravation and worry over the past couple of years if I'd hit him."

"You really amaze me, Milo." Ivers leaned forward across the table, momentarily neglecting the attractive young woman. "When was that?"

"Not quite three years ago. He was out riding on horseback—well, he'd just married that uppity white bitch who ought to have had better sense, and I couldn't stomach him anymore, riding roughshod all over town, and thinking he's better than everybody else. Anyway, that's ancient history. This time I've arranged to have somebody do it in New Orleans—somebody who knows his business and won't miss."

"You'd better be careful that it's not traced back to you, Milo. That could be dangerous for both of us."

"I don't know why you're getting the wind up, Carleton. I'm the one taking all the risks. You've never been involved. The only thing he's got on you is the way you treated that juicy octoroon you had to let go."

"Don't remind me." Ivers's lips tightened in a sneer of savage hatred. "I'd gladly see him dead and buried six feet under just for that—she was really a piece, and I haven't had anything near like her since then. But go on, tell me why you think this time you've made sure he'll be out of the way once and for all!"

"Never you mind about my being sure, Carleton." Henson sat back with a self-contented smirk and twirled his waxed mustache. "I'll tell you what I've done," he said at last, "and I'm so sure this time that I'll bet you my house if it doesn't come out the way I want it."

"I'll admit I covet your house, but I think I covet this Laney of yours more than that," Ivers dryly chuckled, and reached over to apply a third pinch to the young woman's thigh. Surreptitiously rolling her eyes in resignation, she moved closer to him, shifting her chair, so that he would have easier access to such libidinous caresses. At the same time, she gave him a provocative look, which made him lick his lips and chuckle softly with anticipation.

"Why, I'd almost bet her, too," the land speculator boastingly declared. "Now listen. A couple of years ago, when I had to take a trip to Natchez to file a claim on some property I was after, I met a fellow who called himself George Delton. He'd been a Confederate deserter who holed up there till the war was over and then got himself a cushy job helping a semiretired madam run a very profitable crib. Anyway, we got to talking over some good Maryland whiskey—I'd paid a visit to the crib and had the prettiest girl there—and George told me that he'd once had to leave his home in Baltimore because he'd knifed a man who owed him some money over cards. He's right handy with a knife, and as we got more into our cups in Natchez, he told me that he likes to kill. It's a real kick for him, the kind of kick a man usually gets from an accommodating whore like Laney here."

"Oh, Milo honey, you oughtn't to talk about me like that! What will Mr. Ivers think?" Elaine whiningly protested, turning to the elderly banker and clinging to his arm as if wanting both reassurance and protection from such calumny. Ivers leered at her, and with one arm around her back, he boldly cupped one of her large, pendulous breasts with the other, as he murmured, "You're not that at all, my dear—you're obviously a fine lady. When we're alone later tonight, I'll show you how much I think of you!"

"Oh, you're just a card, you are, Mr. Ivers," she giggled. Carleton Ivers sighed and reluctantly drew himself away from this salaciously intimate conversation to say to his host, "The history of another rogue doesn't particularly concern me."

"But it should and it will, Carleton. You see, we kept in touch with each other. Fact is, now that Brickley's elaborate scheme boomeranged, I wish I'd asked George Delton to handle the job from the beginning. You can be sure that Lopasuta Bouchard would have gotten a quick knife in his ribs, been put into a sack weighted down with rocks, and thrown into the Mississippi. Anyhow, the long and the short of it is that I've written to George, because he's moved to New Orleans. He's got himself the same sort of job he had in Natchez, running a bordello on Gallatin Street. I described Bouchard to him and told him to keep on the lookout for the Injun—and that there'd be four hundred dollars in hard Union cash as soon as he sent me Lopasuta Bouchard's write-up in the *Times-Picayune* death notices. You get my meaning?"

"I do indeed. Do you really think he'll do it for you?"

"I already sent him a hundred dollars on account. We use a code when we write each other, and so nobody could ever connect the two of us, I gave him a post office box number for replying." At this point, Henson fumbled in his waistcoat pocket and drew out a letter scrawled in pencil. "Here's what he wrote me back—I just got it a couple of days ago. Read it for yourself."

He tossed the letter across the table to Ivers, who caught it deftly in the air, unfolded it, and read it. Then the banker whistled. "Now I'm beginning to believe you. I'll even go so far as to say that I think this time Lopasuta Bouchard's goose is finally cooked—and it's long overdue."

"I second that. Don't you worry; for the money I'm paying George Delton, he'll get it done right. And if he does it smartly enough, there won't be anything to compromise anyone. Believe me, Carleton, a knife in the back in the dark of night—nobody could trace it. Well now, would you care for some more bourbon, or possibly a snifter of brandy?"

"Oh, I don't think so, Milo—not if I'm going to try to console this charming young lady here after the nasty thing you called her." Carleton Ivers rose, swaying unsteadily, from his chair and turned to hold out his hand to Elaine, who took it and rose with him, favoring him with a simpering smile of acquiescence.

"Look, Milo," the banker hoarsely added, "just to make the cheese more binding, I'm going to contribute a little something to the business at hand." He fumbled for his wallet, extracted it, and drew out a fifty-dollar bill. Tossing it in front of Henson, he went on, "Send it off to this George Delton of yours. Tell him it's a present from an admiring friend. Tell him I want Lopasuta Bouchard just as dead as you do, and I'll sweeten the kitty even more when he pulls it off."

"I'll send it out to him in a letter tomorrow," Henson promised.

"Well, now, if that's all the business we've got to discuss, you won't mind if I accept your very gracious hospitality and take this charming damsel upstairs with me to one of your guest rooms?" Ivers sniggered.

"Go ahead, with my blessing. Laney, you make my friend happy because, if he gives me a bad report on you tomorrow morning, you're going to be mighty regretful."

"Oh, don't worry, Milo honey, I'll take real good care of him. I like older men, anyway," she ingenuously blurted. Carleton Ivers triumphantly chuckled, his right arm curving around her lissome waist as he escorted her up the winding stairway of his host's elegant house.

312

Henson leaned back and closed his eyes. He played with the tips of his ornate, waxed mustache, using thumbs and forefingers of both hands to make that hirsute decoration even more spectacular.

When he opened his eyes again, Ivers and Elaine had disappeared. He smiled to himself. "Maybe I won't have to go west after all. I'm sort of comfortable here in Montgomery, and there's still plenty of land around the outskirts I can get my hands on and turn into a nice little profit—once I'm sure that goddamned Injun is really done for!"

## Thirty

The morning after Laure Bouchard had met Leland Kenniston, she wrote a lengthy and detailed letter to Father O'Mara of St. Timothy's Academy in Dublin, and after breakfast she walked to the post office with Geraldine to mail it. She had told the headmaster a good deal about herself and Luke, and had given him as objective an analysis as she could of her son Lucien, so that he would know something about the boy and in what direction his talents lay. She asked him to write her at Windhaven Plantation in Lowndesboro and declared that if her son was accepted, she would forward a draft for the first term's tuition. Leland Kenniston would then accompany the boy to Ireland in time for the opening of the fall term.

Laure and Geraldine spent the remainder of the morning wandering through the streets of the French Quarter, peering at window displays and making some purchases in the more irresistible shops. Lopasuta, meanwhile, had gone with Leland to supervise the opening of the store on Chartres Street; afterward, he intensively studied the correspondence and other data pertaining to his employer's difficulties with the New Orleans Hauling Company.

Later that morning, Lopasuta went over to the firm in

question, and politely introduced himself to the owner, Abner Dalloway, a broad-shouldered, paunchy man in his early fifties, who belligerently and utterly denied that Leland had in any way informed him of the fragile nature of the goods his firm had hauled.

Lopasuta replied in his most diplomatic vein that the facts as he understood them did not confirm Dalloway's version and that unless the contractor was willing to settle out of court and indemnify Leland Kenniston for his monetary loss for the breakage of the shipment and the consequent loss of sales, he, as attorney for the importer-exporter, would have no recourse but to take Dalloway to court.

"Take me to court and be damned to you, my fine bucko!" Dalloway snarled, pounding the table with his fist for emphasis. "I'll get up on the stand and swear on the Bible that your fine Mr. Kenniston talked in circles around Robin Hood's barn and didn't pinpoint the exact method of handling he wanted. That's my defense, sonny, and you might as well know it in advance, because you can't possibly win."

"You are, of course, entitled to your viewpoint, Mr. Dalloway," was the Comanche lawyer's tactful answer. "However, you leave us no choice but to file suit in the Circuit Court of Louisiana for breach of contract."

Dalloway snorted and turned his back on Lopasuta, who shrugged and left the office. He met Laure and Geraldine in the French Quarter, and took them both to an intimate Basque restaurant, where they heartily enjoyed a late lunch of *tapinade* as an appetizer, followed by chicken cooked in white wine with raisins and chopped pecans. As they sat sipping glasses of an excellent bottle of Vouvray, Geraldine plied him with questions about his work and the oncoming lawsuit—the very first he would try for his new employer.

Laure sat quietly as her friends talked, still troubled by the diametrically opposed emotions which had arisen within her as a result of last night's dinner at Antoine's.

Her opinion of Leland Kenniston was that, being the forceful type, he might well have made blatant overtures toward her: had she been as naive as a teenaged virgin, she still would have known from the way he looked at her last night that he was fascinated by her. And yet to the contrary, he had behaved modestly, even was subdued toward her, for which she was grateful. And although he was ob-

314

viously extremely wealthy, he did not crassly or vulgarly show off his affluence in an effort to win her favor. For that, too, she was grateful.

Laure uttered a contented sigh as she thought about last night. She hoped that the next time they met, there would be a repetition of that evening—another dinner engagement during which she would be matched with Leland, to listen to him and get to know him better, perhaps to thereby gauge her own troubled, as yet indeterminate feelings. She knew only one thing for sure: the prospect of long years ahead with no man beside her as a companion—and this in no way implied mere sexual gratification, since that would inevitably accompany a total, harmonious commitment and devotion of one to the other—was bleak indeed. John Brunton had been very nearly a father figure in restoring her shattered self-esteem when he had married her after the traumatic loss of her virginity by force and her father's suicide. Luke Bouchard, because of his age, could equally have represented a father figure, but happily and surprisingly he had not at all turned into a prototype, as might have been expected in such a relationship. A man like Leland Kenniston, if he continued to ring true and to be his own individual and responsible self, seemed to be at last the kind of man whom she had subconsciously dreamed of all her life. And because she realized this so early in their acquaintance, she understood the implicit precariousness better than most.

Laure was disappointed that he did not call that evening, but a courier did deliver a dozen beautiful roses to her at the house, with a note saying simply, "In memory of an enchanting evening, which I shall always treasure—Leland Kenniston."

Geraldine refrained from making any teasing remarks when she saw how Laure colored once the roses had been unwrapped. Instead, she merely smiled as she put them into a vase, and then went back to the kitchen to help Mei Luong prepare their evening meal. It was a cozy, pleasant dinner, and Lopasuta's happy mood at being involved in purposeful work with a real future to it warmed Laure greatly, as did his and Geraldine's obvious fondness for each other. She was so pleased that this intelligent young woman harbored no rancor over Lopasuta's unintended, prolonged absence from her side. Watching Lopasuta playing with his sons was both a pleasure for Laure and a poignant reminder of her widowhood, for there was no man in her life now to take her children on his knee, make a fuss over them, and show that he loved them as deeply as she did.

When Laure had gone to bed, Geraldine lay in Lopasuta's arms and whispered of the indelible impression Leland Kenniston's roses had made. "I'd just love to see her marry a man like him, Lopasuta, dear," Geraldine confided. "He's intelligent, energetic, he loves to travel, he's honest and decent, and he expects the best of those he's involved with—that's why he hired you, of course. Laure needs exactly a man like that. And he's just the right age for her, too. Oh, yes, Luke was wonderful, one of the finest men I've ever known—but maybe he was just a bit too perfect, almost more of a god than a man. Somehow I think that Leland could make Laure even happier—and I certainly hope it happens."

"He won't rush it, I can be sure of it," Lopasuta told her. "I think I know him pretty well now. He thinks things out a good deal: though he's young enough to yield to impulse, he often lets his brain govern his heart. And that's a very wise course to take with Laure. Oh, yes, I'm sure he could sweep her off her feet, but then she might fault herself for it, thinking that she wasn't being faithful to Luke's memory."

"My gracious, you've become very wise all of a sudden about women, darling," Geraldine quipped. But a long, passionate kiss effectively silenced her bantering, and at last, drowsy with the languor of fulfillment, they turned to look at each other happily.

"You're remarkable, Geraldine. I'm so happy with you. I hope someday soon Laure can find the same happiness you and I share," Lopasuta murmured as he kissed Geraldine good night.


While the Alabama legislature had taken its summer vacation, Andy Haskins had gone on to Tuscaloosa to work diligently in his new post as director of the sanatorium. He had rented a pleasant house on the outskirts of town for Jessica and the children, and as soon as he finished out his term next spring, he would devote full time to this humanitarian project. Already he had become aware of a practice that appalled him: the attempts by selfish young people to have their aging, ailing parents certified as mentally unbalanced and shunted away forever into a state institution.

Happily, this sanatorium was endowed through private means—though it had a state license to operate—so Andy could, as director, exercise more influence and investigate cases far more thoroughly than could a state sanatorium for the insane.

However, during this fourth week in July, he had received a letter from William Blount, the chairman of the Republican party in Montgomery. Blount, who had been instrumental in getting Andy to run first for the House of Representatives and then for the Alabama Senate, was at his most eloquent and persuasive:

Dear Senator Haskins:

As you know, Rufus W. Cobb of Shelby County, another Democrat, succeeded Governor Houston last year. We who believe that Republicanism is vital and valid in Alabama ask your formal approval to begin backing you to succeed Governor Cobb as our leading candidate on the Republican ticket three years hence.

Your unblemished record as a politician speaks volumes for your integrity and honesty. I do not have to remind you, Senator Haskins, of the corruption that has prevailed among the Democrats, and how they have used coercive force through the outlawed Ku Klux Klan to deter Republican—especially black Republican—votes in statewide elections. I believe that you owe it to the people of Alabama to reconsider your avowed intention of retiring from politics at the conclusion of your term next spring. My associates and I hope that you will give us your approval to go to work behind the scenes on your behalf for the gubernatorial post you so richly deserve.

Yours admiringly,
William Blount

When Andy received this letter, he at once penned a brief reply:

Dear Mr. Blount:

I'm deeply honored and flattered by the confidence you and your associates place in me. But I have made a decision that I will not revoke: I am stepping down from politics at the last session of the current Alabama Senate.

317

The sanatorium I now head gives me more of a chance to work for people who truly need help, and I am weary of the grind and harassment and greediness of politics.

I am most appreciative of everything you have done for me, and I fervently hope you will find a suitable candidate more available than I, who remain,

> Your devoted servant,
> Andrew Haskins
> State Senator

This same week of July, Maxine Bouchard received a long letter at Windhaven Range from Laurette Douglas in Chicago that would have an unexpected influence on her and Lucien Edmond's decision concerning the future of their two oldest children:

Dear Maxine:

It's been far too long since I've last written to you, so I thought I'd compensate for my negligence by sitting down and taking the time to fill you in on what's been happening with Charles and me.

My mother may have told you how successful our Galveston stores have been—as a matter of fact, she and Henry just wrote to say that they hope to get there soon to take me up on my offer that they can buy anything they need at the store at cost. Well, now for the really exciting news: Charles is planning on opening up a new branch in New York City!

After having Lawrence Harding do some checking on the realtor, Charles recently signed a contract for a plot of land and, hopefully, the new store in our nation's biggest city will be ready in time for Christmas business. He's chosen that nice young Alexander Gorth to manage it, and I'm looking forward to going there at Christmas with Charles, because it'll be the first time I'll have ever seen New York.

Still in all, dear Maxine, it's almost unbelievable to think how Chicago has grown since the great fire. Wonderful things are starting up, like the new Chicago Academy of Fine Arts. They take students from all over the country who want to paint or sculpt, and they give them a very fine education. There are many new galleries here now that sell some of the best stu-

318

dent work—I bought a painting of the old Water Tower that survived the great fire, and it's in my parlor right now.

Well, I've just gone over what I just wrote and I have to laugh: Here I am, a born-and-bred Alabama girl, and I'm certainly beating the drum for my new home town! Of course, one day I must go back to visit Laure Bouchard at Windhaven Plantation. I know how terribly hard it must be for poor Laure right now, being both mother and father to her children and missing Luke as she certainly must be.

We have a brand-new neighbor—a young doctor who's on the faculty of Rush Medical College. Although everybody talks about the great hospitals and schools back East, Dr. Thornberg says Rush is better. It has quite an interesting history, too, he's told me. It was established in 1937 by a Dr. Daniel Brainard, who came from the East and found Chicago to be nothing more than a remote settlement with lots of Indians around. And just two days before the settlement became incorporated as a city, Dr. Brainard got a charter from the Illinois Legislature to found the state's first medical college.

He named the school after Dr. Benjamin Rush of Philadelphia, the only formally trained doctor to sign the Declaration of Independence. To his great credit, Dr. Rush also stood for women's right to education and for the abolition of slavery. He was also the first American to describe mental illness as a disease.

Back in 1843, Rush Medical College began its first session of a mere sixteen weeks with all of twenty-two students. But its faculty included Professor James Van Zandt Blaney—he discovered chloroform simultaneously with C.H.Y. Simpson in England, and he also helped organize the Chicago Board of Education, as well as the Chicago and Illinois Medical Societies—and a husband-and-wife team, Drs. George and Gladys Dick, who worked out ways of diagnosing and immunizing against scarlet fever. Dr. Thornberg says Rush was founded with the creed of providing the finest possible medical service to a needful community—the real meaning of the Hippocratic Oath, as it were.

Gracious! Just listen to me spouting off to you about matters which probably don't interest you at all!

But it's just one of the many reasons I'm proud to be a Chicagoan now. Anyway, Maxine, I do hope you and Lucien Edmond will pay us a visit. I want to take you around to the lovely shops and daydream about what we would do if we only had the money to buy all the things we'd love! And of course, if you do come, Charles and I would escort you and Lucien Edmond to all the concerts and museums that Chicago has to offer.

We are both in excellent health—although, of course, we're getting older. Here I am forty-two now, but Charles assures me I've kept my looks and don't look a day over thirty. He just better say something like that, if he knows what side his bread is buttered on! The twins, Arthur and Kenneth—you wouldn't imagine how much they've grown in just a year or two—they're almost fourteen now. Howard is ten, and sweet little Fleur is six—my gracious, how time flies! Maybe the secret of long life is to keep happy all the time so you're never conscious that you're growing older.

Anyway, I've rambled on long enough, but I want to stress my invitation for both you and Lucien Edmond to come see us one day. Just send a telegram, and we'll put you up in style!

Your loving "cousin,"
Laurette Douglas

That evening at dinner Maxine let Lucien Edmond read her letter from Laurette. After he had finished, she declared, "You know, I've been thinking that, instead of going to art school in New Orleans, Carla might very well look into that Academy of Fine Arts. Personally, I think Chicago's a healthier town than New Orleans, especially in the summer when yellow fever always seems to be raging."

"That's true, my dear."

"And if by some chance Hugo finds that working on the range isn't to his liking and if he prefers working indoors, he could do much worse than learning the department store business, don't you think?"

"That's not such a bad idea," Lucien Edmond pondered. "I personally think that our children ought to know more about the rest of the country. And let's face it, Maxine, New Orleans is still the Deep South. Granted that it has wonderful tradition and history, but a Midwestern city like Chicago, vigorous as it is—well, it's very possible that Carla might get a great deal more out of a few years there than she ever could in New Orleans."

"I'll tell you what I'm going to do, darling." Maxine rose from the table and went over to kiss him and put her arm around his shoulders. "I'm going to write Laurette and ask her—just in case it should work out that both Carla and Hugo would go to Chicago this fall—where they could stay and who would look after them. I wouldn't expect the Douglases to put them up—big as their house is, they have all those children. And yet I wouldn't want either Carla or Hugo to be entirely without supervision."

"Understandably, darling."

"Going away to a new city would be a very good thing for them at this time in their lives. But all the same, you and I would both feel more at ease if we knew that some-one reliable was watching to make sure they didn't—you know."

"Get carried away by the temptations of the big city," Lucien Edmond chuckled. "I don't really think we have to worry about our children—they would behave according to their own ethical code. But I know what you mean. Go ahead and write the letter. Incidentally, now that my leg's fine, I think it's time I drive those cattle to Santa Fe as I mentioned."

"Lucien Edmond Bouchard!" Maxine bristled. Then, in-stantly softening, she leaned down to whisper, "This is the loveliest time we've had together in longer than I care to remember, darling. Please don't rush off—or I'll think you're tired of my company."

"Never that. You know better, Maxine. Well, maybe I'll let Joe Duvray sell the cattle in Santa Fe."

"That's a much better idea," she grinned. As she sat down again, she sighed, "I do so hope Hugo's getting along well."

## Thirty-one

During his remaining time in New Orleans, Leland Kenniston arranged to see Laure twice more. On his fourth evening in town, he and Laure went with Lopasuta and Geraldine to enjoy the light entertainment at a popular music hall. But on the night before he was to leave for New York and Laure was to return to Windhaven Plantation, Lopasuta and Geraldine decided to let her be alone with the energetic Irishman. As Geraldine so succinctly put it to her husband, "They ought to be allowed to discover just how they act when they're by themselves. And if anything's going to come of their acquaintance, they should at least have one evening to themselves to find out."

Lopasuta had wryly agreed with this, admitting to himself that since returning from Hong Kong, he was discovering in Geraldine new depths of perspicacity, droll humor, and not a little independence. They had grown closer together than ever, and now Lopasuta Bouchard had even more reason than before to be grateful for Geraldine's support as a wife and partner. At the outset, he had not often discussed the nuances of his legal cases with her. Now, he found himself working up hypothetical cases, detailing his defense or prosecution, the references he would use to back up his argument, and finally his speech to the court by way of summation. And he had come to welcome Geraldine's criticism of these scenarios because he knew her opinions would be honest and unprejudiced.

And so it was that, on their last night in New Orleans, Leland and Laure were finally alone together, first dining at an intimate bistro, and then going to St. Phillip Street Theater to see a performance of Shakespeare's *The Merchant of Venice*. Laure was pleasantly surprised to find that Leland was so conversant with Shakespeare, whom she had often read and whose magnificent drama and powerful usage of the English language had always engrossed her.

During the intermission after the second act, as they went out to the salon to partake of white wine and cheese and tea biscuits, she turned to him and casually asked, "Is this your favorite Shakespearean play, Mr. Kenniston?"

"In some ways, Mrs. Bouchard, it is. I think Shylock's plea to be understood as a man, and not as a Jew, strikes closely to my own feelings. You know, of course, that in many American cities Irishmen are still reviled. It used to be quite common in sections of Chicago and New York for stores to actually have signs in their windows reading, 'No Irish need apply.' And you have only to change the word 'Irish' to 'Jewish,' or 'Chinese,' or 'Hungarian,' or anything else you wish to designate a people or a race you have no great admiration for, and there you find the very crux of hatred and bigotry. I confess—and I beg you to forgive me for indulging in a polemic, Mrs. Bouchard—that this is one great flaw I find here in the South. I have read enough history to understand its origins—the institution of slavery was essential to the production of cotton, the South's principal industry. I know also that England backed the Confederacy during the Civil War, at least at first, because they needed the cotton for their mills. Yet they did not dare show their partiality too strongly, and perhaps that is why the Confederacy lost."

"You know, Mr. Kenniston, you continue to amaze me. I hadn't thought that a businessman would be well versed in Shakespeare, or history, or some of the other things that you've shown a familiarity with."

"It wasn't always that way, Mrs. Bouchard," he amiably chuckled. "When I was a brat of a boy back in County Mayo, I was lucky if I had half a potato and a cup of very weak tea after a hard day's work in the field with the hoe. Or sometimes just a turnip and heated water, which I pretended was tea."

"Was it really so dreadful?"

"Oh, yes. The English landlords were not particularly generous to their Irish tenants. That's one reason that Ireland wants its independence from Great Britain. I believe in that myself, but it must be achieved through education and peaceful means—never violence. I must apologize again—I never meant to impose my personal opinions upon you—"

"But you haven't. You've given me some very stimulating notions, Mr. Kenniston. I'm very grateful to you for that. You see, I was born here in New Orleans, and since I married Luke Bouchard, I have lived in a very small town in Alabama where there isn't too much culture or stimulating conversation—and certainly no gourmet restaurants like Antoine's." She gave him one of her dazzling smiles, and as Leland stared intently at her, the gong sounded to summon the audience back to their seats.

When the play was over and the audience had rousingly applauded the actress who played Portia, Leland Kenniston and Laure Bouchard turned to each other with smiles of pleasure. "Extremely well done, didn't you think, Mrs. Bouchard?" he ventured.

"Oh, yes, delightful! I think Portia could have won just about every case she went to court with—just as I hope that Lopasuta will win every case which concerns you, Mr. Kenniston," she replied, her smile deepening.

Leland stared into her eyes for a moment, then forced himself to look away. "It's getting late," he finally said. "I'll get a carriage and take you back to Lopasuta and Geraldine, Mrs. Bouchard. But I'm looking forward to seeing you again in New York and to meeting your son Lucien."

"It's very good of you to take such an interest. He's a remarkable boy, though of course you'll think I'm prejudiced in saying so."

"Not at all. I'm sure he displays the best traits of his parents, which would make him a most unique lad. I hope you will schedule arrangements to allow you both to spend some time in New York before we sail to Dublin, because I'm very much looking forward to showing off my city. There's much that both of you would enjoy there, including several very outstanding restaurants and many wonderful halls where concerts, operas, and vaudeville are provided for a discerning audience, such as we had here this evening."

He offered her his arm, and Laure unhesitatingly took it. The magnetic contact between them made her tremble, and she felt herself physically stirred by this vigorous and candid man. Still, she appreciated his restraint. In no way had he sought to take liberties with her or assume that, simply because she was widowed, she would be vulnerable to him. Such discretion and tact seemed to her indications of his security with his manhood.

Laure perceived also that he was not acting, not affecting a pose to make a good impression. He seemed to be quite comfortable with people, and he did not egotistically seek the spotlight of attention. With a start, she was aware that she had begun to analyze him as if he were vitally important to her, something she had been totally unprepared for. She thought of his behavior during these three occasions they had met, and remembered the heroic rescue of that cat in the street. Obviously he couldn't purposely have planned that dramatic gesture as a means of impressing her. But she had been impressed when he had reacted so spontaneously and swiftly. No, he was not a Don Juan whose campaign to overcome a woman and win her total surrender was through the artificiality of creating situations in which he would always emerge the triumphant hero in her eyes. She found herself, somewhat to her own distress, obliged to consider what he could or might mean to her life in the future. And she very nearly wished that it was time for her to take Lucien to New York so that she and Leland would meet him again and spend more time together. She hoped she might then learn who and what he really was, so far as it would concern her personally.

As they sat side by side in the *fiacre* taking them from the theater to the house on Greenley Street, Leland was silent, yet attentive, and when their eyes did meet, he smiled at Laure, and there was no trace of either automatic reflex out of mannered politeness, or smug assertiveness. It was, rather, the smile of a sensible man who wishes to say to a woman, *"Te voglio bene,"* meaning that he is pleased with their being together and wishes her well as a person. It was a comfortable aura.

When at last the *fiacre* stopped in front of the house, Leland got out and helped Laure down to the curb. He glanced up at the coachman and pleasantly said, "If you will wait a moment or two, I shall go back with you to the St. Charles."

"Very good, m'sieu."

He led Laure to the door and, lifting the brass knocker, struck three times. Lopasuta, who had been studying law books to prepare for his case against Abner Dalloway, responded to the knock.

Leland smiled at his protégé, then jested that his lovely house guest was being returned safe and sound. Turning back to Laure, Leland declared, "It has been a rare privilege for me to have met you, Mrs. Bouchard. As soon as you hear from Father O'Mara, please telegraph me at my New York office to give me time to make the necessary hotel and steamship arrangements." He glanced back at Lopasuta and said, "I think you would all enjoy traveling up to New York on one of the luxury steamers—it would be far more comfortable than a train. And while you, my boy, may have had a good deal of sea travel lately, it would probably be a treat to your lovely wife."

Lopasuta laughed, then quickly agreed to this decision.

Leland then put it, "As a matter of fact, I should return to New Orleans and consult with René Laurent one last time before I go off to Europe, so I'll time that visit to coincide with your schedule, Mrs. Bouchard, and then we can all travel to New York together."

"That's a wonderful suggestion, Mr. Kenniston," Laure responded, and then added, "I have enjoyed meeting you, and I know Lucien will be thrilled at the idea of going abroad to study. Thank you ever so much."

"Thank *you*, Mrs. Bouchard." He hesitated making any overt gesture, yet the admiration in his eyes was not lost on Laure. She suddenly found herself wishing that he would take her in his arms and kiss her goodbye, while at the same time she was grateful that he did not. If the truth be known, Leland Kenniston was already falling in love with Laure Bouchard, but it was his fear of rushing her and the risk of losing her forever that held him back—apart from his natural reticence in not wishing to make any romantic gesture with Lopasuta there to watch.

So he contented himself with doffing his top hat and saying, "Good night, Mrs. Bouchard, and thank you for a wonderful evening. If all goes well, I can look forward to escorting you to New York at the beginning of August."

"I promise to let you know the moment I hear from Father O'Mara, Mr. Kenniston. And thank you again." Laure's green eyes were warm and her smile almost wistful as she watched him incline his head toward her.

He said good night to Lopasuta and urged the young lawyer to communicate the news about the Dalloway case as soon as a decision had been reached, and then got back into the *fiacre*.

"It was good of you to stay up so late to let me in, dear Lopasuta," Laure said tenderly to her adoptive son.

326

"I was studying—preparing myself for my first case for Mr. Kenniston. I want to win it for him."

"I know you do. I know you will," Laure murmured.

## Thirty-two

Eight days after Leland Kenniston had gone back to New York and Laure Bouchard to Windhaven Plantation, Lopasuta appeared in the Circuit Court of the State of Louisiana to prosecute the plaintiff's suit against Dalloway & Company, Conveyors and Haulers.

Lopasuta opened his case by presenting to the judge as evidence the signed contract from the New York lawyer, and Abner Dalloway glumly and profanely admitted it was his own handwriting. This clearly showed that Dalloway had indeed been aware of the fragility of the cargo his men would be handling for Leland Kenniston.

Dalloway's attorney, a gray-haired Creole, feebly protested that this could not be admissible as evidence, but the judge overruled him. Within forty-five minutes, Lopasuta Bouchard was awarded damages on behalf of his client plus court costs. The judge, to be eminently fair to all concerned and since Dalloway had a reasonably good reputation as a handler of merchandise, ruled that an impartial appraiser agreed upon by both plaintiff and defendant should adjudge the actual cost of the damaged goods, to make a proper settlement.

"Lawyer, you can tell your smart-ass client, that fine and fancy Mr. Kenniston, that it's the last time I'll ever handle his cargo," Abner Dalloway snarled, as Lopasuta left the courtroom.

Lopasuta could hardly conceal the warm glow of triumph he felt; the case was in itself insignificant, but it represented a notable milestone in his career. The judge had been impressed by his courtroom manner and his presentation of facts, carefully marshaled and cited with a legal formality rare in the newly formed Circuit Court of New Orleans. Indeed, Judge Ephraim Stowbridge, nearing seventy and having orginally come from Boston where he had been a successful trial lawyer, leaned over the bench at the conclusion of the trial to say to Lopasuta, "Young man, you argued your case well. You are certainly one of the most well-prepared attorneys whom I have encountered in my twenty years in a courtroom. My congratulations to you, sir!"

Lopasuta's first act was to stride to the telegraph office and send Leland Kenniston the news of the victory and the details of the damages Dalloway would be obliged to pay him. When he emerged from the telegraph office, it was almost twilight. Geraldine, along with Mei Luong and the boys, had been invited to dinner by a friendly widow who lived across the street from them, so he decided to go to a tiny Creole restaurant he had accidentally discovered on his way to court. A glance through the window had revealed a cozy, delightfully furnished setting, and the handwritten menu fixed in the window for all to see featured the house specialty, *canard à l'orange,* an exotic dish that Lopasuta had always wanted to try.

The only drawback was that the restaurant was located near the notorious Gallatin Street, which René Laurent had told him was an area to be shunned at night. Yet strong and tall, and exhilarated by his first legal victory in New Orleans, Lopasuta was willing to waive the risk.

When he had left the courthouse, a towering brute of a man in his mid-thirties, with jutting, craggy jaw whose low forehead, massive shoulders, and long, well-muscled arms gave him an almost simian cast, had moved out of a narrow alleyway and had begun, very slowly, to follow Lopasuta.

Lopasuta had no reason to look behind him, fearing nothing and buoyed by both the judge's praise and the knowledge that he had begun to justify Leland's confidence in him. He walked leisurely, anticipating in advance the gustatory treat he would have at the restaurant called La Flambée.

As Lopasuta turned the corner, the man behind him quickened his step till he was only a few feet away from the young Comanche lawyer. Then suddenly, in a low, in-

328

sinuating tone, the giant muttered, "Say mister, I know where there's a nice house with the prettiest girls in town. How's you like me to take you there?"

Lopasuta turned to confront his interlocutor, and his eyes widened at the sight of the towering stranger. The man's intense dark-blue eyes fixed on him as if memorizing his face, and then he muttered, "Say now, I know you, don't I? Weren't you in the courthouse just now, and isn't your name Lopasuta Bouchard?"

"You're right, and it is," Lopasuta declared curtly. "If you'll excuse me, I'm starved, and I was going to have dinner at La Flambée."

"Not so fast, I figger you'd sort of like to celebrate tonight. Yeah, sure, I heard all about how you handled that case against Dalloway. Real clever, Mr. Bouchard."

"Who are you, anyhow?"

The man grinned hideously, then swiftly put his hand into his coat pocket and drew out a bone-handled knife with a gleaming, sharp blade.

Instantly, Lopasuta's senses quickened, and he swiftly appraised the giant who menacingly confronted him.

"I'm not interested in a house with girls," he said coolly.

"Yeah, I forgot—you're married to a white squaw who stands to be very grateful if she's made a widow, wouldn't you say?"

"Not exactly, friend," Lopasuta sarcastically parried, his eyes fixed on the gleaming knife. "Now if you'll step out of my way, I'd like to eat."

"I don't think you've got time left to eat, Mr. Bouchard. You can starve in hell!" was the snarling answer, as the man lunged at him with the bone-handled knife.

Lopasuta instantly grabbed hold of his assailant's wrist and attempted to wrench it back, but the giant just smirked at his intended victim and pulled his hand out of Lopasuta's reach. But in that same instant, Lopasuta leaped like a cat, his left hand catching his assailant's right wrist and twisting as he dug his fingernails as harshly as he could into the man's flesh. Closing his right hand into a fist, Lopasuta slammed it with all his force into the man's belly.

Taken by surprise by the unexpected defense of his intended victim, the giant stumbled back with an agonized grimace, sinking down on one knee. Lopasuta kept desperate hold of the man's right wrist, holding the long, deadly

329

knife. With a swift glance behind him, he ascertained that there was no one else on this deserted street, and that he must defend himself against this unknown attacker.

With a bellow of rage, the giant stumbled to his feet and wrenched his wrist out of Lopasuta's grip, while at the same time slashing at the young Comanche's face. Nimbly, Lopasuta leaped to one side to avoid the knife and once again, with an unexpected forward lunge, caught the man's wrist with all his strength, while at the same time doubling his left hand into a fist smashing it against the giant's jaw.

There was a strangled "Ouff!" as the man again stumbled. Aware that he was dealing with no mere tyro, the giant tried to kick out with his right foot, shod in a heavy brogan, but again Lopasuta had anticipated the maneuver and twisted to one side so that the kick went aimlessly by. At the same time, he twisted the attacker's wrist and turned the knife blade back upon its owner, as he forced himself forward.

"Christ, you goddamned Injun bastid, you cut me! Jesus, I'll kill you for that, so help me!" the man cried out in a frenzy. He stumbled back, glancing down at his left side where the sharp point of his knife had lacerated his dirty clothing and drawn blood from the flesh beneath. Now he came forward, again slashing with the knife toward Lopasuta's face, his eyes malevolently narrowed, his lips twisted in a savage grimace of murderous hate.

This time he kicked out with his left foot, momentarily catching Lopasuta off guard, and the heavy brogan banged against the lawyer's right shin. Now it was Lopasuta's turn to grimace, and he stumbled back himself, then leaped to one side just as the man was upon him, striking down with the knife to end the fight swiftly. Ducking his head and advancing from the giant's right hand, he came in under the flailing arm and again with his right hand caught the man's wrist and viciously twisted it with all his strength.

There was a howl of pain, and the knife clattered to the sidewalk. Again, Lopasuta drove his fist into the man's belly, but the giant remained tenaciously standing, though he groaned aloud in pain and vituperatively swore his intention to disembowel his adversary.

Now his hamlike fist struck Lopasuta on the cheekbone, numbing the Comanche lawyer for a moment. The giant stooped down and retrieved the fallen knife, then lunged from downwards up, intent on eviscerating his opponent.

But once again instinct told the Comanche lawyer how to avoid that death-dealing blow, and he leaped back and to the left so that the knife went harmlessly through the air. Lopasuta immediately caught hold of his adversary's wrist, but this time fiercely twisted it back, and a shriek of hideous agony burst from the man. The wrist had fractured and, furious, the assailant transferred the knife to his left hand as his right arm dangled uselessly.

Once again Lopasuta looked around, but there was still no one in view. This corner was dark and gloomy with no gaslight on it. A feeble moon, almost obscured behind a scudding rain cloud, cast a pallid light on the isolated scene. There was no use waiting for help from the civil guard, Lopasuta knew. Most of them avoided the area bordered by Gallatin Street as they would the plague, and many civil guardsmen who had gone there to apprehend a known criminal had ended up in the Mississippi.

At last, the giant got to his feet and snarled, "I've played with you long enough—now I'm going to cut your tripes out and feed them to the dogs, you hear, Bouchard?"

"You've the advantage of me. You know my name, but I don't know yours."

"I might as well tell you, because you're not going to live to repeat it to anybody. It's George Delton. That's enough talk, Injun. The next sound I'm gonna hear will be you begging me to take my knife out of your dirty guts!" With this, he lunged at Lopasuta and his left hand balled into a fist; he struck out at the Comanche lawyer's jaw, making Lopasuta reel and stumble backwards, completely off balance.

"Now I got you!" his assailant triumphantly guffawed as he rushed headlong at his victim with his left hand lifting the knife high, intent on plunging it into his victim's heart.

Desperate, Lopasuta knew he had only seconds to avert that blow by whatever means he could. He had no weapon except his hands and feet, and he was beginning to be winded from the long and furious duel at such uneven odds. Swaying as he was with his injured right leg, he brought up his left and, with the point of his shoe, kicked hard into his assailant's groin.

The man let out an inhuman screech; his face screwed up into a mask of contorted agony and fury, his fingers twisting on the bone handle of the knife to take a better grip of it as he fought for breath. Then, barely daunted, he moved forward again with a relentless purpose, like a jungle predator that does not fear even one stronger than itself in its unreasoning desire to kill.

Lopasuta pretended to again repeat that cruel but resourceful kick, and as he had hoped, the giant twisted half around and then struck at him from the side. This time, Lopasuta kicked out with his right foot and his shoe bit with all his might into the man's shin.

Another frenzied screech shattered the night as the giant went down on one knee, the knife held in his hand more tightly than ever.

Before the man could get to his feet again, Lopasuta kicked him in the jaw and heard a loud click as the man's teeth snapped together. There was a gurgling cry, as the giant was rocked backward and sprawled on the ground. But like a cat with nine lives, he rolled over, got to his knees, and then stumbled to his feet. Weaving, the knife playing in cruel little circles in the paltry light, he came menacingly, inexorably forward toward the young Comanche lawyer.

Blood oozed from the corner of his mouth where his teeth had clenched against the tip of his tongue. It made his face the more hideous as he came toward Lopasuta, mouthing the foulest obscenities the Comanche lawyer had ever heard. Suddenly, as if he had regained his strength like the giant Antaeus of mythology who, each time he touched the ground derived new strength from it, he swept his left hand up in a swift arc, and the sharp knife scored Lopasuta's coat, tore into the fine cambric shirt beneath, and drew blood near his nipple.

"That's just a start—I'm going to cut you to little bits and feed you to the caymans!" the attacker mouthed.

Though he was in superb physical condition and younger as well, Lopasuta knew that he could not endure much longer. The incredible resourcefulness of this giant, his ability to withstand the severest pain, and his constant advantage with that murderously sharp knife intensified by his berserk desire to kill—for what reason, Lopasuta could not fathom—gave him a tremendous advantage. The man beat off pummels and kicks that would have paralyzed or maimed an ordinary man; to see him still coming with that knife held and to have tasted already its sharp viciousness clouded Lopasuta's courage and optimism. But he shook off this feeling, knowing that against all these odds he must somehow win and kill his opponent in the winning, or he himself would die. There was no other possible outcome. If only he could wrest that knife away and use it—

And even as he thought this, the giant charged again with a bellow of rage, slashing near the Comanche's throat. Lopasuta nimbly leaped back, but in so doing, stumbled over an uneven board of the wooden sidewalk, lost his balance, and sprawled on his back.

"Now I got you where I want you, you dirty Injun bastid!" the man hissed. His eyes glittering with malice, he moved slowly toward the fallen Comanche, and then, in an excess of overconfidence, swiftly reversed the knife in his left hand, holding it by the point and lifting it on high to hurl it down toward Lopasuta's heart.

At the last instant, saying a prayer to the Great Spirit, Lopasuta rolled over just as the knife left the man's hand. With a thud, it buried itself in the plank, quivering from the force of the throw, two inches away from Lopasuta's body. As quickly, he rolled back onto his side and pulled out the knife at the moment the giant hurled himself upon him.

Crushed by the man's weight, his arm pinned between their bodies, Lopasuta suddenly relaxed to create a little space between them, then pushed the knife up with all his remaining strength into the giant's belly.

There was a hideous roar of agony. Lopasuta rolled the man onto his back, panting. Both hands grabbing for his bleeding middle, the man gasped for breath. "You tricked me—might have guessed a goddamned Injun would trick me—never happened before—oh, you son of a bitch—I'll kill you—I'll—"

Lopasuta pulled out the knife and, kneeling beside the dying giant, hoarsely whispered, "You've been following me, haven't you? I remember that I've seen you before. Who are you? Why did you try to kill me? How do you know my name?"

The man closed his eyes and arched his back, as a spasm of pain seared his intestines. He tightly compressed his fingers as he futilely tried to stanch the flow of blood from the mortal wound. He breathed heavily, and then opened his eyes and wanly muttered, "It was Mr. H—Henson did it—he wrote me—paid me good—damn your ugly Injun hide anyway—oh, Jesus—" A last spasm seized him, wrenched him, till he slumped in death.

Lopasuta staggered to his feet, aware that he was bleeding, his clothes torn and muddied. As he fought for air, in his mind there was the dying man's voice: "It was H—Henson did it—he paid me good—"

Henson . . . Milo Brutus Henson. That dapper man who had so often smugly smiled at him when he went to the courthouse in Montgomery. So he had been one of them. And maybe it was he who had started the whole thing with William Brickley. Now he knew. And Henson was still alive.

His mind now clear, Lopasuta decided he would go to a Turkish bath. The steam would revive him; the wounds, being superficial, could be easily healed with some bandages and salve. The attendant at the bath could minister to his clothes. Thank God he had been wearing a heavier frock coat than usual for his appearance in a court of law. He had settled one score—or rather, Lucien Edmond Bouchard had settled William Brickley's account forever. But it was up to him, Lopasuta, to go back to Montgomery and confront the man who was perhaps the real instigator of this whole nightmare that had very nearly lost him Geraldine forever and had also very nearly destroyed Windhaven Plantation and Laure Bouchard with it.

## Thirty-three

It was nearly midnight when Lopasuta Bouchard returned to his house. Geraldine had left a lamp burning in a front window, and its light streamed out onto the sidewalk as the calash stopped before the door. He paid the driver and, drawing a deep breath, walked to the door and inserted his key in the lock. Geraldine, wearing a wrapper and a shawl around her shoulders, was sitting on the sofa in the parlor. She ran to him, uttering a cry: "Oh, darling, I was so worried—I expected you home long before this." The dim light in the room concealed most of the damage to Lopasuta's apparel, so Geraldine was spared a bigger fright before Lopasuta had a chance to explain all that had happened.

"Listen, sweetheart, something occurred tonight. It all links up with my abduction."

"Lopasuta!" she declared, her eyes wide, "what do you mean? Oh, my goodness, I completely forgot about your case for Mr. Kenniston—"

"I won it, Geraldine. Do you feel like some coffee? I know I'd love some."

"I'll heat some up right away. Oh, you won—how marvelous!"

"When I left the courtroom, I sent a wire to Leland to tell him. At least I got that much done before—go ahead and heat the coffee please, Geraldine, darling."

She shot him a concerned look, and then, seeing his face drawn as she'd never seen it before, hurried off to the kitchen.

Lopasuta drew a deep breath, and slowly paced a circle around the parlor till Geraldine returned with two cups and saucers. He seated himself on the sofa, and she beside him, setting their coffee on the glass-covered tabouret before them. Geraldine sensed that it would be better for him to volunteer what had happened rather than for her to pry. Presently, he said, "After I left the courthouse, I headed for a restaurant I'd found, knowing that you'd be out with Mei Luong and the boys—a place near Gallatin Street."

"Oh, darling, you should know better than to go to that neighborhood! Everyone says it's peopled with all sorts of thugs and ruffians!"

"I know, sweetheart. But the restaurant wasn't all that close to Gallatin, and I thought it would be all right. Anyway, suddenly I was confronted by a man, a giant of a man. I'd noticed him before but thought nothing about it. Well, he apparently was lurking around the courthouse this afternoon and when I got out, he followed me. The next thing I knew, he called me by name and said he was going to kill me."

"Oh, dear God!" Geraldine ejaculated, putting a hand to her mouth, her eyes very wide with fright.

He reached out to pat her shoulder and to smile wanly. "He had a knife, and he was a lot stronger and bigger than I was, but I was very fortunate. When we were struggling for the knife, I got hold of it and managed—well, before he

335

died, he swore at me and said that Henson had sent him, paid him to put me out of the way for good."

"Milo Brutus Henson? Oh, no—do you mean—"

"I do, Geraldine," Lopasuta solemnly nodded. "It all hangs together now. I'm convinced that it was Henson who contacted Brickley and set me up."

"Thank God they failed, because I love you so!" she murmured, and cupped his face and kissed him on the mouth. She held onto his hand as she reached for her coffee cup. "What are you going to do now?" she finally asked.

"Geraldine, that man in Montgomery hates me because I've fought for the oppressed and the blacks. And I don't think it was just Henson. There's one other man, and the more I think about it, he fits into that plot, too. The banker, Carleton Ivers. You remember how I interceded on Amelia Coleman's behalf."

"I'll never forget that."

"Well, I'm sure he never forgave me for that. And I'm convinced now that he and Henson were partners in that entire scheme. So, darling, I ask your forgiveness for leaving you again, but I have to go back to Montgomery and confront Henson and Ivers. I have to tell them that I know everything now, and that if they don't stop their vicious attacks on the Bouchards, I'll have them put in prison for criminal conspiracy. I'll make them confess, and then, if I need to, I can bring suit against both of them and win it, too."

"I understand." She sighed, closed her eyes a moment, and then took another sip of coffee. "I know you must. But please, my darling, be careful. When I think that you might have been killed tonight—oh, Lopasuta, I just couldn't bear it if anything happened to you again—"

"But it won't; the Great Spirit will watch over me. I should be back within a week, I promise. Can you and Mei Luong get along without me?"

"Of course, honey."

"I'll see René Laurent tomorrow and tell him to look in on you both and make sure you have everything you need. Besides," he permitted himself a humorless chuckle, "I rather think I've earned a small vacation after winning my first case."

\* \* \*

336

Lopasuta took the ferry to Mobile and the steamboat upriver to Montgomery. He had coldly planned what he would do: once having compelled his enemies to admit the truth, he would give them the alternative of leaving town forever, or else he would go to the *Advertiser* and have the story printed in all its details. Thereafter, he would bring suit for malicious conspiracy. He did not think that either Milo Brutus Henson or Carelton Ivers would be stupid enough to demand a court hearing on such charges with such weighty evidence against them.

It was late morning when he arrived in Montgomery, so he went to the restaurant where he had liberated Amelia from the banker's tyrannical enslavement of her. The elderly black couple fussed over him, giving him the best table in their small establishment. Lopasuta told them that he was now living in New Orleans and was a lawyer there as well. He assured them he had not forgotten his old friends in Montgomery and would always be at their service if ever they needed legal help.

Smiling with pleasure after this warm reunion, Lopasuta walked over to the courthouse, where he spent a few hours looking through the deeds until he found the information he was seeking. He then went immediately to Henson's office. It was unoccupied, and when he inquired of a shoemaker next door, the man volunteered the information that Henson was most likely home and gave Lopasuta directions.

It was too far to walk, so the Comanche lawyer hired a horse from the town's livery stable and cantered down the road to the outskirts of town till he came to the white-columned house. Tethering his horse to the hitching post, he stepped onto the porch and rapped the knocker at the front door. A few moments later, Henson's blond inamorata, Elaine Fairfield, opened the door and gave him a wondering look. "If you're looking for Mr. Henson, mister, he doesn't want to be disturbed. He's taking off this week from work. Maybe you ought to see him in his office next week."

"He'll see me now, miss," Lopasuta commanded. "Tell him that Lopasuta Bouchard is here."

"All right, but I don't think he'll like it," Elaine retorted peevishly. She left the door partly open and hurried back to the bedroom, where her mustachioed protector was at his

337

ease, waiting for her to rejoin him. She was wearing only a silk wrapper, and her feet were bare, for when Lopasuta had knocked on the door, she and her lover had been playing the game of the two-backed beast.

Lopasuta did not wait for her to return to tell him he might enter; he slipped inside, closed the front door behind him, and went down the hallway, just in time to see her emerge from the bedroom. Elaine stopped short, and indignantly exclaimed, "Say, mister, you've sure got your nerve! He says he doesn't want to see you!"

"That's too bad; he's going to—and I'd appreciate it if you'd leave us to talk alone together, miss," Lopasuta told her coldly.

"Who do you think you are? Come barging in here—"

"Never mind, Laney," Henson called from the bedroom, "since he's in, I'll see him. Do what the man says. Go to the kitchen and fix us some coffee or something."

"No thank you; nothing for me. Just conversation, Mr. Henson." Lopasuta pushed open the bedroom door and entered. Milo Brutus Henson was lying in bed, the sheet pulled over him, and he shrank back on the pillows as Lopasuta silently stared down at him. Finally, he stammered, "I don't understand why you've come all the way from New Orleans to see me, Mr. Bouchard."

"So you know I live in New Orleans now, eh? You seem to know many things about me, don't you, Mr. Henson? I venture you know even more. Such as knowing all about the plot to get me shipped off to Hong Kong and out of Montgomery forever, and then to have William Brickley insinuate an overseer on Mrs. Bouchard to try to have her plantation destroyed. I'd say that's conspiracy on a grand scale, and any jury in this state would convict you and Ivers for your participation in it."

"Now see here!" Henson blustered, "I don't know where you got this absurd idea, but I had nothing to do with it!"

"I'll tell you the real reason I'm here now, Mr. Henson. You tried to have me killed. A few evenings ago, I was accosted by a big, burly man who had followed me from the courthouse, and told me he was going to kill me. I was very fortunate; in defending myself, I wounded him fatally. Before he died, I asked him why he had tried to kill me and how he knew who I was, and he said that you paid him to get me out of the way once and for all. And I just did some checking to verify a theory I had—which proved

338

to be correct. I know you and Carelton Ivers were partners, and your partnership extended to this conspiracy."

As he was speaking, Lopasuta watched Henson's face, and had his answer. The latter licked his lips, grew very pale, shifted himself further into the pillows, and then whined, "But you can't prove anything. The man's dead; you said so yourself. He can't testify against me. And I've got a good reputation here in Montgomery; I can get up in court and deny everything—you know I can. I know that much about law, Mr. Bouchard."

"I'm sure you do. Scoundrels like you always know more about law than decent, honest citizens who never get into trouble. I'm going to give you one chance to escape prison: you'll leave Montgomery forever, as soon as possible. Sell your house, pocket the money, and be off—but not to New Orleans, Mr. Henson. If you don't agree to this, I'm going right over to the *Advertiser* and tell the editor everything that's happened since I got that letter from William Brickley inviting me down to New Orleans to discuss a legal case."

"If—if I do leave, you—you won't prosecute—you won't give the story to the newspaper?" the man quavered, looking suddenly quite sick.

"No, but I'm going to stay in town until I make sure you keep your part of the bargain. I don't care if you have to sell your house at a loss. It's either that or prison, and perhaps for a very long time—not only for conspiracy, but for abduction and attempted murder."

"All right, all right! I—I'll do what you want. Now I'd appreciate it if you'd leave my house."

"I'll be happy to. But remember, if in a few days I don't see any sign of your preparing to leave, what I said I'll do, I'll do. And I should think that the least you'll get will be ten or twenty years."

"All right, I said I would! Now for God's sake, get the hell out of here!" Henson whined again.

Lopasuta gave him a contemptuous look, and then turned his back and started to leave the bedroom. Hardly had he done so, when Henson slipped his hand under the pillow, drew out a clasp knife, opened the broad, sharp blade, and then, springing out of bed, hurried after the retreating lawyer.

A premonition natural to one who has grown up in a Comanche stronghold made Lopasuta whirl around, just in

339

time to see Milo Brutus Henson, his yellowish teeth bared in a snarl of hate, come at him with the knife. Lopasuta swiftly ducked to one side of the erratically sweeping lunge, caught his assailant's wrist, and twisted it so painfully that Henson let out a shriek of pain and dropped the knife with a clatter on the floor.

Lopasuta picked up the fallen weapon from the floor and disdainfully remarked, "That was extremely stupid of you, Henson. I was willing to give you a chance—despite your knavery. However, you obviously are incorrigible; therefore, you leave me no choice but to immediately file suit against you—and to let the entire citizenry of Montgomery know of your perfidious nature through the means of the press."

Lopasuta started turning away from Henson, but he suddenly whirled around again. "You're damned lucky, Henson, that I'm not going to thrash you within an inch of your life here and now. But there's already been enough violence, and I'm not going to add to it—as much as I'd like to." His hands at his sides kept clenching and unclenching, as if the restraint was proving too much for him.

Henson stared at Lopasuta for a moment, then he suddenly cried out, "You can't do this to me! I'm an honored citizen of this town! You'll destroy me! You goddamned Injun—"

Suddenly his face was suffused with a livid color, then it turned blue. His eyes bulged, and with a gurgling moan, he clutched at his heart and sank down on his knees. Shallow, strangled breaths emitted from his mouth for a minute or two, and then Henson rolled over to one side and lay inert.

Lopasuta reached down and felt the man's heart. A barely perceptible beat lasted for a few seconds, and then it stopped completely. Milo Brutus Henson was dead. The shock of being found out, plus his years of high living, had finally taken their toll.

Elaine Fairfield had been listening to the exchange between the two men from outside the door. Now, when the room had become so quiet, she peered in and to her horror, saw her lover lying on the floor. She came running into the room, her hand clapped to her mouth and her eyes bulging with fright.

"Wh–what happened?" she stammered.

"I'm not a doctor," Lopasuta began, "but my guess is

that he's had a massive coronary. I don't think he felt any real pain," he told her, not unkindly.

"I—I heard everything you said to him from out there," she quavered, gesturing toward the door. "I—I guess it's best this way; he wouldn't have lasted long in prison. Gosh, it's hard to believe he's dead. I didn't like him much, but he was sort of generous in his own way—you know what I mean. Well, I guess I'll have to find somebody else to look after me now, won't I, Mr. Bouchard?" she said glumly.

Despite the fact that the young woman was a common tart, Lopasuta felt sorry for her. She had no other skills to fall back on, now that her benefactor was dead. "I'm sure you'll be resourceful," he said sympathetically. "Well, I'd best be off to the police and tell them what happened. I assure you I didn't harm him, miss."

"I—I believe you, Mr.—Mr. Bouchard. He was always eating too much, and he was always—well—" She suddenly colored and lowered her eyes.

He nodded in understanding, then strode out of the house and, untethering his horse, mounted it and rode toward the police station.

Elaine Fairfield looked down at her lover's dead body. Then she sighed, and walked across the room. Taking his trousers off the back of the chair where he had neatly draped them, she went through the pockets till she found his well-filled wallet. "You won't need this any more, Milo honey, and a girl just has to live," she said aloud.


As Lopasuta directed his horse toward the police station, he had a sudden thought and, instead, turned and rode in the direction of the Montgomery County Courthouse. As he passed that building, he smiled reflectively, thinking how his life had radically changed because of it: it was there, after Jedidiah Danforth had taught him the rudiments of the law with unrelenting discipline, that he had begun to accomplish all that was within himself; it was there, after the conclusion of a case, that Geraldine Murcur had first told him how much she admired his stand against oppression. Yes, it had begun there, and now there was one last score to settle from the past. When it was done, he would be free to recommence in New Orleans under the best of auguries, for he had not sought Milo Brutus Henson's death. He knew that what had happened had

341

been a manifestation of the Great Spirit. Perhaps it was thus that justice was finally attained on the eternal balance sheet, and he, the offspring of a Mexican mother and a Comanche brave, was only the humble instrument of the will of the Great Spirit.

After passing the courthouse, he rode another two blocks farther, then stopped before the one-story brick building of the Montgomery Central Bank & Trust Company. He tethered the horse's reins to the hitching post at the curb, stood a moment before the door, and then entered.

An elderly bank guard addressed him: "Do you want something, mister? Want to see somebody?"

"Yes, thank you. I'd like to see Carelton Ivers, the president."

"Yes, sir! Go right to the back, and you'll see his office over to the left. He just stepped out for a moment, but he'll be right back. You can go in and wait for him. It'll be all right."

"I thank you for your courtesy," Lopasuta said with a nod.

He walked into the plush furnished office and stood with his back to Carleton Ivers's desk, facing the open door. He folded his arms in an attitude of intent deliberation, and when a moment later the white-haired, bony-faced bank president entered, the man stopped short and uttered a strangled "Oh, my God!"

"You seem surprised to see me, Mr. Ivers," Lopasuta Bouchard calmly declared.

"I—I didn't think—I'd heard you went on to New Orleans," Ivers stammered, as he made his way to his desk and seated himself. "This is an—an unexpected pleasure, Mr. B–Bouchard."

"Come now, Mr. Ivers. There's no need to be hypocritical. I know you've hated me since I saved Amelia McAdams from your clutches."

"I—you must surely be mistaken—I don't hate you, Bouchard. I—well, I'm just surprised to see you, that's all. As I said, I'd heard you were in New Orleans."

"Just as you thought that before then I was in Hong Kong." Lopasuta suddenly leaned across the desk and looked his enemy squarely in the eyes. "Ivers, you're in shock because you thought by now that I died in New Orleans—and this time for certain."

"I—I don't know what you're talking about. Now you

342

really must excuse me, I've a good deal of work to do. I have to approve an important loan transaction—"

"You'll spare me a few minutes," Lopasuta demanded. "After that, I don't think you'll want to take the time to make the loan, Mr. Ivers. I've found out a great deal since I went down to New Orleans on the strength of a letter from Mr. William Brickley. All the time I was sailing to Hong Kong, after being shanghaied, I kept trying to figure out why this had been done and by whom. I'm sure I was expected to die in Hong Kong, but I didn't—as you see. And I came home, still wondering.

"After one of your associates found out that I'd gone to New Orleans, he arranged for an assassin to kill me there. But once again, your scheme failed. I have just come from the house of Milo Brutus Henson. I told him I knew all about it now, and gave him a choice: either leave Montgomery or I'd bring charges against him. His reply was to try and stab me in the back."

"He—you—" Ivers was almost apoplectic. He stared at Lopasuta Bouchard, open-mouthed, his eyes wide, disbelieving.

"As you can obviously deduce, Mr. Ivers, that idea also failed. Instead, he's the one who's dead. He suffered a coronary. You might say he caused his own death: his terror at being exposed for his role in a diabolical plot made him react in a manner too strenuous for his heart to bear. And now, Mr. Ivers, I offer you the same terms I offered him: you will arrange to leave Montgomery forever, and you will not attempt any further retaliatory action against me or mine in New Orleans. If you will not agree, I shall go to the *Advertiser* and tell them the entire story. You see, before he died, the New Orleans assassin told me who had paid him. And I also know that you have been affiliated with Henson since you advanced him a sizable loan for a land speculation—from which you also profited. As you can see, I have done some checking of the courtroom records."

"You—you haven't got any proof—I didn't—get the hell out of here, Bouchard! I'm not afraid of your blackmail!"

"You're very wrong, Ivers. It isn't blackmail. When I told Henson all that I knew, I can assure you that he did not clear your name. So as I told you, either you will leave Montgomery, or I shall give the story to the *Advertiser*, and after that, I shall seek an indictment from the grand jury on charges of criminal conspiracy with the intent to murder, slander, and defame—for, as I'm sure you know, Brickley involved my adoptive mother, Laure Bouchard, as well."

Carleton Ivers loosened his cravat. He stood rigid with shock and hate. He stared at Lopasuta Bouchard, his eyes burning with vindictive anger, his breathing harsh. Then he said, in a voice choked with mingled rage and fear, "You talk so high and mighty, you goddamned Injun bastard— coming in here making threats to me, the president of a bank, a respectable citizen! I'll see you in hell first! I didn't think Henson would get the job done, but I will, this time! Your luck's run out, Bouchard—and I feel like biting my tongue using a white man's name on the likes of you, you by-blow of a Mexican bitch and a dirty Injun!" With this, Ivers wrenched open the drawer of his desk and drew out a derringer, aimed it at Lopasuta's heart, and pulled the trigger. But instead of a report there was a click, as the derringer misfired. Lopasuta had been taken by surprise by the swift action of the elderly banker, but in the moment after the derringer failed to fire, he leaped to one side and came around the side of the desk, grasping Ivers's bony right hand and twisting the derringer away.

"I'll kill you," Ivers mouthed, "I'll settle your hash—you son of a bitch—take Amelia away from me—ruin my whole life—damn you—" Ivers's voice was hoarse and shaky, as he tried with his last remaining strength to turn the derringer back against the Comanche lawyer. There were beads of sweat on his forehead as he fought Lopasuta's grip, and then suddenly there was a sharp blast. His eyes bulged, then turned glassy, and his head bowed. The derringer had at last gone off—and the bullet had lodged in his own heart.

Lopasuta Bouchard let go of the dead banker's wrist and watched his would-be assassin slump forward onto the desk. The bank guard came running into the office with a drawn pistol, having heard the sound of the shot.

"Mr. Ivers tried to kill me. I'm Lopasuta Bouchard; I'm an attorney at law. Many important people in this city will vouch for who and what I am. I suggest you call the sheriff while I wait here."

"Jesus, Mr. Bouchard—I guess you'd better wait. Oh, my God, Mr. Ivers dead! You say he tried to kill you—I wouldn't have believed it of a nice old gentleman like him!

Yeah, you'd better wait here, Mr. Bouchard," the guard nervously repeated.

The sheriff of Montgomery County arrived a quarter of an hour later. He listened patiently to Lopasuta's account of Ivers's death—as well as to the preceding death of Milo Brutus Henson. The sheriff shook his head slowly in disbelief and declared, "There'll have to be a hearing, of course. But I'll give you good odds that you'll be cleared without a fuss. There's no evidence to suggest that what happened here and at Henson's were anything more than accidents. And frankly, Mr. Bouchard, knowing your excellent reputation here—as well as the esteem of the Bouchard name—I doubt that any jury will find cause to bring charges against you. But still in all, Mr. Bouchard, I'll have to ask you to stick around Montgomery until this matter is cleared up."

Lopasuta readily agreed, informing the sheriff that he would only be going as far as Windhaven Plantation, to see his adoptive mother, Laure Bouchard. "If necessary, sheriff, she can testify in my behalf regarding some of the facts I've told you."

The sheriff looked down at Carleton Ivers's body a final time, shook his head, and intoned, "My Gawd, you don't know who you can trust these days, do you, Bouchard?"

"Only in Him who makes all of us, sheriff."

The day after the demise of Milo Brutus Henson and Carleton Ivers, Lopasuta again hired a horse from the livery stable and rode downriver to Windhaven Plantation.

His knock at the door of the magnificent plantation house was answered by Laure Bouchard herself, who ushered the Comanche lawyer into the study and ordered refreshments for them both. Lopasuta then described for her all that had taken place and assured her that so far as he could determine, all of the conspirators who had plotted against them—all the enemies of the Bouchards—had been summoned before a Supreme Court from which there could be no possible appeal.

Laure insisted on writing a statement that could be used as testimony in Lopasuta's defense. Seating herself at Luke's old escritoire, she wrote out page after page of details concerning William Brickley's attempts to bankrupt Windhaven Plantation. When she had finished, she declared, "There! This may not be a sworn deposition, but it says enough good things to satisfy any jury worth its salt."

Lopasuta, who had been sitting very quietly in the paneled study of the chateau, stirred from his reverie. "It seems so odd, Laure. This house just isn't the same without Luke's presence, is it?"

She sighed and looked down at her lap. "No, there's an enormous emptiness here now. It's strange that you should mention it, because I've been feeling more and more lately that even though I've lived here and it's been my only home for all these years, now that Luke is no longer here with me, the house somehow doesn't seem to be mine any more." She noticed Lopasuta's quizzical expression and smiled. "Perhaps what I feel is that one has to be born a Bouchard in order to feel that one possesses the house rather than the other way around. I must confess to you that at this point, I'd much rather live somewhere like New Orleans—in the middle of an exciting, growing city—than way off here in the middle of nowhere." She smiled again, this time her face splitting into a grin. "Oh, yes, I'm quite envious of you and Geraldine!"

Lopasuta laughed and clasped her hand in his. "You know that anytime you wish to visit our new home, the door is always open. As a matter of fact, we are both looking forward very much to you and Lucien staying with us again before going off to New York."

Then, rising, Lopasuta declared that he had best be getting back to Montgomery—but first he would pay his respects to Luke. They embraced a final time at the front door, and then taking his leave of Laure, Lopasuta climbed the towering bluff. Standing before the graves of the founder of Windhaven and his grandson, Luke Bouchard, Lopasuta was reminded of his extraordinary good fortune in going from the oblivion of a Comanche stronghold across the Mexican border into a life of service and influence, as well as love, affection, and satisfaction.

And when he had said his prayers of thanks and of respect to the immortal dead, he went back down the bluff and rode back to Montgomery.

Lopasuta called on the sheriff the next day and handed him the lengthy statement that Laure had drafted. The man told Lopasuta that a coroner's grand jury was to be convened the following morning, and suggested that the

Comanche lawyer be on hand to await the results of its deliberations. Lopasuta sent a messenger to Laure, telling her of this and promising to let her know the outcome.

The next morning, when he entered the Montgomery courthouse, he was startled to find his adoptive mother, with her son Lucien, awaiting him. She was determined to be with him, she said, until the outcome of the jury's deliberations was known—even to read her statement in person, should that be required of her.

Lopasuta smiled and assured her that such was not the usual procedure; however, he was grateful for her presence as he awaited the verdict—which in fact was not long in coming. Just before noon, he was informed by a smiling court officer that the jury had cleared him of any criminal wrongdoing.

Laure's written statement, together with Lopasuta's own reputation in the Montgomery courthouse as an honest and able trial lawyer, had contributed much to this fortunate decision. Not even a mild reproof was voted by the coroner's jury, because the day after Carleton Ivers had tried to kill Lopasuta Bouchard and died in the attempt, a state auditor discovered that Ivers's bank was in arrears by over $150,000. When the auditor compelled the head clerk to make the bank's records accessible, an incriminating note was discovered indicating that Carleton Ivers had lent Milo Brutus Henson $42,000 as a bank loan for "land investment pursuant to discussed terms," and then, a year later, inscribed on the note, "paid in full for services already rendered and those yet to be rendered, re: Lopasuta Bouchard."

Lopasuta stood outside the courtroom with Laure and young Lucien. The tall teenager was quiet of demeanor, but inwardly excited over the prospect of studying abroad. When Lopasuta looked into that young, sensitive face, he thought to himself that the boy had not only Luke's eyes, but also something of his father's deliberate and yet intense awareness of what went on around him. In the few casual remarks that Lopasuta exchanged with young Lucien, he unmistakably perceived that Lucien grieved for his dead father and sought, with a controlled but still discernible intent, to achieve the maturity necessary to be the man of the family, one who could help his mother and be of reliable strength to her, instead of being only a child dependent upon a parent.

The threesome arrived at the wharf where Lopasuta would take the steamer to New Orleans. Laure clasped the Comanche's hand and said, "Lopasuta, you'll never know how dear you are to me, how I respect you and love you. I miss having you so close to me—you and Geraldine and your two adorable sons—yet I'm comforted by the knowledge that it's only two or three days' journey to where you and Geraldine are. Perhaps, every now and again, I can take off a week to visit you. Clarabelle Hendry is such a treasure, she'll readily substitute for me with the children."

Lopasuta kissed her on the cheek as he prepared to board the steamboat. "At any rate, Geraldine and I are looking forward to your visit when Leland Kenniston comes back in August."

"I'm looking forward to that, too, Lopasuta. He's a remarkable man—I've never quite met anyone like him before," Laure said, and a telltale flush suffused her cheeks. Quickly, as if to hide this significant proof of the impression that the mature Irishman had made on her, she reached for him and hugged him. "Give Geraldine a kiss for me, Lopasuta. Take care of yourself, and God bless you," she said.

Solemnly, he bowed his head to her and then, after a long, tender look, he turned and went up the gangplank.

Upon reaching home, Lopasuta gave Geraldine a long, detailed account of everything that had happened to him in Montgomery.

"I have to agree with you, Lopasuta," she declared. "It doesn't seem possible that these events could have occurred the way they did—and ended the way they ended—without believing that there was intervention from God. You know, it's funny," she mused. "Before that man tried to kill you here in New Orleans last week, I had completely ignored the possibility that anyone else could have wanted to harm you. And then when you went back to Montgomery to see Henson and Ivers, it almost seemed like the whole nightmare was about to begin again. But now it's over, my love, isn't it? I mean, *really* over?"

Lopasuta took her into his arms and held her gently. "Yes, Geraldine," he whispered into her ear, "it *is* really, finally over."

## Thirty-four

By the end of July, Laure Bouchard received a gracious, urbane letter from Father O'Mara of St. Timothy's Academy, a letter so detailed and full of candid information that she felt certain this would be an excellent school for young Lucien. Father O'Mara stressed the principles of his institution: maturity through growth and communal living; pupils having the opportunity to engage in wholesome class discussions; doing class projects in unison that would convey to them the tenets of teamwork, which they would need when they took their places in adult society; and at the same time, a good leavening of humility. "It is very simple, Mrs. Bouchard," he wrote, "to take a precocious boy and make a prig or an obnoxious genius out of him. The real skill in teaching, as my associates and I unwaveringly believe, is to make him amenable to suggestion, to give him a tolerance which enables him to understand and recognize the many sides of a question, and to be able to make his own wise choice through what he has learned and what he has experienced with his fellows."

That, indeed, was precisely what Laure Bouchard knew young Lucien must have in order to find himself and his rightful place in life. He could, of course, be the heir apparent to a rich estate and inherit it without understanding any of its responsibilities and its obligations—very much as she had done herself when widowhood had been thrust upon her. But she had resolved that Lucien would not make mistakes out of transient emotion or impulse: he would learn to reason and to use the tools of logic so that his decisions upon reaching manhood would be in keeping with his own inherent nature.

She sent off a draft for the tuition for the first semester, which included his room and board, plus an allowance for such extracurricular activities, including sports, as would make his life in Dublin more comfortable and, at the same time, more challenging.

She received a wire from Lopasuta, telling her that Leland would be arriving in New Orleans in ten days' time. This whirled her into action, and she spent several days with Clarabelle Hendry, giving the genial nurse some special instructions for her other children, whom she would leave at home while she took Lucien to New Orleans and thence to New York. This done, she began to pack her finest clothes, and prepared Lucien for his stay across the Atlantic. The boy was as excited as she was, and because of the new experience in store for him, thought very little of the problem of homesickness. He promised Laure that he would write several times a week to tell her all about the school, his companions, his studies, and Dublin.

All the workers of Windhaven Plantation saw her off at the wharf. Lucien, standing tall and poised beside her, was flushed with self-consciousness, his eyes bright with eagerness for what was to come. And that look alone assured Laure that she had not made an error in so swift a decision to send her oldest son abroad to complete his education.

Thus, when they boarded the boat to Mobile, where they would take a ferry to New Orleans, both mother and son looked forward with keen anticipation and with relish— though for vastly divergent reasons. For Laure, it was an awareness that she wished to define Leland Kenniston's influence on her own future: she candidly told herself that she was smitten by him, but also that she knew the danger of such swift infatuation. Always recurrent in her thoughts was the memory of how glib, conniving William Brickley had insinuated himself into her affections. To be sure, her feverish grief over Luke's death had then delivered her vulnerably into Brickley's conspiring hands—whereas now she was far more the mistress of herself, far more able to judge with calmness and rational evaluation.

As she lay in her berth that night, she kept herself awake wondering if this handsome, self-made, mature Irishman was really interested in her, or whether it was simply innate courtesy that had prompted his attentions to her during their first meetings.

Just as Laure and young Lucien embarked for New Orleans, Judith Marquard had been delivered of another girl

350

whom she had promptly named Augusta, after her husband's mother. Her blind husband made no objection when she told him, just after Augusta had been born, that she hoped to go back to work soon.

She had mentioned to him several months before that Lopasuta had told her he would be in need of a confidential secretary who would, just as she had done at the bank, analyze and investigate industrial development and financial transactions in the city. Bernard Marquard now reaffirmed, "I think you will be happy working for him, my dearest. Lopasuta Bouchard has already won himself a great deal of respect among the lawyers of this city, and the cases he has handled have shown a clarity of outlook and a wholesome grounding, not only in the letter, but also in the spirit of the laws of this state. I think each of you will be good for the other, and you have my blessing."

Judith had told Lopasuta that she would be delighted to accept a post as aide to him by the middle of November. The middle-aged factor, René Laurent, had told the Comanche lawyer, "Mrs. Marquard has entrée into the highest financial circles, because of her reputation with the Brunton & Barntry Bank. She will be most valuable to us, and it must also be admitted—particularly by one of French extraction like myself—that her beauty will admit her to the innermost circles of society and commerce, so that she will learn many useful business secrets from which our esteemed employer can ultimately profit."

Laure Bouchard and her stalwart son Lucien arrived in New Orleans on the Thursday of the second week in August. Waiting at the dock were Lopasuta and Geraldine, as was Leland Kenniston, who had arrived the day before. When the honey-haired widow saw the tall Irishman standing at the end of the gangplank just behind Lopasuta and Geraldine, her pulse quickened and color flamed in her cheeks. Instantly, she rebuked herself for this spontaneous reaction: it was much too soon, it must not happen yet! Lucien took her arm and she calmly led him down the gangplank, poised with her head high. Yet she felt herself trembling, and the beat of her heart quickened even more as Leland's blue eyes fixed on hers and a smile curved his frank, honest mouth. The effect from that smile and that look made her realize that her initial feelings for Leland Kenniston had not altered in these last months of absence

351

from him. Her senses were more deeply stirred than they had been by any other man since a long-ago evening when Luke Bouchard had overcome his self-control and made passionate and almost vengeful love to her.

Geraldine hurried up to Laure and embraced her, then stood looking admiringly at the tall boy who self-consciously lowered his eyes. "Lucien, you're just about a man now! How handsome you look in that new suit!" she murmured by way of welcome, then kissed him on the cheek. Lopasuta came forward to greet Laure and to shake hands with her son. During this exchange of amenities, Laure's eyes strayed again and again to Leland, who had not yet moved, but who had continued to look at her with an eager smile on his lips.

Then at last he came forward and said with the most gracious tone and unaffected manner, "Mrs. Bouchard, when someone like you comes to visit it, I know why the Queen City is so named. And you, young man," turning to Lucien, offering his hand which the boy at once took, "you're exactly as your mother described you. As Geraldine just said, you're practically a man now."

"I—I'm very happy to meet you, Mr. Kenniston."

"I'm flattered. It will be my pleasure to escort you and your mother to New York, and then you and I will rough it alone on the Atlantic all the way to Dublin. The prospect doesn't frighten you, I hope?"

"Oh no, sir, this time of year the ocean should be very calm," young Lucien Bouchard riposted, "and I'm looking forward to accompanying you, sir!"

Leland burst into hearty laughter. "By the Eternal, there's a young man after my own heart! And of course he's right about the ocean, you know. Well now, Mrs. Bouchard, I've arranged a suite of rooms for you and Lucien at the St. Charles."

"But I had thought to stay at Geraldine's till we were ready to leave for New York, Mr. Kenniston," Laure dubiously interposed, her eyes widening with surprise.

"I should have been most happy not to have shown myself too dictatorial in making any of your travel arrangements, Mrs. Bouchard. But you see, as I explained to Lopasuta and Geraldine, if we all take the steamship *Pomerania*, which will leave the day after tomorrow, we can have that much more time for me to show all of you around New York. And I thought that the comfort and service of the hotel would be easier for everyone. Please forgive me, if I seem presumptuous in this."

"Not at all, Mr. Kenniston; you're very thoughtful. And since my son has never been away from home before, I think it will be fun for him to experience all the luxury and comfort to be found in large hotels before settling down in a school so far away from home," Laure replied with a smile.

That night, all five of them had dinner at Antoine's, and Leland Kenniston again showed himself to be the perfect host. There were flowers in vases beside Laure's place at one end of the table and at the head of it, where Leland sat. These seating arrangements, too, she regarded as discreet and considerate—though she would not, she admitted to herself, have objected if he had arranged to sit at either her right or her left. Instead, he had her son at her left and Lopasuta at her right, and then Geraldine beside her husband.

"We shall have ten days in New York before the steamship *Kilkenny* lifts anchor for Dublin, Mrs. Bouchard," he informed her. "So all of you will be able to see many of the wonders of our largest metropolis. If we're fortunate, we'll have the opportunity to hear the opening salvo in a campaign for the mayoralty of New York City by a remarkable, enterprising man, William Russell Grace, He has been called the 'Pirate of Peru,' but be that as it may, he may very well become the very first Roman Catholic mayor of New York City. I think that some of the citizens of New Orleans wish they could have a mayor like him."

"And why should that be, Mr. Kenniston?" Laure asked with interest.

"He intends to attack the evils of the political system, among other things. He's a born reformer, and he's dead against Tammany Hall—the powerful political organization rife with corruption, which men like Boss Tweed perpetrated upon the luckless citizens, who had to bear the brunt of extortionate taxes." Leland spoke with animation, his eyes sparkling, and Laure was again impressed.

"I think that's admirable. But the life of a reformer is fraught with danger, don't you agree, Mr. Kenniston?" she asked.

"Yes, I've no doubt of that." His voice was gentle, for her remark had reminded him that her husband had died in the attempt to prevent the assassination of an elected official who had sought to heal the wounds between Democrats and Republicans of the embittered South. "But this man Grace has a personal history completely unlike most reformers. Of course, I'll admit I'm prejudiced in his favor because he came from a good family in Queenstown, Ireland. As a boy, he wanted to gain a commission in the Royal Navy, but his father opposed this, wanting him to take part in his own business. Grace's father, as a matter of fact, had risked his life and his fortune in supporting the struggle of Venezuela for independence. Well, William Russell Grace ran away to sea and traveled around the world for about two years, till his father bought him an interest in a Liverpool firm of ship's chandlers. Understandably, he was bored with that, and of his own volition he went on to Callao, Peru, where his father had helped place him in a similar firm. There, his brother Michael joined him, and the two brothers increased their fortune and influence in Peru. About nineteen years ago—he was then twenty-eight—he was obliged because of ill health to give up his residence in Peru, but he left his brother there to keep up the family interests. And then, right after the Civil War, he settled in New York City to organize W. R. Grace & Company, forming it originally to serve as a sort of correspondent for Grace Brothers & Company of Callao."

"He sounds like a very determined man," Laure put in.

"Yes," Leland's face was aglow with enthusiasm, "and when Peru built its railway system, the Grace concerns secured contracts for practically all the supplies. William Russell Grace himself became a confidential advisor to the Peruvian government, and between 1875 and now, he has been handling the business of arming and equipping the Peruvian army and also enabling the country to purchase a large part of their navy. You see, they're engaged in a war with Chile at the moment. Unfortunately, I think they're going to lose it, but I shouldn't be surprised if Mr. Grace has a few tricks up his sleeve to help the country out. And now that he's in New York, he wants to become mayor on a reform ticket."

"From what you've said of him, I rather think he'll win," Laure declared.

"Nothing would please me more, Mrs. Bouchard. I confess I'm a very patriotic Irishman, and a good Catholic. And by that I don't mean that I go to church on Sunday and expect to have my sins expunged so that I can sin the other six days of the week. It's the spirit of the religion that imbues me, not the ritual. Forgive me if I overwhelm you with my own personal views—I hadn't meant to—but my admiration for William Russell Grace is such that I let down the boundaries for once," he explained with a grin.

"I certainly admire a man's enthusiastic convictions—as long as he isn't bigoted about them," was Laure's gentle answer. She looked steadily at Leland until at last, because his gaze did not waver, she turned away, only too well aware that a blush was suffusing her satiny cheeks and as much as telling Leland that she was already beginning to respond to him. Inwardly, she cried to her conscience: *Oh, God, I don't want to make a mistake again—certainly for my children's sake I mustn't! And yet—and yet—oh, he's so candid and has a wonderful sense of humor coupled to his seriousness—there's something of Luke, a tiny bit of it in him. But he's his own man—he doesn't parade his virtues, or his wealth. He's a kind man, too. And I'm sure that he didn't undertake to accompany my son to Dublin in any underhanded hope that it might make me dependently grateful to him.*

Aloud, she said, in as level a voice as she could maintain, "Can you tell me something of Irish schooling in general, Mr. Kenniston? I've made arrangements with Father O'Mara, of course. I confess that I'm thinking ahead to higher education, as well."

"I'll try to give you as honest an answer as I can from my own knowledge, Mrs. Bouchard. British statesmen for some time have been attempting to tinker with the problem of higher education in Ireland—which I daresay is to be expected, since the English have always wanted to rule and dominate my country. Six years ago, Prime Minister Gladstone tried to settle the question that had been raised in Parliament of a specifically Catholic university. He proposed a bill which would affiliate the Queen's Colleges of Cork and Belfast and the Catholic University to the University of Dublin—which consisted of Trinity College—and to abolish the Queen's College of Galway. What he sought was a university that would be not a mere examining board but a teaching university, with a proper provision of lecture rooms, fellowships, and full professorships. The Catholic bishops declared war against Gladstone's proposal, and it was rejected by only three votes, with some sixty-eight Irish members of Parliament voting against it."

"I can see that politics has been mixed up with education in your country, Mr. Kenniston," Laure observed with a sigh.

"Oh, yes, Mrs. Bouchard, that's always the case. When there is the slightest attempt to give Ireland any kind of freedom, whether it be in the choice of raising their own crops or keeping a modest percentage of the profits, the English landowners strenuously object. Anyway, fortunately, there were enough Catholics in England with influence enough to petition the Pope and obtain full sanction for Catholics to attend the Universities of Oxford and Cambridge. And I will freely admit that, when your son Lucien is of an age to attend the university, if he wishes to enter Oxford or Cambridge and is accepted, he would receive a splendid education there. As for St. Timothy's, all of the teaching is done by young and middle-aged men who have known enough of the world, before they entered the order, to have much more understanding and practical tolerance than you might find in a backwater country school where stiff-necked priests and elderly nuns impose education with a birch rod and a ruler and allow no discussion or open questioning of the tenets they set forth before their pupils. Oh no, St. Timothy's is as progressive as any school you will find in England or, I feel certain, in France or Belgium or Switzerland or even Italy—wherever there are Catholic schools of international reputation."

"You relieve my mind to a good extent by telling me this, Mr. Kenniston. You perhaps know that the original Lucien Bouchard was French-born, from Normandy, who came to Alabama to seek a new life on the frontier. At times I've wondered if a French school would not be more *à propos* for his namesake."

"Historically, the French have usually been against the English." Leland gave her a whimsical little smile. "The French, for example, backed poor Mary Queen of Scots, though they could not save her. Be that as it may, Mrs. Bouchard, I can promise you one thing for certain: Father O'Mara will regularly write to you concerning your son's progress at St. Timothy's, and he will not write anything which is ambiguous or hypocritical. And if your son is not happy there, both he and I will see to it that young Lucien receives placement in a school to his liking, as well as to yours."

"I could ask for nothing fairer, Mr. Kenniston. Thank

you so much again." Laure eyed him steadily now, and tried to control the almost automatic blush which came to her. The sound of his voice was pleasing to her, with its baritone resonance, and she could not help but admire his decided enthusiasm for his convictions.

After dinner, Leland Kenniston rode back to the St. Charles Hotel with Laure and Lucien, while Lopasuta and Geraldine took a calash back to their house on Greenley Street.

As they rode home, the vivacious brunette turned to her tall husband and pensively said, "You know, now that I think of it, it would have been very easy for Mr. Kenniston to have us accompany Laure and her son to New York, as was originally planned, and be there waiting for us. Wouldn't it have been less of a bother to deal with René Laurent by wire?"

Lopasuta reached for his wife's hand and tenderly squeezed it as he gave her an indulgent look. "I've a feeling that Mr. Kenniston is very interested in Laure, and he's using business as an excuse to spend as much time with her as possible."

"Well I think that's wonderful. I think Laure needs a man to guide her—much more so than I would ever desire. It doesn't mean I don't love you, but I wouldn't just merely do anyone's bidding—not even the handsomest, richest man in all the world."

"You've made that quite evident," Lopasuta laughed. "And you don't have to worry, Geraldine; I wouldn't want you to be any other way, believe me." He leaned to her, an arm around her shoulders, and kissed her gently on the cheek. She turned so that their lips met, and her arms linked around his shoulders and she drew him to her in a prolonged kiss.

"Oh, my," she murmured at last when the kiss was over, "I don't doubt your word at all—not at all! And I'm so glad that you've adapted yourself to the ways of the *wasichu*, as you call us, because I did some reading in a book about Indians, and I discovered something that just about shocks me."

"And what is that, dear Geraldine," he innocently asked.

She glanced around to make certain that the driver of the calash was not eavesdropping, and then murmured to him for only him to hear, "In some Indian tribes, like the

Apache, when a wife is pregnant, her husband may not go to bed with her until after the child is weaned—and sometimes that may be as long as two or three years! Can you imagine?"

Lopasuta was both amused and mildly embarrassed by Geraldine's candid outburst, but he knew that her boldness was a characteristic part of her nature and totally unaffected.

As Lopasuta stepped down from the calash before the door of their house, he paid the driver, then took Geraldine's arm and led her to the door and there turned to say to her in a teasing voice, "You forget that I am a Comanche, not an Apache. And so far as I know, the tribal customs of the People do not specify that a husband must ignore his wife during the time she is carrying his child and after she is delivered of it. I do not think the question will arise between us, my dear one."

Geraldine tilted back her head and laughed gaily, as she hugged him. "Well them, I'm glad I had the good sense to marry a Comanche instead of an Apache. Now let's get a good night's sleep. I want you to hold me in your arms so that you can feel our child." She sighed, and declared, "I can't wait till we go to New York and watch dear Laure and that absolutely charming Mr. Kenniston discover what they should already know—that they're absolutely perfect for one another."

Now it was his turn to laugh as he unlocked the door and ceremoniously ushered her in. As she ascended the stairway, he followed behind her, an arm around her waist. He leaned over to kiss the nape of her neck, and Geraldine shivered and turned to him. "Oh, no, you're definitely not an Apache!" she whispered, and then, her eyes luminous, took his hands and led him up the stairs to their bedroom.

The *Pomerania* was the very largest steamboat which Laure, Geraldine, and Lopasuta had ever seen. It was powerful enough to cross the Atlantic, and indeed, eight times a year it did exactly that. As the group stood on the dock staring at the majestic ship, Leland turned to the Comanche lawyer and remarked with a smile, "That's an even larger vessel than the one on which you and I met—and probably than the one that took you to Hong Kong in the first place."

Lopasuta nodded, his eyes fixed on the majestic, sumptuous outlines of the steamboat. Its decks were broad and long, and the sailors aboard it were nattily dressed in uniforms of white blouses and trousers and blue seamen's berets. The *Pomerania* reposed at the end of a long dock, dominating the entire harbor.

Geraldine turned to look at her husband, and saw that his eyes were fixed upon the steamship. And she, so sensitive to him and understanding more about him than she had ever done before their prolonged separation, reached for his hand.

When he turned back to smile at her, he knew indeed he had become almost as *wasichu* as Comanche, had cast off the stoic obduracy with which his tribesmen endured the blows as well as the blessings of fate; he felt so great a swell of joy and pride and thanksgiving for being here with Geraldine. Yes, he had bridged the two worlds, and he was grateful for it.

Leland had shrewdly noted Lopasuta's expression, as he had Laure's and Lucien's: both of them stared at the massive steamship, and then turned to whisper to each other. Leland, tingling with anticipation at the chance of prolonging his time with the beautiful widow, turned to the purser of the *Pomerania*. He verified with him the location of the three staterooms he had engaged: one for himself; a larger one with a connecting door between two cabins for Laure and Lucien; and one for Geraldine and Lopasuta.

He went down the carpeted hallway following a neatly uniformed cabin boy carrying his luggage, watching as Laure and her son went ahead with another who opened the door of their stateroom and took their luggage inside. His room was across the passageway from hers, and after he tipped the cabin boy and genially thanked him and the boy closed the door, he looked at the luxurious furnishings and the comfortably wide bed and then walked slowly to the porthole to take a last glimpse of New Orleans before the *Pomerania* lifted anchor and made its stately way out of the bay, down the Gulf, and up the seaboard on to the Port of New York.

He was a romantic; he wanted love, to be given freely, without question of affluence or social status. Now mature, he had waited all this time for the right woman—a woman who would fulfill not only his amorous fantasies, but also show herself to be inwardly beautiful of spirit and character. The beauty of the flesh was ephemeral, and although it

359

was powerful and often coercive, he knew that physical love in and of itself was transient and often disappointing.

Among his sycophantic New York friends, there were many who had glibly advised him to take this or that young dancer or chorine from one of the vaudeville shows and set her up in an apartment of her own as his mistress. That did not appeal to him because she would have only a body to offer him, and at this time in his life, the comfort and consolation of mere physical communication was insufficient. Yet conversely, precisely because he was such a romantic, he desired the culmination of physical love as the very essence of love between the sexes. When physical love was granted in joyous, spontaneous avowal, it was the perfect conclusion to the intimate awareness of a man and a woman who knew how deeply they cared for each other beyond mere infatuation, or the bodily attraction of one for the other in hedonistic conclave. And this was why he yearned for Laure Bouchard, for to him she epitomized all that was desirable in a woman—mind, spirit, physical beauty, and because he sensed that once she accepted a man of her own judicious choice, what she had to give would be far more rewarding than the affection of a younger, perhaps more outwardly attractive woman.

Lopasuta and Geraldine stood at the rail as the steamship, pulled by two small tugboats, was slowly drawn toward the opening of the bay and on into the Gulf. His face was somber as he watched the receding outline of the huge levee and wharf and the buildings beyond. Geraldine did not speak, knowing that he was thinking of that long-deferred voyage back home from Hong Kong. He was thinking to himself that the long months taken out of his life could never be replaced, and yet they had not been in vain: there had been a purpose to this beyond his reckoning. Considering it as a Comanche would in the settling of accounts between enemies, he had completely avenged the honorable name that had been given to him by Luke Bouchard. And if it had not been for that absence from Geraldine, he would never have met Leland Kenniston. In the balance scale of life, among the *wasichu* as with the People, the scores seemed to be evened.

The daytime temperatures were hot, but there were always cooling breezes from the Atlantic by late afternoon as the steamboat moved around Florida and past the Carolinas. The ships's officers devised sociable gatherings, from shuffleboard on the decks to musicales. For the first time in his life, Lopasuta heard a Beethoven piano trio, a Haydn quartet, and a potpourri of tunes by Rossini, Donizetti, and Verdi. The meals in the luxurious dining room were lavish, offering many courses and fine wines and liqueurs, and Lopasuta humorously remarked to his lovely wife that, if he succumbed to all the culinary temptations aboard the *Pomerania,* he would surely no longer look like a Comanche by the time he reached New York, for his waistline would have expanded to that of a middle-aged, gluttonous *wasichu.*

Lucien Bouchard was spellbound by this leisurely, luxurious journey by sea, yet he chaperoned his mother gracefully and enthusiastically, much to the admiration of Leland Kenniston. Leland, purposely keeping himself in the background so as not to appear overly aggressive, saw in this amity of mother and son a commendable trait of the boy's character.

Twice during the voyage, Leland permitted himself the delicious privilege of dancing with Laure in the ship's ballroom. Each time he took her in his arms, he felt himself trembling with an eagerness more fitting to a callow adolescent who was experiencing his first infatuation—but he continued to impose a rigorous self-discipline, so as not to embarrass or disconcert the beautiful widow. Nonetheless, by the time the *Pomerania* approached the New York harbor, he knew that he was unequivocably in love with her, and that he intended to propose marriage to her at a suitable time.

For her part, Laure felt herself more and more drawn to the black-haired Irishman. His tact and consideration had already marked him as a man of sensitivity and probity. And when, at midnight on their last evening out, she was escorted by Leland back to her stateroom, she felt herself hoping that he would kiss her and tell her of his desire for her—yet he did not. Gravely, he thanked her for the pleasure she had given him during the dance, made small talk, and wished her a pleasant goodnight. As she let herself in and closed the door, she did not see that Leland stood on the other side of the carpeted hallway looking after her, his eyes glowing, his face bemused, wishing that he had given her some understanding of what he truly felt for her.

*　*　*

Geraldine had found the sea voyage somewhat trying. Each afternoon, the pitching and rolling of the steamboat had made her extremely nauseated. This she attributed to her pregnancy, to be sure, but nonetheless she began to wish that she had stayed home. Still, not wishing to be a spoilsport, she had said nothing of this to her husband. But the thought of spending over a week gallivanting around New York made her wonder if it might not be wiser, for the sake of the child, to go back to New Orleans. She turned her thoughts to her friend. It was her belief that Laure was falling in love with Leland, and Geraldine already knew that he was in love with Laure. She wished that she could be there at the moment they both accepted each other in trust and love—and it would happen, she was certain.

It was a bright, hot day when the *Pomerania* entered the New York harbor, and Laure, Lucien, Lopasuta, and Geraldine stood at the rail for their first view of this magnetic, bustling city of which they had heard so much.

As they steamed around the southern tip of Manhattan, Leland pointed out to his guests Bedloe's Island, where the Statue of Liberty, a gift from France to her sister country on the occasion of the Centennial, would shortly be erected. "And do you see there, to the north? Those towers on either side of the East River are for the new bridge that will link Manhattan with Brooklyn. eliminating the need to travel by ferry. If you peer very closely, you can see the wooden footpath strung between the towers for the workmen. However, it's become a most popular form of diversion. If you all like, we can stroll across it during your stay. I've done it once myself—it's quite an adventure, I assure you! Not for the weakhearted, by any means!"

Geraldine, standing to her husband's right, gasped at the thought of such daredeviltry and quickly spurned the offer. Lopasuta laughed at Geraldine's reaction, but inwardly agreed with her. He was greatly impressed by this skyline, though, and asked of his employer if he could identify some of the buildings, in particular the remarkably tall one with what resembled a church spire at the top. Leland informed him that that was the Tribune Building at Nassau and Spruce streets, the home of one of the most successful newspapers in the city. Its ten stories, not including the clocktower spire, made it one of the tallest structures in the city. Leland then told him anecdotes about the city's contrasts of wealth and poverty and tremendous, never-ending growth. But even as he did so, Lopasuta noted his employer from time to time casting sidelong glances at the beautiful woman standing at the rail with her tall young son beside her; Lopasuta said a fervent prayer to the Great Spirit that Laure and this man who had been so kind to him would find permanent happiness in and for each other.

At last the gangplank was let down, and one of the stewards piped the horn indicating that it was time for the passengers to disembark. Leland Kenniston engaged the services of two stewards to take charge of all the luggage, and went down ahead of them to arrange for a coach to take them to the Fifth Avenue Hotel at Madison Square.

When the luggage had been put atop the coach and roped to the roof, Leland handed them all in. The coachman started up the two horses, and they were en route to their hotel.

At the desk, Leland saw to it that their reservations were honored, and had young bellmen take up the luggage. He himself had traveled with only a single valise, for the luggage for his European trip was packed and waiting at his New York town house, an elegant three-story brownstone.

Geraldine, Laure, and Lucien found it novel to take their first elevator ride, for none of the New Orleans hotels had yet installed such devices. When the bellman opened the door of the suite Leland had reserved for Laure and her son, she exclaimed at the sumptuous oriental carpets, the damask-covered chaise longue and sofa, and all of the other elegant furnishings. There were a sitting room, two adjoining bedrooms, and two small bathrooms—an unheard-of luxury that Lucien was gleefully examining. Geraldine and Lopasuta had similar though somewhat smaller accommodations, and Leland had contented himself with a single room with bath at the end of the same floor.

They had arrived in midafternoon, and as he took leave of his friends, Leland said cheerfully, "I've taken the liberty of reserving a table for us at Delmonico's, and then we shall go to the theater for some excellent vaudeville. There is a trained dog animal act that is utterly captivating, plus a pair of Yugoslavian jugglers who have already captured the fancy of all New York. It will be diverting, I'm certain."

Geraldine and Lopasuta expressed their enthusiasm for

these plans and then excused themselves, with Geraldine airily exclaiming, "My unborn child is telling me that it's high time I rest! But I will certainly be delighted to partake of tonight's festivities. We'll be ready by six o'clock." Then, with a wave of her hand, Geraldine closed the door behind her.

"You're certainly most thoughtful, Mr. Kenniston," Laure warmly told him. "And Lucien is very much drawn to you, I'll tell you that much. He can hardly wait till he boards the *Kilkenny* with you for the voyage to Ireland. He's dying to have you tell him stories about Ireland, for he's quite a student of history, you see."

"We Irish have quite a rich history, though, alas, there's not always a happy ending to many of the chronicles," Leland at once replied. "Your son and I will have a great deal of talking and getting acquainted to do on the journey to Dublin, and I'm looking forward to it as much as he is. Well now, you'll want to freshen up. So I shall see you at six."

"Till then, Mr. Kenniston. And thank you so very much again for all your hospitality," Laure said gently as she held out her hand to him. Quite unlike his previous deportment with her, the black-haired Irishman took her hand and, staring intently at her, brought it to his lips and quickly kissed it. "Till then," he murmured, and surprised by his own audacity, he quickly turned and walked down to his room at the end of the hallway.

He did not look back as Laure stood looking after him, and then down at her hand, which she put to her lips. He did not see the furious blush that colored her cheeks as, with a last look, she slipped inside the suite and closed the door.

Geraldine was exclaiming with wonder at the magnificent furnishings of their suite, passing her hand over the fabrics covering the stuffed chairs with ornately scrolled backs and arms. The sitting room even had a dining-room set, in the event the guests should wish a repast served from the hotel's dining room. Geraldine, who had never known such resplendency, exclaimed, "It must cost a fortune, darling! What a generous man Mr. Kenniston is!"

"It is expensive, my darling, but apparently this hotel isn't typical of New York. For Mr. Kenniston has told me about the Buckingham Hotel at Fiftieth Street—right below the just-finished St. Patrick's Cathedral—where they have single rooms decorated in English style at a modest seven dollars a week. The Buckingham is a hotel for conservative people in uptown New York, whereas here, of course, we are in the very hub of things. My guess is that the cost of this suite is between five and ten dollars a day—but that includes four meals."

"My gracious, that's a fortune! Why, one week here would pay our food bills for three months back in New Orleans, Lopasuta!" Geraldine gasped.

He came to her and took her by the shoulders, smiled, and kissed her. "I'm glad you're so practical." His face grew serious. "I intend to establish trust funds for Luke and Dennis, and put aside a trust for you as well, my beloved wife. However, although money is a medium of exchange used to procure the things one desires, it is never a substitute for spiritual needs. I may never be rich in the material sense—certainly not like Leland Kenniston—but that's not important to me. We shall always have a comfortable life, but most of all, we shall have each other's trust and love, and the knowledge of the trials we've gone through and that you so bravely faced. I will never forget how you forgave and understood my actions while I was forced to be away from you."

Her eyes were wet with tears as she clung to him, and wordlessly they pledged a sacrament of undying devotion each to the other.

When at last, a deliciously rosy-hued Geraldine disengaged herself from his embrace, she bantered, "Well, my dear, I wish your fine Mr. Kenniston and Laure could feel just like this."

"I think that she's starting to fall in love with him—at least, I certainly pray for it. He is the very salt of the earth. He is a man who could make any woman happy—and he can especially make Laure happy because he respects her. It's already evident by the way he's acted toward her. I shouldn't be surprised if she secretly hopes that he will be more demonstrative than he has been."

"Yes, he's been a perfect gentleman—maybe too perfect!"

"Of course he has, because that's his nature. I'm hoping that before this week is out, before he and young Lucien sail for Ireland, Laure Bouchard will discover that his absence will cause her distress—and when she does, she will know that she is truly in love with him."

## Thirty-five

Three mornings before Lucien Bouchard and Leland Kenniston were to sail on HMS *Kilkenny*, Geraldine put her hand over her face and uttered a long, tremulous sigh. The waiter who was serving the couple breakfast discreetly turned away.

"What's the matter, darling?" Lopasuta solicitously asked, handing the waiter a tip, then covertly gesturing to him to leave.

"I'm really exhausted, dearest," Geraldine confessed. "We've been on the go constantly. Mr. Kenniston has a great deal more energy than I have! I can barely keep up with the way he takes us all over the city, acting as a guide, taking us to fabulous dinners, concerts, and vaudeville—I really am tired. And you know, I don't want anything to happen to the child I'm carrying. I think that you and I should make plans to go back home as soon as possible."

"If you feel that way, of course I'll arrange it, my darling. I'll talk to Leland right away. Try to eat some breakfast—at least the fruit and the cereal. It'll help settle your stomach."

"All right. Please tell him that I'm very grateful for his hospitality. It's just been too much." Geraldine looked at him forlornly.

"Don't worry, I'll use my most diplomatic manner, and besides, I'm sure he won't feel put out in the least. After all," he winked at her, "if you and I go back to New Orleans, Laure and he will have at least two nights together before he takes the boy to Ireland."

"Oh, my goodness, that hadn't crossed my mind at all! All I thought about was my health and our baby's! But that's a wonderful idea—all the more reason you should try

366

to make your apology for me sound convincing, darling," Geraldine insisted.

"I'll go see him directly after breakfast, I promise," Lopasuta told her.

Half an hour later, Leland, in his nightshirt and bathrobe, opened the door and genially greeted the Comanche lawyer. "Good morning, Lopasuta! Tonight, I've booked a table at Lüchow's, a really fine German restaurant, and after that, we'll go to a chamber-music concert at the Academy of Music, which is just a block away, near Union Square. Trios by Mozart and Mendelssohn, and a new string quartet of Brahms. Restful and gracious music."

"Could I talk to you a moment, Leland?"

"Of course—come in. Have you had your breakfast?"

"Geraldine and I just finished, thanks." Lopasuta moved to the spacious, overstuffed couch and seated himself with a sigh. Leland Kenniston picked up a Havana panatela, lit it, and then, puffing at it to make sure that it drew well, declared, "I can tell you've something on your mind. Anything wrong?"

"Oh, no, Leland, nothing really. But Geraldine's rather overtired from all the excitement—and because she's pregnant. She wonders if you would be distressed if we went back to New Orleans immediately."

"I'm sorry to hear she's out of sorts. Good Lord, I'd no idea I was rushing you around New York so strenuously. Under the circumstances, it might be best if you returned by train. Wait—I've got a schedule in my billfold." He opened his wallet and extracted the schedule, scanning it intently for a moment, then declared: "There's one leaving this evening at seven. It will get you back to New Orleans in about three days."

"That will be fine."

"I'll have the desk clerk get the tickets so there'll be plenty of time for you to pack, have a leisurely lunch, and perhaps do a bit of sightseeing this afternoon if Geraldine feels up to it. There's something I would like you both to attend, if you think that Geraldine would enjoy it."

"What's that, Leland?"

"Mr. Grace is having a precampaign rally not far from Tammany Hall—a most appropriate location, I'd say." Leland permitted himself a wry smile. "I'd like you to listen to just a bit of what he has to say. It'll be at three o'clock. Think you could make it?"

"Yes, I think I'd like that. I must admit I don't know all I'd like to about your city's politics, Leland, but I can understand why you'd support a man like Grace."

"Of course. He not only talks of reform, he's a doer. I suppose because I'm in a way cut from the same mold, I admire him more than most would. And of course, he's as Irish as Paddy's pig, as we say back in Dublin." Leland gave Lopasuta a quick smile. "I plan to invite Laure and Lucien to attend the rally, too. After it's over, we'll all see you and Geraldine off at Grand Central Station. We can have an early dinner at the Grand Union Hotel, across the street from the terminal. So you see, you and Geraldine can still have a last taste of New York and a glimpse into what I think is going to be a most exciting political campaign next year. If Grace wins, and I'm sure he will, it may change the whole outlook of commerce and culture in this big, teeming city. I've also a notion that Mr. Grace will try to do something about the slums of New York. There are far too many. Well then, as soon as I've dressed, I'll go downstairs and have the clerk get your tickets."

"I can't begin to thank you enough for your hospitality to both of us, Leland."

"It's been my pleasure. Besides, you earned this and more. You've won three cases for me already, and René Laurent wrote me that you're fast becoming something of a legal force to reckon with in New Orleans. That'll help my image when my company really begins to operate as a major venture. Incidentally, there's something you can do when you get back—I'd like you to check with the port authorities in New Orleans on tariffs. See if you can get a leveling off on the tariffs for a company that intends to draw a great deal of cargo into the city. I should think the customs officials would welcome high-quality merchandise coming in regularly and be willing to make a few concessions."

"I'll do that for you. I just hope I haven't spoiled your time in New York by cutting short our visit," Lopasuta solemnly declared.

"You haven't in the least—and I'll let you in on a little secret." Leland sat down beside Lopasuta. "You've probably already guessed that I'm very much in love with Laure Bouchard. I've no reason yet to believe that she feels a reciprocal love, and I don't intend to make myself too obvious. But I'll admit very frankly, man to man, that by you and Geraldine going back this evening, I'll have three nights alone with her and the boy. And perhaps if the occasion presents itself, I'll be able to tell her what I really feel."

"Geraldine and I wish you every success. We think you're the right man for her, Leland."

"Thank you, Lopasuta. I value that as a compliment. I've come to a time of life where I look around and I find that all my friends are married with families, and I have no one. I'm not expressing self-pity, to be sure; it's only that I'm more appreciative of my situation now than I would have been ten years ago in thinking about finding a woman who really cares for me and whom I can respect and love—in short, with whom to share my life."

"I certainly hope Laure feels as you do. Geraldine and I would like nothing better, Leland." Lopasuta rose and shook hands with his employer.

Laure Bouchard was wearing a green satin gown, heavily embroidered at the three flounces and paniers, with lace-trimmed cuffs and neckline. The shade of green matched her lovely eyes and set off her honey-gold hair with éclat. She was upset when Geraldine visited her suite about an hour later to tell her that she and Lopasuta had decided to go back to New Orleans. "My dear, I'm so sorry! Lucien and I will miss you! I'd no idea that you didn't like New York."

"Oh, no," Geraldine instantly protested, "it's not that at all. With all the excitement and running around we've done—well, I think for the sake of my child, I should be a little more sedate."

"Good heavens, I can't imagine your ever being sedate, dear Geraldine," Laure gaily laughed; then she put her hands on her friend's shoulders. "Of course, I understand, dear. Well, we'll all miss you. You'll be leaving some time today?"

"Yes, this evening. Before we catch the train, though, Mr. Kenniston says he'd like to take all of us to a rally for the man who's going to run for mayor of New York next year. He thinks it might be interesting."

"I remember how highly he spoke of Mr. Grace. I'd very much like to see what sort of man Mr. Kenniston so admires," Laure mused.

\* \* \*

369

A platform had been erected, with bunting and signs extolling the virtues of William Russell Grace, and the slogan, "In '80, New York's Saving Grace!" proclaimed his candidacy on a program of reform and honesty that would battle the corruption of Tammany Hall. That hoary institution was housed just two blocks away, and not a few clerks from that building had sneaked out of their jobs to attend the rally.

Leland Kenniston had instructed the carriage driver to draw to one side, where they would have an unobstructed view and be able to hear the speakers clearly. A gray-bearded politico rose to make a pompous, long-drawn-out speech about the evils of Tammany Hall and the necessity of finding a man who could take the helm of New York's ship of state and guide it through the turbulent channels into a safe harbor. His successor did not mouth so many inane metaphors; rather, he came right to the point, drawing applause for a five-minute speech in which he pointed out the benefits to the ever-growing metropolis if W. R. Grace were elected mayor. This done, he turned to introduce the candidate himself, and Laure saw a portly, distinguished-looking man of forty-seven come to the podium and look out over the audience.

Lifting his hand to acknowledge the applause, William Russell Grace spoke in the silence that followed: "I thank you for this show of faith and interest. I am sure I am unknown to many of you, although I have been in the field of international commerce for some years now. Some of you may have read in the journals many colorful accounts of my South American exploits. While I am known to many as the 'Pirate of Peru'—because through the efforts of my company, a large part of that country's navy was purchased to do battle with their neighbor, Chile—my interests are now much closer to home. In fact, my major concern *is* my home, my beloved New York, not a South American country. Let me tell you what I feel about this great city and what I want to do with it, and for it, if you will help me with your votes next year."

Laure Bouchard turned to Leland Kenniston and whispered, "He certainly is a forceful, direct speaker."

"Yes. And he's sincere. You know, he probably has a better concept of international affairs than many a governor and possibly even more so than our esteemed President, the Honorable Rutherford B. Hayes." Leland spoke with a tinge of scorn to his words, as he referred to the colorless man who had wrested the Presidency away from Tilden in an election that many still thought had been stolen by the Republicans.

"Indeed, Mrs. Bouchard," Leland added as he leaned toward her, "I intend to make a sizable contribution to Mr. Grace's campaign. Even if he may be accused of having his finger in too many international pies, the fact is that he has already shown how civic-minded he is. Besides, he's wealthy enough in his own right, thanks to his activities abroad, that he won't have to cheat the taxpayers and the voters, as a Tammany Hall candidate would almost assuredly do. The fact is, this city urgently needs an honest mayor, someone who wants to drive the rascals out and will not be afraid to try it. He's a man who, despite his wealth and position, seems to have genuine concern for the common people. In short, I think he's a remarkable man—just the kind of man a remarkable city needs as its leader."

He spoke so eloquently, his dark eyes bright with animation, that Laure stared at him, almost hypnotized. He was a compelling, magnetic man, and in many ways very much like Luke. He, like Luke, believed in integrity and honesty, in imagination and hard work; these were virtues that Luke had had in abundance, together with a deeply ingrained belief in a just God. What she had admired about Luke's religious concepts was that he did not have to attend church for ritualistic, ceremonial demonstrations of his beliefs, but rather that he automatically pursued them in the ethics of his own daily life. And somehow she knew that Leland Kenniston had very much the same inner dedication, needing no ostentatious, specious parading of his faith.

Their eyes met, and she could not help trembling. She had a yearning to express herself to this man who had already shown her how desirable he felt her to be. And this time she did not feel the prick of conscience, telling her that she must beware because perhaps this would be another William Brickley: she had already crossed that Rubicon by testing Leland Kenniston and finding him true and credible.

"Well now, I'm grateful to all of you for your indulgence in allowing me to hear my favorite candidate," Leland declared with an apologetic smile when the rally was over. Turning to young Lucien, he asked, "Do you have any opinion of him, young man?"

"I like the way he talks. He's straightforward and to the point, unlike most politicians—although I've only read their speeches and didn't hear them in person."

"Bravo!" the black-haired Irishman applauded. "Mrs. Bouchard, your son is going to make an absolutely rewarding companion for me aboard the *Kilkenny*. I can foresee many an afternoon and evening of avid conversation on many subjects. Lucien appears to have some decided ideas all his own, which I admire in a young man. You see, Lucien," he turned to the boy, "it's good to establish your own convictions when you're in your formative years. One by one, you'll discard the half-truths and the creeds by which men lived and died over the centuries, till you find your own self, till you find a way of life that is comfortable, that hurts no one, and, indeed, aids those with whom you come into contact. To me that seems to be the real purpose of life. However briefly we're here, we want to make some impression—and not only out of ego. We should feel concerned with the welfare of others. 'No man is an island, entire of itself'—tell me, have you heard of John Donne?"

Lucien shook his head and flushed self-consciously.

"Don't look so abashed. I shouldn't have expected you to know of him at your age. But you will, and Father O'Mara will make sure that you read all the great English-language poets, as well as some of the others, too. He's not prejudiced in that direction. You see, Lucien, men of good will abound in every climate under the sun. The differences between all nations are created by the envious, the greedy, and the powerful, who want to control and limit knowledge, so that they will be free to do what they want under the guise of humanitarianism. You will study the history of the great wars of the Middle Ages, like the War of the Roses, for instance, that lasted over a hundred years. It left both England and France devastated, with the flower of their youth slaughtered, all over an obscure chauvinistic belief by each royal house that theirs was the worthier and hence deserved the support of all their citizens in battle. Today, we're wiser in some sense. Most of our battles take place against plague, famine, and poverty. We haven't yet succeeded, but at least we're trying."

"My gracious, you'd have made an excellent teacher

yourself, Mr. Kenniston," Laure couldn't help putting in admiringly.

"Actually, Mrs. Bouchard, I think that if I hadn't been what I now am, I'd really have enjoyed teaching. To take a group of boys about Lucien's age with sensitivity, imagination, and limitless potential, to help channel their ideas to find the fullest expression and so that they know themselves to be truthful and honest in what they uphold— that's a teacher's reward. It's not monetary, certainly; it's spiritual, cultural, if you like. Yes, I should have been very happy as a teacher. And that's why I'm so looking forward to these discussions your son and I are going to have, Mrs. Bouchard."

She smiled at him, and she found herself deeply impressed by the fervor of his beliefs. The intensity of his words marked them as utterly sincere. This man had the idealism of Luke and perhaps even that of old Lucien Bouchard. Curiously, although he did not seem to be an impractical and rash idealist, still she sensed a touch of Don Quixote in Leland Kenniston.

He gave directions to the carriage driver to take them to the railroad station near where they would all dine and then see Lopasuta and Geraldine off for New Orleans. He leaned back, caught Laure's gaze and smiled at her, then turned away—not out of rudeness, but because he did not trust himself to say anything more at the moment. Inwardly, although he was very grateful that Lopasuta and Geraldine were cutting short their stay, he found himself increasingly anxious at the prospect of finally wooing this woman he so desired. He was not afraid of being rebuffed, but only of offending her and thus destroying what chance he might have for the future in establishing a life which they could share. Wanting to be totally honest with her lest she sense that he was not being completely candid, he had an almost perverse determination to confront Laure with the very worst of his background. He turned back to her now and casually asked, "Would you think ill of me if I told you that I was a Fenian?"

Her beautiful green eyes widened with curiosity. "You must explain what you mean, Mr. Kenniston. The term is new to me."

"Very well, I shall. For an Irishman in America, to be a Fenian is to declare himself body and soul for the Irish cause against the usurpation of our land by English law and landlord domination. Perhaps you would understand better if I gave you some historical background."

"I should like that very much."

"I, too," Lopasuta chimed in, having followed this discussion with growing interest, and Geraldine nodded her own assent, her eyes sparkling as she observed, with all her womanly intuitive instinct, that such a discussion was serving to bring Leland and Laure closer together.

"Well then, briefly, between 1849 and 1856, about a million and a half people left Ireland because of evictions that followed the passage of the Encumbered Estates Act in 1848. The stated purpose of the act was to facilitate the sale of mortgaged estates to solvent, resident landlords who would be more in touch with the common people and thus, it was hoped, more likely to treat the tenants better than the insolvent, absentee owners whom these new landlords were intended to displace. That, as I said, was the theoretical hope of the act. Instead, it led to the confiscation of Catholic land by English Protestant invaders, and thus the very tenants whom the act was created to protect were forced to flee because they couldn't pay their rents."

"How dreadful!" Laure sympathetically murmured.

"You may well say that. There were terrible riots, especially in the slums. And there were dreadful acts of retribution by the English soldiers who naturally protected the rights of the English Protestant landlords. But these acts of retribution turned the stomachs of many Irishmen like myself, who immigrated to America, and some sixteen years ago, a secret society was formed in Chicago, aimed at correcting these abuses. Named after Fioinn, who was a celebrated Irish clan leader of the early Christian era, that society calls itself the Fenians, the men of Fioinn, a kind of standing militia. The society is comprised of Irish-Americans bound by oath to the objective of establishing a free Irish Republic. The Catholic Church has denounced it—both Irish and American Catholic bishops and priests— yet it still flourishes. And I am proud to say that I am a Fenian."

"I do not think it wrong for a man to love his native country so much that he wants to help in its fight for freedom." With this, Laure looked at him with a steadfast, frank gaze, and Leland felt his heart beat faster. Now he chose his words carefully—words directed at her—and his speech had a romantic eloquence to it which went far be-

374

yond the mere words themselves. "Such a comment on your part heartens me greatly, Mrs. Bouchard. I sense in you a kindred spirit. And I think your boy is, also. After all, he is a scion of the founder of the Bouchards. As Lopasuta explained it to me, the original Bouchard came here during the French Revolution to break away from the tyranny of the French nobility upon the citizens in the hope of living upon land that was free, to reap its bounty and to replenish the soil with what he had taken from it. He was a true landholder, a patriot in the deepest sense of the word. I respect and admire him, just as I do my countrymen who endured martyrdom because they sought only to take a meager living from their Irish soil and to enrich it by their presence upon it. Those who fought their greedy landlords—who barely fulfilled the specious terminology of the Act of 1848 insofar as being 'residents' was concerned—were looked upon as outlaws, the worst kind of revolutionaries, nihilists like the abused peasants under the czars of Russia who resort to the bomb to express their indignation and helplessness over oppression."

"You speak very strongly, Mr. Kenniston," Laure murmured, thinking to herself that she was beginning to understand why she had sensed a quixotic impulse in him.

"Yes, and I know that I go beyond the bounds of polite social badinage when I do, and I beg your indulgence. But I am so caught up in it that I want you to know it—so that you will know me the better. I am an idealist. I abhor violence. But if I am attacked, I will fight back as best I can—that is an elementary law, and it has been since the dawn of time. The tragedy is that so many decent people are forced against their will to take up the very weapons which the encroachers use against them. Then they are condemned roundly in the journals and by the capitalistic lords of the earth, hypocritically damning them as rebels and scum and all the rest."

"Are you not afraid that, when you go back to Dublin and it is known that you are a Fenian, you may be in danger yourself, Mr. Kenniston?" she asked, not quite keeping the concern out of her voice.

"No. Thus far, I have made financial contributions anonymously, for food, supplies, and, yes, for arms. I would not personally take up a gun and shoot down a man with whom I had no quarrel only because he was on the other side. I am pacifistic—but I am a patriot."

"Go on. Tell me more about this society, Mr. Kenniston." She seemed to drink in every word, and Lopasuta and Geraldine exchanged a knowing look as they listened, absorbed.

Leland Kenniston shook his head, his face shadowed with a sudden sorrow. "Unhappily, Mrs. Bouchard, there were several aborted attempts to establish an Irish Republic, and the time wasn't right, and violence was used. I do not condone this, you understand, but I understand the reason for its almost inevitable application. You see, if the leaders of the world could be induced to sit at a table and to express themselves frankly and without hypocrisy, points of issue could be raised, calmly debated, sensibly resolved with honorable compromises. But when rebels appear to reject any kind of logical, dispassionate discourse, those leaders instead seize upon an obscure incident, a kind of convenient peg on which to hang all manner of charges to suit their own purposes and convince the world that they are in the right, and the rebels criminals."

Lopasuta had never heard Leland speak with such fervor, nor had Laure: her eyes were very wide and luminous, her lips were parted, as she sat listening to him.

"But again I digress. Well then, some fourteen years ago, a man named Thomas J. Kelley, who had been a colonel during America's Civil War, was sent by the American Fenians to Ireland. There, he convinced the Irish patriots that an Irish-American expedition of a good five thousand men armed with Spencer repeating rifles and backed by artillery could be landed on their shores; further, that the American movement owned a fleet of ships and had soldiers in their employ with the secret connivance of the American government. His story was that France and Russia were also going to cooperate, and that the finest generals in the world would come to Ireland's aid.

"Unfortunately, Colonel Kelley and a compatriot, Captain Deasy, were arrested under the Vagrancy Act. It was planned to rescue these two Irish-Americans as they were to be taken by prison van from Manchester to Bellevue. The van was held up by rebels, but when there was trouble in unlocking the door, one of the would-be rescuers put a revolver to the lock and pulled the trigger. The shot killed a sergeant standing on the other side of the door who was guarding the two men.

"Three men were captured and put on trial for murder,

convicted, and executed. Technically, of course, they were guilty of murder, but it was a very grave injustice and psychologically only served to fuel the flames. Of course, the English had a case of what we might call the jitters, and so the trial was not deliberated calmly, and passions were aroused on the side of the unfortunate victim, who happened to be English. But of course, as can be understood, the Irish patriots were sent into an absolute frenzy of rage and hatred. So this unfortunate incident of firing at a stubborn lock resulted in riots and deaths and drew the Irish and the English still further apart, making it absolutely impossible to conduct any sort of sane, passion-free argument on the subject of an Irish Republic."

"How dreadful! And there can be no appeal to Parliament, or even to the Queen?" Laure asked.

"Queen Victoria decidedly has no great love for the Irish, and her prime ministers have never argued that she should, Mrs. Bouchard. She was brought up to believe that things must proceed in an orderly fashion, and that rebellion is akin to treason—perhaps the most heinous crime under the sun. No, there can be no hope for an Irish Republic under the Queen of England, I'm afraid.

"But getting back to the situation of the Irish farmer, I should say that most of the small ones, especially in the south and the west, live in dire poverty, and they are not particularly skillful, I admit that also. They have been asked, God knows, time enough why they did not improve their agricultural skills, adopting better methods of farming, and the invariable answer was that, if they made improvemens, the rents would be raised, and they would be worse off than ever. The larger landowners among the Irish farmers are not, of course, the principal sufferers. But ever since 1876, there has been a potato famine. Consider this: three years ago, the potato crop in Ireland was worth twelve million pounds, or, sixty million dollars—I am told that now it is worth little more than three million pounds, or fifteen million dollars. How then, you may well argue, can the poor Irish farmer pay his rent and subsist? That is why they must have freedom, and not be under the yoke of the wealthy English landlords—or, for that matter, even compelled to farm, if they cannot make a living at it. And that is why I am a Fenian."

"You are certainly most eloquent, Mr. Kenniston. I'm grateful to you for acquainting me with a great many facts

I didn't know. And I think, in the process, I have learned something about you, also," Laure permitted herself to say, and then blushed violently when his eyes fixed hers in a long, questioning look.

## Thirty-six

Leland Kenniston spent the next two days taking Lucien and his mother to colorful points of interest in and around New York—Castle Garden at Battery Park; an excursion steamer out to the beach at Coney Island; carriage drives through the winding roadways of Central Park. Laure Bouchard was able to witness the contrasts of this teeming city. On the one hand, she saw its tall buildings, elegant shops, and fine restaurants; she saw, too, superbly gowned women entering and leaving luxurious hotels, to the obsequious bowings of hotel doormen, and climbing into carriages attended by liveried coachmen. On the other hand, she saw crowded, filthy tenement-lined streets with pushcarts and half-naked children sleeping in alleyways and crates. Leland, acting as their guide, colored his remarks with many of his own personal opinions and beliefs, so that Laure had further insight into his convictions and his character. His enthusiasms were refreshing for a man of middle years, and he very definitely could not be called an "old sobersides" by any stretch of the imagination.

Lucien did not interfere with them one way or the other. Laure felt that in some ways he acted as a catalyst, for surely Leland Kenniston's efforts to please were directed at him primarily as his imminent traveling companion across the Atlantic to Dublin. But what delighted Laure most was that Leland continued to address her son as he would an adult, and in no way condescendingly; actually, it was as if he knew in advance that young Lucien Bouchard would be quite capable of following the mercurial jumping about of his own mind and his probing commentaries on the New York, as well as the national, scenes.

On the last night before he and Lucien were to board the *Kilkenny*, Leland took them for supper to Delmonico's, where he engaged a private room. The waiter attending them had sandy-red hair and bright blue eyes, and when he spoke, his brogue betrayed his origins even before he introduced himself as Michael O'Grady. The man looked at Leland and did a comical double take. "By all the saints that's holy, if it isn't Leland Kenniston in the flesh, praise be!"

Laure was taken aback and stared first at the man, and then at Leland, her lips quivering as if she were uncertain whether to let her expression grow into a smile or a frown of outrage. But Leland swiftly put her at ease by remarking jocularly, "By all the saints yourself, Michael Aloysius O'Grady—and who would have thought that you would be employed by a place as high class as Delmonico's after your wild Fenian diatribes in our fair city?"

The lanky, jovial waiter burst into laughter, slapped his thigh, then clapped Leland Kenniston on the back and turned to Laure Bouchard with an apologetic "Begging your pardon, madame, I forgot myself. Sure and I didn't expect to see this fine broth of an Irish lad here. We've been old friends ever since he helped me leave me poor father's potato patch in County Clare and come to find work in America so I could send money back to the old country."

"It was my pleasure, Michael," Leland said simply. "But tell me, how is your mother?"

"Faith, she's with the angels now, Leland—ah, I'm forgetting me manners—it's Mr. Kenniston now. Yes, I had a letter from the parish priest just three months ago—me mother was all of eighty, and she died in her sleep holding the crucifix, the blessed crucifix. She had been writing a letter, which she never got to finish, bless her soul, and her priest, Father McGrew, was kind enough to send it to me. And it was he who saw to the service for me poor mother."

"I'm sorry to hear that, Michael," Leland responded kindly. Then, changing the subject, he continued, "But now, these people are my guests. This is Mrs. Bouchard, who is spending her last night in New York, and I'm taking her fine son Lucien here off to Dublin with me to Father O'Mara's St. Timothy's Academy. So if I can prevail upon you to make some suggestions, let us plan a memorable supper such as only Delmonico's can prepare for those who can appreciate it."

"Certainly, Mr. Kenniston. You have me complete attention." The waiter took a pad from his formal coat pocket and solemnly poised a pencil above it. "If I might suggest, Mrs. Bouchard," Michael O'Grady said in a professional tone quite unlike his earlier brash manner, "we have fine mussels and clams. Perhaps you would care for a dish of these to start your dinner, with some chilled hock, or, if you fancy it, a nice Chablis."

Leland hid a smile at this sudden transformation of personality. "You see, Mrs. Bouchard," Leland whimsically interposed, "my friend here is a prince of waiters—when he can be drawn to remember his duties and to forget, at least for the moment, that he is one of the officers of the New York Fenian Society."

"I see. And were you instrumental in bringing Mr. O'Grady into that society?" Laure inquired of Leland.

"Begging your pardon, Mrs. Bouchard," the waiter cut in with a grin, "I was a member of the Fenians long before this good man, this Mr. Kenniston, paid me passage to America. But he doesn't believe in charity—no real Irishman wants that, now!—rather, shall we say, it was an investment in souls and in their growth. That's precisely the way he put it to me. He said that I'm to pay him back by me good conduct and becoming the best waiter in all New York—although I will admit I am a long way from being that, at this moment."

Now Laure could no longer contain her laughter, for she was greatly amused, and she saw also that between the lines of this almost farcical dialogue, which one would normally not expect at so elegant a dining establishment, the two men were the best of friends, despite the difference in their social and economic stations. And this in turn served to make her realize that Leland Kenniston was a man of many fascinating parts, all of which she had not yet learned, and that tonight would be her last chance to get to know him better before he would sail with her son across the Atlantic.

"Are they sweet clams, do you think?" she gently asked.

"As sweet as the song from a colleen in Kilarney, who sings to her true love on the mountaintop," the waiter poetically responded.

"Now those I should like to try," Laure replied with a girlish giggle. Catching Leland's approving eye, she found herself not so much wanting to blush as to wink at him, and she very nearly did. "Well then, Mr. O'Grady, what is your suggestion for an entrée?"

"You might consider sirloin tips sautéed in butter and burgundy, on a bed of wild rice with just a hint of almonds and precious herbs. With this, tiny roasted potatoes—"

"I knew that you would work in potatoes somehow," Leland interrupted with a laugh.

"Faith—that's all that Ireland can produce, that and polemics condemning the English landlords, as well you know, Mr. Kenniston." The waiter drew himself up solemnly and almost stared Leland down by way of rebuke.

"That will do very well," Laure interjected. "And some fresh vegetables—new peas and glazed carrots perhaps?" she hinted.

"Consider them already prepared and simmering in butter for you, Mrs. Bouchard."

"That sounds like heaven."

"And to that heaven let me add a bottle of Meursault," Leland now put in.

"A perfect choice, if I may say so, Mr. Kenniston," the waiter agreed, writing industriously on his pad.

"We shall think of dessert and the appropriate accompaniment after we have gorged ourselves on this Lucullan banquet. Oh, heavens, I'd forgotten—" Leland clapped his hand to his forehead, then he turned to young Lucien: "A thousand apologies, Lucien. I forgot to ask you what you would like."

"What you are both having sounds fine to me, Mr. Kenniston."

"I applaud your good judgment. And I think this evening, we might indulge the young man on the eve of his first Atlantic crossing with a sip of wine," Leland declared.

Michael O'Grady snapped his notebook shut with a flourish and avowed, "What a pleasure it is to be serving the likes of a beautiful woman such as this fair lady. Tell me, Mr. Kenniston, perchance does she have some of old Eire in her?"

"I don't believe so. All the same, she's at least as beautiful as any Irish colleen. Now enough of conversation and go to the cook and tell him to outdo himself," Leland commanded with a wave of his hand.

Scarcely had the waiter left the private dining room when Laure put her hand to her mouth and was convulsed with laughter. Tears came to her eyes till at last, controlling herself, she gasped, "I have never in all my life heard such nonsense and yet been so delighted to see how democratic you are, Mr. Kenniston."

"Speaking of democratic, shall we apply our own democracy, and let me call you Laure, while you call me Leland? It is hardly a time to stand on ceremony, what with my escorting your son to Dublin. Can you not, therefore, put an end to this formality between us and let us know each other by our first names?"

"Your point is well taken—Leland."

Leland Kenniston quivered, and his eyes were bright as he smiled back at Laure Bouchard across the table and said very gently, "Bless you, Laure. I have never before heard my name sound so well on anyone's lips."

Dinner was an immense success. For dessert, Leland ordered an English trifle for young Lucien, while Laure decided on assorted cheeses and seasonable fruits, with imported crackers accompanying the cheese.

As the waiter served dessert, he leaned forward and, in almost a conspiratorial whisper, proposed, "May I suggest, Mrs. Bouchard, that you round off your repast with our world-famous Irish coffee—black coffee laced with Irish whiskey and a dollop of clotted or whipped cream? True, it may be more appropriate for a wintry night than a summer one, but it will give me great pleasure to have you try so patriotic a conclusion to the most delightful meal I have yet been privileged to serve anyone."

Michael O'Grady stood grinning from ear to ear. Throughout dinner he had assumed a demeanor of swift, observant efficiency, and even if Laure had wished to be critical of his familiarity, no one could have found any fault whatsoever with his service. So she nodded her acquiescence, and this time the waiter permitted himself a broad wink at Leland Kenniston's direction as he went off to have the order filled.

Through the meal, Laure had observed that her handsome escort was directing a good deal of his conversation toward her son, prompting him to draw forth his own feelings and thoughts on a variety of subjects. For his part, Lucien was hugely flattered by being made an active par-

382

ticipant in this conversation, and his own regard for the man who was to take him to Dublin greatly increased. Even Laure was pleasantly surprised to discover some of the concepts that her son harbored in his mind and of which she had had no knowledge until this evening. Leland pleased her with his attention to her son and the level of his discussion.

"And what did you think of the Irish coffee, Laure?" he asked her when she had set down her empty cup.

"It's absolutely delicious! I've heard of it, of course, but until tonight I'd never had any. Thank you for everything. This has really been a magnificent treat for both of us— don't you agree, Lucien, dear?"

"Oh, yes, Mother! The only trouble is, I'll probably think about it at every meal I'll be served at my new school, because I'm sure their food will be nothing like this," young Lucien Bouchard wistfully confessed.

"Not a bit of it!" Leland broke in, his eyes sparkling with merriment. "You're not to think that simply because it's a Catholic school, you'll be confined to stale bread and tepid water. Quite the contrary. St. Timothy's boasts an excellent cook who, I understand, was offered a very lucrative post at Simpson's, one of London's really great restaurants. And she refused it. No, when you've had some of her Irish stew, or her Irish soda bread with raisins, you may remember Delmonico's, but it won't be out of envious despair. And during the winter holidays, Mary Meaghan is said to make plum pudding that would tempt an emperor himself, and rich eggnogs warmed and sprinkled liberally with cinnamon—so you see, Lucien, you won't have to send home to your mother for supplementary rations, I assure you."

Laure burst into silvery laughter at this, and again her eyes dwelt on the Irishman's handsome, intent face. He had echoed her laughter, but when her eyes fixed on him, the laughter died away, and he found himself returning her gaze with an almost poignant yearning. He told himself that while young Lucien Bouchard would certainly brighten the voyage ahead of them, he would not have minded it at all if Laure Bouchard had come alone to New Orleans to meet him and thence to New York for trysting. A most honorable tryst, to be sure: he knew now beyond any shadow of a doubt that he wanted to marry Laure, to be motivated by her own needs, and to channel his energetic enterprises into ways that would gratify her and help her and her children prosper.

After dinner, a leisurely carriage ride took them down Fifth Avenue past the shops, the buildings, the fine hotels—a portrait of New York by gaslight. The silhouette of the skyline in the twilight was magnificent, more enchanting than by day, since the merciful darkness concealed the slums beyond all these elegant establishments. On this August night the humidity from the Atlantic Ocean had come over the city and almost made it seem to Laure Bouchard that she was back in New Orleans, where she had been born . . . back where she had met Luke Bouchard.

The coachman reined in his horses in front of the hotel, and the uniformed doorman came forward, doffing his top hat, to help Laure down first and then Lucien, while Leland, shaking his head with a gracious smile, disembarked by himself and watched mother and son go ahead of him into the lobby. He turned to pay the coachman, and then followed.

As they stood waiting for Leland, Lucien was first to speak. "This vacation has been just wonderful, Mr. Kenniston. I'll remember it all my life! Thanks for taking Mother and me to such exciting places, and thanks for treating me the way you have."

"You're more than welcome, but no thanks are needed— you deserve it, Lucien," the black-haired Irishman genially told him. "Well, you'd best get a good night's sleep. We've a steamship to catch tomorrow."

"He's already packed and ready, Leland," Laure explained. "We can have a leisurely breakfast, I assume?"

"Oh, yes. You can have room service bring it to you. Or if you prefer, we can all meet downstairs in the hotel's dining room." Turning to Lucien, he remarked, "Young man, they'll fatten you up aboard ship if you've a mind to be. They serve a hearty breakfast, then bouillon and crackers at eleven, a heavy lunch at one, afternoon tea—a habit of the English, you understand!—then dinner, and, around eleven o'clock at night, the steward lays out a buffet with all the cold meats not eaten that day. If one wants to put on weight, a ship across the Atlantic is assuredly what the doctor would call for. Well then, I'll bid you both a very pleasant good night." He turned to Laure and held out his hand. "Thank you for your trust in me and for confiding your son to my care. You have my word of honor I shan't let you down."

"I think I know that already, Leland. Good night to you."

He let them go ahead of him in the elevator, and then lit a cigar and went outside again, for the humid night had begun to cool as a salty breeze wafted in from the Atlantic. He puffed at his cigar, watching the neatly formed rings slowly rise, break apart, then disappear. His mind was full of fantasy and longing for Laure, and with it there mingled an excitement over the thought of returning to his homeland, of going back to the very hut where he had been born, and where now an aged aunt lived. He sent her money frequently, urging her to come to America. But she stubbornly refused, saying she had been born in Ireland and she was going to die there. And that was why he was so dedicated to the cause of the Fenians. The lot of the Irish must improve—it must! Perhaps this new man, Parnell, who was making visits to America on behalf of the Irish cause might be the one to solidify all of them back home into something that would not involve bloodshed, or fan the flames of bitter, unforgiving hatred between the English and the Irish. Would God such a thing might happen in his lifetime!

He suddenly realized that the doorman was quizzically studying him, and somehow it irked him because it interrupted the nostalgic, bittersweet mood in which he found himself. With an abrupt gesture, he curtly declared, "I think I'll take a constitutional before I turn in. I'm fine, thank you." And with this, he headed down the sidewalk toward the south.

He thought to himself that his compatriots might describe his feelings at this moment as being those of a man who felt that someone was walking over his grave, or, more poetically, that somewhere in the astral spheres beyond his ken, nebulous spirits were meeting far above this spinning planet and holding discourse on the foibles of mortals far below. He did not know what they had in store for him, only that he was more moved than he had ever been before, feeling a haunting and compelling kind of yearning for Laure that was at once physical and spiritual. Yet he knew that he would not pursue it, because he would not force himself upon anyone—unless he knew that he was wanted. There were, he reflected cynically as he strolled along, advantages in being self-sustaining, self-made; yet for all the discipline and the dedication he had given to shaping his life after the death of his parents, Leland Kenniston had known hours of agonizing loneliness in which not even the knowledge of his own achievements sufficed to content him.

At last, he turned abruptly and walked slowly back to the hotel. There was no purpose in looking backward tonight. It was the night before sailing, and for the next several months he would be plunged into the warm sentimentality of going back to the country of his birth, of accompanying a young man of great promise and seeing that he was settled and comfortable and not plagued by homesickness. He had already appraised young Lucien Bouchard and believed that there was much stern stuff in the youngster. In some ways, Lucien reminded him of himself—except that, when he was Lucien's age, he already had to cope with economic tensions that were beyond his power to ameliorate.

He swore under his breath remembering the waiter at Delmonico's. O'Grady was only one of thousands who had uprooted themselves to come to the United States in the hope of economic freedom, only to find menial work and the grudging condescension of those who supposed themselves to be a man's betters simply because they were affluent and fortunate in the materialistic scheme of things.

He began to examine his own conduct tonight, and he took umbrage against his polemics for his native land: doubtless, he had set Laure Bouchard to thinking him a firebrand, when actually he was merely an idealist who loved Ireland because it was his native land. Then he shrugged and chuckled, for even in the depths of despondency, the Irish have a sense of self-mockery, which allows them to transcend the dour misery of their situations. The fact that he had fixed on Laure Bouchard as the solution to all his needs was exactly the way an idealistic dreamer would behave. He could easily find a mate of any kind to lessen the loneliness of his hours and to give him the illusion of communication and companionship. He could make this trip and find somewhere a young colleen, who would be impressed by his wealth and accept him as an escape from the dreadful drudgery and impecunious realities of her daily life. That was not what he wanted at all; he knew it better than anyone else, and it tortured him to find himself so much the idealist that he was not willing to compromise.

The doorman gave him another strange look, doffed his hat, and wished him a good night, to which Leland Kenniston bade him as much in as genial a tone as he could muster. Then he walked slowly to the elevator and let the liftman take him up to his floor, where he took out his key, entered his room, and began his preparations for sleep.

It was nearly midnight. Lucien had gone to sleep in the adjoining bedroom after an animated and affectionate conversation with his mother. He was excited about the sailing the next day in the company of a man whom he respected and admired, but as a dutiful son, he expressed the hope that his mother would not miss him too much because "I really want to make something of myself. There's so much to learn, so much I don't know, and it's a part of the world I've never even thought of, until now. I'll write all I can, Mother. And you write, too, and tell me about how everyone's doing on Windhaven Plantation. I love you very much, Mother."

She had gone back to her bedroom and hauled her luggage onto her bed, deciding to pack everything but her essentials now, for as soon as she bade her son farewell on the *Kilkenny*, she would return to Windhaven Plantation. She briefly wondered if Geraldine and Lopasuta had arrived back in New Orleans yet, hoping that her friend was feeling better now. How proud Luke would have been of both of them, staunch and courageous against bigotry and the worst kind of prejudice. Thinking about Geraldine and Lopasuta and then, concurrently, about Luke made her remember Luke's house in New Orleans—the one he had occupied in New Orleans when he returned from Windhaven Range following Lucy's death. For a long moment, she thought of that house, and she thought how strange it was that Lopasuta and Geraldine should have rented a dwelling so close to it and so similar in appearance that one might easily at night mistake one for the other! That was where she had come to give Luke the gift of love, with no strings attached, with no stipulations or binding agreement. That night she had known herself to be closer in spirit and in flesh than with any other man she had ever known. There had been a blending of aristocratic intellect and forthright, honest candor in Luke Bouchard, and the one offset by the other had left him unpredictable and yet so very dear to her. With this man, Leland Kenniston, she also sensed a powerful intellect, and, too, on every score he rang true to his ethics, from his patriotism to his feeling for her son, from his beneficent treatment of Lopasuta to arranging to meet Laure in New Orleans to accompany Lucien all the way to New York, and then to taking up the role of guardian—for such he would be on this voyage across the Atlantic.

She caught sight of herself in the oval-shaped framed mirror at her dressing table. Her evening dress of shaded turquoise blue lampas made her look younger than her years, and she knew herself to be desirable. As yet, this enigmatic and yet honest man had shown her no real sign of carnal desire. Was it that he did not wish to be involved? Or was it that he was afraid of her rejection? Or was it because he was considerate and, knowing her to be a widow, refused to prey upon her vulnerability? If the last was true, then he was the most honest and honorable man she had known since Luke's death—and certainly by far the most fascinating.

She turned her attention back to her packing, then paused. For a long moment, she stood staring at the open portmanteau on the large double-sized bed, then her lips curved into a sensuous smile and she stooped to retrieve a lacy chemise. She hurriedly undressed and drew the chemise over her head, being careful not to disturb her chignon; then she moved to the boudoir table. She leaned forward, inspecting herself. The reflection in the mirror was generous: she did not look her thirty-eight years, nor were there any longer hollows under her eyes from the weeping she had done when Luke had been martyred. Now she was stronger, and she felt even younger because desire rose within her, an irrefutable desire insidiously mounting to an ardor that told her she was still a woman capable of desire, and of being desired in turn by a man who was too courteous to express his own needs.

She pulled on a beautifully embroidered cambric wrapper and hastily fastened it. If she were to appear at his door attired thus, at such a late hour, he could not possibly mistake her meaning. It would be the perfect solution, since it solved nothing and yet everything: it would tell her now what he wished of her and also what he would mean to her, and yet because she would be the one making the overtures, he would not have to feel compelled to make a formal declaration. For her, it would requite the loneliness, without binding her to be his for the rest of her days. She could not do that yet, though she knew that she wished for it. For now, she just longed for him as a man. It was in a similar way that she had estimated Luke Bouchard, and if there was a pattern in all of this, then she would abide by it. And if there was no pattern and only the immediate, transitory illusion of yearning flesh, she would not feel sullied or abused or rendered captive to his will.

Once again, she searched the mirror and uttered a long, languorous sigh in the knowledge of what she was about to attempt, and then she smiled at herself almost impishly. She was once again the young, almost giddy girl of New Orleans, of days when the Civil War was still a romantic duel of honorable cavaliers, before the brutality and the deaths and the smuggling and the contemptible greed of contraband runners.

Under her chemise, she was divinely naked, her long legs outlined yet masked by the delicate folds of the sheer cotton lawn. On her feet she placed delicate embroidered kid slippers whose open-heeled design showed off her lovely feet.

Silently tiptoeing to the door between the bedrooms, she listened, her heart pounding. Her young son slept. She turned and moved toward the door of the suite, opened it, and looked carefully down the hall. There was complete stillness. A single domed gaslight sent an eerie brightness along the carpeted hallway.

Leland Kenniston's room was beyond the bend in the hallway, and Laure mused that this, indeed, was a turning point for them both. She could not control the warm glow of her skin, which she could feel penetrating through the two layers of fabric, and the quivering of her muscles and the tenseness in her shoulders as she willed this to happen. She knew that an insatiable and overpowering curiosity had led her to this overt act of seeking him out, rather than letting him make the first approach toward her. And because she could do this, she could tell herself that it meant only what the moment meant, nothing more and nothing less, and thus she was absolved from the burden of a guilty conscience.

She had tucked the key to her suite in the little side pocket of her dressing gown, and she felt for it now. Its cold firmness was reassurance that she was free to turn back, even now—and he would never know what she had almost attempted. Or if she crossed that Rubicon, making the first approach to him and daring the danger of having him consider her a mere sensual wanton, then the key would return her to the normalcy of her widowhood, and no one except the two of them would know what would transpire between now and the hour of dawn.

She drew a deep breath and closed her door till she heard the click of the lock. Then she moved noiselessly down the carpeted hallway till she came to the numbered room she knew to be his. Glancing warily to either side of the hallway, she raised her right hand and knocked quickly and softly, once, twice, and after a tiny pause, a third time.

For a moment, she was afraid, and she very nearly turned back to her own suite; then she heard Leland's footsteps. The knob turned, the door was opened, and he stood there in his nightshirt staring at her, incredulous, his eyes wide with surprise. "L–Laure—I—" he began, his voice hoarse and trembling.

She put a finger to her lips, shook her head, and moved inside, putting her hand to the knob of the door and closing it. Then she turned to him, and she whispered, "I had to know. I wasn't sure, but from the way you spoke and the way you looked at me tonight . . . I'm here now. I know that you want me—or at least, I think you do, Leland."

There was a moment's pause, which seemed to her an eternity, as she saw several expressions pass in quick succession over Leland's face. Then at last he spoke in a hoarse whisper.

"Oh, my God, *want* you! Oh, my beautiful Laure—oh, yes, yes, my dearest darling—you don't know how I've dreamed this might happen—but I couldn't and wouldn't tell you—I had no right—"

"Hush," she whispered, putting her fingertip to his lips. "Don't talk. Make me feel wanted. I need to feel wanted, Leland."

"As do I, my beautiful Laure." His fingers gently, reverently, brushed her shoulders, moved down her lissome back, and he sucked in his breath as he felt that, under this thin covering, she was completely naked, his for the taking.

Then with a groan of pent-up desire, his arms locked around her, and his mouth sought hers. Instantly, with an answering moan of desire, of need and of yearning so great

390

it could not be expressed in words, Laure Bouchard met his kiss, and her lips opened, flowering, moist and warm and desirous.

His hands began to explore her, and finding the fastenings of her wrapper, he swiftly undid the hooks and drew the delicate garment from her shoulders. Clad now only in the sheer silken chemise, Laure realized there was no profane impetuosity to the way his fingers moved: they were adoring, hesitant, worshipful, and as yearning as she had dreamed they would be. He slipped the lacy straps down her arms and she felt her bosom bared, felt the frock slip to her hips and uttered a groan of torment as her need rose swiftly within her.

Their lips fused, and his fingertips touched and lingeringly palpated the warm hollow of her sculptured, naked back, then brushed with reverent adoration the highperched, still flawless globes of her swelling breasts.

There was no further need for words, there was nothing save their mutual desire for each other—to serve and be served, to love and be loved, and above all else to share.

He lifted her in his arms and carried her toward the huge bed. She closed her eyes and shivered, wishing it with all her might, hoping he would not condemn her for such audacity. And yet, intuitively she understood it was the only way to draw him from his self-imposed denial of her ardent womanhood.

He had been all she had dreamed he might be, and more: virile and yet considerate, reverent and yet ardent. In the throes of passion, she had felt her nails dig into his back, heard him gasp with the sweet pain, and in her turn had arched to the maddening fusion of their bodies.

He turned to her afterwards, and his voice was hoarse and trembling as he said, "Please, Laure, marry me."

"Leland, you don't have to say that. I'm a widow with children, not an innocent girl."

"But I want to marry you. I love you, I want to be with you the rest of my life."

"My sweet," she whispered, as she linked an arm around his neck and turned to merge herself against him. As his hands grasped her waist, as she felt the thrilling nearness of their bodies, she murmured, "Leland, I care for you more than any other man I've met since Luke's death. But you must give me time. I admire you and respect you for all you've done, and for the way you've taken to Lucien—I can't tell you what it means to me. I know you mean every word of it, but—oh, please, don't rush me!"

"I won't. But, is there hope?"

"I—I'll say only this: there—there isn't any other man I'd marry at this moment—if I felt ready to marry."

She heard him sigh. The darkness was sweet and good to them as lovers for the first time, each alone with private thoughts, yet mindful of the other's yearnings. And then he murmured, as his lips fixed on her shoulder, "I'll have to be content with that, my dearest Laure. But there'll never be any other woman for me. I can't tell you in words what I feel—but believe me when I tell you that I'm not saying these things just—just to be with you—"

"I know that, Leland. I already knew you weren't a man who pursued a woman just for his own pleasure. But you know, too, that, in this day and age, a woman has every right to her own self-indulgence. Let's say that, because I was so drawn to you, I came to you. But take heart in the fact that I wouldn't have gone to just any man—I came to you."

"Yes. I'll remember this all my life. But my dear Laure, one day I'll make you admit that we could be very happy together. Believe that, because I pledge it."

"I believe you. Now hold me again. It will soon be dawn, and this day will part us—you to go to Ireland with my son, I back to Windhaven Plantation."

## Thirty-seven

A waiter delivered breakfast to Laure Bouchard and her son at ten o'clock the next morning. When Laure opened the door after the waiter had identified himself, she was startled to see the splendid service of white linen tablecloth and the finest silver and Delft china, and, most elegant of all, a silver vase in which a single yellow rose was placed. "The compliments of Mr. Kenniston, madam," the waiter deferentially explained. "May I come in and serve you?"

"Why—yes—over here by the sofa will be fine. Lucien, breakfast is here—are you dressed?"

From the adjoining room came a hearty, "Yes, Mother, I'll be right there!"

Laure looked for her reticule to give the waiter a tip, but he, anticipating her gesture, politely interposed, "Mr. Kenniston has most generously taken care of everything, madam. I trust you will enjoy your breakfast."

As the door closed behind him, Laure stared at the yellow rose and a warm flood of crimson suffused her cheeks. It had been a night of utter ecstasy. Perhaps she should be feeling more audacious, more wanton, in having sought out a man who had been a virtual stranger—but he was a stranger no longer. Even if she had been only a coquette seeking a transient hour or two of carnal pleasure, she could not have forgotten him: he had been the most considerate of lovers, tender, passionate, and eager, grateful for her response, which matched his own, and never overtly possessive or smugly triumphant over what many men would have called a "conquest." He had evinced as a lover those same admirable characteristics that she had observed in his behavior and his conversation and his thoughtfulness as host and guide. She thought back to what she had told him just before they had parted, when she had slipped back to her room and gone back to bed and lain there for hours, cherishing her memories of that idyllic night: although she was not yet ready to remarry, there was no other man she would rather take as husband. Yes—it was surely, candidly true.

She found herself ravenously hungry as she looked over the breakfast Leland had ordered. There were kippered herrings, a large platter of assorted omelets, delicate sliced potatoes fried to a golden brown, pumpernickel and rye toast, together with a pitcher of chilled, freshly squeezed orange juice.

Their luggage was ready, for Lucien's school trunk had been carefully packed before Laure and he had left Lowndesboro. She had taken along a valise for the nominal changes he would be required to make during the week they had spent on board ship and in New York, and now that, too, was ready. A bellman appeared and took the luggage, and

Laure turned to look down the carpeted hallway toward Leland Kenniston's room. Seeing her movement, the bellman volunteered, "The gentleman is already in the lobby, madam. He has a carriage, which will take you and young Mr. Bouchard to the pier."

"Why, thank you, that's very kind of you."

Leland had engaged the hotel's coach, for like all luxury hotels, the Fifth Avenue had its own stable of carriages for its guests, to carry them to and from railroad terminals and piers. He gave the driver the directions, and the coachman flourished his long carriage whip and flicked it above the two roan mares.

Leland had, with the utmost tact, seated himself at the far right, with young Lucien placed between him and Laure. He chatted amiably of the other sights they had not yet seen, but perhaps one day, when all of them had more time, could be enjoyed. Then, turning to Lucien, he gently asked, "You don't feel any last-minute hesitation, do you, Lucien?"

"Oh, no, Mr. Kenniston! I'm very anxious to make this trip." Then, almost contritely, the tall youth turned to his mother and murmured, "Of course, I'll miss you, Mother. But I'll be so busy working at my studies that I probably won't feel homesickness so much."

"Of course; I understand, my darling," she replied gently.

She glanced warily at Leland, and for an instant their eyes met. She could read the adoration in them, and she lowered her gaze at once, adjusting her traveling bag in her lap and turning to look through the window. Thus far, he had shown the utmost discretion and thoughtfulness, and there had been no wayward gesture or embarrassing word that might have mystified young Lucien. She mentally marked this down as still another point on the ledger in his favor.

The coach reached the pier, and Leland Kenniston got out and beckoned to two stevedores from the *Kilkenny* to take the luggage and place it aboard. His own steamer trunk was already on board, having been sent from his town house by his maid. Laure retained her large portmanteau; her own ship back to New Orleans was at a nearby wharf, and although she was not scheduled to leave until evening, Laure knew she could board it whenever she wished. Leland helped her get down from the carriage, and the touch of his hand sent tingling waves of excitement through her, reminding her of their magical night together. He had made her feel so totally a woman, and his adoration of her body had restored all her physical self-esteem. He had given her no reason to regret the maturity of her body; as a lover, he had complimented her so intensely on her beauty that she had wondered if even the darkness could hide her blushes.

An arm around young Lucien's shoulders, Leland moved toward the gangplank. Just then, two stevedores appeared carrying a heavy wooden crate between them, and Leland saw the shipping label, his eyes widening as he turned back to Laure. "I would bet anything that this is a shipment of rifles from the Fenian Society in Chicago to the Irish patriots in Belfast, Laure. It's a dangerous fight they're waging."

Overhearing this, a young bearded man contemptuously broke in, "Here's one of those fancy snobs who wish the Irish would be buried in their own potato fields and doesn't want to see guns sent to them so they can put some of those damned English landlords six feet under!"

"I'm not a snob, and I'm as Irish as you are—I was conceived and born in County Mayo," Leland replied hotly. "I simply wish there were another way. There is a need for a forum, an exchange of ideas between representatives from the governments involved—the English as well as the Irish—the best, wisest spokesmen on either side."

"Sure, and by that time, there won't be an Ireland left, mister!" the hotheaded young man angrily retorted. "You may be an Irishman, but you're not my kind!"

"Nor are you mine, if you think the only solution is through blood and death," Leland retorted indignantly. Then, apologetically, he said to Laure, "I'm sorry. I begin to see that my idealism is at times misplaced. I know that educational processes take long years, and in fact the young man may be right—violence may indeed by the only weapon the poor have against rich usurpers who have all the laws on their side."

"I think it's exciting," young Lucien Bouchard murmured as he watched the two stevedores carry the heavy crate up the gangplank and disappear down into the hold of the steamship. Then, addressing Leland Kenniston, he asked, "It's really true, then, that there are a lot of Americans who send arms to the Irish in their struggle for freedom?"

"Yes, Lucien. But when you get older, you'll learn that no one ever wins a war except the munitions makers, the profiteers, and the top government officials who find it expedient. Father O'Mara will teach you about the Crusades. You'll learn that under the guise of Christian salvation, the knights who went off to punish the infidels were even more barbarous than the Saracens. And you'll read about the Children's Crusade, blessed by the Pope himself, in which all those poor children were sent off as a mission, only to be sold into slavery. No, we simply don't learn from history. There was a man by the name of Malthus, who conceived a theory that holds that if there are too many people in the world, war or famine or pestilence will level the score and make things all right again. It is an abominable theory, but then Malthus was an English clergyman and economist, which may explain it—and I shall never subscribe to it. Forgive me again, Laure. I seem to be standing upon a soapbox." He gave an apologetic chuckle and a shrug, then turned to Lucien. "We'd best get aboard. Say your goodbyes to your mother."

Laure hugged her son, and exclaimed, "I hope you have a wonderful time, Lucien, and write as often as you can. I want to know everything you're doing and thinking, and how you like your teachers, and what you think of Ireland. Mr. Kenniston will be your good friend, like a kind of uncle."

"I shall, indeed! He's a fine boy, and he'll be a still better man. But then, he has a wonderful mother," the black-haired Irishman murmured. Laure Bouchard's heart-shaped face crimsoned as she lowered her eyes at this effusive compliment.

Young Lucien Bouchard disengaged himself from his mother's embrace and turned eagerly to Leland Kenniston, his eyes shining. "I'm ready now, Mr. Kenniston."

"Good! Well, Laure, it's been wonderful meeting you and knowing you. You can be sure I'll take very good care of your son. He's going to be a delightful companion on our journey across the Atlantic, and I rather think that I'll learn a great deal from him." He came to her and held out his hand, and she shook it. Once again, the tingling in her body told her that this man was one of the most fascinating and magnetic she had ever known. She did not know where their destinies would lead them, but she knew that if she was fated to remarry, here was the man who would fulfill her every yearning and every need.

## Thirty-eight

After having concluded the deal with Maxwell Grantham, purchasing the necessary supplies, and resting up sufficiently, Ramón ordered the Windhaven Range outfit to head back for home without delay. Though the July weather boded well for their return, Ramón knew that sudden summer storms, flash floods, even tornados, could impede their progress. This, plus the fact that they still planned to stop at the Creek reservation, dictated that they should leave as quickly as possible. Grantham had paid in both gold and a bank draft, adding considerably to the army draft. Ramón had no desire to lose any of it to bushwhackers, remembering only too well the attack launched upon them by Jack Hayes and his renegades. Accordingly, he had cleverly hidden the drafts, as well as the gold, in a secret compartment in the false bottom of one of the chuck wagons, and he let Hugo Bouchard drive it, while Francisco Lorcado drove the other. They headed due east, and on the second day out, near the little town of Las Animas, they crossed the Purgatoire River, a tributary of the mighty Arkansas River, along whose banks they rode.

The men were in good spirits, but they still mourned their companions who had been killed by the bushwhackers. Lucas acted as second in command, warning all the vaqueros to keep their carbines and rifles and pistols loaded and ready, in the event another attempt should be made upon them. To be sure, the alteration of the route back would minimize the danger, although they had over one thousand miles to journey. The only real encumbrances were the two chuck wagons, but because there were no tiring hours of watching the herd and worrying about stampedes and difficult river crossings, they could easily average from thirty to thirty-five miles a day. With luck, Ramón had estimated that they should be back by about the first week of September.

Lucas was acting as scout, riding ahead of the other vaqueros, when he suddenly reined in his mustang. He shouted and waved his sombrero. "There's a man lying over there by a spruce tree, Ramón! He's not moving."

"Felipe, you go along with Lucas and keep your carbine handy, in case it's some sort of decoy for an ambush," Ramón shouted to the sturdy vaquero, who nodded, wheeled his horse to the south, and galloped toward Lucas. The two riders then rode one hundred yards and approached the still form. Lucas dismounted, cocking his weapon and advancing in a wary crouch. He turned back to Felipe. "He's an old man. There's no sign of hoofprints—poor devil, what in the world can he be doing out here? He doesn't have a weapon, not even a holstered pistol. You'd better go back and tell Ramón."

Lucas detached the canteen from the pommel of his saddle and hurried back to the unconscious figure. The man lay on his side, one hand over his weather-beaten, angular face as if to shield himself from the bright July sun, the other holding his knee.

Very gently, Lucas put out his left hand and touched the old man's shoulder. He had a grizzled, shaggy beard nearly to his waist, and on his left temple there was an ugly, purple bruise. Again, Lucas gently touched him, and was rewarded by a twitching of the old man's eyelids. "Here now, you'll be all right. You're with friends. Drink this. I'm here to help you, mister," Lucas said in a soothing voice.

The old man groaned softly, slowly rolled over onto his back, and, his hand still over his eyes, murmured vaguely in so feeble a voice that Lucas had to bend down to hear it, "Thank God—help me sit up. I'm just about done in—"

"Sure, stranger, I'll help you. I'll put my arm around your shoulders and lift you up slow and easy," Lucas assured him. The old man groaned again as Lucas carefully lifted him to a sitting position, his strong arm bracing the bony, narrow shoulders. He proffered his canteen to the old man's mouth, carefully tilting it.

The old man emitted a feeble cackle. "I 'preciate your

ministerin', sonny, but I got all the water I need right here in this river. Now, if you got a spot of grub in your saddlebag, that'd revive me right quick, I reckon!" He laughed again, then continued, "Don't get me wrong, sonny—you're a real lifesaver. I was just about givin' up hope of ever seein' anybody again. I ain't got no food an' my leg's hurt so's I couldn't get me to any place other than this here tree." With a heavy sigh, the white-haired man blinked his eyes and at last stared at Lucas. "Why, you—you're a nigger—"

"I may well be," Lucas responded dryly, "but as you said, I've also saved your life! I'm with an outfit that just took a herd from Texas up here and we're on our way back home. Luckily, I happened to see you lying here. What happened to you? You don't have a horse, and there's a bad bruise on your head."

"Sure oughta be." The old man cackled again. "Three fellers came on me a couple of days back—I don't even know what day it is, for a fact. See, I was on my way back north after visitin' a friend's ranch when they jumped me. They took my horse, what vittles I had, and the bit of money I had in my poke—everything. I tried to fight them off, but the biggest feller—the head of the gang, I s'pose—he kicked me real hard in my leg, then he whacked me on the noggin with the butt of his Colt. I heard him say to his partners as they rode off that I'd be meat for the buzzards purty soon—an' I guess I sure would have been, if you hadn't found me."

"Tell you what—I'll help you climb onto my saddle and we'll ride over to the chuck wagons. There you can lie down and rest a while. We'll be making camp pretty soon, and then we'll fill you up with some real good beef and beans and biscuits and whatever."

"Ain't words enough to thank you for what you're doin' for me, stranger."

"My name's Lucas—Lucas Forsden."

"Me, I'm Frank Scolby. Prospectin's my trade. Been all through Colorady for the last ten years. Would you believe I was in that gold rush back in Californy when old Cap'n Sutter found out there was gold by his mill? I was just a young buck then, 'bout twenny-five, near's I can recollect. I had me a wife then, but she died and my kid died a year later—so I just went on prospectin'. Never hit nothin' much till a couple of weeks back—then I hit it big!"

At this moment, Ramón rode up with Felipe. Dismounting, the two men came over to where Lucas was kneeling beside the prospector.

"Ramón, this man was left out here to die, but I think he'll be okay."

Lucas briefly told Ramón all that the prospector had said, turning to look at the old man every now and then for confirmation. "I told him he could lie down in the chuck wagon and rest, and then we'd let him eat his fill."

"Of course we will. Here, I'll give you a hand with him, Lucas. Easy now, Mr. Scolby, we've got you safe and sound now," Ramón assured the prospector. The two men carefully mounted the bearded old man onto Lucas's horse, leading the animal slowly over to the chuck wagon driven by Francisco Lorcado. They eased him off the horse, then Lucas spread a bedroll on the floor of the wagon before helping the prospector lie down. "There now. I'm sure I can rustle up a couple of biscuits or something just to take the edge off your hunger. Then you should get some rest—and be sure I'll wake you in time for chow," Lucas declared with a grin.

"Mighty grateful—thank you, Lucas. I—I'm real sorry I called you a nigger—"

"It doesn't matter. I know you didn't mean it disrespectfully. By the way, this is Ramón Hernandez. He's the trail boss." Lucas gestured toward Lucien Edmond's handsome brother-in-law.

"If that don't beat all—a Mex and a—well—anyhow, it's sure funny, 'cause you two have treated me better 'n I've been treated in a helluva long time, I can tell you that. I'm grateful for your offer—I'm plumb tuckered out."

"Sure you are. Like I said, I'll wake you up when the beef's ready for you, old timer." Lucas grinned as he closed the flap at the back of the chuck wagon.

Several hours later, just after sundown, Lucas and Ramón went back to the chuck wagon with plates of cooked beef, biscuits, and beans, and found Frank Scolby sitting up and wanly rubbing a hand over his deeply lined, sun-bronzed forehead. His eyes brightened at the sight and the smell of the food. The two men handed him one of the tin plates, a knife and fork, and watched as the prospector ate as if it had been the first time in weeks. With hardly a moment's pause, he seized the second plate and fell to it with an unabated appetite, while Ramón and Lucas exchanged a pitying look. Finally Ramón genially interposed, "*Amigo*, I think you've had enough. You mustn't overdo it. There's more if you want it later, but slow down now."

"Sure—you're right. God, that was good! Ain't had vittles like that in years." He laughed with glee and declared, "You fellers saved my life, and now you treat me like a king. Won't ever forget it, not Frank Scolby. You got my word on it."

After a brief pause, he spoke again, with more animation now. His eyes were gleaming as he stared at both Ramón and Lucas, and then he chuckled almost grimly. "I thought for a spell there those bushwhackers would steal my fortune—but they didn't find it. You fellers saw to it that I'm still alive and rich."

"Rich?" Lucas echoed, mystified, as he glanced at Ramón, who shrugged.

"Sure. Listen, like I told you, I've been minin' for years. Never found much—just enough to get by, buy supplies, keep on goin' all the time, hopin' I'd make a big strike. Well, I finally did. I'm tellin' you this because you fellers saved my life, that's what. I ain't had much learnin', but I know enough that when somebody does me a good favor the way you fellers did, it's up to me to pay 'em back. That's what the Good Book says, anyhow, and that's what I'm gonna do."

"You don't owe us anything. We wouldn't go off and see anyone die, so don't talk about paying us back, *amigo*," Ramón assured him.

But Scolby shook his head and then leaned forward, a crafty look coming into his faded blue eyes. "Lookee here. I told you I made a strike, a big one. No, it ain't gold—it's silver. See, I got me to Leadville when word got out of all the strikes bein' made up that way. Well, miners was thicker'n flies on a hog an' I thought my chances was damn slim at best of findin' anything. But I was sludging up a stream that nobody had worked nigh unto a month ago, and I came across this placer, and I couldn't believe it. I tracked it down to a sort of hill with a lot of heavy rocks and boulders and caves. There'd been a stream running from there—it's mostly dried up now—and I guess some of the silver worked loose and came down in this placer, down to where I was sludging. Well, sir, there was a vein there, way at the back of the cave. I guess it was nature did it— we don't ask questions when we find somethin' like that;

we're just mighty grateful. Anyway, I chiseled me off a hunk of rock out of the vein, got me back to Leadville right quick, and—after verifyin' that the spot hadn't been staked out yet—recorded my claim. Then I took that old chunk of rock to the assay office and—well, lookee here. Ain't no sense my tellin' you when you can see for yourselves. Help me off with my boot, will you?"

Mystified, Lucas did as he was bidden, and took hold of the old man's outstretched right leg. Grabbing the heel of the worn boot, he pulled until it came off. Wordlessly, Scolby reached into the boot and pulled out a creased piece of parchment and handed it to Ramón.

Ramón almost ceremoniously unfolded the paper, glancing up to watch the old prospector's grinning face, then read aloud: "Adolph Schmidt's Assay Office. And it's dated May 15, 1879. 'I hereby certify that the specimen of ore said to have been taken from Leadville County Lode, Nevada District, Colorado, assayed by the undersigned for Mr. Frank Scolby gave the following result: Silver, per ton of 2000 lbs.—2300 ounces per ton'—*Madre de Dios!*" Ramón broke off to exclaim, "that comes to almost three thousand dollars per ton!"

Frank Scolby chuckled at the shocked expression on Ramón's handsome face. "Yep! Told you fellers I finally struck it rich." He cackled with laughter and pointed a bony forefinger at the paper. "Now, if those bushwhackers had been a little smarter, they might've found that there paper with my claim number on it, made tracks back to Leadville, and stolen my mine out from under me. They'd have been a damn sight richer than they could ever get by holdin' up a lot of folks along the trail!"

Ramón quickly asked, "What were you doing out here, anyway, Señor Scolby?"

"Like I told your friend here," the old man began, "I was comin' back from visitin' a friend of mine who has a small ranch some twenty miles east of here. See, I plumb ran out of money, so I needed a grubstake to work the mine. I thought of this friend of mine, thinkin' he might have the capital to invest for equipment and the like and we'd go partners. Turned out he's just barely makin' it. Anyway, I got on my horse and was headed back to Leadville where I figgered I could find me someone who was lookin' to back a claim—hell, there's been twenty thousand miners pourin' in the place in the last two years. And last year alone some twelve million dollars worth of silver was shipped out of the district. Then those three bastids jumped me—well, that brings us up to date. And I want to make you fellers a proposition: for savin' my life, if you put up the grubstake, I'll cut you in fifty-fifty. How's that sound?"

"Señor Scolby," Ramón replied, "I wouldn't think of taking silver from you in return for food and rest. I'd be no better than those bushwhackers if I did that. But I would like to propose that you come back with us to Windhaven Range and meet my partner and brother-in-law, Lucien Edmond Bouchard. I'm sure that Señor Bouchard will put up all the money and the men needed to do the mining. He's an honest man, I give you my word on it; you'll be rich, Señor Scolby, and you can take it easy for the rest of your days.

"If you decide to become partners with Señor Bouchard—and you can work out the details of the partnership with him when we reach the ranch—he'll make sure that you get every penny that's due you, and you won't ever have to go prospecting again," Ramón concluded.

"Suits me fine." Frank Scolby uttered a long sigh and then grinned, "I paid my dues all these years lookin' for a really rich claim, and now I figger I'm a mite too old to work this mine that way it should be, so I'd just as soon let you go ahead with the hard work."

Ramón shook his head slowly, then inquired, "I am reluctant to let you give up so much money, Señor Scolby. Are you really sure you want to be so generous?"

"Damn right I am, Mr. Hernandez. Like I said, you and Lucas here saved my life—and you didn't ask any questions or nothin'. Sure I want to divvy it up with you. You just take me to this partner of yours. By that time, my leg should be okay, and I'll ride back to Leadville with him myself to show him the mine personally. Incidentally," the old prospector suddenly looked embarrassed and sheepish, "I'm sorry I called you a Mex, Mr. Hernandez. And I'm damn sorry I called you a nigger, Lucas."

"*No te preocupa, amigo*. Forget it. Now, perhaps another cup of coffee?"

"Sure wouldn't mind it."

"And a little *aguardiente*. Lucas, ask Felipe if he will part with some of his brandy for Señor Scolby. It'll help him sleep like a baby," Ramón directed with a grin.

\* \* \*

403

On the way over to Wichita—the first leg of their journey back to Windhaven Range—the old miner regaled the vaqueros with tales of prospectors and his own adventures. He had regained much of his vitality, thanks to plenty of nourishing food and rest, and he spoke loquaciously. "You know, everybody was talking back in Leadville about old Horace Austin Warner Tabor. He started out as a stoncutter back in Vermont, and then back in the 'fifties, there was talk of gold strikes in Colorady—me, I was too busy mining out in the Sierras to take much heed of that. Anyhow, this feller, Tabor, he had a wife, Augusta, and she ran a boarding house, then a bakery, then a grocery store, and she thought her husband was plumb loco to go dreamin' about strikin' it rich. But a couple of years back, old Horace bought a third interest in the Little Pittsburgh Silver Mine. And darned if he didn't get a bonanza strike. When I started out and found me this here strike I'm tellin' you about, there was talk in Leadville that old Horace was goin' to sell his interest in the minin' company for a million dollars. He'd already taken an option on what he called the Matchless Mine, and he owned a half-interest in the First National Bank of Denver. Land's sakes, they said he was takin' in a hundred thousand dollars a month and backin' every mine and prospector around him for miles!"

He chuckled and shook his head. "You know, it's a funny thing. An old prospector pal of mine, Dan Robbins—he never had much better luck than I did till I found this here mine—anyhow, just before I started out on this trip, he said that old Horace's wife, Augusta, didn't take kindly to his bein' so rich, and that there was going to be plenty of trouble. Hee, hee, mebbe that's why I never got myself hitched up again, though I can tell you there were lots of purty gals around the minin' camps in them days." He uttered a sigh of nostalgia. "But then was then and now is now—and now is when all of us are gonna be rich!"

Hugo Bouchard was pleased that Manuel Olivera—thoroughly convalesced by now from his wound—was keeping him company and relieving his boredom by taking turns handling the horses of the chuck wagon, tying his mustang to the back of the wagon. The vaquero was still profoundly grateful to young Hugo for the medical skill he had shown, and had told all the other vaqueros that "If it hadn't been for the young Señor Bouchard, I wouldn't be going back to Windhaven Range with you, *mis amigos.*"

Despite the knowledge that the drive was over, and that he was at last going home to his parents and to his sisters, young Hugo was more impatient than he'd ever been in all his life. For now he knew that he would never again go out on a cattle drive, and that he wanted no part of ranch life, and he therefore wanted this journey over with as quickly as possible. He had found himself. He had actually helped to save human life, and that made him determined to pursue medicine as a career. He knew that he would ask his father if he might go to medical school in the fall.

One thing was certain: from now on, Hugo Bouchard was going to be his own man. He was stronger, wirier, in better health than he had ever been before. He had had the companionship of men with completely different backgrounds and been accepted by them. He had sought no favors and been granted none; he had shared the dangers and hardships of a cattle drive and, though inwardly disenchanted with this particular type of life, he was deeply grateful for the experience. Without it, he might never have known what his career was really to be. And the leisurely pace set by Ramón very nearly exasperated him, so eager was he to announce his decision to his parents.

### *Thirty-nine*

Ramón Hernandez was almost completely silent during the two days since they had come upon the old prospector. Ramón was doing a great deal of thinking, some of it nostalgic with a retrospective look into the past, but most of it toward the future. In his view, the sprawling cattle ranch near Carrizo Springs was now well established and the Bouchard name a byword for prime beef and honest dealing. With railroad feeder lines certain to be extended within the next year or two, there would be far less open range than ever before. Long drives such as the one they had just completed would become more difficult or more infrequent. Perhaps it was time to think about diversifying the Windhaven operation. Perhaps it was time to look elsewhere for new ventures and enterprises that would develop additional resources for all those who worked and lived on Windhaven Range.

Ramón was an idealist and had been since his boyhood, when he had been obliged to watch his father being put to death. Out of his desire for vengeance against such oppression, he had joined the guerrilla army of a man who had claimed to be a liberator, but who instead had been a ruthless opportunist who preyed on the poor and the vulnerable. Thanks to the Bouchards, Ramón's life had been saved, and now he was one of them by marriage to Mara Bouchard.

There stirred in him the thought that Frank Scolby's silver mine might well offer an entirely new livelihood, perhaps even a new way of life for his relatives by marriage, for Mara, and their children; but most of all, it would be a long-deferred payment of a debt which he owed the Bouchards for having saved his life and given him a chance to begin all over again. He had been really surprised that the old prospector's story was not simply one of those fantasies that frustrated old men often have after a lifetime of wandering and searching for gold, or silver, or jewels, or the Fountain of Youth, as Ponce de León had sought to find. He understood that all men have dreams that inspire and motivate them. For some, it was the cross of religious freedom; for others, the more materialistic ones, it was the glint of gold and silver and precious stones; and for still others, the uncelebrated and the unheroic, it was the longing for a purposeful life—a family, a home, love and loyalty and devotion. When all was said and done, perhaps that last treasure was the richest of all.

Still, Ramón smiled wryly to himself, having a large share in a silver mine was not something he would turn down! Especially this mine, one that—from the assayer's statement—might prove to be one of the richest silver mines in Colorado . . . a mine not to be compared with John Tabor's Matchless Mine, to be sure, but one that would provide a constant source of wealth to its owners for at least the next five years.

When the men reached Wichita, they stopped half a day to buy another wagon to be loaded with food, blankets, clothing, and trinkets for the people of the Creek reservation. While the vaqueros were seeing to the purchase and loading of the wagon, Ramón and Hugo went to Dr. Ben Wilson's house, where they were greeted warmly by Elone and the Wilson children. Hugo in particular was disappointed to learn that Ben Wilson himself was out of town for a few days, paying calls on patients whose farms and ranches were more than a day's journey from Wichita. The Quaker doctor had begun, in the past year or so, to make such swings through the surrounding counties on a regular basis, for the region was still short of qualified physicians.

Elone insisted upon serving Ramón and his nephew a hearty lunch, and she assured them that Ben would be eager to see Hugo one day soon, particularly now that he was planning to study medicine. Then, in the early afternoon, the two Texans took their leave, rejoining the vaqueros and riding with them toward the village where Sipanata was now *mico*.

At the village, the sturdy chief of the Creeks ordered the villagers to prepare a feast at which the vaqueros of Windhaven Range would be honored and welcome guests. Young Hugo Bouchard, sitting beside his uncle, heard from Sipanata the story that Lucien Edmond often told: how the Bouchards had helped the displaced onetime rulers of the South, and also how the white-eyes shaman, Dr. Ben Wilson, had come to live with them to heal their sick and to prove the goodness in his heart, so that the Creeks would not hate all white-eyes. Ramón added, "You may recall, Hugo, that after Dr. Wilson left, he arranged to have a regular army doctor visit here every month. And he did that through the honest Indian agent whose appointment Ben Wilson ensured by writing an angry letter to the Indian Bureau in Washington. That letter demanded a replacement for the greedy, evil man who, taking the money allotted by the government for these poor people, got them only the worst food and clothing and pocketed the difference."

"Yes, Ben Wilson is a remarkably kind and caring man, Uncle Ramón," Hugo thoughtfully said. "I wish he had been there when we stopped by to see him in Wichita."

"Yes, I know," Ramón replied, "and unfortunately there

really wasn't time this trip—because of Frank Scolby's mine—to stay overnight and await his return. But let's hope that the Wilsons will be visiting the ranch again someday soon. Or it may be that we'll all have occasion to visit Dr. Wilson in Wichita, one of these days."

Late in the morning of the sixth of September, Ramón and Lucas were riding at the head of the outfit when they suddenly took off their sombreros, waved them wildly, and let out loud cheers as they saw the hacienda, the bunkhouses, the church, and the other structures two miles away. They had been gone longer than they had expected, but to Ramón's way of thinking, the luckiest and perhaps most valuable encounter of the entire journey had been meeting the old propector.

As they neared the ranch, the vaqueros who had remained behind saw them and came out to welcome them. Lucien Edmond Bouchard, hearing the loud cheers, went to find his wife. "Maxine honey, Ramón and Hugo are back! Let's go welcome them and all the others."

"Oh, yes, darling! Let's go meet Hugo—oh, I wonder how he is! He's probably changed—oh dear, I hope not too much. I guess we'll finally know how he feels about ranching life, won't we?" Maxine said with an anxious smile as she rose and, tucking her arm around Lucien Edmond's waist, accompanied him out to the porch of the hacienda.

As Hugo leaped down from the driver's seat of the chuck wagon, he saw his father and mother standing on the porch of the ranch house, and he bit his lip and flushed self-consciously. There had come into his mind, at this instant of reunion, the guilty thought that perhaps in having made his decision not to continue life as a rancher, he would be letting Lucien Edmond down. After all, he was his father's only son: there was no other male to take over the ranch and to manage it when Lucien Edmond would want to stop working, or, as could happen, die. And what then? Who would run this vast, sprawling ranch and continue this community the way his father had done? And what about the school? And Catayuna, and Joe Duvray and Eddie Gentry, and all those others dependent upon his father? Perhaps he had made a mistake; perhaps he was being too selfish.

"Hugo, it's good to have you back! You look wonderful!" his father suddenly called, and began to stride forward.

Maxine hurried forward to catch up with Lucien Edmond, her arms open to embrace her son.

"Hello, Father." Hugo put out his hand, and it was warmly gripped and held. Then Lucien Edmond put his arms around the youth's shoulders and hugged him affectionately. "Hello yourself!" He stood back and admiringly exclaimed, "My God, you've gotten so suntanned and strong I almost didn't recognize you! You're a man now, Hugo!"

"Oh, yes, he is! You look wonderful, Hugo. Did your journey go well? Was there any danger?" Maxine anxiously inquired, as she hugged her son.

It was Ramón who, now coming forward, had overheard this dialogue and thought it best to explain Hugo's achievements on the drive. "This son of yours, *amigo*," he said to Lucien Edmond, "he is *muy hombre*. Do you know what he did? He saved the lives of Felipe Sanchez and Manuel Olivera. We were attacked by bushwhackers—I think they were sent by that crooked Indian agent, Jeb Cornish, in Dodge City—"

"Oh, my God!" Maxine clapped a hand to her mouth, her eyes wide.

"It is all right, Maxine," Ramón soothingly hastened to interpose, "Hugo wasn't even scratched. But Manuel Olivera took a bullet in the shoulder, and when it was dug out, Hugo had the idea of sewing up the wound with needle and thread. And then Felipe was gored by a steer that had been frightened by a storm on Trinchera Pass, and Hugo did the same thing again. There is not a vaquero of the outfit who does not admire your son, Maxine. As I do."

"That's wonderful! I'm so proud of you, Hugo, dearest!" Maxine embraced Hugo again, who put his arms around her and grinned self-consciously.

Lucien Edmond, watching his son closely, cocked his head a bit and declared, "Hugo, I have the feeling that there's something on your mind—or is it that you're just tired, understandably, after your journey?"

Hugo, strengthened by his uncle's praise, decided to take the proverbial bull by the horns. "Father, I know this is very sudden and you probably won't like it, but I don't want to be a rancher. When I was helping Felipe and Manuel, I felt that I knew at last what I wanted to do. Father, I want to be a doctor. I hope this doesn't upset you too much."

"Quite the contrary! I think that's marvelous. Saving lives is a fine, rewarding profession, something to inspire a man, even when things are humdrum and dreary—as I suppose the cattle drive was for you, Hugo," Lucien Edmond unexpectedly told his son.

Hugo started, his eyes widening. "You really mean that, Father? I—I'm very glad. I can be better at that than riding along with cows and steers—but are—are you really sure it's all right?"

"Of course it is. It will be good to have a doctor in the family. But we'll talk further about this at dinner, because your mother and I have been thinking about not only your future, but Carla's, as well," Lucien Edmond said.

Hugo gently disengaged himself from his mother's embrace and went to his father and shook hands firmly with him, smiling, his eyes bright with happiness. The problem he had burdened himself with had been lifted from him, and with it the guilt. Now he felt that he could begin his own life and still be loved by his parents, a concern which had greatly worried him all the way back from Colorado.

"I have some extraordinary news for you, too, Lucien Edmond," Ramón now gently intervened. "It's something that may alter the futures of us all."

"That sounds mysterious, Ramón—very intriguing, indeed. But as curious as I am, I think it would be best if we talk at dinner. Right now, let's get the men back to the bunkhouses and the horses put away—and then, of course, we'll transact that little business of Maxwell Grantham's. I assume it went off satisfactorily?"

"Quite well. Unfortunately, the stampedes caused by the bushwhacker attack and a few other incidents cost us a number of head. Before those occurrences, I sold four hundred and fifty head to the two army forts for a very good price. But we'll talk of that later on," Ramón explained.

"Good! Come to my study as soon as you've been to your house and gotten settled. Then we'll have a drink— no, two: one to your success, and one to Hugo's finding out what he wants to do with his life. I think, indeed, we have good reason to celebrate." Lucien Edmond clapped Ramón on the shoulder.

As Ramón Hernandez hurried back to his house, anticipating his loving reunion with his wife, Mara, and their children, he suddenly heard his name being called. Expecting to see one of the vaqueros who had stayed behind on the ranch, he was startled when he turned and found himself staring at an unfamiliar face.

His perplexity grew into astonishment when the man standing before him declared, "Mr. Hernandez, don't you remember me? I'm Robert Markey—you know, the man you saved from being strung up last year."

"Señor Markey! Of course! How are you? What are you doing here? Forgive me for not recognizing you, but you look so different—you have changed a great deal."

"Well, you had a lot to do with that, Mr. Hernandez," Robert said, and then described the circumstances that had led him to seek out his benefactor. "You see," the young man continued, "I knew that finding you would be my only hope for getting someplace in life. I felt that since you had been so kind to me back in Kansas, you would understand my dilemma and would let me make it up to you by giving me a chance to pay you back." He smiled wryly and scratched his head. "I suppose in a way I've done just that, because your partner, Mr. Bouchard, says I've done a damn good job here. Anyway, I'm now one of your vaqueros, Mr. Hernandez!"

Ramón clapped Robert on the shoulder and grinned, warmly telling him, "Well, my friend, it is indeed a pleasure to see you again—and under such good circumstances! I am doubly glad that I didn't let my vaqueros string you up," he laughed. "Now that you are *muy hombre*, you are truly one of us, *no es verdad?*"

"Carla will be so glad to see you, darling." Maxine turned to Hugo and gestured for him to come abreast of them as they walked into the hacienda. "Incidentally, she wants to go to art school. First I had thought New Orleans would be just the place, but I received a letter from Laurette Douglas and what you just said about wanting to be a doctor has given me a wonderful idea. And I think your father will go along with it."

The girls came into the living room, and Carla ran to her brother, kissing him on the cheek. "My goodness, Hugo, you look just wonderful! Was it very hard for you?"

"Yes, but that was the best part of it. You're looking beautiful, Sis," he said.

Carla blushed and lowered her eyes. "I can tell you've

been out on the trail, saying a pretty compliment to me like that. You learned that from those Mexican *caballeros*, I've no doubt."

"You can tease me all you wish, Carla," he chided her. "The fact is that I've come to know those men—and there's a lot more to them than just the pretty compliments they make. I respect them tremendously for what they have to go through every day of their lives. And speaking of lives, I now know what I want to do with mine. I didn't before, but now I do. I want to study to be a doctor."

"Why, Hugo, I think that's marvelous! You know, Mother and Father and I discussed my going to art school, but I think she and Father were holding off on a decision for me until they found out what you thought about the cattle drive. Now that you're back, maybe we can find schools in the same place and not miss too much of the fall term!"

"I'd like that a lot, Carla. I'd like to be with you, to be sort of a big brother to you."

"I'm older than you are!" she twitted him. Then she hugged and kissed him, and said very gently, "But you certainly look older than I do, and I overheard what Ramón was saying about you outside. I'll bet Mother and Father are so very proud of you. They practically did nothing else but talk about you when you were away. And you know Mother—she was so worried you'd get bitten by a snake, or something—"

"No snakes, but I did run into a Gila monster—and when I shot it I caused a stampede. I thought to myself that right then and there the entire outfit was going to send me back home as fast as the horse would carry me!" Hugo ruefully said, and then laughed, his sister joining in wholeheartedly.

"Here is all the gold and the bank drafts from Maxwell Grantham, from Fort Sumner, and from Fort Bascom, Lucien Edmond." Ramón put them down on the escritoire; then, at Lucien Edmond's suggestion, he helped himself to a glass of fine port from a decanter on the sideboard.

"A very profitable transaction. Unfortunately, it hardly makes up for the loss of so many men in that murderous attack. How can you be so sure it was Cornish who directed those bushwhackers?" Lucien Edmond asked.

"There's really no proof, Lucien Edmond. I could write

to a federal marshal and tell him that I suspect Jeb Cornish and go into the particulars about the attack—for all I know, there may be wanted posters on some of the survivors. We took a good toll of them, in return, but I wish to *el Señor Dios* that we hadn't lost anyone. Poor young Tomás—he became Hugo's good friend. When he died, I think that put some steel into Hugo's backbone because from then on, he wasn't a tenderfoot anymore."

"There is a meaning to everything that happens to us in life," Lucien Edmond philosophized. "I'm glad that Hugo went with you. Without this experience, he would have had a more difficult time making his decision. And now—I confess I can't wait any longer: what is this extraordinary news you were going to tell me?"

"It's about a silver mine, Lucien Edmond. After we'd concluded our deal with Maxwell Grantham and were heading back, we found an old man—without food or a horse—lying on the trail not far from Las Animas. His name's Frank Scolby—incidentally, we brought him along. He's been prospecting for years, ever since the California Gold Rush days, and he's found a silver mine at Leadville, Colorado. The renegades who robbed him and left him for dead didn't learn about it. Anyway, he showed us the deed plus the assayer's certificate—Lucien Edmond, the ore tested out as yielding almost three thousand dollars a ton! And Señor Scolby insists that because we saved his life, we are to have half of it."

"This is incredible! Silver! Of course I've heard about the enormous mining operations going on in Colorado. Well now, I congratulate you on all you've achieved. And be sure to have Mr. Scolby in to dinner with us."

"He says he wants to take you back to the mine so that you can see for yourself, Lucien Edmond."

"Do you know, I wouldn't mind that at all. I've been chafing at the bit here all these months. I've begun to feel like an old man from all this inactivity. It would be good to go off on an adventure like this and to hear men's talk again," Lucien Edmond chuckled, and slapped his thigh. "All right, Ramón. Go tell Mr. Scolby I'm looking forward to meeting him, and he's going to have a very special dinner in his honor."

At the conclusion of dinner, Maxine briefly excused herself while she shepherded her younger daughters off to bed. When she returned and sat down in her chair, Frank Scolby, sitting at Lucien Edmond's left at the dinner table, apologized for his shabby clothes and the unkempt appearance of his long beard. "Now, Mr. Scolby, don't you downgrade yourself," Maxine declared, laughing. "With all your hard years of work, you've earned the right to look just the way you want. And we don't stand on ceremony here at Windhaven Range, anyway."

"That's mighty friendly of you, ma'am. My, this is wonderful grub! Whoever cooks it—would you tell them I ain't had a meal like this in longer than I remember?"

"Of course I'll do that." Maxine received a covert sign from her husband, indicating that he wanted to discuss the silver mine with the old man.

"Mr. Scolby, what I don't understand is why you're willing to share half of your mine with us simply for saving your life," Lucien Edmond leaned forward and remarked.

"Look, Mr. Bouchard, it's right easy for me to tell you why. For more years than I care to remember, I've been a loner. All the time I was prospectin', I was bamboozled by just about everybody. Finally I'm knocked on the noggin and left to die, and your Señor Ramón here and that nice Lucas feller, they rescued me and fed me up real good. I'd have died if it hadn't been for them. So I figger they got a right to it. You being the head man, it's you I'll deal with. Besides, I haven't got the *dinero* to get all that fancy mining equipment, so that's another reason I'm willin' to split fifty-fifty. It'll take a lot of equipment and men to get the ore out, run it, and melt it down to real honest-to-God silver, Mr. Bouchard. If you're willin' to do that, seems to me like you got a right to half the mine."

Lucien Edmond Bouchard was thunderstruck. He looked at the old man, then back at Ramón, who nodded to confirm that this was not merely talk, and then added, "Señor Scolby couldn't be talked out of this. I told him that was too high a price to pay—even for a prime beef dinner!" Everyone at the table, including the old prospector himself, joined in laughing. "But he has stuck to it," Ramón continued. With this, Frank Scolby drew out his deed from his inner coat pocket and presented it to Lucien Edmond with a flourish.

Maxine stared incredulously first at the paper, then at her husband—who sat with a thunderstruck look on his face—and finally at the bearded prospector. At last she stammered, "This—this is almost like a fairy tale, Mr. Scolby. But do you realize that, if it's as rich as the assayer thinks it is, you might be throwing away many, many thousands of dollars?"

Frank Scolby shrugged. "You're a real nice woman, Mrs. Bouchard, ma'am, and you got a real nice family. Me, I'm completely alone, as I said. My folks split up when I was just a kid and I lost track of my brothers and sisters after I headed out West when I wasn't out of my teens yet to take up prospectin'. I had me a wife and son, but they both died years ago. Well now, I feel right homey and peaceful-like with Señor Ramón and Lucas and now you folks, and since I haven't got anybody at all—well, what would I do with so much money? And besides, nobody would have even known about this mine if I'd been left out there to die, that's for certain. Let's just say it's 'cause—well, I ain't never been to church, but I do believe in God, and I figger that God, He gimme another chance when Ramón and Lucas saved me. And because they're part of your outfit, Mrs. Bouchard, I want to divvy it up. Then I'll feel right, understand?"

Maxine was too filled with emotion to speak; she could only nod, her eyes brimming with tears. She reached across the table to squeeze the old miner's hand and whispered, "God bless you. No one in this family or anyone who works for Windhaven Range will ever take advantage of you in any way, Mr. Scolby. You will always be protected by my husband—his honesty, his reputation, and his men."

"I sort of figgered all that out aforehand, ma'am," Frank Scolby nodded, and then, reaching for a dusty red bandanna, loudly blew his nose, for he, too, was choked with feeling.

Lucien Edmond couldn't wait to go to Leadville at the end of the next week with Frank Scolby, his other partner, Joe Duvray, and two vaqueros to investigate the mine. The old prospector had assured them that he was quite up to the stagecoach and train trip all the way to Colorado and back and, indeed, looked forward to it.

All through dinner Hugo and Carla had been eyeing each other, obviously bursting with impatience to talk to their parents. Noticing this, Frank Scolby very tactfully took his napkin, wiped his mouth, and then huskily declared, "Beggin' your pardon, Mrs. Bouchard, ma'am,

Mr. Bouchard, I think it's high time an old feller like me got his beauty sleep. Anyhow, you folks want to talk among yourselves, and I know when I'm in the way. If you'll just show me a place where I can lay my old bones down, I'd be mighty grateful."

"You'll have a room right here, Mr. Scolby. Ramón, would you take Mr. Scolby to the south guest room and make him comfortable? Thank you. I'll see you two in the morning," Lucien Edmond promised.

Hugo and Carla patiently waited until Ramón escorted the old man from the dining room, exchanging conspiratorial glances. When at last they had left, Hugo turned to his father and asked, "Did you really mean what you said, Father, about letting me study to become a doctor?"

"Of course I did. Hugo, your mother has been saving something to tell you about all evening, so I think it's time to turn the floor over to her. Maxine, my dearest, would you do the honors?" Lucien Edmond smiled at his wife and blew her a kiss.

Maxine acknowledged the compliment by blowing back her own kiss to Lucien Edmond, then turned to her two oldest children with a delighted smile. "You probably know that while you were away, Hugo, Carla came to us and said she wanted the chance to study for a career in art. At first, I thought of New Orleans—they have an art school there as well as finishing schools. Now that you've told us of your own decision—well, maybe you can call it fate, but I received a letter from Laurette Douglas. In it, she told me about a wonderful new art school in Chicago, the Academy of Fine Arts, and she also described Rush Medical College, an institution with a history of outstanding faculty and remarkably advanced medical research. One of the staff members at Rush is Laurette's neighbor across the street, Dr. Max Thornberg. I wrote Laurette back, telling her of the possibility that you two might wish to study in Chicago. Dear Laurette started making inquiries, and just last week I got her answer!"

With this, she unfolded a sheet of paper and read to them both:

Dear Maxine:

I was so pleased to receive your letter mentioning that Carla might enroll in the Chicago Academy of Fine Arts. As you may recall, you thought that if

416

Hugo did not care for becoming a rancher, he might find an educational institution here in Chicago, too, so that the two of them could be together and not feel quite so lonely in a strange city.

Well, I talked to Dr. Max Thornberg—he's the man at Rush I wrote you about—and it turns out that his sister, Cordelia—a spinster in her forties—says she would be very happy to act as a chaperone for both your fine children. As it happens, her brother is going on a two-year sabbatical leave to Europe this fall, in order to visit some of the leading European hospitals so that he can acquire more knowledge that will be of benefit to his work here in Chicago. Cordelia said that if you were interested, she could therefore give Carla and Hugo room and board in their house across the street.

Do let me know if this is of interest to you.

Your faithful friend,
Laurette Douglas

"Oh, what a wonderful idea, Mother!" Carla gleefully clapped her hands. "How clever of you to think of this solution! Although it's exciting to think of being on our own, still it's nice to know we'll have family right there if we need them. Oh, Mother—can we really go?"

"Yes, my dearest," Maxine beamed at them, "that is, of course, if you are both accepted by the schools. Hugo, I don't think that you could find a better school anywhere in the country than this Rush Medical College that Laurette has written about. And yes, the living arrangements would be absolutely perfect—don't you agree?"

"Oh, yes, Mother!" Carla and Hugo happily exclaimed in unison.

Maxine turned to Lucien Edmond, with a thoughtful expression on her face. "You know, my dear, although we've always taken great pains to educate our children properly, still they haven't had the benefit of much formal schooling. But according to the literature that Laurette was kind enough to enclose with her last letter, both the Academy of Fine Arts and Rush Medical College have excellent preparatory classes. I presume that Carla and Hugo would be admitted to the school on a probationary basis, until they are able to make up any deficiencies of not having had more formal education."

417

"Yes, I read that, too," her husband replied. "And, knowing Carla and Hugo, I'm sure that they'll work very hard at their studies to gain regular admission in the spring term."

"Well, then," Maxine put in, "we should all sit down right now and compose a letter to each of the colleges. Perhaps if we explain the circumstances, the deans will understand why we're so late in contacting them and will make exceptions for our children. Then, if it wouldn't be too much trouble, one of the vaqueros could ride to San Antonio and post them."

"That would be no trouble at all," Lucien Edmond assured her. "As a matter of fact, I was going to send some men to San Antonio anyway, to deposit the proceeds of the drive." Turning back to his children, he said, "I hope you two won't find this abrupt change too upsetting and that you won't be disappointed."

"I'm sure we won't, Father," Hugo responded. Then, rising from his chair, his eyes bright with happiness, he declared, "I'm very grateful, Father, and I'm truly glad that I'm not letting you down. I'm going to study hard and be as good a doctor as I can possible be—I promise."

"And one day," Carla said with a faraway look in her eyes as she leaned back in her chair, "maybe I'll have some of my work exhibited in galleries in cities like New York and Chicago. I'm certainly going to try."

"The most important thing anyone can do in life is trying to do one's best, my darlings," Maxine assured them with a smile.

## Forty

It was a Thursday, a few days before Lucien Edmond Bouchard, Joe Duvray, and Frank Scolby, along with two armed vaqueros, would set out for Leadville, Colorado. It was a time for rejoicing, and this morning, old Friar Bartoloméo Alicante had held a late morning mass in the church that the vaqueros had built. He knelt at the altar to thank the dear Lord for the bounty and blessings that had been bestowed upon Windhaven Range and on all the Bouchards, wherever they were now.

In his sermon the portly friar alluded to the newfound riches that had almost miraculously been bestowed. "We are humble people, all of us, and our lives are but a brief span upon the earth. He who created us, He who watches over the smallest, as the greatest of His creations, He who sees the fall of a tiny sparrow from His heavens, is responsible for the most incomprehensible mysteries. My children, the world is full of such mysteries, and we shall know the answers to them only on that final day when we are summoned before Him. Humility becomes us all in the presence of the wondrous workings of Him from whom we came, out of dust, out of Adam's rib, into a world we cannot forsake because He created it—and He has entrusted us to work its good against the forces of evil."

Everyone listened to his words in hushed reverence. Lucien Edmond and Maxine, who sat together holding hands, looked at each other and smiled tenderly, feeling the aura of love and gentleness that the old priest evoked.

Bartoloméo Alicante spoke again in a quavering voice, lifting his eyes toward the ceiling. "This church was built by men of good faith—uneducated, yet devoted and dedicated—to honor Him in whom they believed with all their hearts and souls. And it did not matter that there was a difference in sect or race or creed. For in all of you who sit in this church there is a belief which transcends any creed, any race, any color; a universal reverence for the Creator. As old Lucien Bouchard sensed a century ago, it has not mattered whether he and his descendants were Catholic or Protestant: they have lived in a spiritual blessedness, for they are truly the children of God."

After a pause, Friar Bartoloméo Alicante continued his discourse: "He who made us all and who made the world and all its wonders, does not examine us to see what church we attend, nor does He hear the terms of our prayers and measure them, as mortal men might. No, my children, He is all knowing, and He is kind and good and indulgent. He understands that it is enough that we lead lives that do no harm to our neighbors, that we strive eternally for good and the destruction of evil. That is what He meant

419

when He taught Adam and Eve the lesson of the Garden of Eden: it was man's error that condemned us to a life on earth filled with scourges and tribulations. And yet, He will still redeem us, if we are willing to hear His eternal message. I tell you, my children, I rejoice in my soul. Even though I am old and perhaps coming to the end of my days as measured out by Him, I have seen love and gentleness and compassion and humanity here on this very stretch of earth so far from the large cities where men covet and lust and thirst for power and material wealth. But we here on Windhaven Range know that there are greater things in this world than the acquisition of power and possessions. Let us pray that we shall always be in a humble state of grace to receive His love. Amen."

Just as he concluded his sermon, there was a sudden, terrifying, distant keening. Lucien Edmond ran to the chapel door, looked in the direction of the sound, then turned to the others and uttered a cry of alarm: "To the south, it looks as though—oh, my God, it is—it's a tornado!"

Everyone in the church rose immediately, and Lucien Edmond called out to Friar Alicante, "Padre, I must go and warn everyone to take shelter in the cellars."

In the front row, the sisters, who had come from Mexico City to found a school here, crossed themselves and began to pray, expressions of terror on their gentle faces. But Catayuna, strong and ardent, called to them, "Sisters, let us find shelter! *El Señor Dios* does not send this wind to take our lives, but to test us. Come, I will lead you to a safe place!"

They followed her, the younger nuns trembling and tearful, sustained by the older ones, who murmured soothing words and reminded them that they were like the children of Israel—God had led them, too, to safety across the Red Sea and destroyed Pharaoh's legions.

Rushing out of the church, some of them turned and saw a huge black funnel cloud, ominously lowering from the sky in the southeast and heading toward them.

Almost a decade earlier, having heard that Texas was sometimes subjected to cyclonic winds, Lucien Edmond Bouchard had ordered his vaqueros to dig cellars, places of refuge against violent storms. Catayuna now led the nuns to a door by the auxiliary bunkhouses—a door that looked like that of a shed, but, when opened, led down a narrow stairway to a well-fortified cellar. She gestured to them, urging them on, as the black cloud came closer—a sinister, whirling darkness, like the maw of a cave in which all manner of demons and loathsome creatures dwelt.

Catayuna stood staunchly, herding them all into the shelter, waiting for the youngest nuns, who came last. When they had entered, she pulled the door shut with all her might and thrust the bolt through. When she reached the safety of the cellar, she knelt and prayed aloud—praying for the Bouchards and the *trabajadores* and the vaqueros; all of the kind and courageous people who had made her feel so welcome here.

Lucien Edmond, Maxine, and their six children hurried through the kitchen of the hacienda and down a flight of narrow stairs to their own cyclone cellar. They pulled the trap door shut, thrust the bolt home—and waited.

The tornado struck with unbelievable fury. The black funnel cloud descended first upon the main bunkhouse and then the church. Within seconds, the little church was leveled, and the old priest who knelt before the altar was felled by a huge beam from the nave. He died with a prayer on his lips: "Almighty God, deliver us from evil—unto Thy hands, I commend my spirit—"

In the Belcher house, Henry lay abed, for he was suffering from rheumatism. Maybelle was in the kitchen, making him a hot poultice. She had heard the wind, had heard the shouts from the church and the bunkhouses and the hacienda, but she had not understood their significance. Bent upon relieving the pains of her suffering husband, she failed to recognize the warnings to take shelter. Even as she hurried into the bedroom and began to place the poultice upon Henry's shoulder, the funnel struck, and the walls of the house caved in. Maybelle flung herself upon her husband, trying to protect him with her own body against the violence of the elements—and they died together, without pain or knowledge of that death as the oxygen was sucked out of the air.

The vaqueros had been warned, and they hurried—singly or with their families—to a shed beside the main bunkhouse, opened the door, and hurried down the steps that led to their own protective cellar. But beyond, to the west, three young vaqueros who were tending the cattle were picked up with their horses and flung into the air, then dashed down hundreds of yards away.

Joe Duvray, Margaret, and their children, having been forewarned by the howling of the wind and the darkening of the sky, had entered their own cellar and bolted the door a moment before the funnel cloud whisked away their home, leaving only a few broken timbers where once there had been a farmhouse.

With the same suddenness that it had come, the tornado departed. Slowly the sun came out again into an eerie stillness. It was over. Yet perhaps it marked a new beginning.

## Forty-one

Lucien Edmond Bouchard walked with his arm protectively around his sobbing wife, Maxine, as they surveyed the aftermath of the tornado. A weary sigh grew into a groan of despair as he assessed the destruction.

The school building, where the nuns and Catayuna had taught the young children of the ranch and neighboring settlers, had been totally destroyed. The small chapel was in ruins. His eyes turned to the leveled bunkhouse, then to their own hacienda from which the roof had been hurtled away by the violent wind. He stared in disbelief at the pile of broken timbers that had been the charming home of Henry and Maybelle Belcher.

Lucien Edmond squinted across the compound. He saw Ramón standing with Mara and their children by the cellar entrance of their house. They waved at Lucien Edmond and Maxine, indicating that they were unharmed. Oddly enough, their house had been left standing intact.

"Maxine," Lucien Edmond turned to his sobbing wife, "we have suffered a terrible blow, but all is not lost. If there's truly a rich lode of silver in that mine, we can rebuild the ranch—our house, the church, everything. Why, there'll surely be money enough for a new school, perhaps even for homes for poor children and deprived Indians. We must seriously think of all the possibilities. It's just unfortunate that our plans to leave for the mine immediately will now have to wait until we have done some necessary reconstruction here."

More and more people were coming out of the shelters, walking around the compound with a dazed look in their eyes. The dignified Mother Superior, who had come from Mexico City with her nuns in search of sanctuary and who had founded the school, now approached Lucien Edmond, dabbing at her eyes with a handkerchief.

"Mother Superior," he said, devoutly crossing himself, "you and the sisters will stay with us while the vaqueros put up a temporary shelter of good Texas wood. I hope to be able to give you very good news in a few months—when we have had a chance to survey the silver mine and plan accordingly. Perhaps—who knows—we may wish to resettle. But this is not the time to make a decision. . . ."

Over four hundred head of cattle had died or been so badly hurt by the tornado that the vaqueros had to shoot them to end their suffering. The vaqueros had also gone valiantly to work—making repairs, rebuilding the bunkhouse, the hacienda, and any of the houses that had suffered damage. Some, like Joe Duvray's, had been totally destroyed.

The dead of Windhaven Range were buried. Humble Pablo Casares—who, with his Kate and their children, had escaped the fury of the tornado—acted as surrogate priest at the burial of Friar Bartoloméo Alicante, Maybelle and Henry Belcher, and his fallen comrades. Though he was Episcopalian, Robert Markey joined in the prayers for the dead, kneeling with Eddie Gentry and Walter Catlin. The young farmer murmured a special prayer in gratitude for what Lucien Edmond Bouchard and Ramón Hernandez had accorded him.

Two weeks after the tornado wreaked its havoc on Windhaven Range, Carla and Hugo received word from their respective colleges that they had been accepted for admission. Since Hugo's classes were scheduled to begin on October fifteenth and Carla's a week later, Maxine was abruptly hurled into a flurry of activity, for which Lucien Edmond was immensely grateful. She was so busy shopping with her children in San Antonio, mending those items

423

that need attention, ironing, and packing, that grieving was forgotten.

The entire Bouchard family assembled before the hacienda to see Hugo and Carla off on their new adventure. They would go by carriage to San Antonio, to catch a train for St. Louis and then Chicago. Tears were mingled with yelps of laughter, and as the carriage carrying Carla and Hugo pulled away, accompanied by an escort of two vaqueros, Maxine shouted some last-minute instructions to her children. Turning round in their seats, the two waved and shouted their goodbyes, until at last the carriage was lost from view in the dust thrown up behind it.

Afterward, Maxine was uncharacteristically quiet. She gave a particularly plaintive sigh, and Lucien Edmond softly asked, "Are you missing your two chicks already, my dear?"

"No, it's not that," she wistfully replied. "I've suddenly realized that since I have two college-aged children, I'm no longer a young woman."

Lucien Edmond put his arm around her shoulders, kissed her lightly on the cheek, and assured her, "Maxine, my darling, to me you'll always be the same beautiful young girl I fell in love with when we first met."

The following morning, Lucien Edmond, Joe Duvray, and two vaqueros rode off with Frank Scolby to San Antonio, where they would make the first of their many stagecoach and train connections to Leadville. If all went as planned, they would be back in six weeks—hopefully with the future of Windhaven Range secured. . . .

## Forty-two

By the middle of October, Laure Bouchard had received her first letter from young Lucien, enthusiastically declaring that he was happy in his school and had made many new friends—not the least of whom was Father O'Mara. A telegram from Lucien Edmond arrived in the latter part of October, telling her of the disaster that had befallen Windhaven Range, and of his determination to rebuild it. "Perhaps," he had written, "after investigating a silver mine in Colorado that has rather miraculously become part of our holdings, we may transfer some of our operations to that northern state."

Maxine Bouchard received a letter during the last week of November, jointly signed by Hugo and Carla, eagerly detailing their respective studies, telling their parents that their regular admission to Rush Medical College and the Chicago Academy of Fine Arts seemed assured, and praising their chaperone, Cordelia Thornberg.

Also during this last week of November, Lucien Edmond Bouchard, Joe Duvray, Frank Scolby, and the accompanying two vaqueros arrived back from the mine in Colorado to Windhaven Range with the news that the vein of silver was truly as rich as the assayer had indicated. Lucien Edmond immediately wrote a long letter to Dr. Ben Wilson, in which Lucien Edmond told the Quaker doctor, "My son respects and admires you, Ben; as a matter of fact, he's now in Chicago studying to be a doctor. He hopes that, one day, he will be as useful to people who need him as you have been." He then asked Ben if he would go to the Creek village. "You see," he wrote, "we have come into ownership of a silver mine that will make us very rich, and I plan to give Sipanata a sum of money that will ensure that his people will never go hungry, no matter what the government does. I would very much like him to know this. Well, say a prayer for all of us that all will go well."

It was the first week of December of the year of 1879. In a New Orleans hospital, Lopasuta Bouchard knelt at the bedside of his young wife, Geraldine. She had been delivered of a baby girl whom she and her husband named Marta, after Lopasuta's Mexican mother. Geraldine lay on the pillows, ashen and exhausted from a long and difficult birth.

The tall, red-haired surgeon who had delivered the child approached the bedside now and whispered into Lopasuta's ear, "May I see you outside the room, Mr. Bouchard? There's something I must tell you."

Lopasuta nodded, leaned forward to kiss Geraldine's pallid cheek, and whispered, "Dr. Eastland wants to talk to me a moment, darling. I'll be back right away."

Her eyelids flickered as she looked at him, and she smiled wanly as she said, "I suspect the doctor is hiding something from me—he's not very good at masking his concern. You know how much I trust you—and I'm trusting you now to tell me what Dr. Eastland says."

"I promise you, my darling, I'll tell you. Now try to rest," he whispered as he leaned forward and kissed her forehead.

Then, moving quietly out of the room, he closed the door behind him and stood facing the red-haired doctor. "What do you wish to tell me, Dr. Eastland?"

"It's not good news, Mr. Bouchard, Oh, no, don't mistake me—your wife is totally out of danger. But I'm afraid I must tell you that she can never have a child again. It was touch and go between her and the baby, and it was a miracle the infant survived. Your wife will have to accept the fact that she can never bear children again."

Lopasuta frowned, then looked at the doctor with a sad smile. "I understand, Dr. Eastland. Thank you for telling me so frankly."

"Do you wish me to tell your wife?"

Lopasuta shook his head. "That's for me to do, Dr. Eastland. Thank you again, and I'm very grateful to you for saving both my wife and daughter. But you look awfully tired yourself. Get some rest."

The doctor chuckled, "You're a remarkable man, Mr.

Bouchard. Most fathers worry about themselves, and here you are worrying about me. I admire you—and I admire your wife. She's a wonderful woman, very courageous and determined. Try to give her strength—you've enough for both of you."

"I thank you for your kindness. I will do whatever I can. Good night, Dr. Eastland."

Lopasuta turned and went slowly back into the hospital room. Softly closing the door behind him, he went to sit at the edge of Geraldine's bed. She blinked her eyes open and asked him, "What did he say, my darling?"

"Geraldine, our little Marta is fine, and so are you. But she is the last child we can ever have. The Great Spirit has willed it so, my dear one."

"I see." Her eyes, dull with fatigue and pain, fixed on his handsome face, and then she again murmured, "I see. . . ."

"I love you, Geraldine. We now have two wonderful children. We shall always be together to rear them properly. They will be fine people who will earn their places in life."

"Lopasuta?"

"Yes, my sweetheart?"

"I think you must be very upset by what Dr. Eastland told you. You've miscounted our children, my love. You said our 'two wonderful children.' Surely you mean three!"

"Geraldine, my dear one!"

"It's true. After all, my beloved husband, Luke is your child, but I love him as if he were my very flesh and blood. And if you hadn't been taken away from me, I should truly have been his mother."

Lopasuta did not even try to conceal the sudden tears springing into his eyes as he leaned forward to cup Geraldine's face with his palms and to kiss her gently on the eyelids. "Dearest Geraldine," he said in a trembling, broken voice.

She sighed deeply, closed her eyes a moment, and then slowly turned to stare at him: "Do you know—while you were talking to Dr. Eastland, I fell asleep. And I had the most remarkable dream: I saw our Dennis go off to West Point and become an officer. He was at the head of his class, Lopasuta dear, and enormously respected. Anyway, then he was sent out to the West, where he was an officer in charge of troops. Only, he told them that they were

427

never to kill Indians, because Dennis is one-quarter Comanche, proving that Indians are not savages. Oh, how I hope my dream comes true!"

"I believe it can come true. You and I will do all we can to see that it does, dear one." He took her hand between both of his and held it to his heart.

It was December 18, 1879. On the top of the towering bluff which fronted the Alabama River, Laure and Lopasuta Bouchard stood together before the graves of old Lucien Bouchard and his Dimarte, and that of Luke, close beside his beloved grandfather.

It was the one hundred seventeenth anniversary of Lucien Bouchard's birth. Through more than a century, the Bouchard fidelity and love and honor had persevered. It had touched strangers wherever the Bouchards had found new places to live their lives: in Chicago, Houston, Galveston, in Wichita, in Carrizo Springs, Texas, and now in New Orleans.

Lopasuta turned to his adoptive mother and smiled meaningfully at her. He then turned to the grave of the man who had given his life to save that of the governor of Alabama.

"My father, I kneel before your grave now, and I pray to the Great Spirit that He will look down with favor upon us and grant us the strength to triumph over evil and to do good unto our neighbors—for this is what you taught me, my father. So long as I live, I shall never forget for a waking moment the purpose of your life upon this earth."

Lopasuta Bouchard turned to Laure again, took her hand, and brought it to his lips. "In his name, I humbly salute you, Laure, and pledge to you that the name that you and he gave me will never be sullied and will be triumphant through my love and homage."

# The Windhaven Saga
### by Marie de Jourlet

AMERICA'S #1 PLANTATION SAGA · OVER **7** MILLION COPIES IN PRINT!